Days
of the
Dead

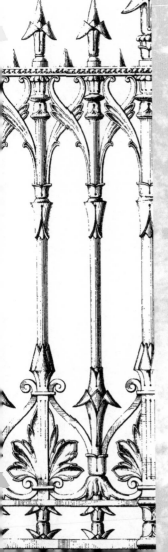

BANTAM BOOKS

New York

Toronto

London

Sydney

Auckland

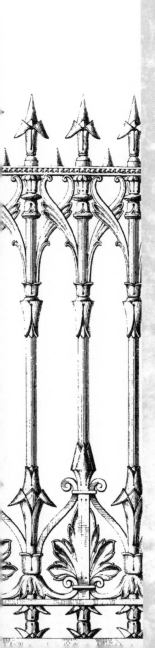

Days
of the
Dead

Barbara
Hambly

DAYS OF THE DEAD
A Bantam Book / July 2003

Published by Bantam Dell
A Division of Random House, Inc.
New York, New York

LIBRARY OF CONGRESS CATALOGING IN PUBLICATION DATA
Hambly, Barbara.
    Days of the dead / Barbara Hambly.
    p. cm.
    ISBN 0-553-10954-5
    1. January, Benjamin (Fictitious character)—Fiction. 2. Free African
Americans—Fiction. 3. African American men—Fiction. 4. Americans—
Mexico—Fiction. 5. Mexico—Fiction. I. Title.

PS3558.A4215 D39 2003
813'.54—dc21   2002038571

Manufactured in the United States of America
Published simultaneously in Canada

BVG   10 9 8 7 6 5 4 3 2 1

For Victoria

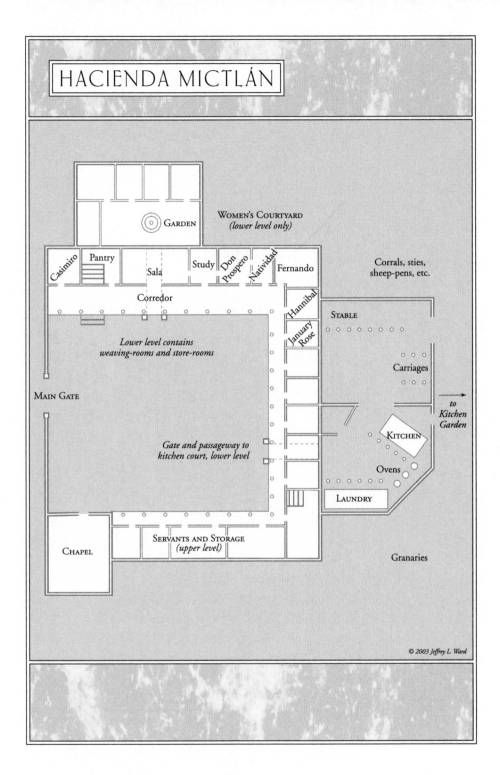

HACIENDA MICTLÁN

WOMEN'S COURTYARD
(lower level only)

GARDEN

Casimiro | Pantry | Sala | Study | Don Prospero | Natividad | Fernando

Corredor

Hannibal

January Rose

STABLE

Corrals, sties,
sheep-pens, etc.

Carriages

*Lower level contains
weaving-rooms and store-rooms*

MAIN GATE

*to
Kitchen
Garden*

KITCHEN

*Gate and passageway to
kitchen court, lower level*

Ovens

LAUNDRY

CHAPEL

SERVANTS AND STORAGE
(upper level)

Granaries

© 2003 Jeffrey L. Ward

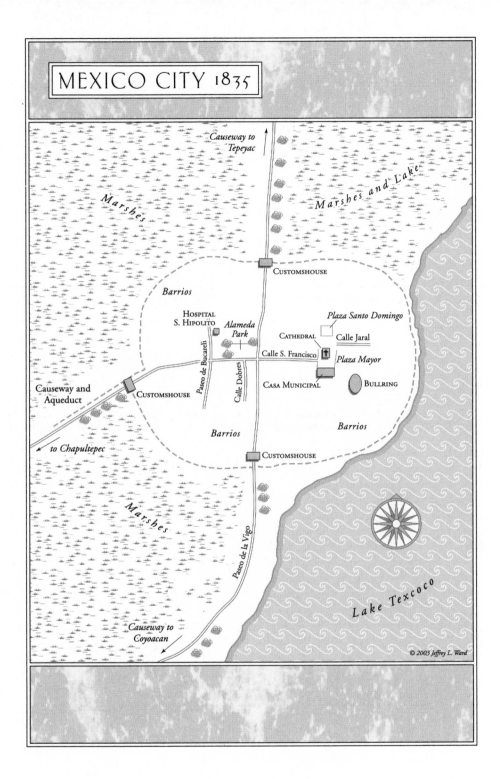

MEXICO CITY 1835

Causeway to
Tepeyac

Marshes

Marshes and Lake

CUSTOMSHOUSE

Barrios

HOSPITAL
S. HIPOLITO

Alameda
Park

Plaza Santo Domingo

CATHEDRAL

Calle Jaral

Calle S. Francisco

Plaza Mayor

Paseo de Bucareli

Calle Dobres

CASA MUNICIPAL

CUSTOMSHOUSE

Causeway and
Aqueduct

BULLRING

to Chapultepec

Barrios

Barrios

CUSTOMSHOUSE

Marshes

Paseo de la Vigo

Lake Texcoco

Causeway to
Coyoacan

© 2003 Jeffrey L. Ward

Don Prospero de Castellón and His Children

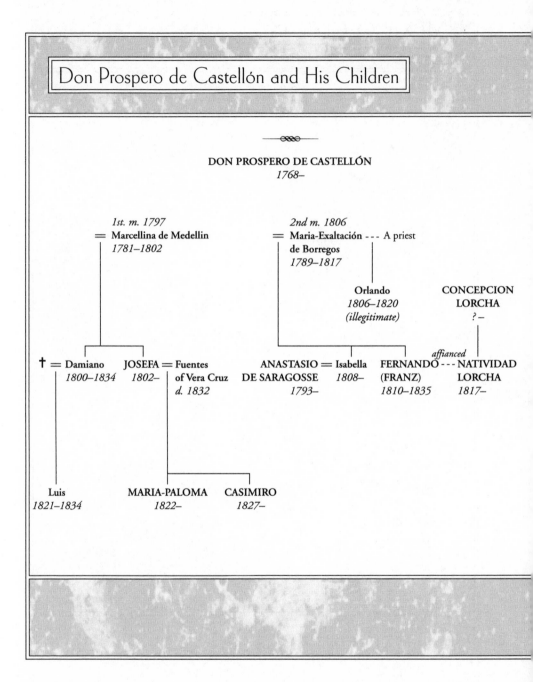

DON PROSPERO DE CASTELLÓN
1768–

1st. m. 1797
= **Marcellina de Medellin**
1781–1802

2nd m. 1806
= **Maria-Exaltación** - - - A priest
de Borregos
1789–1817

Orlando
1806–1820
(illegitimate)

CONCEPCION
LORCHA
?–

affianced

† = **Damiano**   **JOSEFA** = **Fuentes**   **ANASTASIO** = Isabella   **FERNANDO** - - - **NATIVIDAD**
1800–1834 *1802–* **of Vera Cruz**   **DE SARAGOSSE** *1808–*   **(FRANZ)**   **LORCHA**
                     d. 1832   *1793–*   *1810–1835*   *1817–*

Luis
1821–1834

MARIA-PALOMA   **CASIMIRO**
1822–   *1827–*

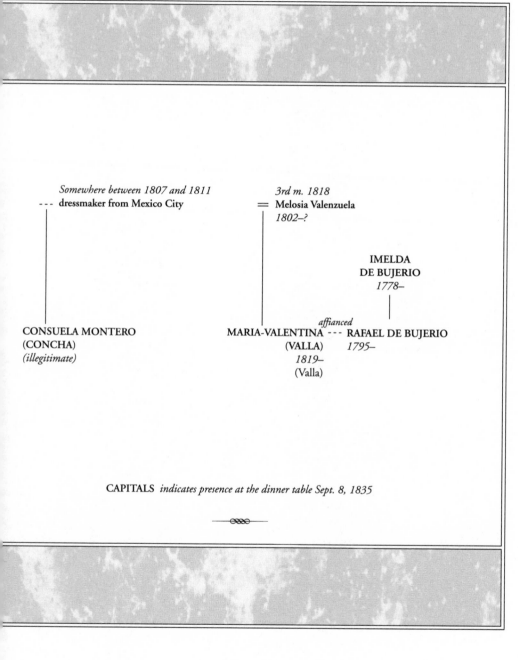

Somewhere between 1807 and 1811
- - - dressmaker from Mexico City

3rd m. 1818
= Melosia Valenzuela
1802–?

IMELDA
DE BUJERIO
1778–

CONSUELA MONTERO
(CONCHA)
(illegitimate)

affianced
MARIA-VALENTINA - - - RAFAEL DE BUJERIO
(VALLA)   *1795–*
1819–
(Valla)

CAPITALS *indicates presence at the dinner table Sept. 8, 1835*

Days
of the
Dead

ONE

Hacienda Mictlán
Outside the City of Mexico
September 16, 1835

Amicus Meus,

Enclosed with this missive you'll find a draft for what I hope is sufficient money to pay your passage here by the speediest available transport. My host at the moment is being so good as to hold the minions of Justice at bay, which is quite generous of him given that I am widely supposed to have murdered his only son. Were Don Prospero de Castellón even marginally sane, I would probably already have been executed—the evidence is fairly damning. By remarks the Don has made, however, I have the uncomfortable conviction that after the first of November—the second at the latest—he will fall in with the popular view, not that I killed the fellow, but that I deserve to be punished for the deed. In company with most of the rest of the household, he believes that young Fernando will re-visit the house, along with various other deceased relatives, at that time, the only difference between his belief and that of his daughters and their families being that he thinks he will be able to ask the murdered man outright—and receive an answer *in no uncertain terms—about what ought best to be done with yours truly.*

The local constabulary is also in fairly steady attendance. If ever I have earned your regard or affection, please come and engage in a few sleuth-hound tactics. I am at a complete loss to imagine how anyone but myself could have made quietus for young Fernando—who certainly deserved what he got—and if you do not prove otherwise, I shall soon be forced to begin suspecting myself. Please come. I am in fairly desperate straits, though, as I said, I believe I shall be safe enough until the Days of the Dead.

Your friend,
Hannibal Sefton

Postscriptum: I don't know whether they still garrote heretics like myself here, or hygienically shoot them as they do in the countryside. You understand that I don't really like to ask.

Benjamin January folded up his friend's letter after its perhaps seventy-fifth reading in the three weeks since its arrival on the morning of his wedding, settled back against the jolting seat of the Vera Cruz *diligencia,* and wondered—again—if he was going to make it to Mexico City alive, and if he did whether Hannibal would still be alive when he got there.

At every inn en route, the innkeepers had whispered darkly about "bandits in the mountains," prompting the passengers of the *diligencia* to ride with rifles cradled in their arms and pistols at their belts: their fellow-passenger Mr. Dillard of Tennessee seemed to take January going armed as a personal affront. But then, Mr. Dillard had not ceased glaring at January since the coach had pulled out of the baking, vulture-haunted streets of Vera Cruz. "You're not gonna let nigras ride *inside,* are you?" Dillard had demanded of the driver.

"He paid for his ticket like everybody else," the driver had retorted in a nasal Yankee twang. "Something he's permitted to do in *this* country, which has had the courage to strike down the foul abomination of slavery . . . unlike some nations which *purport* to be free."

"Damn Whig abolitionist," had snarled Dillard.

"Godless fleshmongering Democrat," the driver had replied.

It had not been an auspicious beginning to a journey that rapidly got worse. In addition to the threat of bandits—which had not, in four days of travel, so far manifested itself—there was the more clearly present threat of the inns themselves, ancient, filthy structures of adobe-brick, primitive beyond belief and inhabited by nests of scorpions and centipedes as well as the more usual fauna of chickens, pigs, and village dogs. There was the food—mostly greasy tamales, inadequately cooked beans, and the national staple of tortillas, unleavened corncakes cooked on an open grill. Born in the slave-quarters of a cane plantation upriver from New Orleans, January had eaten worse, but not recently.

Most deadly of all, there was the Yankee coachman's driving, as he lashed his team of four skittery little mustangs at crazy speed over the high yellow passes of the Sierra Madre Orientale, causing the *diligencia* to sway and jolt and causing January to wonder if he shouldn't have damned his friend Hannibal to whatever penalty the government of New Spain—*Pardon me,* he corrected himself, *MEXICO*—thought fit to dole out, and stayed at home to enjoy the wonderful state of having actually, finally, against all odds, married Rose Vitrac.

A particularly savage rut hurled the coach nearly sideways and precipitated his new bride nearly into his lap. Covered with yellow dust, sweating in the crystalline heat of these parched gray peaks, her soft snuff-colored curls skinned back tight into unflattering braids for travel . . . it took everything in him not to seize her in his arms and cover her with kisses.

That would really give Mr. Dillard something to complain about, he thought. And it would shock the other passengers—two German merchants, their doddering Swiss valet, and a young priest—speechless. Instead, he remarked, "At least, at this rate, we'll get there soon, and learn what actually happened." He gestured with Hannibal's letter and tucked it back into his pocket.

Rose removed her spectacles, sought vainly for some portion of her clothing not thick with dust in order to clean the dusty lenses, then sighed and resignedly replaced them on her nose. "You don't think Hannibal actually did it, do you?"

This was a question they'd asked each other for three weeks now, when not occupied with the logistics of honeymoon copulation in a stateroom bunk barely the size of a particularly stingy coffin. (The *Belle Marquise,* out of New Orleans to Vera Cruz, transported pineapples, tobacco, and the insect life that invariably accompanied them, and the floor was not an option.) Mostly they wondered if their friend—of average height and skeletally thin from the ravages of consumption—could have physically accomplished murder.

And the answer, of course, was yes. Even were "young Fernando" as tall as January and, like January, built upon what English novelists liked to call Herculean lines, there was always poison, there were firearms, there was the possibility of a stiletto in the back in a darkened room. January and Rose had whiled away many hours evolving such hypothetical scenarios ("What if Fernando habitually wore a steel breastplate to bed?" "One can mix sulfate of mercury with candle-wax and make a poisoned candle that when burned will kill the person in the room. . . .") as they strolled the decks of the *Belle Marquise,* waiting for a northern wind to fill the sails for those last few maddening miles into Vera Cruz; and, latterly, as they'd had the marrow pounded out of their bones by the frantic pace of the *diligencia* over rutted mountain roads.

In the absence of the slightest information about the victim, the circumstances, or any conceivable motivation for the murder, it was as good a way as any to pass the time.

But that wasn't what Rose meant now, and January knew it.

His mind returned to the reeking heat and darkness of the waterfront at New Orleans, the tail-end of summer, 1832. Even at that hour of the night—and he'd heard the Cathedral clock strike three as he'd left the garçonnière above his mother's kitchen—there was activity along the levee, stevedores unloading bales from the big, ugly flat-sided steamboats, filthy ruffians in coarse calico shirts and heavy Conestoga boots driving pigs from the flatboats by the light of torches, whores in tawdry dresses plying their trade in the shadows. Music jingled from the saloons along Rue du Levee, where men gambled through the night; somewhere a slave gang hauling wood onto a boat wailed a primitive holler. Roaches the size of mice crept on the sides of the warehouses, or flew with roaring wings around the flaming cressets; the warm air breathed and blew with the storm that flickered far out over the Gulf.

New Orleans. The home January had fled sixteen years before, seeking education and freedom in France.

He'd made his way along the levee, away from the docks where the steamboats waited three deep and toward the taller masts of the ocean-going ships. The *Duchesse Ivrogne,* on which he'd come from France only two days before, would not even yet have left port. When he'd risen, sleepless, dressed, and gone out, he'd told himself it was to see if the *Duchesse* was still in port, and to learn what her captain would ask to take him back to France again, though what the man would have been doing up at three in the morning January hadn't considered—perhaps in his heart he'd known that wasn't his intent at all. Around the ships the dark was thicker, and there was little activity beyond the scur-ryings of rats. Between the wet hulks, the river gleamed with the reflec-tion of the distant torches, the occasional riding-light.

January found an empty wharf and walked out along it, the stink of the river pungent in his nose with a thousand memories. Hereabouts, where the river bent, the current was ferocious.

He didn't think it would take him long to drown.

He could barely see the wharf's end when he reached it. Occasional heat-lightning outlined the sable clouds of trees on the opposite river-bank, but illuminated nothing nearer. He'd advanced feeling his way with his feet—an absurd precaution, he thought, with the part of his mind still aware of the world of the living: wasn't the point of his com-ing here tonight to walk off the end of the wharf in the dark?

But when he reached the end he only stood there, looking out into the blackness, with the electric whisper of far-off storm-winds passing like silk ribbons over his face.

Whether he would have jumped he still didn't know. He knew—even three years later—that he'd been close to it.

But behind him he heard music, the light sweet embroideries of a single violin, playing a Mozart air in the dark.

And he turned back.

A white man was sitting on a bollard about halfway between the wharf's end and the levee behind them, a thin man of medium height whose long dark hair hung straggling over his shoulders like a di-sheveled mermaid's. He played like an angel, dismissed from the Heavenly Choir, for drunkenness, perhaps, because a squat black bottle of gin sat on the wharf-planks at his feet. He didn't look up as January came back toward him out of the night, only embellished the little dance-tune till it sparkled, calling secret rhythm and resonance from it until it seemed to speak of all joy, all light, all life.

He hadn't been there when January had walked out onto the wharf. He must have followed him, and sat down to play.

Then he looked up at January with the darkest eyes January had ever seen, and said: "You look like a man who needs a drink."

He was the first white man since January's return to his home city who had addressed him as a man, and not some lower form of life. When January had departed in 1817 the town had been mostly French, and the Creole French had long ago come to accommodation with their half-African *libre* cousins who made up most of the town's free-colored community. To Americans, who seemed to have taken over the town in their thousands, all blacks were potential slaves.

January said, "I do."

The fiddler nudged the bottle at his feet with the toe of one battered boot. "Try this. They lie, who say drafts from the River Styx bring oblivion. *Who knows what dreams may come, when we have shuffled off this mortal coil....*"

"*Aye, there's the rub,*" January had agreed, and bent to pick up the bottle. He answered in the English in which the fiddler had addressed him, the white man's voice not the twangy rasp of all those Americans who had told him all those things that a nigger couldn't do these days, and who had asked him for his free papers, to prove he had the right to walk around by himself: rather, it had the slight lilt of the educated Anglo-Irish, overlaid with the whispery hoarseness of consumption.

"Or do you think you'll find someone that you've lost in those waters?"

With cholera walking the dark streets of every city in the world that year, it was a reasonable question. January saw again what was, at that time, his last clear recollection before the long haze of grief and agony in which he'd taken ship for New Orleans from Paris—his wife Ayasha's body, stretched across their bed in their grilling-hot room in Paris, her long black hair trailing down into the drying pools of vomit on the floor. The disease had spared her nothing. She had suffered and died alone.

"Not think," he'd replied, the whole conversation with this slight fantastic figure feeling to him like something from a dream. As the past two months, since finding Ayasha's body, had all felt like a dream. "Hope."

"Hope is something the living do." The fiddler coughed, switching the bow into his other hand so that he could press his hand to his side. "... *to hope til Hope creates / from its own wreck the thing it contemplates....* It's too silly an occupation for the dead."

January took a sip of the gin—which was cheap and unspeakably bad—and said, "You may be right about that."

The *diligencia* jolted, bringing him back to the present. To the knowledge of money in his pocket, and Rose—whom he had not known existed on that hot storm-whispering night three years ago—at his side.

Slowly he said, "Hannibal has been my friend for three years. Drunk or sober, I don't think you could find a more peaceable soul in creation—or a more hapless one." He spoke French—across from him the two German merchants muttered together in their native tongue and glanced worriedly out at the gray and yellow landscape of stone, distant pines, and dust. The entire journey had been a series of translations and recapitulations, and even in the close confines of the swaying coach January and Rose had a curious sense of privacy, as if everyone else were trapped within their own linguistic worlds.

"But it is also true," he went on, "that I have no idea what Hannibal did, or even what his name was, before the night I met him." The morning after that encounter on the waterfront January had gotten his first music pupil in New Orleans, and two nights after that had been hired for his first job playing at a quadroon ball. Hannibal had been playing as well, as usual the only white among musicians who ranged from musterfinos—men who were considered to be "of color" on the grounds of one African great-grandparent—down to January's nearly-pure African blackness. For this reason alone the fiddler was considered rather degenerate by the whites in the town.

"No," said Rose softly. "No... He's never spoken of his family, or where he comes from, not even when he's drunk."

January nodded—Hannibal had never mentioned what *he* was doing in the deserted darkness of the New Orleans levee, contemplating the River Styx.

"Oh, he'll mention that he was up at Oxford, and his speech gets very Irish when he's drunk. He turned up in New Orleans about a year before you did; he'd teach the girls at my school to play violin, piano, and harp, and would correct their Latin in exchange for supper. I couldn't pay him in cash, of course."

Her mouth quirked reminiscently as she spoke of the school she'd taught on Rue St. Claud, the smile fleeting away the next moment like the silver flash of fish among reeds. January well recalled the old Spanish house to which she'd first led him on a night of wind and rain during the terrible season of yellow fever in the summer of 1833. Most of her students—daughters of quadroon and octoroon plaçées by their white protectors, even as she was herself—had left the city then. Only six remained, four of those desperately ill with yellow fever. He remembered Rose's bitter tears at their death. Two years later, she still grieved for them, and the loss of the school had been like the loss of her family.

January's hand sought hers, its tightening an unspoken reassurance. *We will have a school again.* She flashed him another quicksilver smile. Their wedding-night had been spent in the big old house on Rue Esplanade that was, miracle of miracles after years of mutual poverty, their own. It was still a matter of astonishment to him that though he daily missed Ayasha still, his grief did not lessen the wonder of his love for Rose.

Her hand tightened in return, and in a lighter voice she said, "So for all I know, Hannibal could have left a trail of corpses from here to Ireland and on across the Continent. Unless . . ." She hesitated, genuine doubt springing into green-gray eyes that were her legacy from a white father and a white grandfather. "You don't think he could have done murder while under the influence of opium, do you? And not remember?"

"My nightingale, do you have *any idea* how much opium it would *take* to render Hannibal unconscious?"

"Hmmn," said Rose. "There is much in what you say."

"Even supposing he—or *anyone*—could lay hands on such a quantity," went on January—who had considered the possibility already—"there wouldn't be a question of his having done it. And it sounds like there is. Though why he would be staying on a hacienda evidently operated by a madman, when we last saw him running off with the prima soprano from that Italian opera troupe . . ."

January saw the bandits and heard the shots at the same instant that the clattering rhythm of the coach-team broke. A bullet punched through the side of the coach, and the old Swiss valet on his jump-seat opened his mouth as if to protest, but no sound came out, only blood. As he toppled over, the guard's voice yelled from above, "Bandits!" In the same moment, the coach itself lurched, swayed precariously; there was another salvo of shots and Rose dropped forward, scooping up the rifles that had been put ready in the coach at the previous night's stop in Perote.

One of the team's been hit, January thought, in the second before the coach bumped, slewed, tipped in what felt like a horrible slow dream-like somersault. . . . He grabbed Rose around the waist and caught the wall-strap with the other hand—the Swiss valet pitched from his seat, dead-weight flying, smashing into January's back as the big vehicle went over. Dillard was the only other passenger who braced himself for the impact, and the two German merchants plunged and tumbled in a whirlwind of dust, hats, and spattering specks of blood: horses scream-ing, a blurred jumble of dark shapes glimpsed through the reeling win-dows, the warning shout of the Indian guard on the box above.

The impact of something or someone drove the breath from January's body; gunfire cracked all around.

He drove himself up at the windows above him before the coach stopped skidding—it didn't occur to him till later to wonder what would have happened had the attack come in one of those places where the road swung along the brink of a gorge. Young Padre Cesario shoved a rifle into his hands, and January flipped up the window like a trap-door, and fired at one of the forms that came pounding toward him through the dust. January ducked down, caught another rifle—Rose was loading—popped up, and fired. "Where'd you learn to handle a gun, boy?" demanded Dillard, emerging like a gopher from the win-dow beside him. Anywhere in the United States it was illegal for a black man to own or use firearms. A bullet plowed the window-frame near his hand, spraying splinters.

"Fighting for Jackson at New Orleans." January could almost hear the Tennessean's brain crunch as it assimilated the hero-President's name. "British didn't run around like this, though." He fired, and a looming horseback shape flung out its arms and fell.

"Sure is like tryin' to shoot weasels by starlight," Dillard agreed, and spat tobacco.

Behind the fallen coach the Indian guard yelled something: January turned and got off a shot at more ragged, wolf-like shapes clambering over the rocks above the road, heard another bullet strike the coach roof. A man inside cried out. A rider loomed out of the dust, bloody spittle stringing from the barbed Spanish bit in the horse's mouth. January glimpsed a scarred, bearded face as black as his own under the wide-brimmed leather hat, the flash of silver on the pistol the man aimed down at him; Dillard's gun roared in double thunder with the dark-faced bandit's. Both shots went wild, and in the next second the coach driver sprang up almost under the hooves of the bandit's horse, swinging his empty rifle like a club, while on the ground by the coach in a tangle of harness the two surviving horses kicked, screamed, thrashed.

The dark bandit wheeled, plunged into the dust, shouting *"Vamanos, toros!"* to his men. One unhorsed bandit tried to mount a fallen comrade's horse, and Dillard coolly shot him in the back; the animal whinnying, backing, reins tangled in a thicket of creosote-bush in the ditch beside the road. As the bandits rode off, the Tennessean swung himself up through the coach window and went to get the horse; January ducked down into the coach again. Strange, he thought, that one of the first men of African blood that he'd seen in this country had been trying to kill him.

Then he smelled blood down in the coach and saw Rose with the breast of her dress all crimson with gore....

She was knotting one of her hat-veils around a wound in Padre Cesario's wrist and the blood clearly belonged to him—or to the poor valet Da Ponte, crumpled in a huddle—but the sight of it nearly stopped January's heart.

It could have been Rose.

Like that, in a second, everything we could have had together, all the years of our happiness, gone...

He began to shake, as if with malarial chill. "Are you all right?" He hoped his voice didn't sound as hoarse to her as it did in his own ears.

She nodded. Her hands were black with powder and her long hair—beautiful walnut-brown and curly, more like a white woman's than a black's—stuck with sweat to her face and hung down in strings where it had escaped chignon and hat.

We're going back to New Orleans and to hell with Hannibal.... *YOU'RE going back to New Orleans and I'll join you there after I've wrung his neck for him. . . . We'll open the school on Rue Esplanade and live happily ever after forever unless you get kidnapped by slave-traders or die in another cholera epidemic or in childbirth. . . .*

He drew a deep breath and looked around. "Anyone else hurt?"

The two merchants shook their heads. One of them bent over Da Ponte, tried to straighten him; January and the other merchant opened the coach door above them like a trap-door, and gently helped out first the priest, then Rose, then lifted out the valet's body. He was old and fragile and had spoken only Italian; January wondered what he'd been doing in Mexico, and if he had family back in Locarno. He'd been shot through the throat.

It could have been Rose.

Dillard and the guard came back, each leading a bandit's horse. The bandit January had shot lay sobbing some distance from the coach. He'd been dragged, and then trampled, by his terrified mount. Blood bubbled from his mouth and spread over the crotch of his thin, ragged peasant breeches. His unshaven face contorted with agony; January fished his rosary from his pocket, knelt beside the man and twined the blue glass beads, the battered steel crucifix in the filthy hands.

The bandit couldn't speak but brought the rosary up to his lips and kissed it.

"Your sins are forgiven you," whispered January in Spanish, and made the Sign of the Cross. Standing, he took from his pocket the pistol he'd purchased in Vera Cruz. "Go with God."

And shot him through the head.

He was wiping the blood off his rosary when the Indian coach guard came over and said in Spanish, "Don't waste your powder on such a one, Señor. El Moro may attack us again before we reach the city."

"Sorry."

The other men were unharnessing the surviving horses, dragging the dead ones clear. Checking hocks, knees, tendons. Already the *sopilotes*—the gray-headed black vultures—were circling, waiting for the living to clear the hell away and let them eat. January heard, far off on the still, thin air, the ringing of church-bells. It was Sunday, he remembered. They had climbed into the *diligencia* at two in the morning in Perote, and he had been so sleepy, he had barely been able to murmur his prayers.

He walked a little distance from the coach with its scattered debris of luggage, hat-boxes, letters from a burst mailsack, and the book one of the Germans had been reading, past the towering knee of gray rock that had concealed the bandits' attack. He felt dizzy, with the sun's heat rising off the stone and the road and the clear, brittle desolation of these oak-dotted mountains, but the air nonetheless steely with chill.

I've been in this country a week, he thought, *and already I've killed a man.*

He wondered if Hannibal was still alive at all.

Coming to Mexico, it had been in his heart to wonder about what it would be like where slavery had been done away with, as the abolitionist Yankee driver had said.

And now he knew.

Born a slave, for sixteen years of his manhood he'd lived in France in a world completely free. Free to study medicine, free to study music, free to wed a woman he loved . . . free of the ghastly burden of being the black son of slaves in Louisiana that he had carried like a slab of stone all his life.

And he'd learned that freedom made no difference whatsoever when Death came calling.

Past the rocks the road turned, falling away steeply before him into dry abysses of yellow air that seemed to magnify everything like crystal. He saw below him a long dun landscape splodged with thorny green, broken here and there with anemic trees, feathery with autumn. Mountains gouged the sky southward to his left, black rock meringued with marble white, trailing drifts of white smoke. Farther off to the south and west the noon sky glared silver in sheets of water, fringed with green that was darker still.

January felt he could see every tile of every roof of the city that rose, it seemed, from the heart of the lake, red and blue and gilt; could name every horse and cow, every burro and child and pig in the thatch-roofed villages that lay between dry rangeland and endless, gleaming acres of bird-skimmed marsh. Could distinguish every voice of those multi-tongued bells one from another as they sent forth over the lands their eternal message: each soul, no matter whose, is equally cherished, equally precious in the sight of God.

Behind him he heard cursing—German, English, Spanish—and the jangle of harness-ware. A long whip cracked as the men righted the coach. He supposed he should go back. Padre Cesario would need his arm looked at before the wound turned nasty. And it wasn't beyond the realm of possibility that the bandits would return, and he was out of sight of the others. But for a long time he only stood, looking down over that high, barren valley, watching the geese and the ducks, the hawks and the vultures, free as the angels of Death in the jeweled air.

Once they reached Mexico City itself, it took them hours to get inside.

Lake and marshland surrounded it. After a night in abominable accommodations in the village at the foot of the pass, they spent most of the morning tearing along at top speed between sheets of water prickled with reeds, coming at last to one of the causeways raised by the Indians from whom the Spanish had stolen the land. These causeways being the only means to cross the marsh, they were the ideal places for the government to set up customs barriers and extract tolls from those bringing merchandise—or anything else—into the city, with predictable results.

Familiar for years with the customs barriers around Paris and their jam of carriages, carts, pack-animals, and basket-toting vendors all waiting to be passed by the bored and overworked bureaucrats of the customshouse, January minded the wait less than some members of the party. But even Dillard, though he muttered about how Old Hickory would deal with tariffs, by God, didn't seem surprised.

By which January deduced the man from Tennessee had been in Mexico City before.

He could only be glad that they'd decided to have the valet Da Ponte buried at the church at the mountain pass yesterday afternoon. Otherwise the customs inspectors would almost certainly have levied duty on the body.

Besides the enormous lines of ox-carts, coaches, burros laden with charcoal and firewood, and herds of long-horned cattle and grunting swine, there were unexpected numbers of soldiers on the causeway, even for a country that had been in a state of internal warfare, on and off, for the past twenty-five years. When January asked his fellow-passenger Herr Groellich about it, the German replied, "Had you not heard, then? Every day new levies come in from the countryside, from as far off as the Yucatán. Generalissimo Santa Anna gathers his Army of Operations, the greatest army of the world, he says, to march north and punish the rebellious Americans who have seized the province of Texas."

At the mention of Texas, Dillard turned his head from gazing out at the crowding men in their red-and-blue uniforms. Watchful anger flickered in his dark eyes.

"I understand the Texians claim that the Generalissimo's young brother-in-law, General Cós, made concessions to them," the German went on, nervously straightening the bow of his green silk neck-scarf. "Including that the government of Mexico would respect the rights given them under the old constitution of ten years ago."

"Of course, he had neither the right nor the authority to concede anything of the kind," put in his partner, angling his head to peer over his spectacles. "If indeed he ever said any such thing at all, which he now says he did not."

"What does he say about Texas?" demanded Dillard of Rose. "Does he mention that we—*they*—don't have the right to govern themselves as we were promised? Or that the so-called government of *this* country—that's *supposed* to believe in independence the way we do—is so mismanaged, a man can't hold his own property safe there anymore?"

January knew that a reasoned discussion of governmental jurisdiction under the principles of federal union as set out by Alexander Hamilton would only serve to make the situation worse, and so held his peace. Rose replied tactfully, "Herr Groellich only remarks, sir, that the Americans at Béxar appear to have defeated one army and that General Santa Anna is preparing to send another, which certainly shouldn't come as a surprise to Mr. Houston. Do you now live in Texas, Mr. Dillard?"

"Er—no. M'am," he added, clearly not sure whether to address a woman of color by even that slight honorific. "That is, I'm one of

Mr. Butler's secretaries here—the American chargé d'affaires." But at the mention of Texas, Dillard's face softened and his eyes lost their anger—a lover hearing the name of his beloved. January guessed that the denial of Texian—and therefore Mexican—citizenship was a lie.

"And is it as treeless as they say?" Rose asked. "I was raised in the bayou country; everyone speaks of Texas as if it were a desert."

"Oh, no, m'am. Once you get above the valley of the Nueces, you're in the high plains, with nuthin' but sky and Comanche. But in the hill-country around San Antonio de Béxar, it's soft and green, like paradise. It's as beautiful a land as God made, m'am, open and sweet; a land for free men. And we don't—*they* don't—aim to be run out of it."

By *free men* January assumed Dillard meant *free white men*. One source of friction between the Mexican government and the Americans who had been flooding into the northern part of the state of Cohuila-Texas was that Mexico forbade the institution of slavery that so many Americans considered essential to cotton farming.

Even after Herr Groellich took up a collection toward a substantial bribe for the customs inspectors, it was still nearly two in the afternoon by the time they were led past the line of waiting beasts, soldiers, and vehicles of the poor and into the vaulted stone room where every valise and portmanteau was shaken, prodded, looked into, and levied upon. Dillard declared himself to be a resident of Tennessee and refused, as a diplomatic secretary, to have his single carpetbag searched. When the clerks insisted, causing a long delay, he grew indignant at Rose's whispered suggestion that a bribe would settle the problem and instead simply stormed out of the customshouse into the jammed and squalid street beyond.

"Welcome to Mexico," murmured Rose under her breath as she and January climbed back into the coach and it lurched out through the iron-strapped customshouse gates. "I hope Hannibal is well and truly grateful to us."

"I'll settle for finding him alive."

The Vera Cruz *diligencia* terminated its run in the Calle Dolores, not far from the city's great Cathedral square. Beyond the customshouse lay a tangle of narrow streets, unpaved and trampled into unspeakable soup by the constant stream of traffic. Even in the slave-quarters where he'd spent his early childhood, January had never seen squalor such as that visible through the coach windows. The mud-brick huts that defined the lane made the two-family cabin of his earliest recollections seem palatial, and the fluids leaking from the garbage-heaps between them rendered the clay underfoot to puddled, piss-smelling, wheel-gripping ooze. Flies swarmed. Dogs tore at the half-gutted carcass of a goat. Incredibly ragged men, black with filth and clothed only in cotton breeches so thin as to clearly outline the genitals—or so ragged as to flashingly display them—crowded around the coach, reaching out groping hands to beg, or gazed sullenly from the garishly painted *pulquerias* that adorned every intersection.

Twenty-five years, thought January, both aghast and deeply sad. In 1810, when New Spain first rose in revolt against the mother country of her upper classes, she had been one of the wealthiest lands in the world. The source of cattle, silver, gold, corn and fruits, coffee and sugar-cane. A peaceful and prosperous hinterland whose subjugation had kept Spain's economy above hatches for centuries.

Dillard doesn't know how lucky his people were in the British colonies. Eight years of fighting and then it was over. Creole British rulers who were educated in government and who hadn't been brought up with the necessity of keeping an enormous population of displaced and angry Indians as agricultural slaves. And a military commander with the integrity not to succumb to the temptation of dictatorship. Even France hadn't managed that.

Around them the ramshackle adobe slums gave way to taller houses of stucco and light-red *tezontl* stone. Pilasters, medallions, elaborate baroque arabesques of marble adorned windows and doors, bright against paintwork of cherry, orange, lapis, or green. Tiles gleamed on the fronts of the taller houses; saints stared disapprovingly down from niches. Between those tall fronts were wedged shops no bigger than closets: *pulquerias* abounded, gaudy with murals of flowers, bull-fights, semi-nude women, and bearing names like *The Wandering Jew* and *With You Until Death.* As they passed the open doors, January could smell the mild, yeasty pungence of the beverage, and saw figures sprawled on the benches or amid peanut-hulls on the floor.

And everywhere, brilliant color under the brilliant sun.

When they stopped at last before the offices of the *diligencia* company, January asked the young priest Padre Cesario where the Calle Jaral lay. There Hannibal's latest known inamorata, the opera singer Consuela Montero, had her house. "You cannot mean to walk there, surely?" asked the priest, shocked.

"If it is not far," said January. "We can hire porters. . . ."

"By all means, hire porters," agreed the priest as quickly and as self-evidently as if the question were whether January should wear trousers. "But hire also a hack and a driver," he said, and he nodded across the street to the several decrepit-looking mule-drawn coaches waiting on the other side. "Understand, Señor, that in Mexico a man is treated according to how those about him perceive him being treated by others. Even you—if you will pardon me for mentioning your race—even *negros,* who are everywhere treated with scorn in my country, a part of that at least is that they have no money, no family, no influence. Influence is everything here. But you and your lady are well dressed, and have money. If you lower yourself to walking, men will say, 'See, in spite of his fine clothes he is only a *negro* on foot—and he may have stolen the clothes.' If you arrive in a hack, to *show* that you are not poor, all will be different."

January nodded. He had already observed something of the kind in Vera Cruz, and had slipped the customs officials at the barrier an enormous bribe not to search his baggage last, which he guessed they ordinarily would have done. It could, he supposed, be called an investment. "Thank you," he said.

"Moreover," the priest added, "it is several streets to the Plaza Mayor—the Cathedral square—and the Calle Jaral lies beyond it. The *léperos* are everywhere, and will be upon you like flies on meat if you are afoot."

"*Léperos*...lepers?" He used the French word, *lepreux,* and the padre shook his head.

"Not actual lepers, no. But this is what the beggars of the capital are called, *léperos*—*pelados*—as filthy as lepers, and more dangerous." Padre Cesario sighed, genuinely distressed. The priest was a man of fair complexion and European features, almost certainly full-blooded *criollo*—Creole Spanish. He had a small parish church in the city, he had said on their journey; he looked far too well fed and well clothed to be living off that income alone.

"These are men driven from the villages by poverty and starvation, and by fear of being drafted into the Army, where conditions are truly terrible, Señor. Day laborers when they can get work, who starve when they cannot. With the fighting that has raged over my country all these long years, they have flocked to the capital by the thousands, so that there is neither work nor food for them, and most spend their days pursuing oblivion in the *pulquerias.* No one in Mexico City ever walks if he can pay to ride."

January looked around him. Lines of mules passed by, guided by muleteers—*arrieros*—in striped serapes and wide-brimmed hats of glazed black leather; water-sellers with huge pots slung before them and behind on head-straps, and soldiers in red and blue. But no gentlemen on foot, he saw, and no women save the Indian women, or the countrywomen—*poblanas*—in their short bright two-colored petticoats and satin vests, jingling with silver ornaments. Even these were importuned by beggars at every other step. In every doorway, in every alley, he glimpsed still more wretched human bundles of dirty rags, waiting.

"Thank you, Padre," he said, and signed for a cab.

"Lastly," said the priest, "if I may be so bold as to advise you, Señor, hire servants as quickly as you can. Wherever you go, have them follow you. And that, my friend, will do more than anything can to make people . . . if not forget your race, at least not turn up their noses at you as being of no worth. Ah!" His face radiated into smiles as a high and spindly carriage known as a *volante* appeared around the corner and drew up before the *diligencia* offices. "One of my—er—parishioners, come to welcome me. Señor—Señora . . ." He shook hands with January, bent to kiss Rose's glove. Then he sprang to the open carriage, in which waited an extremely fashionable-looking lady who greeted him with a most unparishioner-like kiss on the lips.

As January helped Rose into the cab—and looked down his nose as haughtily as he could manage to while he tipped an Indian porter to load up their baggage on it—he wondered if Consuela Montero was still in Mexico City at all, and even if she was, whether the opera singer would be concerned with Hannibal's fate. She was, if he recalled Hannibal's letters correctly, the illegitimate daughter of the wealthy *hacendado* Don Prospero de Castellón, and therefore the half-sister of the murdered man.

Yet she was the only one he knew who might know exactly how matters stood.

In his letters, Hannibal had described the house on the Calle Jaral as "once the palace of a local marquis of impeccable heritage, now let—to the family's enduring chagrin—to a silk-merchant and a coffee-seller on the ground floor, and to my most scandalous and beautiful Concha upstairs." In addition to the aforementioned establishments, there was a shoemaker operating in what had been the coal room, a manufacturer of cigars operating out of—and apparently raising his family in—what had been the wood room, while the coffee-seller's wife ran what appeared to be a public cook-shop in the palace's old kitchen, with benches set up in the front courtyard for her customers.

This lady was the only one still in evidence when the hack pulled in under the broad arch of the gate, just clearing up after the *comida,* the leisurely early-afternoon dinner that preceded the daily siesta. The afternoon sun poured hot rays down into the courtyard so that the very air felt smothered. "Do you think anyone will be awake to let us in?" asked Rose, looking around her at the crude chairs and tables that occupied the space where the family carriages had been stored in palmier days, and at the laundry hung from the balcony arcades.

"I suppose we can nap in the courtyard until Prince Charming comes along and wakes Sleeping Beauty with a kiss." January paid off the driver, who had set the baggage down near the broad stone stair that led to the upper arcade. No one appeared from any of the many doors visible on that level, so January picked up the trunk, and Rose the hat-box and carpetbags.

"The Day of the Dead is the Feast of All Saints at home, isn't it?" asked Rose as they climbed the stairs. "I remember Mother taking me to her mother's tomb to clean and whitewash it—she'd have her cook make up a picnic lunch like everyone else who came to the cemetery that day, but I don't recall anything about expecting Grandma to come out of the grave and share it with us."

She set the bags down at the top of the steps, put back the veils of her hat, and looked doubtfully at the shut doors and shuttered windows. In the United States it would have been illegal for her to wear a hat at all—women of color being required to wear the tignon, or head-scarf, of servitude—and January delighted in the close-fitting bonnet, the neat, soft swags of her curls.

"Mother would take me to the white section of the cemetery, too, to hang a wreath on her father's tomb and pay our respects to the family. They always pretended to the children that she was a 'former servant,' but of course they all knew. The Americans in New Orleans don't do any of that, do they?"

"That's because Americans breed behind fences like cats and don't have families, according to my mother," remarked January, picking out from the several doors the one with a large bronze knocker. "Not that, as a former slave herself, my mother has a single ancestor in any grave-yard in town—that she knew about, at any rate. That never stopped her from having the cook make up a basket lunch and going down to St. Louis Cemetery to spend the day visiting with her friends."

He was raising his hand to the knocker when the door flew open. A voice inside cried, "Señor Enero! *Madre de Dios,* come in! My house is yours, and everything in it—thank God you have come!" And a small crimson whirlwind bustled forth to catch him in a tight embrace.

"And Señorita Rose!" Consuela Montero turned, her plump hands and ample décolletage still flashing with garnets though she'd loosened her raven curls in preparation for siesta. "The lady who made the fire-works for the opera!"

Rose laughed as they were drawn into the *sala*—the formal and rather bare room common to the inns they had stayed at in Vera Cruz and on the road. Like those at the inns, it contained only a long table running down the middle, and ten heavily carved chairs ranged around the walls. A painting of the Virgin adorned one wall, above a blue-and-white Chinese vase of roses. Elsewhere, rather surprisingly, hung a small Turner in a gold frame.

"Señorita Rose no longer," said January gravely. "Madame... Señora Enero, my wife."

"*En verdad? Felicitación,* Rosita... may I call you Rose?" Consuela tiptoed to kiss Rose's dusty cheek. "Señor, Señora... this is my com-panion Doña Gertrudis de Avila de Caldofranco...." She gestured to the black-clothed woman who had stood beside the door through all of this, a look of impassive disapproval on her high-born Spanish counte-nance. "Though why it is considered correct to keep a chaperone here when all the town knows one is living in sin with a violin-player—that's enough, Trudis, now go fetch us wine and cakes, and have Lita make up the spare bedroom for my guests—you will, of course, remain as my guests? Hannibal will be overjoyed.... You got my letter?"

"We got a letter from Hannibal."

"He wrote one, then? I did also, once it became clear that that im-becile Ward, the minister of the British, was going to do nothing."

Consuela led the way through a door into her own bedroom, which like many in both Mexico and France—and indeed in the older houses of New Orleans as well—was set up as an informal parlor. There were comfortable chairs, a pianoforte—January couldn't help touching a key and found it was in tune—and another small modern painting, an English cathedral beneath an astonishing sky. "That *adoquín* Ylario— the junior intendant of police in this city—has been out to the ha- cienda three times in the past two weeks, watching the place from the arroyos beside the road, waiting for my father to ride out so that he may go in and arrest Hannibal while most of the vaqueros are gone. He has a judge here in town. . . ."

"How much danger is Hannibal in?"

"A great deal, once Ylario should get him into town." Consuela nodded thanks to the manservant who brought in a tray of light wine, coffee, and cakes: *pandolce* sparkling with crystals of brown sugar, camote, hulled peanuts, and flowers wrought of marzipan. "Ordinarily, of course, a man might remain weeks—months—in La Accordada prison before an *alcalde* even sees him, and he might never be seen if Santa Anna sends his Army recruiters through to draft the prisoners. But there are judges who, like this Capitán Ylario, are sick of Santa Anna's favorites, and since they cannot hang my father—who paid Santa Anna's debts for him many times when Santa Anna was still a loyal officer of the King— they will be more than glad to sentence poor Hannibal to death the moment Ylario brings him before them. By the time my father could lo- cate Santa Anna to rescind the order—for *El Presidente* has a habit of running off to his hacienda in Vera Cruz and pretending to be a philoso- pher for months at a time—Hannibal would be dead at the end of a rope."

"What kind of evidence do they have against him?" asked Rose, and Consuela blinked at her in surprise.

"The evidence against him is that he did it, Señora. My brother de- served to be poisoned, and I don't think there was a tear shed for him by anyone in the house except that *mariposa* valet of his who found the body, but . . ."

"What happened?"

The singer shrugged impatiently, and picked apart the hull of a peanut with small, deft fingers, as if the matter of Hannibal's guilt or innocence were secondary to the importance of his escape. "We had all just sat through the most dreadful dinner to celebrate my brother Fernando's wedding on the following day. At the end of it Fernando went into my father's study and locked the door. Everyone still at the dinner-table saw Hannibal take brandy and glasses from the sideboard and go outside—the study has three doors, one from the *sala,* one from the *corredor* outside, and one from my father's room, which was pad-locked because my father had gone mad just then and was locked up in his room. But from the window of his room my father saw Hannibal take a bottle from his pocket and pour something into one of the glasses of brandy, just before he went into the study."

Rose said, "I can see how there would be a misunderstanding."

Consuela shook her head. "There can be no misunderstanding about it, Señora Rose. I came out into the *corredor* only moments later, with my half-sister Valentina and my father's mistress Natividad, who was going to marry Fernando, and with Natividad's mother and Doña Gertrudis, of course. . . . A woman in this country does not neglect her duenna's company any more than she neglects to cast a shadow upon the wall. So we were all there when Hannibal came out of the study, without the brandy or the glasses. The rest of the men all stayed in the *sala* drinking while Hannibal played the violin for us in the *corredor;* then when the men came out the servants were in the *sala,* clearing away the dinner and setting up tables for cards. So you can see there was no way in which anyone else could have entered the study. My father is quite mad, you understand, but when he sees actual things—not talk-ing skulls or feathered snakes floating in the air or the Jaguar-God ma-terializing in his bedroom—he is *most* observant. He didn't like my brother. . . ."

"I don't imagine he did," murmured January, "if Fernando had pil-fered his mistress."

"*Dios,* no! That had nothing to do with the matter. It was my fa-ther's idea that Franz marry Natividad. . . ."

"Franz?"

"Fernando. My brother. From the age of ten he had lived in Prussia, where he went to military school—he was twenty-five when he died. He was a major in the Tenth Berlin Guards, and loved the army of the Prussians. It was clean, he always said, as if less exalted beings lived in filth and fed upon garbage. He did not want to come back to Mexico. He only did so this year, after the deaths of our older brother Don Damiano and Damiano's son Luis from the *vomito negro*."

"So up until this year," said Rose, "this Don Damiano was your father's heir?"

"Just so," agreed Consuela, dusting dark crystals of sugar from her fingers. "My father was married three times, you understand—in many ways that is the reason for his command that Fernando marry Natividad, which Fernando did not want to do at all. Father's first wife was Doña Marcellina de Medellín, by whom he had Damiano and our eldest sister Josefa, who is now a widow with two children. After Doña Marcellina's death my father married Doña Maria-Exaltación de Borregos, a Spanish girl sent here to a convent during all the fighting in Spain, and she bore him Isabella and Fernando. Later still he wed Melosia Valenzuela, who became the mother of Valentina, and who ran off one night when Valla was a little girl with only the clothes on her back, not that I blame the wretched woman in the slightest for doing so.

"My mother," added Consuela, her voice thinning to a wry edge, "he also attempted to imprison as he imprisoned poor Hannibal—she was a mantua-maker—and she struck him over the head with a tortilla-press and made her escape with the connivance of some muleteers. I don't think he ever tried that sort of thing again with a woman. But you see, because Melosia ran away, Natividad's mother did not see any reason why Father could not marry Natividad, and so of course to silence her Father arranged for it that Natividad marry Franz."

While Consuela was speaking, January was marginally conscious of a steady parade of servants past the open bedroom door. They bore the luggage, bedding, ewers of water, and wood for a bedroom fire along the *corredor*. Consuela seemed to employ nearly a dozen servants, far more than even the most lavishly-kept woman would have in France, let alone in the United States. Having seen the sheer numbers of poor in the streets, January guessed there were men and women who would happily scrub chamber pots for food and a place to sleep in an attic.

No wonder anything in this country, from murder to imported point-lace, could be bought with a bribe.

With raised eyebrows, Rose asked, "And your brother agreed to this—er—arrangement?"

"He had to." Consuela poured herself another cup of coffee, and dropped a chunk of pale-brown sugar into its inky depths. "He was a colonel in Santa Anna's army, and without my father's money he could not buy uniforms or guns for his men when they march north to Texas to deal with the *Norteamericano* rebels, for of course the Army has no money to pay for such things. Franz does not like women, you understand, let alone that Natividad is a *cusca* and stupid as a wooden peg."

"So Hannibal is still at the hacienda?" asked Rose. One would never guess to look at her that twenty-four hours ago she'd been loading rifles in an overturned stagecoach with blood all over her dress. She had a long oval face and, despite a treacherous dusting of freckles, a naturally serious expression: in her pale-blue traveling-dress, simple hat, and spectacles, she looked like she'd never done anything in her life but teach geography to schoolgirls.

"Oh, yes. You understand, my father had been holding Hannibal prisoner for six days already *before* the murder. Myself, I was ready to strangle the old lunatic, for I was singing *La Sonnambula* in three days at the Teatro Principal and had to rehearse, and an excellent performance it would have been had the conductor been sober. I cannot think why it was not my father who was poisoned, instead of Franz."

"Holding him prisoner?" asked January, startled. "What had he done?"

The diva shrugged. "Played the violin."

"It must have been quite a tune," Rose remarked.

The smile that tugged Consuela's full lips was both reminiscent and wry. "You know how Hannibal plays," she replied. "As the angels of God would play, did God permit His angels to suffer passion and grief. He also plays picquet—Hannibal, I mean—an old-fashioned game much out of favor these days, but my father dotes upon it. And he can talk to Father of Petronius and Suetonius and listen when Father goes on for hours and hours about the statues of the old gods that he digs up from the ruins of the Indian cities, or buys from every peddler who comes through the village. So when it came time for Hannibal and myself to return from our visit at the end of August, Father said it would suit him better that Hannibal remain as his guest, and play the fiddle for him every night, as the singer Farinelli once did for the King of Spain, and play picquet with him, since the rest of the family were all bores and monstrosities."

January said, "Hmmn."

"I should think," commented Rose judiciously, sipping her coffee, "that the simplest way to discourage such importunate hospitality would be to win heavily at picquet. Hannibal's quite capable of it. I've played with him."

"Oh, he won *thousands* of pesos from my father, and from Don Anastasio—the husband of Franz's full sister Isabella and one of my father's oldest friends. Don Anastasio's hacienda lies just to the west of Mictlán. That doesn't matter to my father. Hannibal took five or six hundred from Franz, which I think was the reason Franz threatened to kill him. Father gave orders to Vasco—the foreman of his vaqueros, who is loyal to him and could not abide either Franz or Anastasio—not to permit Hannibal to leave the hacienda, and when my father came down sick three days later..."

"Can we return for a moment," interposed January, "to the part about your brother threatening to kill Hannibal?"

"Did they quarrel?" asked Rose. Beyond the open door the courtyard had fallen absolutely silent with the hour of siesta, the autumn heat pressing down upon the house and the city around it as surely as any evil fairy's spell upon an enchanted castle. The servants had vanished; with the window shutters closed, the bedroom was stuffy and dim.

"Quarrel? *Dios,* no!" Consuela dipped a fragment of *pandolce* into her coffee. "You know Hannibal never quarrels with anyone, not even when he has taken a drop too much opium. But my brother was a savage, Señora. A cold savage, who never raised his voice. When he was with the Army, Franz had three of his men flogged to death, one of them by his own hand; it is rumored also that he beat one of his servants here in town to death as well." She shook her head, her face in its frame of tumbled black curls suddenly somber and very Indian.

"So—three days before the wedding my father went into one of his crazy fits. God forbid that even the bride should have more attention paid to her on her wedding-eve than he. He began talking to his idols, and wandering about the house in his nightshirt, and thinking that Santa Anna—who as his dear friend was there for the wedding—was the war-god of the old Indians, to whom the ancient priests offered the torn-out hearts of living victims, which always makes the servants nervous.

"Josefa—our eldest sister, as I have said, who does not have much use for me—sent at once for her confessor and for her confessor's confessor, to pray that the Devil be driven out of our father. Natividad's mother, Señora Lorcha, also sent for a priest, and tried to have my father marry Natividad before anyone could do anything about it, but Fernando arrived in the midst of that ceremony with two mad-doctors from town and had Father put under restraint. Hannibal tried to slip out in all the confusion and was caught by the vaqueros and brought back. It is fifteen miles to the city, you understand, and most of it open rangeland, and even with Father locked up in his room Vasco would not take orders from Fernando."

Consuela sighed and broke off another piece of *pandolce.* "So in the midst of all this praying and cursing and conversations with sacred jaguars and people who weren't there, Hannibal was playing cards in the *corredor* upstairs with me and Valentina and Natividad, on the afternoon before the wedding-feast, with all of our respective duennas present, naturally. And suddenly Fernando came out of my father's study and took Hannibal by the throat, and thrust him up against the wall and snarled, 'Know that when I am master here you will pay dearly for your perfidy, *Norteamericano* bastard.'

"And of course Hannibal replied 'My dear Fernando, you're as mistaken about my intentions as you are about my nationality and the circumstances of my birth,' but of course my brother did not listen. He was not a listener, my brother Franz."

She angled her coffee-cup in her fingers; a hot sliver of light from the door touched the dark fluid and glinted in the garnets on her rings. "Since it was clear to all by then that my father was going to be locked up, leaving Franz truly in charge to do as he pleased, Hannibal tried to bolt again before supper but did not get even a mile. He was badly frightened, and with good reason. When Santa Anna arrived I know he asked him for protection and an escort back to town, but Santa Anna said that he would not go against the wishes of his dear friend Don Prospero. I think the situation amused him, and he would not intervene. He is cruel that way."

"Would Santa Anna have simply stood by and let Franz... Fernando... mistreat... a British citizen?" asked Rose uneasily.

"That I don't know, Señora. Santa Anna seeks to please my father because my father paid his debts for him. The general's favor and his friendship are the reasons my father is still rich when most of the other old landowners are bankrupt from taxes and forced loans and losing all their men to the Army. But he is cruel, Santa Anna, and sly. He has no particular affection for Hannibal, and as I said, the situation amused him, like watching a cock-fight, or a bull being baited."

A corner of her lush mouth turned down. "I cannot say that supper was a meal notable for its sparkling conversation. M'sieu Guillenormand, my father's chef, was beside himself for fear that the dinner would be called off altogether or that Santa Anna would go back to the city without sampling his efforts. Guillenormand said that it was just like my father—which of course it was—to go mad just when he, Sacripant Guillenormand, was on the point of serving up a dinner that would make his fame forever, as if anyone could make himself famous forever for doing anything in Mexico City these days. It was like something out of Molière or Goya, with Fernando glaring at Natividad, and Natividad's mother looking daggers at Fernando, and Josefa watching Natividad's mother to make sure she didn't slip away and marry her daughter to my father when no one was looking, and the two mad-doctors trying to make polite conversation with the priests. . . . Josefa ate nothing but dry bread, to prove her sinfulness, and M'sieu Guillenormand threatened to kill himself on account of that, as he had done many times before. Franz got up and announced he was going back to the study to try to make sense of my father's papers; we all heard him bolt the study door. Hannibal took the brandy bottle and two glasses from the sideboard and went out to the door that opens from the study into the *corredor.*

"And three hours later my brother's valet found my brother dead."

THREE

They left Mexico City as soon as it was light enough to see. Consuela and Rose rode in an old-fashioned traveling-coach shaped like a tea-cup and slung on leather straps that made it sway like a ship in a gale, while January rode beside them, surrounded by an armed assortment of male servants and profoundly thankful not to be in the heaving coach itself. Though Rose had evidently been deemed sufficiently respectable to play *dame de compagnie* to a lady going to the home of her father—either that, or Doña Gertrudis, like John Dillard, objected to riding in a coach with *los negros*—both women were accompanied by their maids.

"Of course Rose must have a maid," Consuela had declared after siesta yesterday while supper was being laid on the table. "Your Padre Cesario was absolutely right. And you, Señor Enero, must have a valet." To January's protest that it would not be possible to locate servants of any kind—much less reliable ones—before departing for Mictlán in the morning, Consuela had replied with an airy wave of her hand and the words "We will leave that to Sancho. Sancho is my footman and he knows everyone in town. He will get you servants."

He had, too. For Rose, the wiry, rather wolfish Sancho had located—and vouched for—a slim, dark zamba girl named Zama, and for January he had produced a leathery, silent, elderly Yaqui Indian called Cristobál. At a reale apiece a week, with shabby livery thrown in from the trunks in Consuela's box-room, it was a cheap enough means of establishing their credentials among the respectable: January was amused to see that while Cristobál fitted silently in among Consuela's mounted henchmen, Consuela's mestizo maid Pepita looked down her nose at the darker-skinned Zama and refused to share the same carriage-seat with her.

He wondered how he and Rose would have fared on this journey had they not—through a strange chain of luck and circumstance the previous summer—stumbled upon a moderate-sized pirate cache in the bayous near the home of Rose's white relatives, in the swamplands south of New Orleans. Perhaps, as all the saints attested, money could not buy happiness, but it certainly made the misery attendant on being born of African parentage in Louisiana much easier to deal with.

So they rode out of Mexico City like lords, with servants and a coach, as the flower-sellers were gliding into the town on their barges covered with poppies, singing strange songs in the old Nahuatl tongue.

Within a few miles of the end of the northern causeway, January better understood how his friend could be held prisoner in a private home fifteen miles from the largest city in the Western Hemisphere. Once away from the city and the lakes that surrounded it, the deforested land was utterly desolate. Across the chewed green mantle of what remained of the rainy season's grasses, cattle wandered at will, save where horrific hedges of cactus kept them out of dusty village cornfields. *Sopilotes* circled lazily in the sky. Brush-choked gullies slashed the earth that the coach had to descend, rattling in every joint and trace, then heave free of again; with all his heart January pitied the women inside. Sometimes he would glimpse riders, half-seen in clouds of yellow dust. Free rancheros, probably, who held small farms along the few stingy watercourses, or the vaqueros of the wealthy cattlemen in short jackets and leather knee-breeches unbuttoned halfway up to the thigh, their long hair tied in silk kerchiefs beneath low-crowned leather hats. But the sight of them made January's heart quicken with dread as he recalled the bandits in the pass: as he recalled Rose kneeling in the overturned coach, with blood staining her dress.

It could have been Rose. It could have been Rose they buried in the little cemetery at Chalco—to leave him once more standing on the dark banks of the River Styx, trying to think of a reason to go on with his life alone.

And there was nothing to stop them from being attacked, and robbed, and killed, except their own numbers and their own weaponry. In New Orleans January had grown, if not used to the thought that he could be kidnapped and sold as a slave in the Territories, at least accustomed to taking precautions. He now realized how different it was to be in a place where *no one* would care, or make the smallest attempt to stop violence or murder.

Don Prospero de Castellón was called *hacendado*, but within his realm he was the ruler as surely as the Sultan ruled Turkey. There was, quite literally, no one to stop him—or the bandit El Moro—from doing exactly as he chose.

"The British minister?" said Consuela when the carriage halted mid-morning so that the women could drink a little wine and rest from the endless, sickening jolting. "He looked down his nose when I spoke of Hannibal and said only 'That worthless opium-eater,' as if half the population of England doesn't drop opium in their beer and dose their babies with laudanum to keep them from crying." She snapped open her sandalwood fan and sniffed. A short distance away Pepita and Zama puffed on their respective cigarettos and ignored one another.

January said nothing. Though he had long deplored his friend's use of the drug, he understood it. The racking coughs of consumption could be stilled by nothing else. Hannibal had written to him in August that months of rest in Consuela's flat had improved his condition wonderfully; January guessed that his friend would find, as others had found before him, that the golden key that opened the shackles of pain would prove to lock the gates of another kind of prison entirely.

Provided, of course, that he lived to see the New Year.

"Who was at your brother's wedding-feast?" he asked instead. "You spoke of your sisters—Doña Josefa, the eldest, and another who is married to your father's friend Don Anastasio...."

"Isabella," agreed Consuela. "But she did not come to the banquet. She had a migraine, Don Anastasio said, but me, I think it was that she could not endure to see such a one as Natividad married to her brother. She is a woman much ill-done-by in the world—just ask her."

She spoke flippantly, but January had heard enough about the family—and seen enough of how society worked in Mexico—to guess that life could not be easy for any daughter of the mad and autocratic Don

Prospero. There was no precarious middle ground, such as Rose had for a time occupied in New Orleans, for women who would not be dependent on their fathers or husbands.

Between the loss of her beloved school in the wake of the cholera in September of '33, and the finding of the pirate cache nearly two years later, Rose had eked out a living as a translator of Latin and Greek volumes for the owners of New Orleans bookstores, and had contracted out her skills in those languages to the few boys' academies in the town, correcting examinations. In Mexico she would probably not even have had that chance.

January, trained in France as a surgeon but knowing from bitter experience that his race effectively barred him from practice, understood that her position in those days was far more difficult than his own. He'd made a reasonable living as a musician, saving during the Christmas season and Mardi Gras to pay his rent during the summer doldrums when the wealthy whites left town. For a woman, black or white or colored, there were few things to do besides attaching herself, in some capacity, to a man.

Consuela's voice called back his thoughts as she ticked off names with her plump fingers. "There was Santa Anna, of course, and two, maybe three, of his aides—young friends of Franz's, whose duty it is to go about after the Presidente and add to his consequence. There were the two mad-doctors Franz brought from town, Pichon and Laveuve, and in the opposing camp, so to speak, were the priests: Josefa's confessor Fray Ramiro, the priest she brought in from town to exorcise the demons of madness from my father, and the priest Natividad's mother brought in from town to secretly wed my father and Natividad while no one was looking."

"I'm sure that was responsible for some icy silences over the *coq au vin*," said Rose, climbing back into the carriage once more.

"I felt for the poor man, for even Josefa would not speak to him, and of course Señora Lorcha by that time was trying to pretend that it had never happened." Consuela waved to the two maids to come, and Sancho, with a bow of almost burlesque exaggeration, helped her up onto the high step. "There was also Doña Imelda de Bujerio, and her son Don Rafael, who are also neighbors of my father, though Don Rafael, like Fernando, prefers to remain at his town house in the city, and leaves his hacienda at Fructosa to be managed by the *mayor*. Don

Rafael is going to marry Valla—Valentina—so of course when Señora Lorcha tried to marry Natividad to my father, it would mean my father repudiating Valla's mother, Melosia, and making Valentina into a bastard who cannot inherit."

"I see that the wonder is not that someone was murdered at that gathering," remarked Rose as the carriage jolted into motion again, "but that only *one* person suffered the ultimate penalty." She coughed on the dust but left the glass windows of the coach open. Having spent four days on the Vera Cruz *diligencia* debating whether to be suffocated or grilled, January could sympathize.

"Were it not that Franz was going to have Hannibal whipped—possibly to death—the moment the company left," said Consuela, with a wry twist to her mouth, "I would have derived a good deal of entertainment from watching my family at dinner, for of course Valentina flirted with all Santa Anna's young aides, and Doña Josefa would eat only a mouthful of dry bread, and pray for my brother, and glare like a basilisk that turns men to stone. For two years, since she returned to my father's house on her husband's death, she has begged my father to permit her to retire to the Convent of the Bleeding Heart of Mary—because my father's investments kept her husband from going bankrupt when the *centralistas* took over the government, he controls her money. And of course he refuses to pay the fees required by the Convent. He says he has never heard anywhere that Christ dickered like a marriage-broker over the dowries of his brides, and naturally the cost of a woman's upkeep for the remainder of her life in a place of contemplation has never crossed his mind."

"Would your brother have let her retire?" asked January, leaning a little in the saddle to speak through the window.

"I don't think so. He was a Protestant in his heart, my brother—*en verdad,* he became one, in fact, when he entered the military school in Potsdam, though he recanted once he returned to Mexico. But it was clear that he considered the Mass a foolish superstition, and the saints no more than the old gods dressed up in European clothing. And Don Anastasio, who is a scholar and a heretic, has pointed out that he was not so wrong in this, at least in the villages, where churches stand on the foundations of the old temples, and Saint Michael and Saint Gabriel wear the feathers of the warrior-god Huitzilopoctli in their hair."

·   ·   ·

The hacienda of Mictlán stood at the edge of a small lake, a high adobe wall pale against the dark background of clustering oaks. Watchtowers stood at two corners, grim reminders of the savagery of this half-desolated countryside, and the few windows that pierced the outer wall were heavily barred with iron and wood. Farther along the lake's reedy shore the adobe huts and rough, palm-thatched *jacals* of an Indian village spread amid wide corn-fields, huts, and fields surrounded by hedges of thick-growing cactus. Men in the loose, thin breeches and tunics of *indios* worked at hauling in the field stubble for winter fodder, or hoeing among the bean-plants and pumpkins. Beyond the *casca*—what in Louisiana would have been called the Big House, though it more resembled a walled fortress—five tall, cone-shaped hills reared in far too straight a line to be natural. They were thickly blanketed in thorn and brush through which what appeared to be broken statues or pillars thrust up, like snaggled teeth.

Wide gates stood open into a central quadrangle: dust, straying chickens, saddled horses, smells. On three sides, women sat or knelt beneath the dense shade of the gallery, clothed in the loose cape-like blouses and knee-length skirts of Indians, their black hair braided with ribbons, carding wool or twisting thread on old-fashioned drop spindles. From rooms behind them came the thump of looms; the stink of leather curing and soap being boiled filled the vast court like soup in a trough. As the carriage came to a standstill, a long-haired ruffian in leather breeches came from the shade to take January's horse. At the same moment, a man's melodious voice drifted down from an open door in the upstairs arcade: "Gentlemen, I beg you! Nothing is to be resolved by bloodshed!"

"*Ai!*" muttered Consuela as Sancho leaped from his perch to hand her down. "What is it now?"

Dark skirts rustling, she led the way to a broad sweep of elaborately tiled stairs that ascended to the upper *corredor* as a sharp voice snapped in reply, "On the contrary, Don Anastasio, a great deal can be resolved by bloodshed, most notably the intransigent injustices of those who do not recognize the Principles of Universal Law."

"I will show you a universal law, you pettifogging mestizo scum," bellowed a hoarse bass voice, "if your men advance one step closer to that door."

"Oh, a thousand curses, it's that *baboso* policeman Ylario...."

And as January and Rose followed Consuela through the carved doors into the great *sala,* Hannibal remarked plaintively, "Please don't tell me I'm about to be shot in the name of the Principles of Universal Law."

As viewed by January from the threshold, the battle-lines appeared thus: two men in the blue uniforms of what January guessed to be the Mexico City *guardia civil* had taken a defensive position against the *sala's* rear wall. They held Hannibal pinned between them with his hands manacled behind his back. Two more in similar uniforms flanked them, their pistols pointed at the half-dozen ruffians in the attire of vaqueros—leather trousers, dingy underdrawers, tooled leather *botas,* and short jackets—deployed between them and the door. The *guardia civil* were commanded by a chubby little cock-sparrow in neat black civilian clothing and a violet-embroidered waistcoat that wouldn't have been out of place in the streets of Paris: Capitán Francisco Ylario.

In the center of the vaqueros stood Don Prospero de Castellón, unmistakably: tall, hook-nosed, black-clothed, his long white mane and snowy mustaches bristling and a kind of enthusiastic madness sparkling in his pale-blue eyes.

He had a rifle pointed at Ylario, who to his credit faced the weapon unflinchingly.

In one corner of the room, two men in European tailcoats and stylish cravats were looking around frantically for cover and clearly wondering at what point they should jettison their dignity and dive for it; there was also a priest, fat and unshaven, cowering next to the half-open door at the end of the room, bleating "Gentlemen! Gentlemen!" and roundly ignored by all. Beside Don Prospero stood a slender middle-aged gentleman clothed, like the mad Don, in the short embroidered velvet jacket and close-fitting trousers of a Mexican grandee, saying in the deep, beautiful voice January had first heard, "Prospero, you know that the law forbids..."

This was evidently precisely the wrong thing to say, because Don Prospero said, "The law? The *law*?" and settled the rifle close against his shoulder to fire. "What has the law to do with—"

"Father, you cannot have your vaqueros open fire on the *guardia civil*!" Consuela pushed past January and strode to Don Prospero's side, slapping the rifle-barrel upward from beneath, which, January thought, showed far more experience with such threats than if she'd tried to wrest the weapon from him.

"And why not, girl?" Don Prospero's mustaches seemed to point like fangs, but he didn't re-aim the weapon. Hannibal, who stood almost directly behind Capitán Ylario in the line of fire, shut his eyes in what appeared to be brief silent prayer.

"Because those vaqueros of yours have no more idea of aim than armed pigs, and the *guardia civil* are worse, and they would surely hit the Señora in the serpent petticoat there." Consuela gestured to the Italian marble fireplace directly beside Hannibal's shoulder, upon whose mantel-shelf stood an image, a horrifying demon adorned with a necklace of skulls and, as Consuela had said, a skirt modeled to resemble writhing snakes.

"Capitán Ylario." She walked over to the prim little man, who, January now saw, was younger than he had at first guessed, stiff-backed and rather white around the lips beneath his small, neat mustache: he, like January and Hannibal, had seen that Don Prospero really was going to shoot. "You have no idea how full my heart is with joy and gratitude that there is so little crime in the streets of Mexico City that you can be spared to spend all of a day riding out here and hiding in an arroyo, waiting for my father to leave the hacienda, so that you can arrest a single malefactor. . . ."

"Do you mean the man who murdered *your brother,* Señora?" Ylario's voice was cold. "A crime for which any *natural* woman would have long since wreaked her own vengeance . . ."

"You obviously never met Fernando," remarked Hannibal.

"I sing in operas, Capitán, but I don't live in them," Consuela replied. "Were I a natural woman, I would have married a muleteer when I was fourteen and have had eight children by this time and do nothing with my days but make tortillas for them. Now, Señor Enero here"—she strode back, caught January by the sleeve, and dragged him over to the mantel, apparently oblivious to the amount of armament still primed and ready on all sides—"has been given a mandate from the British minister to look into this matter of my brother's death. . . ."

"What would it matter if we blew that whore to pieces, eh?" demanded Don Prospero suddenly, showing signs of bringing the rifle up to his shoulder again. "She is minor—petty—without power! Coatlique—bah! Let her be shattered into a thousand fragments! You're a slut in any case," he added, apparently addressing the image now rather than his daughter, striding over to the mantelpiece to shake his finger up at the grimacing demon face. "I never believed that story of yours about becoming pregnant from a wreath of feathers, my girl. You women always make excuses, eh? Danaë, eh, that claimed the King of the Gods made her pregnant through a shower of golden coins...."

"Don't speak ill of golden coins," begged Hannibal. "I know quite a number of young ladies who became pregnant after showers of golden coins, and some from silver and even copper...."

"And how would this...*gentleman's*...enquiries," asked Ylario, eyeing January up and down with chill disbelief, "differ from those that I have made into the matter, Señora?"

"Heretic!" The chubby priest—black robe smutched down the belly with food-stains—ventured far enough from the safety of the doorway to shake his crucifix at Don Prospero and the idol. "Apostate!"

"Perhaps," replied January mildly, "because I genuinely believe Señor Sefton to be innocent?"

"Oh, thank God," whispered Hannibal. He wasn't much changed from the last time January had seen him seven months ago: still too thin, his gray-flecked hair braided in an old-fashioned queue down his back, incongruous over the shoulders of the short Mexican jacket he wore. There was a little more gray in his mustache than there had been, and his eyes, dark as café noir, had lost the consumptive glitter they'd had in New Orleans. Either the disease that had crucified him for years had gone into one of its periodic abeyances, thought January, or months of absolute rest in the thin, dry air had done him some good.

"Who do you call heretic?" roared the old *hacendado,* rounding on the priest, who popped back behind the door frame like a gopher into its hole. "How am I called heretic? Since when is it heretical to speak disrespectfully to a slut goddess who deceived her son about his paternity? Her son, now, he was a true god, a great god—"

"Blasphemer!" squeaked the voice from behind the door. Don Prospero strode over to pound on the panels, and the vaqueros, hugely entertained, lowered their rifles and grouped around him: evidently, none of them had much use for the priest. In their corner the two gentlemen in European dress scribbled madly in their notebooks.

"If you have been given a mandate by the minister," said Capitán Ylario smoothly, signing to his men, "you can present your papers to me—and make enquiries concerning Señor Sefton's defense—at the Casa Municipal."

"I am the Lord thy God, and thou shalt have no other gods before me...," shouted the priest from behind the door.

"Nor do I!" Don Prospero flung himself against the door like a maddened bull, and January heard a bolt shoot on the other side. "Coatlique—and even her great son the Left-Handed Hummingbird—I don't hold them before the Lord of Hosts!"

At Ylario's nod the blue-uniformed men caught Hannibal's arms and hustled him toward the outer door, leveling their pistols on January when he moved to stop them. Hannibal braced his feet but was nearly dragged off them; Don Anastasio made a move to close the outer door, but Ylario produced a pistol from his own pocket and pointed it at him: "I wouldn't."

"Prospero!" Anastasio shouted, but Don Prospero was hammering on the study door, shouting, "The Lord of Hosts defeated the Indian gods, rode roughshod over them, conquered them forever.... And as for your nonsense about making graven images, I didn't make those images!"

"Prospero!"

"Father!"

"I've never made a graven image in my life! You lie-monger, you glutton, you troublemaker who tries to separate a loyal daughter from her father, how dare you...?"

Rose, who all this time had stood watching in the outer doorway, now closed the door and placed herself heroically before it. For an instant, January feared Ylario would threaten her with a pistol also, but he didn't—though by his expression he clearly wished he could.

He gestured to his guards to thrust her out of the way, and Rose flattened back against the door, her chill eyes promising the struggle—and the delay—that Ylario clearly wished to avoid.

"Señora," the little man said with steely politeness, "I do not know who you are, but I warn you that you are interfering with the justice of this country. If you and this man whom I assume to be your husband do not wish to spend the night in the jail yourselves—whatever else may transpire—you will let justice take its course."

Rose glanced across the room at Don Prospero, who was still shouting at the priest, oblivious to his closely-guarded guest's imminent departure, and said nothing. Only braced herself and left it to Ylario to make the first move.

January always wondered later what it would have been, because at that moment the door behind Rose opened—thrusting her forward into the room—and the gorgeously uniformed man standing framed in it asked in a voice of aggrieved reasonableness, "Ylario, what the hell is going on?"

The westering sunlight slanting into the *corredor* flared on the curlicued scrolls of gold braid—January's first wife, Ayasha, had called such designs "chicken guts"—that embellished the newcomer's refulgent scarlet jacket, flashed on boots polished to the inner gleam of the newcomer's grave, dark eyes. Don Prospero turned from the cornered priest and threw open his arms in greeting.

"There you are!" he cried. "You tell this small-minded and unfaithful servant of the God of Hosts about being a god, my lord. Tezcatlipoca," he introduced as the priest opened the study door cautiously and peered around it. "The Jaguar-God, the Smoking Mirror.... You tell him, eh, my liege, that I don't worship you before this priest's God."

The newcomer inclined his head with the sweet-tempered tolerance of a martyred philosopher forced to humor his benighted friend. "Of a certainty I am not worshipped before the True God," he told the priest. "That would be a blasphemous thing." He crossed himself, but his eyes danced with unholy amusement.

Ylario stood where he had been, ignored by all, pistol in hand, and did not move, but the cold, still fury in his eyes told January who the newcomer was, in case he hadn't deduced it already from the three uniformed aides standing in the *corredor* with their plumed hats gripped reverently in kid-gloved hands. Voices in the courtyard were calling out, *"El Presidente... El Presidente..."* and there was the jangle of accoutrements and the rising dust-cloud of many more horses. The priest—and the two European gentlemen in the corner—goggled in shock.

"Sir," said the priest—unnecessarily, when he finally got his breath—"Don Prospero, that is no god, but a man: President and Generalissimo *Benemerito de la Patria* Antonio López de Santa Anna."

And while the attention of everyone in the room was fastened on the handsome, broad-shouldered dictator whose election the previous year had precipitated so much furor in the country, January and Rose caught Hannibal by the elbows and silently dragged him from the room.

FOUR

"My friends, Shakespeare himself would boggle at the task of expressing the depth of my joy at the sight of you." Hannibal collapsed onto a stone bench where the *corredor* right-angled into the narrower arcade that fronted the east and south sides of the court; when January put his hand on his friend's shoulder, he could feel him trembling. "Get these damned manacles off me—*Let us break their bonds asunder,* as the Good Book urges, *and cast their cords from us.* Ylario must have been watching the house all morning. He and his bravos—if such they may be termed—turned up the minute Prospero and Natividad disappeared on their ride.

> *Even as the sun, with purple-colored face,*
> *Had ta'en his last leave of the weeping morn,*
> *Rose-cheeked Adonis hied him to the chase...*

"You wouldn't have anything resembling brandy on you, would you, *amicus meus?*"

January took his flask from his pocket as Rose extracted one of the long steel pins from her hair. She thrust the tip of the pin into a crack in the stone bench and bent it into a neat right angle: "Turn around," she ordered.

"He has a judge in Mexico City," continued Hannibal shakily, "an

ally who was ruined when Santa Anna and the *centralistas* took over....
Thank you, I needed that. *Man, being reasonable, must get drunk / The best of life is but intoxication....* Ordinarily a man will wait weeks or months to be tried, but I suspect my neck would be well and truly stretched by morning. I kiss your hands and feet," he added to Rose as she pulled the handcuffs off him—both of them had at various times assured January that the simple locks on the average set of manacles were the most easily picked things in the world. January took their word for it—he'd never managed it. Hannibal took January's flask from him and took a second gulp, his hands still shaking badly, then turned to Rose to suit the action to the word and paused, thin fingers touching her wedding-band.

Then he looked back at January with unalloyed gladness in his face. *"God, the best maker of all marriages / Combine your hearts as one.* No wonder Athene of the Owl Eyes here was able to make such short work of the spancels of Universal Law; it's said love laughs at locksmiths. My dear friends, I wish you both happiness." He hugged Rose and kissed her cheek, got up from the stone bench and embraced January like a brother: his bones under his jacket felt like a bag of sticks.

"Your letter reached us on the morning of the wedding," said January with mock severity. "I assure you we were *not* pleased. Particularly considering I'd been up all night delivering my sister's baby. A girl," he added at Hannibal's exclamation of delight. "Charmian. Healthy and pretty, like a little ripe peach." He took from his pocket the draft Hannibal had sent to pay the ship's passage, and tucked it into the fiddler's short Mexican jacket. "We are also now rich. It's a long story. Now *you* tell *us* a long story, about the night Fernando de Castellón died."

"Ah." Hannibal shivered and sank back onto the bench: January saw that the stone was very old, covered with worn bas-reliefs of feathered warriors, sinister scrolled serpents, glyphs he could not read. Here a kneeling man could be made out, piercing his tongue with what appeared to be an enormous needle. Elsewhere four men held a fifth down upon an altar while a figure in a feathered headdress carved out the victim's heart.

"Consuela tells me you were seen putting something into the young man's wineglass," he said.

"In point of fact," said Hannibal, "I was putting it into my *own* wineglass, and it was laudanum, and not very much of it, either. After sitting for three hours at that table with Doña Josefa glaring at me from one side and Doña Gertrudis from the other, believe me, I needed it. But of course Werther—Fernando's valet—is convinced I poisoned his master. And after three weeks of watching me walking about in a state of what he considers freedom—having himself never been subjected to what amounts to house arrest by a raving lunatic—he got sick of waiting for the Principles of Universal Law to go into effect and took matters quite literally into his own hands. He crept into my room one night and tried to strangle me. Discouraged from that activity, he promptly fled the hacienda, rode straight to Mexico City, and informed Capitán Ylario that when he had found Franz, Franz was not yet dead, and that he died with the words 'The *Norteamericano* has poisoned me' upon his purpling lips."

"Ah," said Rose in a tone more resigned than surprised.

"Is there a chance he could be speaking the truth?" asked January. "Werther, I mean, not Franz."

"Not unless the laws governing the transmission of heat and cold have altered themselves for my confusion," answered Hannibal wearily. "Which is entirely possible, the way things have been going." He drew his knees up and wrapped his arms around them, rather resembling a dilapidated cricket in the westering sun that slanted through the arcade. "Not that there was any doubt, cold or not, that the poor brute was dead. It was...quite obviously a horrible death. The problem is..."

In the court below one of the vaqueros called out something in their nearly-unintelligible *Indio* Spanish; there was a great jingling of traces and the creak and rumble of carriage-wheels. "Ah," said Hannibal, glancing over the turned wood of the rail. "Where the battle is, there will the eagles gather, full of schemes for the Army to pay them for supplies at six or seven times the market rate."

January, stepping over to the rail and following his gaze, saw an extremely handsome traveling-coach draw up in the courtyard, barely to be seen through the dust-cloud raised by its six matched bay horses and innumerable brightly-liveried outriders. A slender, graying, and extremely dandified gentleman in a suit of elaborately-ruched red linen stepped from the vehicle, bowing as he gave his hand to help down an elderly matron with a nose like a hatchet and enough diamonds around her throat to purchase the populations of several villages.

"Doña Imelda de Bujerio," identified Hannibal, coming to the rail at January's side. "The gent in crimson is her son, Don Rafael; he'll explain to you a little later what it's like to be a black slave on a sugar plantation, he knows all about it from reading the novels of the Duchesse de Duras."

A second coach—smaller and plainer than the first—came through the gates. By the way Doña Imelda immediately began giving orders to the man and two women who got out it was clear that these were servants.

"In addition to being betrothed to that minx Valentina, Don Rafael is engaged with Don Prospero in selling cattle to the Army for the invasion of Texas. Doña Imelda was part of the group sitting out with me here on the night of the wedding-feast, along with Valla's duenna Doña Filomena Borregos. *Procul este, severae*... Señora Lorcha was here, too, playing dragon to her daughter the lovely Natividad, like the three Fates accompanying the Graces, though to do her justice, Doña Filomena is a sweet-natured soul, if a trifle fond of her sherry, and mended my shirts for me up until the time I was accused of murdering her nephew. Ah, there's Doña Josefa. . . ."

A woman emerged into the light, dust, and confusion of the courtyard, clothed and veiled in funereal black unrelieved by the slightest brightness of ribbon or jewel.

"There's a gate just beside the stair," provided Hannibal. "It leads through to the ladies' courtyard that lies to the north of this building. Doña Josefa, her daughter Paloma, Valla, and Doña Filomena dwell there in a sort of Catholicized purdah. Up until a few months ago Josefa's son Casimiro was in there as well. Casimiro's eight, and has just been promoted to that room down at the far corner on the other side of the stair. Señora Lorcha, I might add, was livid that she and her daughter weren't allotted rooms in the ladies' courtyard, but there are limits, even in this household. I wonder if we'll be privileged to witness . . . Ah, yes! Here they are now."

Hannibal leaned his chin on the railing, like a man high in the gallery of a theater looking down upon the stage, and January, looking past him, saw another little group of vaqueros ride into the yard, guarding two women in black. The taller, dismounting, seemed to ooze from the saddle and into the arms of the vaquero who sprang to assist her down; her riding-dress was cut so as to leave no one in the slightest doubt as to her charms. The vaqueros sent an Indian servant to bring a bench for the shorter woman to dismount. She was stocky, stubby, and moved with a kind of stiff wariness. Even though she was veiled, January could sense the bitter watchfulness of her eyes.

Doña Imelda's middle-aged son stared at Natividad like a child at a plate of gingerbread. His mother had to speak sharply to him, to wrest his attention away, and she did so without, apparently, even giving the two newcomers a glance.

"And all of them were sitting with you here, at the end of the *corredor,* on the night of Fernando's death?" asked January.

"As far from one another as they could be and still remain in the same group," replied Hannibal. "Concha must have told you about Señora Lorcha's attempt at pre-emptive nuptials. The last time I encountered an atmosphere that glacial was when a cousin of mine married a poacher's daughter by the rites of an inappropriate church and brought her to Sunday dinner. I don't think Doña Imelda even looked at either of them throughout the evening. But this far from town one has very little choice about after-dinner entertainment: it was sit out here or go indoors and contemplate the horrors of the religious art on your bedroom walls."

Rose said, "Hmmn." In every inn and house January had so far entered—including Consuela's—nearly every room that did not contain a painting of the Virgin boasted a crucifix, usually of Indian work, Christ's face and body streaming with blood from graphically depicted wounds.

Just what I want to see the last thing before I blow out my candle at night.

"And no one came in or went out of the study?"

"No. As you see, there's a torch-bracket immediately opposite the door. Josefa dragged Paloma away fairly early, rather than have her exposed to such a raffish crew as Natividad, Concha, and Señora Lorcha; Valentina left as soon as it grew full dark. Doña Filomena dozed off after her fifteenth sherry, and I can hardly say I blame her."

January glanced over the rail again, observing, indeed, how Doña Imelda and Doña Josefa kept their distance from—and their backs turned to—Natividad and her mother. "And no one heard anything from the study?"

Hannibal sighed and shook his head. "The door was shut and

bolted—the window shutters, too. The walls are three feet of solid adobe. From where we sat we could hear Santa Anna thundering on in the *sala* about how he was going to wipe the Texian rebels from the face of the earth. I doubt that if Fernando had cried out at the top of his lungs he'd have been heard."

He winced, sickened with pity for even a man who would almost certainly have had him killed. "But I doubt he had the breath to cry out, once the poison started to work. His face was so swollen, I'm not sure I would have recognized him if it hadn't been for his hair and his uniform. He looked like he'd died of suffocation, mouth gaping, tongue sticking out—his hands were still tangled in his collar, one of those ghastly military ones designed to protect you from inadvertently *breathing* in battle. The room was quite bright. Fernando couldn't abide what he called the 'medieval dark' of candle-light and had a patent Argand lamp on the desk and two more in his room; he'd brought them from Germany."

From somewhere in the courtyard a voice wailed in French, "The President? Here? And no one has thought to tell me this until now, now, when there is nothing to eat for dinner but that pitiful roasted deer, those wretched *vols-au-vent,* and only *three jellies* to offer! It is enough to slay oneself, to fall upon one's sword. . . ."

The chef, thought January. Presumably, the one who had counted on the wedding-feast to make his reputation . . .

"How did Franz look when you spoke to him directly after supper?"

"He didn't look well," said Hannibal. "But of course, for twenty-four hours he'd been trying to make sense out of Don Prospero's financial papers, not a task *I'd* care to undertake sober."

"Consuela tells me he threatened you earlier in the day."

"And so he had." Hannibal sighed and took January's flask for another sip of brandy. "You have to understand that the day had started with Don Prospero standing stark naked in the courtyard, conversing at the top of his lungs with an invisible Jaguar-God. Don Anastasio tried to quiet him and got a *mano* thrown at him—one of those rock pounders that the Indian women grind corn with. By pretending to be Quetzalcoatl, I managed to get Don Prospero back upstairs and into his room, with Father Ramiro telling me all the way I should be garroted as a heretic, but that was followed almost immediately by Señora Lorcha's attempt at a sneaky wedding—there's a door from Natividad's room into Don Prospero's, and Señora Lorcha had stolen the padlock key. Fernando and his two mad-doctors arrived in time to put a stop to *that,* so I understand his being snappish. After supper I went to see him, quite frankly to see if he'd call off his father's thugs long enough for me to make it back to Mexico City. I mean, *he* didn't want me here, *I* didn't want to be here, so it should have been possible for us to find *some* kind of common ground."

"I take it," said Rose, "that matters did not work out that way."

"No," sighed Hannibal. "No, they didn't. You see, the amorous Valentina..."

Within the *sala,* a rifle cracked. The next instant, the two gentlemen in European tailcoats burst through the door and pelted toward the stairs—January noted that one was fair and tall and the other dark and awkward-looking and taller still; both had mustaches and the fair one wore a monocle. Both ran like men who had long ago concluded that it was beneath their dignity to run and had recently changed their minds and were out of practice—they collided at the top of the stairs in a shower of notebooks, pencils, and high-crowned beaver hats, and nearly scratched each other baldheaded trying to be the first one down.

"Drs. Laveuve and Pichon," identified Hannibal in the tone of a gamekeeper helpfully identifying various sub-species of pheasants for the uninitiated guest. "Pichon is one of the chief physicians at San Hipólito, the biggest hospital for the mad in Mexico City; Laveuve runs a private clinic for those unfortunate enough to be both wealthy and insane."

"Piss-scryers!" howled Don Prospero, emerging from the *sala* with a rifle in his hands. "Clyster-jockeys!" In the courtyard, the fleeing medicos seized the nearest horses, scrambled awkwardly to the high-cantled saddles, and spurred through the gate, followed by the laughter and shouted advice of the vaqueros. Doña Imelda's maids and valet, emerging from their rough little travel-coach, sprang back into it for safety, and Don Rafael looked as if he wanted to join them, but Doña Imelda only drew herself up in affront, and none of the other women—Natividad, Señora Lorcha, nor Josefa—even appeared to blink.

"I'm surprised at you, 'Stasio," said Don Prospero mildly as Don Anastasio emerged from the *sala* door behind him and went to gather up the two Europeans' dropped litter of notebooks and pencils. "Bringing in doctors to pick at me like a couple of *sopilotes.* You didn't used to be so solicitous. What, you here, Antonio?" Don Prospero added as Santa Anna and his young aides came out behind Anastasio. "When did you arrive? And Conchita..."

"Papa." Consuela gestured toward January, and he advanced to the group and bowed. "This is Señor Benjamino Enero, a surgeon of the United States, appointed by the British minister to look into this matter of Fernando's death."

The dictator's dark, sharp glance took in January's well-cut clothing, African features, and clean linen, and his dark brows arched in speculation. But Don Prospero merely waved and said, "No need for that, Conchita—though of course it is very kind of you, Señor Enero, and kind of Don Enrico Ward of England as well. But Fernando himself will tell us everything we need to know. Still, a pleasure to make your acquaintance, Señor."

He turned eyes of chill Pyrenean blue, the heritage of centuries of aristocratic *criollo* inbreeding, on January. "Did you know that the surgeons of ancient Egypt were performing cataract surgery before Moses ever marched his Israelites forth from bondage? Surgery is true medicine, true healing, unlike those imbeciles...." He gestured at the dust-cloud still hanging over the court, all that was left of the two mad-doctors. "My dear," he added as the newly arrived guests emerged from the stairway—he strode past Don Rafael and Doña Imelda as if they were invisible, to clasp Natividad's hands. Natividad sighed—to remarkable effect, her half-bared bosoms in their fluff of black lace resembling nothing so much as a blancmange set on a plate at a wake—and glanced smokily across Don Prospero's shoulder to meet Santa Anna's appreciative eyes.

"Hinojo!" bellowed Don Prospero, and a tall and surprisingly handsome major-domo appeared, clad in the fashion of the preceding century in knee-smalls, silk stockings, and a red satin coat. "Fetch out brandy to the *corredor,* and tell Guillenormand to prepare the *boeuf marchand de vin*... I believe it's the *marchand de vin* you liked so much last time, my Eagle?" Santa Anna almost visibly fluffed his plumage at the flattering nickname. "Oh, run along, Ylario," Don Prospero added, and made shooing gestures as the Capitán and his blue-coated men emerged from the *sala*. "No one wants you here pulling long faces and no one wants to hear about the Principles of Universal Law."

"No," said Ylario softly, his bitter eyes going to the President of his country. "I see that clearly, Señor."

Santa Anna waved a gracious dismissal, as if the sun were not sinking and the fifteen supperless miles that lay between Hacienda Mictlán and the city were not haunted by bandits. Ylario bowed, but as his constables filed down the stairs and Santa Anna's aides settled themselves on the rough chairs of Indian work to enjoy their brandy, Ylario himself walked along the shadow-barred arcade to the corner where Hannibal and Rose sat.

January saw him stop before them, and through Don Prospero's booming introductions as the de Bujerios ascended the stairs, he heard Ylario say to Hannibal: "Do not think that you can hide behind your patron forever, Señor. Justice will not be cheated. And you will hang."

Under the circumstances, one could scarcely expect dinner to be a scintillant meal, and it was not. Santa Anna, the Napoleon of the West as he modestly referred to himself a number of times, monopolized the conversation with an air of gracious condescension, speaking of his own exploits and glories—and of his upcoming march to slaughter the *Norteamericano* bandits disrupting the peace of Cohuila-Texas—and making sure nobody listened to anything else. The General's young officers were clearly torn between being a reverent audience and flirting with Don Prospero's angel-faced daughter Valentina, who did her best to distract them. She was, January guessed, sixteen, her fair hair and blue eyes attesting to pure Spanish blood. Clothed in black, with a pair of sapphire girandole earrings sparkling in the candle-light, she was seated next to the elegant Don Rafael, who graciously explained to her—and to the young officer on her other side—exactly why it was important for Mexico that the American colonists be evicted from Texas, and how much he had paid his tailor for his suit.

"The girl will have horns on him before the dishes from their wedding-breakfast are washed," muttered Consuela at January's elbow. "She was flirting with the priest at her First Communion, that one."

In New Orleans—where he had for years earned his living playing the piano at subscription dances and private balls among the Americans, the French, and the free colored—one of January's favorite pastimes had always been watching people. *I don't see why white folks' business is any affair of yours,* his mother would sniff—not that his mother wasn't one of the best-informed gossips in Orleans Parish. But January was fascinated by what went on beneath the surface of all those polite exchanges: by who spoke to whom, and who snubbed whom; by glares and crossed glances and eyelids lowered above the sandalwood filigree of a fan.

Additionally, he realized, most of these people had been present at Don Fernando's ill-fated wedding-feast. They had seen what went on. Was it beyond the realm of possibility that one of them had found some way to slip poison into Don Fernando's food and shift the blame onto Hannibal's bony shoulders?

He leaned over to Consuela. "How was the table arranged on the night of Fernando's death?" he asked her quietly. "Who sat next to him?"

"It was almost exactly as you see it," she replied. "Except that Franz, not my father, was at the head. Like my father, Franz would rather have Santa Anna sit at his right than Doña Imelda, who should by rights be there—" Doña Imelda, ignored on the dictator's right, glared smoulderingly at her host, furious at the snub, as she must have been at the wedding-banquet, too. "Santa Anna would much rather sit at my father's right—or Franz's, that night—than at Josefa's right . . . as who wouldn't?" She nodded toward the foot of the table, where Doña Josefa presided over her single small hunk of bread, her coarse black dress smelling of unwashed flesh and unhealed abrasions underneath, and her emaciated hands folded in prayer.

So Franz had been flanked—as Don Prospero was flanked tonight—by his fiancée, Natividad Lorcha, on his left and President Santa Anna on his right. And judging by the way Doña Imelda and Josefa were glaring at the shapely young woman, he guessed that Natividad would have found it impossible to dump poison onto her intended's plate undetected, had she so desired.

The food was served *à la française:* turtle *en croute,* game-bird hash, glacéed venison *à la Turque,* and a dozen removes cramming the long table, from which the guests helped themselves or were helped by the servants, rather than having the food on the sideboards and a footman behind each chair. January couldn't imagine someone at table poisoning any dish without killing at least several fellow diners as well as Fernando.

The food was very much *à la française* as well: soufflés, *vols-au-vent, boeuf marchand de vin,* followed by Camembert cheeses and tartlets of pears and apples. Having dined marvelously at Consuela's the night before upon an amazing variety of *moles* of chocolate and chilis, tamales sweet and savory, *ropa vieja,* and exquisitely stewed *axolotl* from the lakes, January could only shake his head over his host's apparent contempt for anything that smacked of the food of the countryside. Even the penitential Doña Josefa ate white bread—albeit stale—not tortillas.

After supper the Indian servants kindled lamps on the *corredor,* and lit smudges of lemongrass and gunpowder in iron cressets to discourage the mosquitoes that rose up off the lake. The women repaired to the *corredor* immediately, while the men remained around the table, smoking cigars and listening to Santa Anna on the subject of the perfidies of the American chargé d'affaires—"Spymaster, rather! Hounding me with petitions and protests about what is none of his business—for every one of those so-called Americans in Texas became a citizen of Mexico before he took up land! Harboring dissidents within his household and doing all he can to stir up trouble behind my back..."

Hannibal, January noticed, had departed when the women did, and a few moments later he heard the sweet drift of violin music from the *corredor* outside, mingling with the voices of the vaqueros around their fire at the other side of the great central court, with the deeper notes of their guitars and Natividad's light, empty-headed laughter.

When the men rose to join the women, Don Prospero caught January's arm. "You are but lately come to Mexico, Enero? I could not but note your admiration for my splendid Coatlique."

January had in fact not given the hideous image more than a glance. The breeze through the open door of the *sala* made the candle-flame waver over the image's surface, giving the impression of uneasy movement to the snakes that made up her skirt.

"I dug her up among the pyramids that lie behind this house," the old *hacendado* continued, his eyes, with their queer intensity, locked upon January's face. "They're a study of mine, you know. You must ride out with me tomorrow to look at the pyramids—they were infinitely wise, those ancients, and infinitely powerful. The priests used to wear masks made of the detached facial bones of former victims, exquisitely set with crystal and turquoise. Quite remarkable."

"I should very much like to see them," said January, and the old man smiled, a baring of teeth, like an animal about to bite.

"Ignorant folk seem to think the priests cut through the victim's breastbone vertically to tear out the heart," Don Prospero said. "But in fact they slit the thorax in a horizontal curve just beneath the curve of the rib cage and reached up under the sternum, something that can be accomplished in a few seconds."

Past the Don's shoulder, January saw Don Anastasio, on his way out the door, pause and look back. Concern and something like fear flickered in his dark eyes.

Out in the *corredor,* January had to smile at the way the women had divided themselves up, like liquids in one of Rose's chemical experiments stratifying immediately and automatically, literally unable to combine. Rose sat beside Consuela, talking of stage machinery and how to make fire effects without burning the theater down. Natividad, January guessed, would probably have joined them had her mother permitted her to even acknowledge the presence of a woman of color in the long, furnished arcade, much less exchange words with her: not that Señora Lorcha was much less than three-quarters Indian herself, and her daughter close to that. But as Señora Lorcha snubbed Rose, Doña Imelda snubbed her, forming the nucleus of the *criollo* Spanish group of Josefa, Valentina, and Valla's duenna. All puffed on their cigarettos with little golden clips and ignored the existence of the other women as they would have ignored flies upon the wall.

At the sight of Santa Anna's aides—handsome young men in uniforms as gorgeous as their chief's—Valentina rose, smiling. Doña Imelda was immediately at her side. "See, Vallacita, here is Rafael, your *novia,*" she said in a voice that carried a command to Rafael in no uncertain terms. Torn from his approach to Natividad, Don Rafael came over obediently to join his mother and Valentina on the leather-covered bench and launched into an informative account of the re-upholstering of his carriage. Valentina turned her face coldly away.

Down in the darkness of the courtyard, one of the vaqueros around their fire played a sharp quickstep *baille.* Hannibal's violin caught the melody and turned it, weaving the air into a lilting barcarole and tossing it back into the shadows. The guitar replied, quicker now and challenging; the violin answered lightly, quadrupling each note into cascades of riffles. January heard the vaqueros around the fire laugh at the guitarist's expression, and as the two instruments merged into a lively duet, he realized General Santa Anna had quietly joined him.

"So Sir Henry Ward gave you a mandate to look into your friend's little problem, eh?" The General's teeth gleamed as he took the cigar from his mouth. "That was gracious of him."

January met his eyes. Santa Anna was a man of average height for the United States, though he was accounted tall in Mexico—he carried himself like a king. Had he looked this gracious and noble six months ago, January wondered, when he'd turned his troops loose on the women and non-combatants of the captured rebel city of Zacatecas, after slaughtering the prisoners taken in arms?

"Whether Señora Montero spoke in truth or in anticipation—or merely out of a desire to annoy Capitán Ylario—I will endeavor to see Sir Henry Ward at the earliest opportunity, Your Excellency."

Santa Anna chuckled. "It is true that Capitán Ylario is officious. The pettifogging of bureaucrats did not end when the Spaniards were ejected from my country, and Ylario is the worst of that breed, narrow-minded, unimaginative, and in love with rules . . . bah! You really think your friend is innocent?"

"I do, Excellency, yes."

"Why?"

"Because he is my friend," replied January. "Because a man remains loyal to his friends."

The dictator raised his brows, then glanced across at Don Prospero, who was listening to the music with the first expression of repose January had seen on his face.

"Perhaps because I have heard only a part of the evidence against him, and I have not had time to look around and draw my own conclusions," January continued. "If you were hunting in the mountains, Excellency, wouldn't you rather see the quarry's tracks yourself than depend on the word of a guide? Particularly a guide you do not know?"

The President's smile widened. He had put away an enormous quantity of wine and brandy at supper but seemed little the worse for it. The dark-green uniform jacket he'd changed into for dinner, so covered with bullion that it flashed in the smoky flare-light, was unbuttoned at the throat to show spotless French linen and the red slash of a cravat, like a flow of blood. "You're a wise man, Enero," he remarked. "What do those stupid *Nortes* think of to make men wise like you to be slaves?"

"It is something that happens to wise men now and then," said January. "Aesop was a slave. So was Plato at one point in his life. All a wise man can do is seek the truth."

"And the truth is that every one of us at table that night ate the same food, and drank the same wine and brandy out of the same bottles as Fernando de Castellón," said Santa Anna. "And Fernando believed that your friend murdered him."

"Fernando was dead for hours before his valet found the body," January pointed out. "I'm a surgeon, sir. I think at least I'll be able to prove that if given a chance."

Santa Anna raised his eyebrows, but made a gesture like a fencer conceding a hit.

January asked, "Do you happen to know why young de Castellón threatened Hannibal's life earlier that day?"

The President shrugged, then grinned maliciously. "Perhaps because your friend was making love to *la bella* Valentina." He glanced along the *corredor* to the fair-haired, black-clothed girl who sat with her face turned away from her relentlessly informative fiancé, gazing restlessly into the dark. "A pile of his love-letters to her was on the desk."

FIVE

There wasn't much point in opening *that* subject with Hannibal—not with the damsel in question, her fiancé, and her prospective mother-in-law all within twenty feet, not to mention Consuela, whom January had once suspected of attempting to murder a rival over an opera impresario's affections. Moments later Hinojo appeared in the doorway with the announcement that card-tables had been set up, and everyone settled down to gamble, the invariable pastime of nearly the entire upper class. Don Prospero summarily broke into Don Anastasio's scholarly discussion of agriculture with Rose to demand that his friend partner him at whist. Santa Anna, rather to January's surprise, asked him to make up the fourth at the table, infuriating Señora Lorcha, who thought that her daughter should have had the position. "A most lovely young lady," whispered the dictator to January as they took their seats, "but can't tell a spade from a club." Natividad settled for sitting on Santa Anna's knee and asking questions about his hand ("What will you ever do with all those hearts?") until he sent her over to help his host instead. January heard about nothing but cock-fighting and the revolution in Texas for the remainder of the evening.

January rose early the following morning. The room he and Rose had been given lay on the eastern side of the court, next to Hannibal's and almost directly opposite the main gate. It was massively thick-walled and would have been considered bare by American standards, at least to Americans who hadn't spent their first seven years sleeping on a pile of corn-shucks in a slave-cabin. He knelt in the last hard chill of the lingering night to pray before the cross in the wall-niche, then washed in the dark, moving carefully so as not to trip over something and wake Rose. The water in the can beside the door was warm, and he made a mental note to thank Cristobál. Outside in the court he could hear the muffled clop of hooves, the voices of vaqueros as they received their orders from the hacienda's *mayor,* and the soft chatter of the *indio* women as they took up their carding-combs and spindles. Light trickled through the cracks in the heavy wooden shutters. From the little chapel on the other side of the court, a small bell spoke its musical note.

When January emerged from his room, it was to see Doña Josefa as she came out of the chapel door, a thin, sinister figure in her black gown and veils, trailed by a smaller, slighter figure who had to be her daughter, Paloma. They crossed the court and vanished beneath the gallery, through the smaller archway that led into the realm of the women. The girl, January noted, looked around her with interest at the horses, the vaqueros, the villagers bringing in firewood through the gates, and the men of Santa Anna's bodyguard, and now and then nodded to this person or that, though she dared not stop to speak. Doña Josefa walked with head down, hands still clasped in prayer.

The chapel door closed behind them. They were the only worshippers.

Hands in the pockets of his short brown corduroy jacket, January walked the whole of the *corredor* around the three sides of the court, counting doors and, where possible, glancing into such rooms as were open at this hour, familiarizing himself with the lay of the land. The rooms on the south side of the quadrangle contained only the rolled-up straw mats and heaped woolen blankets of the *acomodados,* the footmen, maids, kitchen-boys who lived in the main house rent-free in exchange for their services. Other than the usual massacred Christ on the wall, there was nothing else in that long dormitory.

Another dormitory contained the beds of the married servants, separated by muslin curtains. The vaqueros, regarded as a lesser breed, slept downstairs in the store-rooms along the lower arcade, or sometimes in the sheds or on the ground among the maze of corrals that stretched behind the kitchen.

The rooms on the east side doubled as store-rooms when there were no guests to occupy them while those along the north side—facing the warm winter sun—seemed to be more or less permanent bedchambers on either side of the *sala,* the small butler's pantry, and Don Prospero's study. The large bedroom at the northeast corner was clearly the best guest room, with one of Santa Anna's soldiers standing guard outside it; alone of all the rooms in the *casco,* it had a lock on its door. It, and every other room along that side, had bars on the windows: ornamental bars of turned wood, to be sure, but quite stout enough to prevent passage. Every other chamber could, once the shutters were open, be entered as casually as through the door. No window in the place was glazed.

Screw-holes marked Don Prospero's door where a bolt had recently been affixed and recently removed. Standing beside the barred and shuttered window, January guessed that it would be possible for someone inside to see a man at the study door. As Hannibal had pointed out, there was an iron cresset on the pillar just opposite. The fire that the servants would have just finished kindling after dinner would have clearly illuminated Hannibal's face. January moved on to the *sala.*

There, a Friday-faced, drooping beanpole in livery was laying out napkins on the sideboard. January nodded a greeting to the man and crossed to the closed door that communicated between *sala* and study. Its jamb was still marked with yesterday's bullet gouges, pale in the soot-stained wood. There were others, he saw, older and repaired with plugs whittled of wood.

The door was not latched. The room beyond was still shuttered, shadowy in the morning cool. Its plastered walls were painted bright yellow and decorated with gay painted borders. Plank shelves covered every wall, overflowing with a higgledy-piggledy agglomeration of books, newspapers, pamphlets, idols, vases, skulls—human and animal—and what appeared to be chunks of rock taken from the fields. Idols stared from every shelf: gold, silver, stone, and terracotta; feathered headdresses, crystal eyes that gleamed creepily in the gloom.

Candle-wax dribbled on everything, and walls, ceiling, idols, and books were splattered with huge gouts of faded black where ink-pots had apparently been thrown. The desk—rough local work, like nearly all the rest of the furniture in the *casco*—was a drifted chaos of letters, documents, and newspaper-clippings that someone had apparently intended to organize into a commonplace-book and then abandoned. A couple of wrought-iron candlesticks reared like cacti among the mess, ringed in blobs of dribbled tallow. Whatever had been done with Fernando's patent Argand lamps, they had not been welcome once his father resumed control of this room.

In addition to the door that led into the study from the *sala,* the room had two others: one going out onto the *corredor,* the other leading into Don Prospero's bedchamber. Both were closed with iron bolts.

"Best you do not go in there, Señor."

January turned and saw the tall footman behind him. Bonifacio, he recalled Consuela had addressed him last night.

"The Don sometimes becomes very angry if things are disturbed."

"Of course. I'm sorry." January stepped back from the doorway immediately: he knew how the wrath of a "very angry" master would inevitably fall on the servants, not the offending guests. "I only wanted to see the room where poor young Don Fernando was found."

The footman nodded understandingly. He looked to be mestizo, with a good deal of Spanish blood. Though his crimson livery was cut in the fashion of the previous century, he did not wear a wig, and like most of the hacienda servants, he wore crude, moccasin-like *zapatos* rather than shoes. His Spanish was good. "I heard them say that you were Don Hannibal's friend. That the English government sent you to help him."

"Indeed they did," said January, casually fishing a silver reale from his pocket, which Bonifacio accepted without hesitation or embarrassment. News traveled as fast, January reflected, through the servants' dormitories here as it did among the slaves back in New Orleans, and for the same reasons. When your life and your livelihood depend on the folks in the Big House—on their whims and preferences—gossip takes on a completely different dimension than mere pastime. You cannot say of a man "His anger is his problem, I don't have to truckle to his crochets" if he has the power to sell your children, or to keep you safe from the recruiters of a voracious Army, or to throw your family off the land that is the only thing between you and the hopeless life of a *pelado* on the streets of the capital.

And every silver reale is one more bright little weapon with which to battle hopelessness and fear.

"Did you see his body?"

"Oh, yes, Señor. I was one of those who helped carry it down to be cleaned by the women."

"Would it be permitted that I speak with some of these women?"

"Of course, Señor. I will take you to them myself."

Bonifacio straightened the last of the napkins and tableware on the sideboard as he passed, and led the way out into the *corredor.*

"On the night of Don Fernando's death, do you think someone could have come into the study through Don Prospero's room?"

"I don't think so, Señor." The footman nodded a greeting as they passed other servants on the stair, carrying up cans of hot water for guests. "The door from the *Padrón*'s room into the *corredor* was locked with a padlock, and the one that connects it with the chamber be-yond—the chamber that used to be the dressing-room between Don Prospero's chamber and that of his wife—was also bolted. I don't think Señorita Natividad would have opened it for any reason."

January glanced back over his shoulder as they descended the tiled stair, mentally raising his eyebrows at the idea of the master of the house giving his son's fiancée—former mistress or not—a bedchamber adjoining his own. "And who has that room now?"

"Señorita Natividad," replied Bonifacio without change of expression. "It is where she always stays."

"I see," said January, wondering—as Consuela had wondered—why it was Fernando who had been murdered and not his father. "And who had the corner room, then?"

"That was Don Fernando's room, Señor," answered the footman. "He stayed there whenever he was at Mictlán, and locked it up and kept the key with him when he was away in town. It was his mother's room, you understand—Doña Maria-Exaltación de Borregos—and after her, that of Doña Melosia, Valentina's mother. It was Doña Melosia who had the lock put on, though she seldom stayed here on the hacienda. Doña Melosia was a woman of great sensibility," the servant added tact-fully. "A woman of the city, unused to the countryside and its ways. She stayed mostly at the town house as Don Prospero came here more and more. When her husband entertained the gods inside his head"—he tapped his temple significantly—"you can see how troubling it would be for her."

January nodded, remembering those glittering blue eyes and the feral smile. He wondered if Fernando had smiled that way.

The kitchen court lay east of the main quadrangle, through an archway like the gate of a young city. The kitchen building was little more than a shed, open at one side and flanked by a thatched shelter for the firewood and, on the other side, by four outdoor ovens like white-washed beehives. There were three open brick firepits whose gridirons sent up waves of heat, a line of rickety store-sheds, and another thatched shelter where half a dozen women ground corn in stone *metates,* chattering among themselves. "Yannamaria," Bonifacio introduced, "this is Señor Enero, Don Hannibal's friend. Señor Enero seeks to know about Don Fernando's death. Lupe, Tepinita," he introduced others, "Xoco, Cihu."

It was not lost on January that Bonifacio introduced him as Señor Enero—Mr. January—but referred to Hannibal as Don, a distinction accorded the penniless violinist for his white skin. At least he wasn't simply called Enero, as Santa Anna had done, the lack of any honorific at all comprising a category occupied by children, Indians, *léperos,* and—in the United States—slaves.

"No good will come of it." Old Yannamaria stopped shoving the granite *mano* back and forth in its stone trough long enough to cross herself and spit. "In two weeks he will be back to visit the house of his family. What will he say when he sees that his father has made a guest of his murderer? What will he do?" Eyes flat and expressionless as a serpent's looked up at January from under thin white brows. "It is for such matters that the dead walk."

"What can one expect?" retorted the woman Lupe. She was big and heavy-boned, her brown face lined with the marks of children birthed and children lost. "When a son has nothing to say but *We keep better count of money in Germany* and *In Germany we hire business managers to make sure there is no stealing* and *No farmer in Germany would be permitted to rob a landlord through laziness like these here,* is it a wonder that the father would not show grief at the death of such a one?"

The other women muttered and nodded and made signs against the Evil Eye.

"Blood is blood," said Yannamaria darkly. She used the Indian word, *eztli.* "And blood is all that the dead understand."

"Money is all that Don Fernando understood," replied Lupe. "Money and the whip. Señor Enero, your friend had good cause to kill that one—it was well done."

One of the other women laughed, and made a remark in Nahuatl; Lupe laughed in her turn. "Cihu laughs," she explained to January, "at

Señor Guillenormand the chef. When they brought poor Don Fernando's corpse here to be washed, Señor Guillenormand flung up his hands and cried that there would be no dead man brought into his kitchen. He was like a nun at an inn when there is only one bed and a party of muleteers come in wanting to share it. The harvest was done, you understand, Señor, and all the store-rooms around this courtyard are full up with corn. So we had to carry Don Fernando back into the main court, and lay him out and wash him in one of the weaving-rooms."

And she chuckled, her black eyes sparkling with the humor of one who had seen much death. She wore not the loose *huipil* but the chemise and skirt of the *china poblana,* like the mestizo women of the capital. She had the authority of one who has earned command—head-woman of the village, January guessed. He had met her African counterpart in the quarters of a dozen plantations up and down the lower Mississippi, and recognized her at once.

"What did Fernando look like," asked January, squatting beside the women and folding his big arms around his knees, "when they washed him? What did his features look like? And his body?"

"His face was swollen." Lupe's gaze unfocused momentarily, as if she looked through a window back at the past, into that lamplit store-room. Her speech was clearer than Yannamaria's—she had more of her teeth, for one thing—but like the older woman's, her accent was thick, a rough patois that was barely Spanish. "Swollen and gorged with blood. His mouth was open and his tongue poked out like a hanged man's, but there was no bruise upon his throat. I know that *mariposa* valet of his, Werther, has said that his master was alive when he found him and said, *The* Norte *has poisoned me.* But his flesh was cool, like a man who has been some hours dead."

"Did he have bruises on his back?" asked January. "On the backs of his arms and the backs of his legs?"

"You mean as men do when they lie dead on the floor?" The dark eyes sparkled mordantly into his, like those of a village child reeling off Bible verses to disconcert the patronizing visitor who calls her illiterate. January returned her small, grim smile and nodded.

One of the younger girls asked, "But why would Werther lie? He loved his master. . . ."

The woman Cihu made another remark in Nahuatl, accompanied

by a gesture that spelled out exactly how dearly she thought Werther had loved Don Fernando. All the women but Yannamaria laughed; the old woman only shook her head and said, "He will be back, Don Fernando. And he will want blood."

"*Mesdames!* Enough of this levity!" A man bustled in from the kitchen door, neat and pudgy and clothed—January couldn't imagine how he managed it in the kitchen's incandescent heat—in full European morning dress of longtailed coat, trousers, and stock. His mouth was small and pinched beneath a close-clipped gray mustache, and his eyes, even at halfway across the yard, had the expression of one who spends three-quarters of his day snapping *Mesdames! Enough of this levity!*

January got to his feet and crossed to the kitchen door, saying as he did so in his best Parisian French, "I beg you will forgive them, sir. It is I who had some questions to ask of them." He held out his hand. "I am Benjamin Janvier, of New Orleans—you must be M'sieu Guillenormand, the artist responsible for that truly remarkable feast last night." The women had gone back to scraping at their *metates,* heads down in dutiful silence. January thought about the amount of corn that had to be ground daily for tortillas—for how many people, counting the servants and vaqueros?—and set himself to distracting the cook from this annoyance. Those women had labor enough.

"After five days of food at the posting inns and two weeks of shipboard messes, I can only thank you, sir, from the bottom of my heart."

Guillenormand, who had initially regarded him with a suspicious glare, fluffed like a mating pigeon. "It was nothing, nothing—no more than one owes one's own sense of what is right." January half expected him to strut in a little circle and coo.

"On the contrary, sir," said January, guessing from the man's stance, accent, and dress that it would be impossible to lay it on too thick, "even in Paris I doubt I have encountered such a subtle hand with *marchand de vin.*"

Had he paid Don Prospero's cook a thousand dollars for it, he couldn't have gotten a more detailed account of the preparation, serving, and timing of the celebratory feast on young Fernando's wedding-eve. Pigeon sausage, glacéed ham, filets of young rabbit ("Ah, M'sieu, allow me to conduct you to the hutches—true rabbits from France, not these lean beasts here that are more goat than coney!"), celery *à l'espag-*

nole, and spicy garlic ratatouille. One of January's biggest joys in life was to listen to almost anybody talk about whatever brought joy to their hearts, so he was able to say things like "Can you obtain a heat even enough for a good flan from a wood fire such as they have here?" and "Where did you find butter enough to sauté the truffles for the ratatouille, if they have no dairy herds in Mexico?"

As he suspected, such questions precipitated an excruciatingly minute account of the preparations (in order to get the true French flavor of butter, Don Prospero maintained a small herd of Guernseys under constant guard by three vaqueros), which left January in less and less doubt that any portion of the feast could have been poisoned, either in the kitchen or between the kitchen and the *sala* where it was served.

"Don Prospero is a maestro where food is concerned," effused Guillenormand. "A true connoisseur! Since I have come into this country—I, a student of the great Carème himself!—I have seen such liberties taken with cuisine that it would reduce you to tears, M'sieu, yes, tears! *Okra* in the place of good honest French aubergines! *Beans* served with *poulet à la Reine*! Chocolate in the sauces—faugh! Tortillas—even at the tables of wealthy men, M'sieu, *tortillas* in the place of bread! It would turn an honest Christian's stomach! Don Prospero is the only man who understands! It is not ready," the chef added as the wan and wilted Doña Filomena appeared in the kitchen doorway.

By this time January was sitting backwards on a rush-bottomed chair just inside the doorway, while Guillenormand whipped up sugared icings for breakfast pastries and checked the slow steaming of the milk heating for chocolate and *café au lait.* Though the kitchen was of the ramshackle construction of every Mexican *cucina* January had seen so far—he could see daylight between the thatch—it was scrupulously clean, the surfaces around the wide hearth and the bank of stewholes tiled and scrubbed, the pans stacked on shelves, and every utensil laid out exactly where the cook could reach them on starched, embroidered white cloths. Knife-box, spice-boxes, sugar-safe, and coffee-tin all had locks; there were at least four French-style water-filters ranged along a high shelf, their big pottery jars glazed bright blue and yellow, like flowers. The sand-box was huge; January reflected that Don Prospero must bring in sand for scrubbing pots by the ton.

Did he import that, too, from France?

Doña Filomena vanished like a startled blackbird. Guillenormand went back to stirring the cocoa, which presumably had been Valentina's duenna's goal.

"Do you have trouble with theft?" asked January with a glance through the kitchen door at the women. "With this many servants coming and going..."

"M'sieu, you do not know! I cannot tell you of my sufferings!" Which meant, of course, that the cook could and would, and January put on his most interested expression and leaned forward.

"People in and out of here all the time— Wipe your feet before you come in from the yard, you ignorant donkey!" Guillenormand whirled from the stewhole where he worked, and the unfortunate kitchen-boy shied as if he'd been shot at. "You would think it a backstreet *pulqueria*! And what *indios* want with butter, or white sugar, or white flour, I cannot imagine, but you may believe I keep a close eye on everything that comes in or goes out! Indeed, when there is a great feast, as there was last night, I will order Hinojo to walk with each course across to the *sala* to make sure that those lazy vaqueros who hang about all evening in the courtyard do not pinch the sugar, which they love like children. I am not finished, Madame, and I will send Joaquin to you when I am!"

It was Señora Lorcha in the doorway this time. She put her hands on her hips and snapped, "And how much longer is my daughter to wait for her cocoa, while you stand gossiping with this... this upstart *negro,* eh?" She barely threw January a glance. "You think because Don Prospero is a gourmand who fancies he's too good to live like other people on tortillas and beans that you can dictate to the members of his household?"

"And are you, Madame, accustomed to living upon tortillas and beans?" inquired the cook haughtily, switching to the Spanish in which she had addressed him. "I had no idea."

Señora Lorcha's face turned bright red, as well it might, thought January. He'd watched the mother of the lovely Natividad scrupulously minding her manners at table last night and guessed by the obvious care she was taking, and by the way she watched her daughter's every move, that her claims to gentility—and to more than one or two rather distant Spanish ancestors—were as false as the paste diamonds in her hair. "You are insolent, Señor!"

"I am also busy." Guillenormand set his spoon down in the cocoa-pot. "But I am at your service, Madame, for however long you wish to prolong this conversation instead of permitting me to finish your precious daughter's refreshment."

Señora Lorcha hissed, "Poisoner!" and turned on her heel—January's eyes cut sideways, fast, to the cook's face, in time to see it blanch and freeze. The next second Guillenormand forced a manufactured chuckle and a rather stiff gesture of scorn, and January asked, *"Ponzoñero?"* He deliberately mispronounced the Spanish word, as if it were unfamiliar to him.

"Oh." Guillenormand cleared his throat and chuckled again. "Merely a spiteful word the lower classes have for Frenchmen, M'sieu."

"What was that all about?"

"The lovely Natividad's breakfast cocoa." He resumed stirring, and January wondered whether the man's self-consequence would run to leaving a piece of skin on the top of the cocoa when it was finally sent in, or whether his pride in perfection would not permit such a lapse even to vex his enemy. "A hag," the cook added, shaking his head. "A veritable *entremetteuse*—you saw the girl at dinner last night! It would have served the old cow right if her daughter had married Franz—pardon, *Don Fernando*...." He put an ironic twist on the Spanish name. "He would have sent her packing in quick order, back to the slums from which they both come."

"But would he actually have married the...the young lady?" January asked. "Somehow she does not seem to me...but then, I know nothing of the family, nothing of the custom of the country...."

"M'sieu," said Guillenormand solemnly, raising his ladle, "I swear by the Blessed Name of Liberty—the only true Deity of the Universe—that I have never seen such a household as this one. But as for young Franz, once his elder brother was dead and he understood that the inheritance of lands wider than many German principalities lay within his grasp, he would have wed anyone his father ordered him to wed in spite of all the glares and puffing and comments of that pretty valet of his. Santa Anna's generals are all borrowing money—some of them at forty-eight percent!—to outfit their men for the march to Texas. Don Fernando would not have been the first man in history," he added, "to marry a midden that he might have the muck."

"You must have been very shocked at his death."

"M'sieu, after eighteen years in this household, nothing can shock me. Name of God," he exclaimed as yet another form darkened the kitchen door, "what must a man do to...? Ah." His voice softened as he saw, along with the somberly-liveried servant who clearly appeared to be somebody's valet, a boy of about eight, dressed in a neat black jacket and breeches with a spreading collar of white lace. "Maître Casimiro. Maître Casimiro Fuentes, may I present to you M'sieu Benjamin Janvier, a physician of the city of New Orleans."

January rose and shook the boy's hand. The child seemed a little nonplussed, but greeted him in good French and used the polite "vous" rather than the "tu" by which even children in New Orleans addressed slaves. As the son of Señora Josefa, the only blacks the child would have encountered in Vera Cruz would have been servants, or the former slaves on the sugar plantations of the lowlands.

The cook went on. "I'll have your uncle's tisane in moments, Maître Casimiro...." As he spoke, he went to the hearth, and with a long rod tilted the kettle at the back of the fire, to pour steaming water into a small pot. This he carried to the table, where half a dozen trays were ranged, each bearing a fine-china chocolate-pot and cup, and a plate of iced pastries. "Joaquin!" he roared, and the rangy kitchen-boy previously addressed as "ignorant donkey" jostled past the child and the valet in the doorway. "Continue to stir that milk—gently!" The cook had switched back to Spanish from the French in which he'd addressed Casimiro. Apparently Don Prospero adhered to the French and English mode of making chocolate with milk rather than the Mexican preference for spices and water.

"And if I find so much as one shred of skin upon it, I will make sure that no shred of skin remains upon your worthless back! Don Anastasio—and Madame Isabella—when she is well enough to accompany him here—prefer tisane in the morning," he added to January in French. "Quite sensibly, as Don Anastasio knows. It is best for the health. Did your uncle ask for anything specific, Maître Casimiro?"

"Please, sir, the chamomile, sir." Casimiro glanced up at the valet who stood behind him, as if for confirmation; the man smiled and nodded. Guillenormand went to a shelf beside the stove, where half a dozen lacquered caddies stood in a row, fishing a ring of small keys from his pocket.

"Don Anastasio keeps chamomile, lemongrass, and a mixture of rose and hibiscus here, for when he visits." The cook unlocked the red chest—polished clean as a noblewoman's jeweled locket, January noticed—and spooned the aromatic leaves into one of the little pots. When he poured the steaming water over them, the scent brought back to January the clean breath of French fields, of a world far separated from the dust and violence of this volcanic land.

"Don Anastasio dries and mixes them himself. A true maestro, save for his fondness for Indian foodstuffs.... Would you believe it, M'sieu? He spent five years trying to convince the world of fashion—or such world of fashion as exists in Mexico City!—to consume peanuts, such as the *indios* eat! Did you ever hear of anything so absurd? Ridiculous, and of course no one of any birth or breeding would touch such a thing, not that there is much of birth or breeding left.... But there!

"I regret to say," Guillenormand added with a sigh as young Casimiro, trailed by the smiling valet, bore the tray of tea-things away, "that when Madame Isabella comes here, she demands cocoa in the morning, like all the rest of these Mexican girls. A filthy habit."

"Who are the others for?" asked January as the cook thrust Joaquin away from the stewholes ("Imbecile! Now you've burnt the milk!") and began to pour out the cocoa tenderly into the various pots to be taken to people's rooms. Four of the tea-caddies looked old, Chinese ware with carved lacquer sides and gold lids. Two were English imitations, new, and of painted tin. "Madame Josefa, perhaps...?" January couldn't imagine her requesting even lemongrass tea. Too sinfully luxurious.

The cook heaved a sigh. "This country," he said, and shook his head again. "The horrors that religion has inflicted upon it, upon the world! Alas, for the failure of the Revolution! No, Madame Josefa will have only cold water in the mornings, and demands that her poor daughter have only that as well. The girl is twelve, M'sieu! And for two years now her mother has worked to train her to become a nun, as she herself wishes to do.... Such a waste of useful intelligence, of women who could raise strong families for the nation! Had the Revolution truly succeeded..."

January listened to the cook's political views uninterrupted for ten minutes, while Señora Lorcha, Doña Filomena, and several assorted valets came in for the cocoa-trays. Counting back eighteen years, he guessed Guillenormand had departed France with the return of the Bourbon monarchy—rather curious, considering the aristocratic nature of true *haute cuisine,* but then, January had encountered far odder sets of beliefs in his time. By a long scenic route of restrictive monarchical trade agreements and the general improvement of world commerce following upon the Revolution, he managed to bring the subject back to the tea-caddies.

"Ah, yes, the tea. Those two on the end were M'sieu Franz's—Don Fernando's—that he brought with him from Prussia. He preferred tea to coffee—coffee made him itch, he claimed—and always bought the finest China green to drink after supper. Myself, like Don Prospero, I prefer a good cup of well-brewed coffee to such rinse-water, and Don Anastasio will have the smoked teas of Formosa. . . . The blue box contains an infusion of jasmine and rose-hips M'sieu Franz would take to settle his stomach. For a man who would flog his soldiers fifty lashes for an unshaven chin, he was like a dyspeptic grandmother about his food! Clean, he said, it must be clean—to me he said this, to *me,* Sacripant Guillenormand! As if in this kitchen. . . What do you want, limb of Satan?"

Father Ramiro drew himself up with dignity in the doorway. "I come only to fetch a little water." The priest held up a plain terracotta pitcher as evidence of his intention.

Guillenormand watched him with wary loathing as Father Ramiro lumbered across the kitchen to one of the water-jugs beneath the purifiers on the shelf. Ramiro, for his part, glared at the cook as he filled up his jug and then departed, ostentatiously walking a wide detour around the table with its pile of pastries.

"He came to see if I was out, that he might steal as many pastries as he could cram into his dirty sleeves," Guillenormand muttered to January, watching the priest cross the kitchen court to the open firepits, where two women were rolling corn dough into neat balls and squeezing them flat in a sort of long-handled iron waffle-maker—the tortilla-press, January guessed, of the sort with which Consuela's mother had cracked Don Prospero over the head. "I should have asked you, M'sieu, to begin with: would you and your lady prefer tea rather than cocoa? I cannot offer you Don Anastasio's chamomile, of course. . . ."

"I would not dream of asking for it," replied January. "But yes, if you could make up a pot of M'sieu Franz's China green, I'm sure my lady wife would much appreciate it."

And I'm sure I can find something in the nature of a stray kitchen-cat or a rat from the granaries, January reflected as he bore a tray, two cups, cocoa for himself, and a number of pastries back to his room, *to test the tea on before Rose or I will touch it.*

The experiment might tell us something interesting.

"I told you the evidence was damning." Hannibal perched tailor-fashion on the leather chest at the end of January's bed while January searched for a place of concealment for the pot of Fernando's tea. When he'd returned to the room, Rose had been gone, the bed made up, and the blue-and-yellow pottery slop-jar emptied and clean. Clearly the servants had been in. All he'd need, he reflected, was for Zama or Cristobál to return and sample the tea while he himself was out looking for his wife.

"You didn't tell me you'd been making love to the virgin daughter of the household," he said to Hannibal.

"That's because I hadn't been. Well, not very much, anyway."

January straightened up, tea-pot in hand, and regarded him in exasperation. The sparseness of Mexican furnishings meant, among other things, that there were very few places in which to conceal anything. The bed was high, and anything under it would be immediately visible. There wasn't even an armoire, such as there would be in a bedchamber in New Orleans or Paris.

"I suppose Cupid wrote those love-letters that were found on Fernando's desk?"

"He might have." Hannibal poured out a cup of cocoa for himself and broke off half a pastry. "But if he did, he wrote them in truly execrable English—from which, God help me, I was fool enough to agree to translate them into Spanish. I find myself inclining these days to the prevailing local sentiment that education only addles women's minds, but over the years Don Anastasio has managed to convince Don Prospero to have his daughters educated. It did nothing but make a novel-reader out of Isabella—and all Doña Josefa will read or permit her daughter to read are prayer-books and the lives of female saints. But Valentina has a brain in her head. I suppose somewhere, some poor American has a collection of her love-letters in my handwriting; God knows what effect *that* will have on my reputation...."

"Where did Valentina meet an American?" January set the pot back on the tray on the thick sill of the window and settled into the chair beside it. "I thought the virgin daughters of the household never left their courtyard unescorted."

"Out riding," said Hannibal. "Like Beatrice passing through the streets of Florence with her duennas, to pierce Dante's heart with love from afar. There was a little encounter with beggars who could have turned threatening—I gather from the vaqueros there were two on the pathway and about a dozen hidden in the rocks near-by. '*Mi corazón*'— the little minx is always careful to ink out her beloved's name before she brings me the latest billet-doux for translation—and a couple of his *norte* friends rode up and turned the tide of the encounter. A few days after that she came to me with a letter to translate."

"Which you did."

"I couldn't see the harm in it." Hannibal licked pastry-icing off his long fingers. Down in the courtyard, Santa Anna's men were preparing to depart, in a great confusion of trampling, shouting, jingling spurs, and dust. As he'd come past the *sala* on the way to his room, January had seen the dictator in conference about Army provisions with Don Prospero, Don Rafael, Doña Imelda, and Don Anastasio, and wondered if Capitán Ylario had made it back to the city unambushed, and how long it had taken for him to get past the customs barrier.

"Which I did," Hannibal confessed. "The more fool I. *Honi soit qui mal y pense.* I was still at Consuela's flat in town—Valla begged me not to tell her. Valla slipped me the letter, I gave her the translation the next time we were here; she must have spent all night writing a reply, which I then took and translated into English.

This wimpled, whining, purblind wayward boy,
This senior-junior, giant-dwarf Dan Cupid;
Regent of love-rhymes, lord of folded arms,
The anointed sovereign of sighs and groans. . . .

"Her shining knight of the north must have gotten her letter some-how—I have no idea how they exchange letters, but if it were me I'd have a drop-box somewhere in the hills—because the next time I came here there was another letter from him, longer but no better spelled. . . ."

"And the correspondence flourished," concluded January grimly. "As such correspondences will. I understand your not wanting to smirch the young lady's name by accusing her of trading letters with a man her father almost certainly wouldn't approve of, but since Fernando had learned already that she was exchanging love-letters with *someone* . . ."

"Why didn't I tell Fernando it wasn't me?" Hannibal leaned back against the bedpost. Like most of the household, he was somberly dressed, his trousers and short Mexican jacket both black out of respect for the family's grief, and a black silk scarf tied over his long hair, vaquero-fashion. "I asked Valla about it first, of course—I had deduced, from being slammed up against a wall and half-strangled, that Fernando had found the love-letters. She then assured me that she had burned the originals, and that she was prepared to swear that not only had I written all the letters to her myself, but that I had sneaked into the women's courtyard at night and attempted to rape her. *The light of love, the purity of grace / The mind, the music breathing from her face* . . ."

January said, "Hmmn."

"You can see why I am extremely glad that somebody showed up who at least believes me." The fiddler fell silent for a time, chewing on a corner of his graying mustache, watching January with somber, coffee-black eyes. "Which I appreciate, by the way," he added. "Especially as I realize that this—er—new addition to the evidence in no way lessens my motivation for killing Fernando. Or offers an alternative source of poison in the approximately three minutes between the conclusion of supper and my entry to his study, glass in hand."

"I'm not so sure about that." January touched the side of the tea-pot with the backs of his fingernails. "What can you tell me about Sacripant Guillenormand?"

Voices in the *corredor*. Don Prospero's: "Their President would never dare to enter into war with Mexico, my Eagle! And the Americans themselves are few and cowardly. You have nothing to concern yourself with."

"I have to concern myself with that scoundrel chargé d'affaires Butler and those troublemakers he calls his secretaries. . . . Ah, my beautiful lady Rose!"

January and Hannibal traded a glance, then both went out into the arcade, January pausing only long enough to stow the little pot of tea in the bottom of the chest, tucked carefully in with Rose's petticoats. Gorgeous in yet another gold-laced uniform, white doeskin riding-breeches molded to his thighs like a lady's gloves, the President bent over Rose's hand while Natividad—who managed to be heavily veiled yet scantily covered at the same time—stood demurely at his side.

"I have offered the escort of my men to the lovely Señora Lorcha and her daughter," Santa Anna informed his host with the air of Socrates about to spend an evening chastely discoursing philosophy with Alcibiades in bed.

Señora Lorcha, hovering protectively at her beautiful daughter's back, glanced at Don Prospero to see how he'd take the news, but was disappointed. The old *hacendado* merely waved a careless hand. "Splendid, splendid, my dear Eagle. High time she went back to town. My dear, I trust we shall meet next week?"

"I would love that above all things, sir," cooed Natividad in her breathless little-girl voice. "That is . . . Mama?"

"We shall see, child," returned Señora Lorcha grimly, her eyes narrow with loathing. January understood: popular gossip indicated that the President went through mistresses like a rat through cheese, so the exchange of an elderly prospective husband for a questionable politician was, in the long run, probably not a profitable one.

"Three thousand head, mind you," said Santa Anna to Don Prospero, "and five thousand of sheep . . ." He stepped aside as two liveried footmen jostled past, carrying Natividad's trunks, trailed by a slatternly maidservant puffing on a cigaretto. "Have the first of them at the camp by Thursday, and I'll send the first dozen soldiers seconded to your silver mines in Catorce by the first of the month. Dare I hope I shall see you at the bull-fight Sunday? By all means do not forget the English minister's reception on the thirtieth; I shall be retiring after that to Mango de Calva, and won't return until it's time to march against Texas."

Hannibal's eyes widened. "Mango de Calva's his hacienda near Vera Cruz," he explained softly to January. "If he's not around to back up Don Prospero..."

"We'll get to the bottom of this before then."

Natividad languishing on his arm, Santa Anna halted before them, inclined his head. "Good hunting, Enero," he said. His expression was that of a man at a cock-fight, knowing that one of the contenders will be razored to pieces and no more than mildly curious to see which. "I await with interest the results of your enquiry."

"No more so than do I, Excellency," responded Hannibal with a courtly bow.

"My dear friend!" Don Prospero draped an arm around Hannibal's shoulders as the President and his party descended to the court. "Don't listen to Antonio, eh? What is he when all is said and done? President of Mexico? Pah! Merely a moneylender's son! I have told you before this not to worry yourself—Fernando shall tell us what he wants done, and we shall do it." He smiled again, like the statues of the Jaguar-God.

As the carriage pulled out of the courtyard in a roiling of dust and clattering hooves, January, Hannibal, Rose, and Consuela returned to January's room. "You got cocoa?" asked Rose, lifting the lid from the pot. "Zama promised to fetch me some and I last saw her engaged in what I can only hope is matrimony with one of the vaqueros."

"I imagine it's stone cold." January poured a cup for her, and another for Consuela, who was shaking dust from the folds of her midnight-blue taffeta dress.

"You had tea also, didn't you?" Hannibal looked around, and January sat on the lid of the chest.

"In a manner of speaking. I just had a rather interesting conversation with Sacripant Guillenormand."

"I'm astounded," retorted Consuela. "Unless you find it interesting to hear an exact account of the difficulties in obtaining fresh peas."

"And I," said Rose, "have had an even more interesting conversation with young Maria-Paloma Fuentes—Doña Josefa's daughter. It appears that young Miss Valentina has been making clandestine rendezvous with a suitor by the garden wall."

"Has she indeed?" remarked Hannibal. "Both she and her *corazón* were remarkably discreet about it in their letters—unless they wrote in some sort of code. Number of kisses equals the date, that sort of thing."

"You know, then?" Rose set down her cup.

"I know she has a lover." With an apologetic glance at Consuela, Hannibal repeated to the two women the account of his career as literary Cupid. Consuela rolled her eyes and tapped him sharply with her fan.

"*Cabeza de burro*. You didn't see her setting you up as a decoy, in case the letters were found?"

"I'm afraid my mistrust of women is insufficiently acute. *Splendide mendax et in omne virgo nobilis aevum....*"

"If Valentina is such a flirt," put in Rose reasonably, "surely there are other damsels willing to marry the—er—*informative* Don Rafael... who took time off from explaining the Texas conflict to Santa Anna last night long enough to tell me that it is not a good idea to be a woman of color living in New Orleans. Particularly if Don Prospero is so taken with the Natividads of this world. Your brother may have stopped him from repudiating his marriage to Doña Melosia on this occasion, but you know there will be others."

"I know it," said Consuela grimly, "and Valla knows it—since our father does not hesitate to threaten her with it whenever she crosses his will. As for Don Rafael, Father bought up all the de Bujerio lands when Don Rafael's father went bankrupt in 1827. He permits Don Rafael and his mother—and all his sisters and cousins and aunts—to live in their old town house in the city, but that is not so very different from one of the *jacals* on the edge of the village."

January raised his eyebrows. "And I thought my old master's family was a nest of snakes," he remarked.

Consuela sipped her cocoa, made a face, then set the cup aside. Through the open door drifted the shouts of grooms and vaqueros, the musical jangle of harness and the stamping of hooves as another carriage was brought into the court: "...sheer, unreasonable willfulness," trumpeted Doña Imelda's voice from the *corredor*. Skirts rustled and two women passed the window, pacing along the arcade, Doña Josefa in her unwashed black gown like the gorgeously-clothed Doña Imelda's shadow: "I search my daughter's room as a matter of duty to her...."

"Of course! Why Valla should put up such a fuss... but there! She has never had the discipline a girl requires. The possession of trinkets is only a temptation to sin. It is good training to be reminded that the soul possesses nothing, not even itself."

"You are truly a saint, my dear Josefa."

No wonder Fernando demanded the corner room with locks on its doors, January reflected.

"How I envy your daughter, Doña Imelda! Every time I hear of the preparations for her entry into the convent, my heart swells to bursting with longing."

"Now, that is only natural." Doña Imelda's voice, blaring as a regimental band, purred with satisfaction. "The Bleeding Heart *is* the most exclusive convent in town. I've heard the Incarnation is accepting just *anyone* these days. You will come to the ceremony, won't you?"

"If my father will permit." The hate in Josefa's voice was as clear as if she had spat upon his name. "What can one expect from a man who..."

Their voices faded, leaving a stain upon the silence of the room.

"Madness has a way of spreading in families," said Rose at length. "I don't mean that the children inherit weak minds, necessarily. But everyone's behavior twists to accommodate the conduct of one member, like beaten horses that shy if a stranger so much as lifts his hand. Things that would be unthinkable elsewhere seem normal. One must either go mad oneself, or flee."

Hannibal said softly, "Or both."

"Or both," Rose agreed. "In any case, Paloma says that on the night of the wedding-feast she slipped out of her bedroom while her mother was praying, and sat in the shadows of the ladies' courtyard by the gate, listening to Hannibal play. She loves your playing," she added, glancing across at the fiddler. "If nothing else, you've brought the poor child great joy."

"I'm glad," replied Hannibal. "I honestly am. But I regret to say that given the choice of being triced up on the stable gate and flogged to death by Fernando, or being hanged for his murder, I'd sooner have sent Paloma joy post-paid from Mexico City."

"I cannot," Rose sighed, "find it in me to argue with you. On the evening of the eighth of September, Paloma heard a man whistle on the far side of the wall, and peeked out of her hiding-place in time to see

Valla climb the grapevines that cover that wall—they're centuries old and some of the stems are as big around as a man's leg. . . ."

> "O wall, full often thou hast heard my moans,
> For parting my fair Pyramus and me,
> My cherry lips have often kissed thy stones. . . ."

Rose picked up Consuela's fan and tapped Hannibal sharply. "According to Paloma, this isn't the only meeting she's witnessed. The most recent one, she says, was ten or twelve days ago: St. Bridget's day, which her mother celebrated with an all-night vigil of prayer because St. Bridget was a widow. I asked Paloma what the tune was that the rider whistles; she said it was this."

And Rose whistled—in an unlady-like fashion—a tune known among the Americans as "Pretty Peggy-o."

"If it was Valla," argued Consuela, "where was Doña Filomena?"

"Tied up in the wine cellar," said Hannibal promptly. "Or locked in the stables. Or with Doña Josefa in the chapel, praying that the lovely Valentina wouldn't accuse her of operating a house of prostitution out of the women's courtyard and produce forged correspondence to prove it. *Did* you bring in tea?"

"I did." January stood, opened the chest, and brought out the little Sèvres pot. "According to M'sieu Guillenormand, this tea was Fernando's special blend. No one in the household was permitted to drink it, and only Werther and Guillenormand had keys to the caddy—not that such locks can't be easily picked, according to nearly every house-servant I've ever talked to. Did Fernando have tea after supper before going into his study?"

"Not before going in," said Hannibal. "He said he wished to put in more work on his father's papers that night, but he may just have wanted to get away from Señora Lorcha. But when I went in, there was a tray on the desk. Meissen ware, apple-green-and-white with a gold rim: cup, saucer, pot, water-pot, milk-pitcher, sugar-bowl, slop-jar, and spirit-lamp, with a little gold strainer and a gold spoon to match."

"Werther took it in," said Consuela decisively. "I remember him coming out of the study door, silent as a cat, and the look he gave Natividad as he passed her would have taken paint off a fence."

"That I can believe. My back was to the study door—and I'm afraid I wasn't entirely sober myself. *What life is then to a man that is without wine?* He must have come into the study with his tray from the *corredor....*"

"Which means," concluded Rose, "that anyone could have put anything into it while everyone else was at supper."

"If you can think of a way anyone could have left the supper-table," remarked January, "without everyone noticing. *Did* anyone leave, Hannibal? Consuela?"

They looked at each other blankly for a moment, then Consuela shook her head. "Except for the servants, of course. They were in and out of the sala." She frowned a little, as if, for the first time, the thought was moving in her mind that Hannibal might not have murdered her brother after all. "And Franz was not popular among the *indios* of the village. He was like the Inquisition—not for God but for money. He was full of plans to reorganize the villages as they are organized in Prussia. On the day of the wedding-feast, the villagers sent a delegation to Don Anastasio, begging him to speak to my father about Fernando, or to cure my father if he could. Don Anastasio is regarded as something of a *brujo* in the villages, and able to do such things. But it would take a brave servant to enter the study when Fernando was sitting so close to its door."

"And the door into the *corredor* was bolted from the inside," added Hannibal. "Franz had to get up and unbolt it, to let me in." The muscles of his jaw twitched, and he settled back against the bedpost, his arms wrapped around his knees.

"Hence my quest for Don Fernando's personal cache of tea," said January firmly. He stowed the tea-pot carefully back in the chest and closed the lid. "I wonder if one of the kitchen-boys could be bribed into stealing us one of M'sieu Guillenormand's rabbits. Or does someone raise them in the village?"

"Lupe does," said Consuela. "You should hear her on the subject of French *mariquitas,* for whom an honest hare isn't good enough. She'll sell you one for a medio."

Footmen were still loading Doña Imelda's luggage—an amazing quantity considering the woman had come only for an overnight stay—into the smaller of her two carriages, when January descended the courtyard stair a few minutes later. The huge quadrangle was filled with not only the mounts of the de Bujerio outriders—stoutly-built Andalusians and Hanoverian warmbloods who towered over the scrawny mustangs of the vaqueros—but with those of the guards who would accompany Don Prospero's proposed expedition to the pyramids. Circling around beneath the ground-floor arcade to avoid being trampled—or smothered in the fog of dust—January encountered Don Anastasio, coming from the direction of the kitchen with several small bundles of dried herbs in his hands, done up with string. January touched his hat to him; the slim, silver-haired *hacendado* checked his stride and bowed.

"Señor Enero," he said. "You play a good game of cards—I'm sorry I had not the opportunity to speak to you as much as I would have liked last night, nor to your lovely bride. A most intelligent and educated woman. A pity we do not see more like her in my country."

January recalled some of Consuela's remarks about Anastasio's own wife, and replied, "A pity we do not see more like her in *my* country, Don Anastasio. For she is exceptional—and the view that women are too highly strung to sustain the rigors of an education is hardly limited to Mexico."

"One would think, in the nineteenth century . . ." The Don shook his head, his glance flickering to January's face. "Is it true that you were appointed by the British minister to look into the matter of Señor Sefton's innocence? For I recall when Sefton was first accused, Señora Montero spoke to Sir Henry on the subject and was told that he could—or would—do nothing. And I thought it most curious that an Englishman would appoint an American to such an investigation."

"It is not for me," smiled January, "to comment upon the truth or falsehood of what a lady says. If I have anything at all to do with the matter, upon my return to the city it will be true."

Don Anastasio grinned, teeth very white and strong above a neatly-trimmed beard. "Whatever else may be said of your friend, it has been good beyond expression to hear music properly played. Do you truly believe him to be innocent?"

"I don't know. Do you truly believe him to be guilty?"

"What makes you ask that?"

"What makes you hesitate in answering?"

The Don said nothing for a time. Then, slowly, he replied, "Truly, Señor Enero, I do not know. Werther Bremer's grief appeared to me to be entirely genuine—the poor boy was utterly distraught at his master's death. My common sense tells me that it must have been one of them or the other, for no one else had access to anything Franz consumed after dinner was done. I hope I am not being prejudiced by the joys of educated conversation...." He gestured with the packet he held: January smelled the summery breath of chamomile and comfrey. "Perhaps I am too much a lover of music to believe that a rotten branch can produce such sweet fruit. My wife's confessor would take me to task on that score, I'm sure. I don't know how else murder could have been done—but I don't believe Sefton did it. Not knowingly, anyway."

"Unknowingly, then?" January had watched Don Anastasio converse with Rose at dinner about botany and the behavior of barometers on the high central Mexican plateau. A *brujo*, Consuela had called him. January was curious what Fernando's brother-in-law would have observed on the night of the wedding-feast.

"I have heard of men drying the residue of certain poisons onto the sides of wineglasses," said Don Anastasio at length. "It could be done in a slow oven, after the baking was finished. But Guillenormand is a fanatic for cleanliness, and the glasses that Hannibal carried into that room he took from the sideboard in the *sala*. They would not have had any residue on them, or you can be sure one of the kitchen-boys would have had a beating. Even more so would that apply to Fernando's teacup, which Bremer cleaned himself. It has crossed my mind..."

He stepped closer to January, and deeper into the shadows of the arcade, away from the clamor of the men and horses in the court.

"However the poisoning was done, it has crossed my mind that perhaps the best thing to do might be simply to wait for the Days of the Dead, and then spirit your friend out of here on the night of *los niños,* while everyone is at the cemetery."

"The cemetery?"

"Here in Mictlán, the first night of the feast—the first of November—is the feast of the Saints, the holy ones who dwell with God, and so by extension that of the innocent ones, the children. People bring food to the graves, to share with the spirits of the dead and with one another: tamales, candy, the sweetest of fresh fruits. The graves are decorated with red coxcomb and yellow marigolds—*cempoalxochitl,* the Indians call them, *the flower of twenty,* though why twenty I've never understood."

Beside Doña Imelda's carriage, Don Prospero was snapping out instructions to Don Rafael. "Have those sheep to the Army by Thursday, you understand. And for the love of God, don't just send whatever beasts you happen to round up! Sort out the healthy ones and turn them back into the pasture. Those imbeciles that buy for the Army won't know the difference."

By his tone he might have been talking to the kitchen-boy, but Don Rafael inclined his head; whether a slave worked in the cane-fields or in the Big House, January reflected, he was still a slave.

"You're not leaving? Nonsense, your mother will get back to town all right! I'm showing Hannibal's Moorish friend the pyramids. Vasco!" Don Prospero shouted to the tallest of the vaqueros, a startlingly handsome man with the long braids of an Indian. "Saddle a horse for Rafael here to come with us."

"I've already seen the pyramids, sir. You showed them to me yourself—"

"I know you've already seen the pyramids, you blockhead!" flared the Don. His pale eyes glared from beneath the white brows. "Are you so stupid you think you've seen all there is?"

"Er—of course not, sir. It's just..."

"Rafael." Doña Imelda stood beside the carriage door, ignoring the footman who waited, hand extended, to help her in. "It is a long way back to town, and we must be going if we wish to reach there by nightfall."

"Do people just go to take one look at Rome, eh? Or Venice?"

"Of... of course not, sir...."

"Rafael."

"These are the temples of gods beyond our comprehension!" shouted Don Prospero, flinging out his long arms. "Of seers and priests and warriors who were reading truths in the stars when Spaniards were still hitting one another over the head with sticks! You..." He jabbed a finger at Doña Imelda. "Your son will return tomorrow."

"They are an uncanny place," Don Anastasio murmured to January, still at his side, "the pyramids of Mictlán." He turned to look at them, framed by the vast arch of the kitchen-yard gate, tawny-gold cones against a bottomless sky. "Most of the villagers cannot be induced to walk among them—many, not even to speak of them. But sometimes after the Days of the Dead are over, I have found altars there, in the crypts that are bored into their hearts. Little shrines decorated with shells and bits of turquoise and glass, with coins and bunches of tobacco. Places where the idols remain, watching over the cenotes—the holy wells—in the dark. And sometimes it is clear that food is not the only thing that has been given to the spirits, for the lilies and the marigolds before the images are splashed with fresh blood."

He glanced sidelong up at January, and in his eyes January saw the same uneasiness he had glimpsed the previous night, when Don Prospero had sung the praises of the ancient priests and explained the techniques of cardiosection. "You say you are a physician, Señor. Have you had to do with the diseases of the mad? The diseases of the mind?"

January shook his head. "I am only a surgeon," he replied. "And for ten years, owing to the prejudices of the white men against my race, I have made my living as a musician and a teacher of music. I've seen lunatics, of course, and spoken to men who tried to study them...."

"You're fortunate," muttered Anastasio. "Here in this country they're as likely to try to drive the Devil out with prayer and cayenne pepper, or call in the local *tlaciuhqui* with his smoke-pot and his mushrooms. There is, of course, every chance that on the second night—the night when *all* the Dead return, young and old alike—poor Prospero will simply decide that his son was murdered by the Jaguar-God or the ghost of Hernán Cortés, and will help Hannibal get out of the country just to spite Capitán Ylario—who is a muddle-headed young prig so enamored of his own abilities that he couldn't catch an urchin pilfering apples. On the other hand..."

Anastasio frowned, and his eyes followed the tall black figure of Don Prospero across the gilded fog of dust in the yard till it vanished beneath the shadows of the stair. "On the other hand, it might be best to get Hannibal out of here before Don Prospero comes back from the cemetery with whatever he thinks his son is going to tell him to do with his killer."

SEVEN

The pyramids of Mictlán lay east of the *casco*, on high ground above a long extension of the lake that stretched in far too straight a line to be anything but man-made. The most easterly, the Pyramid of the Sun, lay some five miles from the last few fences of the tangle of corrals and sheep-pens that marked the farthest extension of the hacienda's kitchen precincts. The closest lay at a distance of about three miles, and was the tallest, a hundred and fifty feet of steep-sided brush and heat-withered acacias, studded with the broken edges of stone steps, the bleached faces of stone-carved skulls that stared up startlingly from the pale earth.

That was the Pyramid of the Dead, for which the hacienda was named.

"Tezcatlipoca, now, he never did get on with Quetzalcoatl." Don Prospero gestured at the broken lumps of brush-covered stone that marked where lesser buildings of the complex had stood. "Seduced three of his nieces, and Xochiquetzal, Tlaloc's wife, into the bargain, not that it would have taken much, from all I've ever heard of Tlaloc. There's a statue of him over yonder...." He waved in the direction of the reed-curtained lakeshore. "Rain-God. The idiot Greeks would have equated him with Jupiter, but that shows all they know. They're all flirts, anyhow," he added darkly. "Women."

Valentina, riding straight-backed as a little black-clad soldier among the vaqueros who escorted the party, was close enough to hear—Don Prospero seldom spoke below a roar—but didn't turn her head. Doña Filomena, her pear-shaped and depressed-looking duenna, only clung to the back of the vaquero behind whom she rode pillion and moaned; when Valentina had announced, back in the courtyard, her intention of joining the expedition to the pyramids, her chaperone had blenched and pleaded a headache, but Don Prospero had insisted on the elderly woman's presence.

He had insisted on Hannibal's presence, too. January wondered, glancing sidelong at the fiddler riding beside him, whether the Don feared that Ylario was still lurking somewhere and waiting his chance to strike again, or merely wanted to have as large an audience as possible.

"Take Tlazolteotl, now," the Don went on. "She seduced the holy hermit Jappan for no better reason than that his virtue annoyed her. He ended up having his head cut off—and his wife's head too, for good measure—and he turned into a scorpion. She turned into a scorpion afterwards as well, a different-colored one. And Maria-Exaltación was no better. Flirted with every man she met, which was astonishing considering she was always down with the vapors or a rash, don't know how she did it. And Valla, of course, is nothing but a little tart, like that mother of hers, what was her name...? Fernando took it all so seriously. Worst thing I could have done, sending him to Germany, but his mother insisted...."

On Don Prospero's farther side, Don Rafael de Bujerio clung to the high pommel of his deep Mexican saddle and tried to look as if he weren't frantic over the effect of the stirrups on the polish of his fine English boots. Having come to Mictlán with no expectation of doing any riding, he had not brought clothes for it. Sweating heavily in his London-tailored tailcoat, he kept grimly at Don Prospero's side, exclaiming in admiration at everything the old man said.

The other vaqueros strung out in a ragged skein around the Don, his daughter Valentina, and his guests, and observing them, January understood, with sinking heart, just how difficult it would be for Hannibal to make his escape from this place. In their leather breeches, faded shirts, short jackets, and leather *botas*—gaiters—they had a ferocious look, not far removed from the bandits who'd attacked the *diligencia* in the pass: young men for the most part, though there were a couple of stringy graybeards among them, thin and scrubby as the horses they rode. There was an animal quality to them, and they seemed to question Don Prospero no more than the pack-wolves question the king-wolf: those whose hearts harbored questions would simply have moved on. They patrolled the gully-slashed rangeland that lay for dozens of miles in all directions around the *casco,* looking for any sign of anomaly that could mean an injured cow. A man could not ride away from the house without attracting their attention: a man alone on foot would probably not make it to the city at all.

"Xipe Toltec, now, the god of the maize—his priests would put on the flayed skins of their victims and wear them until they rotted off their bodies, to show the people how the husk rots from the corn. You'll see, there are some astonishing bas-reliefs. . . ."

January urged his horse—a big black gelding—over closer to Hannibal's, and asked softly, "What became of Franz's tea-service, by the way? I didn't see anything like what you described when I was down in the kitchen."

Hannibal shook his head. "Another of the many things I haven't liked to ask." In the strong sunlight his eyes had a bruised look, as if he had not slept in many nights. "Werther kept it in its own chest in Franz's room—where Werther slept on a trundle-bed in a corner—but now that you speak of it, when they cleared Franz's things out of the room after Werther departed in haste, I didn't see it. I can only guess it's found its way into the Monte de Piedad—the government pawnshop in the city—or the thieves' market in the southeast corner of the Cathedral square. Did you acquire a rabbit to sample the tea, by the way?"

"Lupe sold me one," said January. "She said she'd put a mark on its basket so that none of the servants would touch it. I think she suspected I was getting it to sacrifice."

"As indeed you are. *Dulce et decorum est. . .*"

"Huitzilopochtli, now, the left-handed hummingbird, he was the one they had to fear." The old Don nudged his mount over closer to January's, and shook his horsehair quirt at the two friends. "He needed blood—great quantities of it—if the sun was to rise the next day, and I must say it seems to have worked, because the sun rose on schedule and has continued to rise ever since. What they'll do when the laid-up surplus is spent, I have no notion." From beneath the wide brim of his glazed leather hat his too-brilliant eyes glared like blue topaz. "They sacrificed dogs as well, you know. Ate them, of course, too. Rather than sacrifice a full-sized and perfectly edible dog, they bred them specially for sacrifice, down to the size of rats. Disgusting little brutes. Isabella has them. God knows why Anastasio lets her keep them. Treats them like babies, talks to them—I daresay if Isabella had babies of her own, she'd get rid of them quick enough. One day I'll break the neck of that little brute of Valla's."

They dismounted in the open space that lay at the foot of the Pyramid of the Dead, close by the remains of two broken statues that had once flanked a stair. Huge eyes and incised feathers decorated the domed head that poked up through the tangle of weeds and earth on one side; on the other, all that remained was a broken mass, and a toothed jaguar grin.

"There's a crypt cut into the heart of that one," said Don Prospero, pointing his quirt up at a leveling of the ground three-quarters of the way to the top. "He's still in there, Mictlantecuhtli, Lord of the Land of the Dead. They'd tear out the heart before him, and throw the body down the steps to the people who waited here where we stand. Come along, fool," he added sharply as Don Rafael showed signs of sinking down onto the broken guardian-statue to rest.

The town-bred *hacendado* leaped immediately to his feet and started after Don Prospero, then halted—presumably when he recalled Valentina's presence—and turned back toward her horse just as Hannibal helped her from the saddle. Don Rafael wavered, as if debating whether he should go back to her and offer her his arm, for the hill was quite steep. But Don Prospero snapped at him again, and he hastened to follow.

"I shall die!" groaned Doña Filomena, almost melting from her perch behind Vasco, the tall chief of the vaqueros. "Oh, I must rest . . . I cannot go on. . . ."

"You've only just gotten here," snapped Don Prospero. "No lagging, now! If you cannot walk, Señora, I assure you I can arrange for you to be dragged."

She burst into tears and looked to Valentina for sympathy, but Valla only stood looking around her, her arms hugged about her under the short velvet *manga*—the beautifully decorated riding cape—that she wore. With a sniffle Doña Filomena produced a substantial silver flask from her reticule and drank from it, then stumbled after Don Prospero and his daughter.

"My name is Ozymandias, King of Kings," murmured Hannibal, pausing to contemplate the staring eye of the Serpent-God at the foot of the pyramid. *"Look on my works, ye mighty, and despair."* He produced a flask of his own—laudanum-laced sherry—and set off in Prospero's wake, January walking thoughtfully behind.

"Mostly the Spanish destroyed everything they found here," declaimed Prospero as he led the way straight up the steep, brushy slope. "There used to be little temples on the tops of all of these—you'll see." His blithe harsh voice chopped at the hush of the forenoon. From somewhere in the dry tangle of creosote bush and yellowing weeds near-by came the rattle of an insect, the skitter of a fleeing hare or fox. *Sopilotes* circled, tiny as imaginary specks in the vision, deep in the well of the sky. Under the white glare of the sun, the pyramids loomed eerily, fragments of carving peering from among the rough-barked junipers. On one section of frieze, twisted human torsos cut into the stone in deep relief, detached arms and writhing, severed legs. Above each carved body was a carved head, curls of what looked like ribbon extruding from their half-parted lips.

"Breath," explained Hannibal, panting in the thin air as he climbed. "Or the songs that they sing in dying.

> *All whom war, death, age, agues, tyrannies,*
> *Despair, law, chance hath slain...."*

From the level space they had seen from below, a black cave opened into the heart of the pyramid. "The Inquisitors came here, of course." Don Prospero strolled casually into the low tunnel that stretched into darkness; looking back down the precipitate slope, January saw the vaqueros clustered close around the horses, looking nervously over their shoulders.

Their rifles were in their hands, not at their shoulders. It was not El Moro and his bandits that they feared.

"'Stasio and I explored every foot of these shrines when we were boys, searching for treasure." Yellow light flared in the darkness as Don Prospero kindled a torch. "I laugh now to think that two youths expected to uncover a treasure that would have escaped so expert a looter as Cortés."

January ducked as he entered the passageway, the crumbling corbels brushing the crown of his wide-brimmed hat. Ahead, the torch-light revealed more dead men carved on the brown stone of the walls, dismembered, beheaded, decapitated heads singing or breathing out their final curling ribbons of life between rows of grinning skulls. Then he stepped into the main crypt and froze. Years of rational study among the educated of Paris deserted him in one single chilling breath as he came face-to-face with the Lord of the Land of the Dead.

Mictlantecuhtli, skeletal, crouching, grinning with the bones of his face, fleshless hands folded before the empty cavity of his belly. The horrid shape was cut into the far wall in such deep relief as to seem like almost a statue, the torch-gleam lost utterly in the twin black pits of his eyes. Parted teeth showed only a black eternal hollow. The floor of the little chamber rose at that side of the room, a broken rim showing where steps had been. At the foot of those crumbled steps, empty as the god's shadowed eyes, a circular pit gaped, filled with bottomless shadow. Between pit-rim and outer door stood what had to have been the altar-stone, its carvings all broken, weeds growing in the crevices of its death's-head designs.

"Earth's face is but thy table," said Hannibal, sinking wearily down onto the altar and taking another sip of sherry, *"there are set / Plants, cattle, men, dishes for Death to eat."*

"We nearly broke our necks going down that cenote on a rope." Don Prospero nodded at the black maw of the holy well. "Of course, the Spanish filled it in with rubble, centuries ago. The Indians said that Tlaloc, god of the pulp of the earth, dwelled in its depths; they'd throw virgin girls down, and gold and jewels and balls of copal incense. Me, if I'd been a priest here, you can be sure I'd have had a net stretched on the days when they were just throwing gold and jewels. Tlaloc could have the girls, for all of me. Eh, daughter?"

He glanced wickedly at Valla, who stood beside the narrow entry of the passageway, Don Rafael fidgeting uncomfortably at her side.

"My father was always forbidding us to come here because he said bandits lurked in the ruins," Don Prospero continued. "I never believed him, and we never encountered any, nor even saw signs of their camps. Come on. Don't lag. You have to see the countryside from the top.

"Banditry is ten times now what it was—twenty times—since we kicked the Penínsularios out," he went on as he charged up the remaining slope of the pyramid like a billygoat. "And still they won't come here. Sometimes I ride out here alone, to watch the moon rise from the top of the pyramid, or to bring my telescope and study the stars. And in the hours before the moon rises...Sometimes I'll just lie by the lip of the well and listen. And I'll hear old Tlaloc's voice speaking to me out of the dark."

The view from the top of the pyramid was breath-taking. The red-tiled roofs of the *casco,* the leaves of the trees in the ladies' courtyard, the myriad corrals and pens that sprawled behind the kitchen, the gilt cross at the top of the little chapel—all these things seemed to January as if he viewed them through a microscope, perfect, distant, like miniatures etched in glass. The rangeland spread out around the pyramids in a green-splotched symphony of dusty brown and tawny gold, slashed by arroyos where thorn and trees and brush grew thick. Close to the feet of all five pyramids on the north, a shallow depression of the ground was thick with oaks and paloverde: like the water to the south, regular in shape, the work of men's hands.

"The Indians said when a warrior died in battle, or a woman in childbirth, they return to this world as butterflies," Don Prospero told them. "Myself, I think they become hummingbirds, who fight for their territory like warriors, if two want flowers from the same bush. It is the one thing that concerns me about your murdering Fernando," he added abruptly, turning back and fixing Hannibal with one coldly staring blue eye. "He'll be angry about dying the way he did, like a sickly woman, or a feeble child, instead of in battle like a man. I don't know what he'll have to say about that."

"θεων εν γοννασι κειται, I suppose," sighed the fiddler. "It lies in the lap of the gods, rather like a celestial napkin, and one can only hope death has given him some perspective on the matter. Not that Fernando was ever one to take notice of perspective before."

"Do not jest, my friend." Don Prospero folded his arms and stared out into the shining spaces of the sky, as if reading things written on the air that no one else could see. "Generally I leave the gods and the dead to deal with their own affairs, but I fear my son will be angry. You may find yourself in trouble." Then he set off down the pyramid—straight down its steep side—calling out behind him, "Come along now— plenty more to see...."

The noon sun beat down, reminding January that he'd had no

breakfast, and the thin air had a sparkly quality, like the onset of migraine. Don Prospero insisted on climbing all five pyramids, though the middle three—which had formerly supported the temples of the Moon, the Stars, and the Rain—were much worn down, that of the Stars being barely more than a shallow hill. "I dug up that statue of Tezcatlipoca here.... Here's where I found Coatlique, the slut.... Worse than Helen of Troy, *she* was.... Why Menelaus didn't simply repudiate her I'll never understand. Would have saved everybody trouble. Take a look at that bas-relief: see how the heart itself is singing in the priest's hand?"

Doña Filomena wailed and sobbed and swore she must stop and rest, but when she did so, Don Prospero signed to two of the vaqueros who had accompanied them up the pyramids and they pulled her to her feet and dragged her: Hannibal stumbled along behind them in chalky-lipped silence. Though he looked better than he had the previous winter in New Orleans, he was still not strong; January had to put a hand under his elbow and half carry him up the last slope of the Pyramid of the Sun.

"The beaten road, which those poor slaves with weary footsteps tread," quoted the fiddler faintly, his breath rasping in his throat. *"Who travel to their home among the dead.* Occasionally the thought of the prison in Mexico City does cross my mind displaying certain charms."

"You wouldn't like it," said January as his friend sank to the ground at the pyramid's top. He unslung from around his neck the water-bottle he'd taken from his saddle—nearly empty now—and handed it to him; a few feet away, Doña Filomena clung to Don Rafael and loudly proclaimed that she was about to die. Looking around, January saw that instead of wailing and protesting and demanding to be permitted to stay behind, Valentina had merely fallen back from the others and was nowhere to be seen. He walked to the edge of the pyramid's level crown and looked down the slope, in time to see the girl's slim figure—black against the saffron and buff of the land—vanish into the dense belt of trees that lay along the north.

Curious, he walked farther along the foundation-stones of the old temple at the pyramid's top and caught sight of that black dress again far below. Ordinarily the leaves of the heavily wooded depression would have hidden her, but it was late in the year, and the oak at whose feet she knelt—at least, he thought she was kneeling—stood at the edge of a little clearing where the broken statue of a jaguar lay on its side.

Although he wouldn't swear to it, January thought he saw Valentina take something from beneath her *manga* and slip it in among the roots of the oak.

EIGHT

Returning to Hacienda Mictlán, January found Lupe's rabbit still enjoying rollicking good health.

"Whatever ended up in Fernando's tea," sighed Rose, poking a tuft of maguey-flowers through the cage's bamboo bars and glancing up as January came into their room, "—if it was in fact in the tea—it wasn't put into the caddy in the kitchen. I managed to talk Guillenormand into giving me a sample of the contents of the other caddy—the jasmine and rose-hip blend Fernando drank to settle his stomach—and it seems to have been equally benign."

She got to her feet and staggered, catching herself on the bedpost. January set down the tray he'd brought from the kitchen and caught her arm. "It's nothing," said Rose, rubbing her knees through her skirts. "In between checking on Compair Lapin's health"—she nodded toward the dozing bunny—"and making discreet enquiries about that green Meissen tea-service, I spent the greater part of the day in the chapel with Doña Josefa, which eventually earned me her account of her father's bout of madness and her brother's death."

She sat on the bed and pulled up her skirts and petticoats to feel gingerly at her knee-caps. "They tell me St. Jerome prayed so much, he acquired knees like a camel's, but they didn't mention what his back must have felt like after a long day at the altar." She unclipped her garters and rolled down her stockings, and January exclaimed in alarm at the bluish bruises just below the patella, where the flesh would have pressed to the stone of the chapel floor.

"Paloma told me—she was part of the jolly little gathering in the chapel as well—that both she and her mother routinely faint after a few hours of this. If I hadn't encountered this kind of thing elsewhere, I'd suspect that Doña Josefa was as mad as her father. Did M'sieu Guillenormand send that food along with you? How kind of him... since of course Doña Josefa doesn't eat a mid-day *comida.* ..."

"She's her father's daughter, anyway." January brought the tray over to the bed: a brioche, fresh butter garnished with mint-leaves in a little Sèvres pot, a noble wedge of Brie de Meaux, and two exquisitely sweet French Faro apples, plus a carafe of Reisling that wouldn't have been out of place at a Montmartre inn. "Don Prospero doesn't seem to get hungry and assumes that no one else does either. ... But you didn't have to do that."

"Well, in fact, I did," said Rose. "Another woman I would have asked to tea and gossip, or engaged on a mutual sewing project—much as I hate sewing—but somehow I knew that wouldn't do, with Doña Josefa. One needs to spend time in company before confidences begin to flow. I'm quite all right. Mostly what I felt was boredom, and a nagging consciousness of fraud. But I couldn't very well tell my hostess that I don't believe God has the slightest interest in how many hours human beings put in on their knees."

She buttered a chunk of the brioche as she spoke. Down below them, the steady thump-thump of the workroom looms that made up the daytime heartbeat of the *casco* was silent with siesta; the chatter of the women around the lower arcade was stilled as well. Even the vaqueros had retired to the shade to sleep.

"Thank goodness they decorate their altars like a hashish-eater's dream—at least there was plenty to look at. Though I'll admit I could not avoid the resentful reflection that you, who go to confession and actually enjoy prayer, should be the one to clamber about the countryside in quest of pagan deities, while I—a pagan or the next thing to it— should be condemned to spend the morning in prayer and much of the afternoon admiring Josefa's collection of sacred ironmongery. Do you know she wears a belt of nails under her clothing, with the points turned inward so that they dig into her flesh?"

"I wondered what it was," said January drily. "I can smell infections and blood at five paces. She doesn't make Paloma do that, does she?"

"Not yet. Paloma is 'innocent,' she says, though goodness knows how long that indulgence will last. Innocent or not, she makes the poor girl sleep without a blanket on a bare plank, with a block of wood for a pillow, to prepare her, she says, for her ultimate destination at the Convent of the Bleeding Heart of Mary in town. She spoke with passionate envy of Don Rafael's sister Pilar, who will shortly be taking vows there: Paloma did not express an opinion. Because she *is* innocent, Josefa lets the child sleep on a flat plank rather than one with a one-inch stringer of wood nailed up the middle, and forbears to wake her up three times in the middle of the night for prayers. I will never understand Christians."

Anger tinged her voice, and she returned to buttering her bread and spreading the thick soft cheese upon it. January stepped to the door and listened to the silence of the court, gauging the slant of the hot bars of sunlight that splashed across the red-tiled arcade. Where the arcade angled into the wider *corredor,* the door of the corner room—the room that had been Fernando's—stood slightly ajar, left by the servants who had cleaned it in Santa Anna's wake.

With scarcely a rustle of petticoats, Rose slipped up barefoot to his side.

She saw the direction of his look, and they didn't exchange a word; then, like two mischievous schoolchildren, they slipped through the door and down the arcade, past Hannibal's room, where the fiddler lay like a dead man across his bed in the straw-smelling gloom, and down to that half-open door at the corner.

The tidying hands of the servants had passed over it, stripping the bed, rolling up the carpets of red-and-black native weave. Alone of the bedrooms in the house, this room had an armoire, with marquetry doors that could lock, clearly of European work. The desk contained nothing but neat sheafs of blank paper in several sizes, ink, seals and wax, chamois-leather penwipers and three patent steel-nibbed pens polished clean as a British rifleman's gun. There were also visiting-cards wrapped in paper—*Fernando de Castellón,* with an address on the Calle San Francisco—and a ledger bound in gilt-stamped green leather, which January slipped into his pocket. Ranged across the back of the desk were the three patent Argand-model lamps Hannibal had spoken of, still containing a little oil, and near the window—which was set high in the wall and looked onto the pyramids, not the *corredor*—a small blue-tiled heating-stove of German design.

The armoire was unlocked, and contained only a small satchel that held two white linen shirts, some clean stockings, a volume of Hegel, and von Ranke's *History of the Latin and Teutonic People.* The fly-leaves of both were inscribed, in a rather unformed hand, with the name Werther Bremer. There was no sign of the green-and-white Meissen tea-service or its chest.

"What now?" whispered Rose when they regained the sanctuary of their room. "If I thought there was a single servant awake in the kitchen—except for M'sieu Guillenormand, who sits up reading Parisian liberal newspapers as a protest against local laziness—I'd suggest calling for bath-water, but I think you're going to have to wait for that. Perhaps," she added meditatively, putting her arms around January's waist from behind, "if we both thought very hard about it, we might find something to do of which Josefa would completely disapprove, in revenge for the day we've both had . . . ?"

January grinned and covered her hands with his big ones. "It's an idea, my nightingale, and one we'll have to pursue . . . and God knows I need a bath." He released one hand to brush at the thick yellow dust on his sleeve. "But before it gets dark I want to ride back to the pyramids and see what it was Mademoiselle Valentina cached under the roots of that oak-tree."

Within minutes Rose had changed into riding-clothes, and the two were slipping stealthily across the kitchen yard toward the corrals. "If I thought we could do so without drawing the attention of every vaquero in the place," added January softly, "I'd suggest we steal three horses, leave a note for Consuela, and make a break with Hannibal for Mexico City now. This place is dangerous." He looked back across the silent quadrangle, the bare, dusty ground and the high yellow walls, each archway of the two arcades, upper and lower, a choir of silently singing mouths of shadow, and was reminded of the ranks of carved skulls in the crypt of the Lord of the Dead.

"You feel that, too?" asked Rose, and January looked down at her, hearing the uneasiness in her voice. "It's a completely illogical feeling," she admitted in the tone of one apologizing for error, and he shook his head.

"No: it's a deduction that your mind has made from clues you haven't yet realized are clues." He led the way past the radiant heat of the round *comal* ovens, and out through the wide stable gates. "Don Prospero is unstable—and dangerous. Just because he's protecting Hannibal now doesn't mean he won't turn against him after November second—or even sooner, if he has some dream of the Jaguar-God. And if Werther Bremer turns out not to have done the murder, that means that the real killer is still here on the hacienda. Since we don't know why the murder was committed, that means we have no guarantee that he—or she—won't kill again."

As January had expected, the moment he and Rose emerged from the small postern at the back of the kitchen yard into the tangle of corrals and sheds that constituted the hacienda's stables, a shaggy-haired, scar-faced vaquero materialized from the shade of a paloverde tree and asked, "Can we be of help?" Since it would be foolish to ride through this bandit-haunted land alone, January explained—in his most educated Spanish—that *la Señora* Enero had a desire to see some of the statues and ruins that surrounded the pyramids, though of course neither of them had any desire to wake Don Prospero for another expedition. . . .

The vaquero grinned his understanding, and whistled for a couple of companions, who emerged, yawning and scratching themselves, from where they'd been sleeping on the ground in the shade. While they were saddling horses, January's Indian servant, Cristóbal, joined them, silent as ever, apparently from out of nowhere. As they rode out, January and Rose continued their conversation in French—many of the vaqueros barely spoke Spanish.

"According to Josefa," said Rose, "Don Prospero had been slipping toward mania for several days before his attack on the fourth of September. Generally, she says, his spells last about twenty-four hours. Then he'll sleep for another day, and then he's well, or as well as he ever is. On the fourth he was definitely disoriented, shouting that voices were speaking to him from the air, and unable to recognize his family. Nobody worried much until the seventh, when Don Anastasio sent for Franz; by the morning of the eighth, as Hannibal said, Prospero had to be forcibly restrained."

January shivered at the thought of the four preceding days, of living with Don Prospero roving at large. "No wonder Valentina was making plans to get out of there. I only wonder that Paloma didn't try to bolt, too."

"Josefa wouldn't hear of it," said Rose drily. "Josefa seems to have had the same idea that Señora Lorcha did, and tried to get her father to sign over the ten thousand dollars it would cost for her and Paloma to enter a convent—leaving poor little Casimiro alone in his grandfather's care, though no one seems to have thought of that. Josefa was livid when Señora Lorcha's priest showed up for the clandestine marriage of Prospero and Natividad, because, of course, then Fernando arrived hot-foot with his two mad-doctors in tow and took over everything. Santa Anna and his aides arrived on the eighth as well."

"And Fernando intended to go through with marrying Natividad?"

"After that he had to." Rose drew rein a little, following January as he led the little cortege down into the thickly-wooded depression in the ground that flanked the pyramids to the north. "I think he guessed it would only be a matter of time before Señora Lorcha forged proof that Natividad *had* married Don Prospero on the eighth, and as his wife was entitled to a third of his property in the event of his death."

Here among the trees, the air stifled in the lungs, and the gnats and mosquitoes swarmed. Undergrowth tangled in thickets like thorned wire, and among the close-crowding gray boles of oak and juniper, January seemed to feel the watching eyes of those who had held this land before the Spanish, those proud, secretive faces cut into the stone of the crumbling temple walls.

He nodded at his wife, his mind still filled with the picture of that poisoned and chaotic house in which Fernando died. "Natividad prob-ably reasoned that if she couldn't marry a man who'd be safely locked away in an asylum for the rest of his life, at least she could marry one who might be killed in Texas before she would ever be required to live with him. Given Fernando's proclivities, there was a good chance she'd never be asked to live with him at all."

"It's generous of you to attribute to her the powers of reasoning." Rose ducked a low-hanging oak-branch, the tiny, stiff gray-green leaves snagging at her riding-hat brim. "She may have been doing only what her mother ordered. Josefa says Franz invariably referred to Natividad as 'that cow,' not so much from his contempt for women in general—an attitude he seems to share with his father—as because of the money she cost the estate. But Werther had no such financial admixture to *his* motives. He never let a day pass without some slight or mischief: pebbles in shoes, ink-spots on silk, sometimes worse. Of course, since Josefa never exchanged a word with Natividad or her mother, she didn't know much, and it seems to have entirely escaped her that all that enmity from Werther had any other root than righteous indignation against a harlot. What Natividad thought, I have no idea."

"But it would pay us to find out." January raised his hand to signal a halt, and instructed Quacho, the scar-faced vaquero, to deploy his two companions and Cristóbal in a perimeter around the outer edge of the wooded depression. "And quickly. Don Prospero's instability aside, God knows at what point young Ylario is going to abandon the Principles of Universal Law and feel himself justified in simply shooting Hannibal from the shelter of the nearest arroyo the next time he steps out the gate. There's no way we could protect against that."

"Do you think he would?" asked Rose as January helped her from the saddle—Valla's side-saddle, borrowed along with one of Valla's highly-bred Irish mares. Her riding-boots crunched in the mats of brown oak-leaves underfoot. "He seems most wedded to the Principles of Universal Law."

"So wedded to them that he might feel justified in bypassing the frustrating letter of the law in favor of what he considers its spirit." January took his knife from his belt and cut a sapling for a snake-stick, having grown up in the Louisiana countryside with a healthy wariness about long grass and deep underbrush. It was good even to be able to carry a knife, one of the many things he was forbidden to do in the United States. Bandits, *léperos,* and General Santa Anna aside, there were things to be said for Mexico.

Sighting on the flattened crown of the Pyramid of the Sun—visible as a burning amber trapezoid through the ragged treetops—he made his way in what he hoped was the direction of the clearing at its foot, where the broken jaguar statue lay at the roots of the oak.

"So far it doesn't look like anyone could have poisoned Fernando after dinner but his valet or Hannibal. Werther certainly had reason to—not the logical reason of a police case, but the illogic of a lover. I am very curious as to where Werther Bremer is now, and what he has been doing in the weeks since his flight from Mictlán."

The trees above them thinned where stone pavement broke through the hard-packed earth. Fragments of carving showed among the twisted roots of soapberry and creosote, and at the foot of a hoary-barked oak-tree, a stone jaguar glared with furious eyes. The depression, Don Prospero had said, had in all probability been a sunken ball-court, where teams of Indians had once vied for the privilege of stripping all the spectators of their feathered clothing and gold ornaments, with the added fillip of knowing that the members of the losing team would end up having their hearts torn out on the altars of the gods. He didn't imagine anyone ever wore their best to the game.

"Consuela says that she must leave first thing tomorrow," Rose told him. "She's singing in *L'Italiana in Algeri* Saturday night, and the rehearsal is Friday...."

"Good," said January. "Don Prospero seems to have a habit of hanging on to his guests, and much as I hate to leave Hannibal alone, God knows how long it's going to take us to find out what really happened on the eighth. Hannibal says he should be safe until the second, but if Santa Anna leaves before that for Vera Cruz, I wouldn't lay two medios on his life lasting another twenty-four hours."

He did not add, glancing over his shoulder at the silent woods, already beginning to fill with silvery twilight, that he would feel safer back in the city. Safer to know that Rose was away from this place. The sun was beginning to sink, trailing the glassy sliver of the new moon in its wake. Night, when it came, would be like the inside of a cow. He prodded at the dark hollow beneath the roots of the oak and, when no snake emerged or rattled in protest, knelt to reach gingerly inside.

There was quite a little cache there, tucked deep into the crannies of the stone. Two leather bags, double-wrapped in sacking, proved to contain cornmeal; a third held parched corn. Four empty water-bottles, and a fifth containing brandy: January poured a little of it into one of the empties, to take home and test on poor Compair Lapin, though he couldn't imagine a poisoned decanter going unsampled for nearly two months with such souls as Hannibal and Doña Filomena in the house. Three tiny parcels proved to contain money: small amounts, such as would not be missed from drawers or reticules. The most recent, lying on top, January was amused and exasperated to note, consisted of American coins, clearly abstracted from his own luggage. With them was a pearl bracelet he did not recognize, and the sapphire girandole earrings Valentina had worn the night before at supper.

I search my daughter's room as a matter of course, Doña Imelda had said, and Josefa had enthusiastically agreed. *The possession of baubles and trinkets is only a temptation to sin. It is good training to be reminded that the soul possesses nothing.*

There was no note.

"She's getting ready to run for it, all right." He looked back up at Rose, who stood behind him, holding the horses. "I wonder if Fernando stumbled upon something else, some other evidence of her plans to meet her lover or to flee?"

"If he did, I still can't see how she could have entered the study." Rose swung lightly to the Irish mare's saddle, hooked her right knee around the bar. "She was with others all the way through dinner, and afterwards in the *corredor*. The same goes for Señora Lorcha and Natividad."

"And Doña Imelda," said January thoughtfully. "And Consuela, for that matter."

"Why on earth would Consuela wish to murder her brother?" exclaimed Rose, startled.

January shrugged. "We don't know that," he said. "But the fact that we don't know a reason why Consuela, or Don Anastasio, or Hinojo the butler, or Santa Anna himself for that matter, would have wanted to murder Fernando doesn't mean that they didn't have one, maybe as strong a reason as passion or hatred or fear. All we have to go on was what was actually done, and who could actually, physically, have committed the crime. And at the moment," he concluded regretfully, mounting his heavy-boned gelding, "the only ones who had any contact with anything Don Fernando ate or drank after he left the dinner were Hannibal and Werther."

"And Don Prospero," mused Rose. "Bolts or no bolts on the doors to his room, he had the best of all reasons to want his son dead. And his movements in the hour or so after dinner when Franz must have died are unaccounted for."

The sun had set by the time they returned to the *casco*. The women who worked at spindle and loom were streaming out the front gates of the great court, chattering and laughing and wrapping their long rebosos around their shoulders against the evening chill, as Rose and January, dusty and exhausted, came through the kitchen gates. The long ground-floor workrooms, sheltered by their surrounding arcade, would be deep in gloom now, and the women had to return to their own huts in the village to make tortillas for their husbands and children and parents. The flat cornbread upon which all of Indian and mestizo cuisine was based staled and lost its suppleness very quickly; the women had to bake it anew at every meal.

"I trust and pray there'll be time for a bath before dinner," Rose was saying as they climbed the stair to the upper arcade. Light shone through the cracks in the shutters of Consuela's room; Hannibal's, as far as January could see, was dark. He wondered if the fiddler was recovered from the exhaustion of the day's clamber over the pyramids, and if Don Prospero would insist on his playing after dinner that night. "And I'll speak to Zama about having our things packed at first light."

"Good," said January. "I'd like to be able to at least take the *diligencia* back to Vera Cruz without worrying about the police waiting for us on the dock. But how we're to learn if Don Prospero—"

He stopped, his hand on the latch of their door, every alarm-bell in his mind suddenly clamoring at the smell of blood.

He held up his hand and Rose halted behind him....

Servants had already kindled the cressets along the *corredor,* the smoke thin and pungent against the whining mosquitoes. He took candles from his pocket—experience had taught him to carry them—and he lit one from the nearest flame, then cautiously pushed open the door.

The smell was stronger in the dark. From the wall the massacred Christ gazed sorrowfully at him: January recalled the dead bandit in the pass, the dismembered limbs carved on the temple walls, and thought, *No wonder they show Christ covered with gore and horrors—how else in this land would He get anyone's attention?*

Nothing moved in the room, so he stepped inside, swiftly touched the flame to the wicks of other candles in their heavy iron holder. Golden light broadened. For the first moment he thought that nothing had been changed, nothing touched: the bed still made, the chest still closed, the small travel-trunk in its corner unmolested ...

Then he saw the little bamboo cage that had held Compair Lapin stood open and empty.

And on top of the chest at the bed's foot, one of M'sieu Guillenormand's red-and-white French dishes, half-filled with congealing blood, in which swam what could only be the rabbit's heart.

NINE

January had hoped to consult Don Anastasio about the heart—to ask whether this was a customary form of local juju or a repetition of some common act of Don Prospero's madness—but the gentle, scholarly *hacendado* had departed already for his own hacienda of Saragosse. "He'll be back," replied Don Prospero carelessly when January inquired after him at supper. "I told him to fetch pears for tomorrow night's dessert—he has a most astonishing way with them. True French jagonelles, *here.* . . . The Indians are right, he is a *brujo.* And grapes. My father was very partial to grapes, so I want to make sure there are some here when he comes back." It took January a moment to remember that the father referred to was dead. "Where is that lazy fiddler?" The Don glared around the torchlit *corredor,* where the household had assembled before dinner. "Fetch him," he ordered the butler.

"I'll get him," offered January, and the sharp blue eyes flared like lightning in the flickering yellow light.

"Stay right here—Hinojo will get him. I want to talk to you about the ancient Indians. Little enough decent conversation I get around this place, between the likes of Josefa and Rafael." He jerked his head at Valentina's suitor. "An amazing sight, the pyramids, no? Their priests had calculated the cycles of the stars and planets for thousands of years in the past, and centuries into the future, with greater accuracy than the

Babylonians did. They were able to predict retrogrades in the orbits of Mars and Venus...."

Hinojo and the foreman Vasco appeared with a haggard and ghostly Hannibal between them: "You should be more grateful, eh?" chided Don Prospero with a glaring smile but an unmistakable edge of hardness in his tone. He prodded Hannibal playfully in the chest. "Instead of Guillenormand's veal *à la Reine,* you could be eating stale tortillas in the yard of La Accordada prison. Now, tell me if you don't think tales of that strumpet Helen of Troy parallel exactly the conduct of Xochiquetzal...?"

Although swaying with exhaustion and opium-laced brandy, Hannibal exerted himself to be charming at dinner ("It's obvious Menelaus married Helen only for her dowry—she'd probably been waiting for *years* to show him that nobody treated *her* that way and got away with it. Helen would have run off with Thersites if he'd had the wits to sing her a love-song....") and after dinner played the gentle gavottes and old Scots ballads that seemed to bring the Don the only relaxation his furious mind was capable of grasping.

> *What will your mother say, Pretty Peggy-o?*
> *What will your mother say, Pretty Peggy-o?*
> *What will your mother say when she finds you've gone away*
> *To places far and strange to Fennario-o?*

January borrowed a guitar from one of the vaqueros and joined him in the lively contradanses and the strange old Irish planxties that seemed to be woven of starlight.

"Stay here, Enero." Don Prospero removed the cigar from his mouth and regarded January with deep approval. "The violin alone is the song of the gods, but accompanied... Paradise itself! I will have Hannibal play for *los niños* in the cemetery on the first night of the feast, when all go to the churchyard to make music...."

"Like Compair Lapin," smiled January, but he watched Don Prospero's face as he said it. "Brother Rabbit."

There was no reaction, no flicker of guilt, only a shaken head and an inquiring look: "It is a story of my people," January told Prospero. "Compair Lapin once took his fiddle to the churchyard at a place called

Red Hill, and played the dead up out of their graves, so that they danced on the hillside in the starlight. His music was so wild and so beautiful—and his power so great—that the angels came down from Heaven to dance, and all the beasts of the earth came also, and ringed the hill with song. Then the Devil himself came up out of the ground, and had to dance, and couldn't stop dancing. Compair Lapin wouldn't let him stop dancing, but played on and on, until the Devil swore to leave Compair Lapin and all his family in peace forever.

"And after the Devil swore, they all danced for the joy of it in the Red Hill Churchyard until the sun came up, and the angels fled away into the sky, embarrassed at what they'd tell God about where they'd been all night, and the dead sank away back into the earth, and the Devil went home to Hell with sore feet."

Don Prospero laughed out loud at this, and Hannibal played a strange trace of some ancient tune, like wind through bones.

> *"At the round earth's imagined corners, blow*
> *Your trumpets, angels, and arise, arise,*
> *From death, you numberless infinities*
> *Of souls, and to your scattered bodies go."*

"Even so," said the Don. "Like your Compair Lapin—your little Fray Tochtli—I beg you, at least remain until the Feast of the Dead. You will keep the feast with me, and play the dead up out of the ground— maybe even make my Fernando dance, eh? I'd like to see that."

"I am desolated to be forced to turn down such an offer," said January, leaning his arm over the slender waist of the guitar. "But Señora Montero is pledged to return to town tomorrow, to rehearse for the opera in which she will be singing. I have agreed to assist her with my playing."

"She doesn't need you. I'll tend to her." The old man spoke as if Consuela weren't sitting three feet away, on the bench with Don Rafael, who kept depositing bits of current events and information about his hacienda at her feet like a dog hopeful of favorable notice. January wondered if it would be possible to get out of this place tomorrow before Don Prospero found some means of making him stay.

"I suppose if we were really sensible, we'd steal a couple of horses tonight," he said later when he and Rose followed Hannibal back to his room and stillness descended on the *casco*.

"It would do you no good." Hannibal dropped down onto the bed as if someone had cut the strings that kept him on his feet, and fished under the pillow for another bottle of laudanum. "I've tried it. Vasco and his minions keep a close watch over the corrals. . . . *Where'er yon fires ascend, the Trojans wake,* and one is only watched more closely later. In your case I doubt the American chargé d'affaires, Mr. Butler, would raise much of a fuss if Don Prospero put you in chains: he'd think it only natural. Did you find any trace of the fatal tea-cup?"

January shook his head. "Which in itself is odd, I think. We did find this. . . ." He held up the green-bound ledger he'd taken from Fernando's desk. "Fernando's expenses since June, not only in pesos and dollars but in *thalers, silbergrosschen,* and *friedrichsdor* uniforms, boots from London, horses—he seemed to prefer Hanoverian warmbloods to the local stock. . . ."

"I'd prefer a well-raised Swiss goat to the local stock myself."

"—a rather stingy salary to someone named Laurent. . . ."

"His French cook, back at the town house on the Calle San Francisco. God knows what became of him. Fernando had as little use for the local cuisine as his father does." Hannibal held up his glass of sherry and carefully dripped laudanum into the golden liquid. "And I can tell you that leaving the carved-out hearts of small livestock in people's rooms is no local magic that I ever heard of."

"I didn't think so," January agreed. "There was no writing or symbols around it, as you'll find in nearly any gris-gris I know; no salt or ashes, not even any blood dripped in the cage. I'd be curious to know what was done with the carcass. . . ."

"Don't stay around to look." Hannibal's eyes, sunken in hollows of bruised-looking flesh, were deadly grave. "I'll search, and let you know somehow. Whatever it means, I suspect that like Macbeth's dinner-guests, standing not upon the order of your going is your best course of action. I'm sorry now I even wrote to you—a momentary attack of panic on my part. I never for the world thought . . ."

January stepped over to the bed and laid a hand on his friend's shoulder. "We'll get you out," he said gently, answering, not Hannibal's words, but the fear that lurked in his eyes. Hannibal glanced up at him, and January saw, behind the fear in those coffee-black depths, naked despair.

Then Hannibal looked away and said lightly, "Of course you will, *amicus meus.*" The lilt of the well-bred Irish gentry was stronger now in his voice, with tiredness and drink. "But best you get yourselves clear of the mess first."

"Of course we'll get you out." Rose said it briskly. "Benjamin, at the very least you can come up with one of those mysterious drugs one hears of that counterfeit death in all its particulars, so we can smuggle him out in a coffin. . . ."

"Don Prospero will begin to be suspicious when I don't put in an appearance on All Souls."

"By then you'll be long gone."

"Contrary to Mr. Shakespeare and any number of operas and novels," sighed January, "—not to mention, I am told, a thriving market in patent coffins that can be opened from inside by the twitch of a lever— in all my medical experience I have yet to encounter a poison that reliably induces coma. The closest I've ever heard of is belladonna, and I assure you, you wouldn't like it."

Hannibal smiled faintly. "Another illusion shattered."

Outside, Don Prospero's voice lifted angrily: ". . . my land and I can do as I please!" January had no idea to whom he was speaking—possibly Consuela, though the singer had gone to her room before Hannibal was finished with his playing. Possibly to no one at all. The torches along the *corredor* had burned themselves out, and the moon had set; the Don's voice came deep and harsh out of the utter darkness.

"Think yourself ill-done-by, I'll wager. All women do. Don't know when you're well off, my girl! The King of the Toltecs sent his daughter to the Aztecs as a hostage to ensure their good behavior—a fair trade if I do say so—you're lucky I haven't done as much. They *skinned* her." His voice rang with satisfaction on the words. "When the King came back to speak to their ambassadors, the High Priest was wearing her skin."

There was no reply, but in January's mind he heard the echo of Don Anastasio's voice: *It might be best to get Hannibal out of here before Don Prospero comes back with what he thinks his son is going to tell him. . . .*

He wondered what voice Don Prospero might be hearing in his mind, and what it was telling him.

"Well," said Hannibal into the silence, "that's certainly one that even Euripides never came up with."

January slept uneasily, and dreamed of flight across those hot yellow lands under the burning eye of the sun—the Smoking Mirror—pursued by a gaunt, brown-faced priest, clothed in the rotting skin of a girl. In the morning he rose with the tinny clank of the chapel bell and packed his trunk, then went down to the stables to make sure that Consuela's coachman Juan was in fact putting to the horses as he had been ordered, to be ready for departure at first light.

He wasn't, nor did Consuela herself, dabbing marmalade onto a delicate croissant roll in the *sala,* appear to be in the slightest haste: "Those lazy *conchudos* in the stables are just trying to figure out which strap goes into which buckle. The coach will be along." She looked sleek and well pleased with herself, and there was a love-bite on her neck; January wondered whose.

He emerged from the *sala,* wondering how early Don Prospero would be up and about and if he and Rose might be able to leave on horseback unmolested, and was met by the small black-clad form of the boy Casimiro, who rose from one of the leather-covered benches with a ludicrously tiny white dog in his arms. "Señor Enero?" asked the boy, and January bowed. "Is it true what my Uncle 'Stasio says, that you're a physician?"

"I'm a surgeon," said January, "but I've studied medicine as well." He squatted and held out his hand for the little dog to sniff.

"Do you know about insane people? This is Pequeña," he added, bending to stroke the dog's snowy head. "She's my Aunt Valentina's dog, but Valla doesn't care for her much. I feed her. Did Uncle 'Stasio send for you, to tell if Grandfather is insane?"

He glanced worriedly over his shoulder as he spoke, down into the courtyard in the direction of the chapel, where, January guessed, his mother was still at early Mass. Then he lowered his voice and whispered, "Did you really have a rabbit in your room?"

"Did you find one?" asked January softly, and the boy nodded, his dark eyes big. "Where?"

"Out by the kitchen. Yesterday before supper." The boy sat again on the leather-covered bench, and January took a seat beside him.

Casimiro was thin, like his sister, Paloma. January hoped Guillenormand was managing to slip Josefa's children a little extra food while their mother was occupied with her prayers.

"Pequeña had got out, and I went to look for her, because she could be hurt by the big dogs in the stables. The stable dogs had just found the rabbit; they hadn't torn it up, so I could see..." The child shivered. "I ran and got Uncle 'Stasio and he gave it to one of his own vaqueros to bury, and he said to me, 'Don't pay any attention to this. But tell me at once if you should ever find another like it.' And he looked angry, with his mouth all hard, not looking at me at all."

January nodded and laid a gentle hand on the boy's shoulder. "You've never found anything like it before?"

Casimiro shook his head.

"Does it frighten you when your grandfather has his spells?"

"A little. Mama says God struck Grandfather mad for reading about the devils of the Indians, and that's why he's a heretic. But God wouldn't punish a man for being a heretic if he became one only because he was mad. Would he?"

"I don't know," said January. "I wouldn't think so, because God is wiser than any human being, and understands all the reasons people do what they do. But I don't know."

For a time Casimiro thought about that, gently stroking Pequeña's bat-like ears. There were smudges of sleeplessness beneath the boy's eyes, and January wondered if he, too, dreamed about Indian priests clothed in the flayed skin of children.

"Do you know what happens to—well—what happens to—to people's families when they get locked up for being insane?" asked the boy hesitantly. "I mean, if—if something were to happen to my mother and sister..."

"You mean if they go into a convent?"

Casimiro nodded, his pale little face calm as ivory but the wretchedness showing in his eyes.

"Is that what would happen if your grandfather were to be insane?"

"Oh, yes. Uncle 'Stasio says I could stay with him—would I? When Uncle Damiano and Luis were alive, I was going to go live with them. But then they died, and Uncle Fernando said I'd have to go to military school in Germany the way he did...." His voice shook a little, and he clung tighter to the dog, who licked his chin with a long pink tongue.

"My mother cursed him, and swore she'd never let him make me do that. But if she went into the convent she couldn't do anything about it. She might not even know. They don't let them have visitors there, and they can talk to people only once a month through a barred window and maybe not even then, and they have to wear crowns of iron spikes on their heads so the blood runs down into their hair. I'm glad . . . it isn't a good thing to say, but—maybe it was God who made Uncle Fernando die so I wouldn't have to go to military school? So I could go live with Uncle 'Stasio?"

January was silent, turning the matter over in his mind. At length he said, "Again, Maître Casimiro, I don't know—and I can't know—why God has things happen the way they do. All we can do is thank Him for His gifts to us, even the ones we don't understand or like."

Casimiro nodded—the concept of receiving incomprehensible or unpleasant gifts from God was evidently not a new one to him—and he leaned closer to January, glancing behind him at the *sala's* open doors. In a whisper he asked, "Did Grandfather kill the rabbit?"

"What's that brat doing here?" Don Prospero slammed open the doors of his study and stepped into the *corredor.* He was dressed for riding, and his long white hair lay on his shoulders like a lion's mane. "The woman's turning both those children into impossible mealy-mouthed hypocrites—can't stand brats around. Tlaloc had the right idea. His priests killed them and ate them, and every tear they shed was another raindrop that would nourish the cornfields. All they're good for."

January opened his mouth to protest, but Casimiro had already slipped away like a little dark ghost, hugging Pequeña to his breast.

"You need to see the Temple of Huitzilopochtli." Don Prospero jabbed a finger at January. "There's a truly amazing one at Nemictiliztli Mountain, near the foot of the Chalco pass. Nearly unspoiled, because of the cliffs all around it. You need a rope to get up to it. Simply incredible reliefs. The altar's still standing. I'll have the men bring along torches—it's only twenty miles or so, but it may be dusk before we get back. . . ."

At twenty miles away—with cliffs of unknown height but whose steepness required a rope—it would be black dark and late when they returned after a day's exhaustion. Tactfully, January answered, "Thank you, I truly appreciate the offer, Don Prospero. But they're just bringing our carriage. . . ." He breathed a prayer that this was in fact true.

"Consuela can rehearse on her own," retorted the Don cheerfully. "You really must see the reliefs in the temple. I'm having Vasco saddle horses for you now. But you'll have to hurry and change.... Here, you!" he called to Cristóbal, just emerging from January's room with the trunk on one shoulder as—thank God—Consuela's carriage rattled into the courtyard. "You put that back! Your master isn't going anywhere."

"I'll certainly come with you, with your permission." Hannibal stepped out of his room, deftly halting his host halfway to the courtyard stair, where Cristóbal stood, trunk on shoulder, waiting for orders. Given the strain of climbing the pyramids the day before—not to speak of the amount of brandy and laudanum he'd consumed at night—he looked chalky and ill, but his light voice was fluent as ever. "I've been meaning to ask you if there were any decent reliefs of Huitzilopochtli to study; I'm curious about your theory that there was, in fact, communication with the ancient Greeks that would show itself in similar artistic motifs."

"Really?" Don Prospero's eyes glittered, fascinated.

"It isn't inconceivable that Greek mariners could have made the passage," said Hannibal. "In Wolff's *Prologomena ad Homerum*..."

He took Don Prospero by the embroidered sleeve and guided him back to his study; January, without wasting a second, strode quickly and noiselessly to his own room, where Rose was just finishing strapping up her boxes. He gestured to her imperatively, and Rose, bless her perceptive heart, responded without a sound.

As he escorted her to the stair past the open door of Don Prospero's study—with Cristóbal silently following—January caught Hannibal's eye; the fiddler winked. January didn't even want to think what kind of punishment his friend was letting himself in for with a forty-mile ride, plus cliffs that had proven formidable enough to discourage even the Conquistadores.

For a miracle, Consuela was packed also, and Zama and Pepita were both awake, dressed, and where they could be located. Only when the trunks were strapped up and the carriage had been driven through the gates did January, Rose, and Consuela ascend again to the study to take leave of their host.

Don Prospero, deep in the comparison of half a dozen stone and terracotta statues lined in a row on his desk, only waved impatiently at his guests' farewells: "Good to have seen you, good to have seen you. . . . Hinojo! Have the boys saddle Don Rafael's horse! And get him awake and dressed. He'll come with us," he confided to Hannibal, who was perched on a corner of the desk like a ghost trying to get up enough strength to haunt the house. "Do him good. Valla, too, and that worthless duenna of hers—never heard a woman whine so much in my life."

Hannibal rose to kiss Consuela's hand, but Don Prospero seized him by the arm and pushed him from the study. "You'd best put riding-clothes on if we're to be back by dark." Prospero kissed Consuela's hand himself, but by the time he turned to speak to January, January and Rose were halfway down the stairs.

As the carriage pulled away, January turned to look back at the yellow and red walls of Mictlán, like a band of burning gold at the foot of the gray-green Pyramid of the Dead. Horses were already being led out of the gates, Don Prospero's straight black form recognizable by his gestures as he lectured the appalled Don Rafael about their expedition to the Chalco pass. The vaqueros who would accompany them milled about, hooves raising a glitter of dust that flattened all images into matte shadows in the brittle sun of the forenoon.

As the carriage jolted up the rise on the other side of the village, January thought for a moment he had a glimpse of a black-clothed child in the gateway, watching them out of sight.

"Well." Rose put down the window of the carriage and looked up at him. "At least we're out of there. It was touch-and-go for a time—I wasn't sure we'd make it."

Consuela flipped open her sandalwood fan and said, "Doña Imelda will give birth to twins out of sheer rage when her precious Rafael doesn't return today; I wonder how long Father will keep him there before she comes out from town to retrieve him again."

"I have more and more sympathy for your mother," agreed Rose thoughtfully, and glanced up at January again. "But our time hasn't been ill-spent. We've heard as good an account of the banquet as we're likely to get, and had a look at the house. The question is, what can we do?"

January shook his head. "My nightingale, at the moment I'm afraid I haven't the faintest idea."

"Let me guess." Capitán Ylario's voice was heavy with sarcasm. "Since it is unthinkable that any friend of Don Prospero Ygnacio Bernal de la Cadeña de Castellón should have done so ignoble a thing as poison his host's son, it naturally follows that the crime must have been committed by that sneaking unmanly little *jardinera* Werther Bremer. Oh, and he's a foreigner, too."

Morning light, coming through the single window of the Capitán's tiny room in the Casa Municipal, glinted in the officer's dark eyes and betrayed the hard little folds below and around the rosebud mouth beneath the neatly-trimmed mustache. His hands, resting on the desk, were neat and plump in gloves of white kid, and his clothing breathed the scent of Parma violets when he moved.

"Am I correct?"

"I don't know, Señor," replied January mildly. "That's what I'd like to find out."

Ylario sniffed. "And you came here all the way from the United States just because you'd 'like to find out'?"

From the courtyard below, the voices of clerks and soldiers drifted up, along with whiffs of steam from the coffee-vendors who'd set up shop in the great yard, and smoke from the guards' cigarettos. A soldier's jeering laughter could be heard mocking a prisoner: "Hey, *mari-*

posa, you find the cells here to your liking? You like your mates in there?"

January said, "I came because Señor Sefton is my friend."

"Sefton is an opium-eater and a drunkard, a man whose vile habits result in periods of time when he does not even remember what he does."

"And Werther Bremer was Franz de Castellón's lover. Were he a woman who had the same access to the tea that de Castellón drank after dinner, on the night before he was going to wed, would you hesitate in making an arrest?"

"Man or woman, the jealous lover would have poisoned the girl, not the man whom he—or she—loved." Ylario made an impatient gesture, waving aside the whole topic. "Or murdered that contemptible old madman who seems to feel that all he has to do is hand the President money in order to do as he pleases in this country without regard to justice or the law."

Bitterness rankled in his voice, and January saw him again in the *sala* of Mictlán, dismissed like a servant by that glittering scarlet figure who stood in the sunlight of the open door. Sent away like an importunate child, in the presence of his own men, of Don Prospero's grinning vaqueros, and of strangers.

"Who told you de Castellón had tea before he died?"

January hesitated, seeing what would happen next. "Sefton," he answered, and Ylario threw up his hands. "The French cook, Guillenormand, will affirm that it was de Castellón's habit to drink tea after supper—"

"But that particular night?"

"No." In fact, according to Consuela, she had seen Werther emerge from the study door, but he guessed that saying so would only elicit the observation that Hannibal's mistress was as likely to lie as Hannibal himself.

Ylario paced impatiently to the window, small and set deep in an embrasure in the immense thickness of the whitewashed wall. "The food that Don Fernando de Castellón ate that night was eaten by everyone else in the household. Including Sefton himself. The only thing that the murdered man consumed that the others did not was the brandy that Sefton brought him, brandy into which Sefton was seen to pour something from a bottle. Seen by old de Castellón himself. The door that separates Don Prospero's room from the study was bolted on the study side and padlocked. No one could have entered the study unobserved between the time Sefton departed and Bremer came in to find his master dying."

"Dead," said January. "I spoke with the servants who washed his body, and they all say that he was nearly cold."

"And you believed them? That old witch Yannamaria could have sold Sefton the poison herself. She had no reason to love Don Fernando."

Ylario tossed the words back at him over his shoulder. Standing beside the rough desk, with its worn surface marred by a thousand scrapings of dripped tallow, its sand-pot and inkwell of very old pewter, and its candlesticks of bright-painted *indio* pottery, January tilted his head to read the titles of the books stacked on one side: *Die Welt als Wille und Vorstellung, The Sorrows of Young Werther,* a volume of the letters of Voltaire.

So Ylario, like Werther, was a student of philosophy. Was it only, January wondered, Ylario's sense of brotherhood with the philosophy-reading valet that made him so sure of his innocence? So blind to another view? Or was there something else?

And if there was, why not say so?

"Where is Bremer now?"

And when Ylario hesitated, clearly sorting through what he knew and what he wished to tell, January added gently, "I may be friends with an opium-eater, but that doesn't mean I will lie in wait to murder his accuser. It would help me understand if I could see and speak to the man."

"Would it?" Ylario stiffened again, and threw back his pomaded head. "And what do you think you would see? A weakling philosopher? A pretty-boy?"

January said nothing, waiting patiently, watching him and letting his own words sink back into him. At length Ylario went on in a quieter voice. "I do not know where Werther Bremer is, Señor. After coming to me with what he knew of his master's death—facts that establish not only the means but the motive for Sefton to poison Don Fernando—Bremer has not returned. I sent him a message to his room—a vile place in the barrio of San Juan—but received no reply."

"And the facts you speak of are Valentina de Castellón's letters?"

Ylario hesitated, then said, "Yes."

"Anything else? If I may ask."

"No." Again the hesitation. The Capitán turned from the window, walked back to lay his hands once more on the desk. January was silent for a moment, looking into the younger man's eyes. Seeing there stubbornness, fury—the fury of one who sees in the attack on one whom he perceives as his brother an attack upon himself. To call Werther Bremer a liar on the grounds of the body's post-mortem bruising would be a waste of breath, January reflected. Besides, from what he knew of the venality of the courts, he'd be lucky if he could find a judge who'd heard that the blood circulates, much less that the hour of death could be estimated from its subcutaneous pooling. But the whispered accusations of a dying man would stick in any judge's mind.

"Who is Don Prospero's heir now that his son is dead?"

"Legally it would be young Casimiro Fuentes."

"Under Doña Josefa's guardianship?"

"I presume so, yes. Or, if Doña Josefa were to enter a convent, under that of his aunt, Isabella de Saragosse."

"Are there other grandchildren?"

"No. Don Damiano's son, Luis, was his only child. Doña Isabella and Don Anastasio have no living children."

"Do you know what provisions Don Prospero made for the rest of his family? For Doña Josefa, for instance, or Señorita Valentina? Or presumably for cousins farther removed."

Ylario relaxed so far as to seat himself, and straightened the already-meticulous papers on the surface of the desk. "For that you would need to speak to Don Prospero's man of business, Señor Benedicte dos Cerritos. He lives off the Plaza Santo Domingo. So far as I know, there are no first or second cousins—the Bernal family is not so widespread as the Avilas or the Peraltas or some of the other great *criollo* clans. You will find Señor dos Cerritos a man of discretion—"

The policeman's voice folded drily over the word, making five syllables of it. "He shares his employer's opinion that such mundane considerations as the laws of his country do not apply to him. A Spaniard of Spain—one of those who had too many important friends to return to that country when our Emperor Iturbide cast out the *gatchupins.* You may have more luck with Señor dos Cerritos than I."

"Thank you." January bowed. This young man would have been

a child, he thought, when the *criollo* Emperor had united the pure-blooded nobility of the country to rise against the increasing demands of Spain. He would have come to manhood in that brief era of idealism, before chaos descended as one military strongman after another laid claim to rulership of the wealthy land. No wonder he was angry.

"I shall communicate with you whatever I may learn."

Ylario stood, dignified for all his fussy silk cravat and lack of inches. "Thank you, Señor. I appreciate that."

From the courtyard rose the clamor of drunken voices shouting, as if it were evening instead of mid-morning. A man cursed, and there was the scuffle of feet, the sound of blows, a woman screaming imprecations. Ylario's jaw tightened as if with pain.

"I must go," he told January. "I feel a good deal of concern about Bremer, for he is a man who is unlikely to receive justice once accusations begin to fly. But I saw his grief, and I know it to be genuine, the true grief of manly love, which few these days understand. And I tell you, Señor Enero, Sefton has the cunning of his kind. As long as he could go on milking Don Prospero's madness for his support, he would do it. The girl Valentina was only a side issue. Don Fernando's assumption of control of the estate spelled disaster for Sefton on every level. I assure you, Señor, Sefton is guilty."

Rose was waiting in Consuela's open town carriage, drawn up in the shade of the plane-trees that surrounded the vast Cathedral square. She said "Oh, dear" when January recounted his interview with Ylario. "It sounds as though he's genuinely convinced of Hannibal's guilt, not simply determined to score political points—or genuinely convinced of young Herr Bremer's innocence, anyway. Or both."

"Both, I think," said January thoughtfully. Juan whipped up the horses—a showy chestnut pair with flaxen manes and tails—and the barouche moved into the steady stream of traffic that even at this early hour of the forenoon clogged the paved street that bordered the square. "And I must say I'm not entirely comfortable with the notion of poison being put in China green tea—the flavor of the tea is so light, I'm at a loss to think of many poisons that couldn't be detected, particularly by such a connoisseur as it sounds like Fernando was."

"There is much in what you say." Rose settled back against the deep garnet-red upholstery and contemplated the gaudy chaos of the square:

thatched market-stands displaying pumpkins, corn, chickens, and chilis of a hundred different shapes and hues, hanging under dusty awnings, game-birds, fish, and baskets of axolotl salamanders ready for the pot or the oven. Women in the loose embroidered *huipils* of the Indians or the low-cut white blouses, bright two-colored skirts, white satin shoes, and colorful rebosos of the *china poblana* hawked cups of hot coffee or *pandolce* glittering with dark-brown crystals of sugar; muleteers in striped ponchos and broad-brimmed hats, water-carriers with enormous clay jugs suspended before and behind from straps about their heads, priests in their black robes arm-in-arm with pretty parishioners who made January think of young Padre Cesario and smile.

Carriages clogged the roadway around the square, and the crowding grew worse as the barouche turned into the Platero, the main street of the city. English landaulets and barouches shining with paint and lacquer, drawn by high-bred *frisone* horses from England or the United States and driven by liveried coachmen; high-perched, sporty volantes; heavy Mexican coaches with the crests of nobility on their doors and glassed-in carretelas whose elegantly overdressed occupants peered around the half-closed curtains—all these jostled axles with gaudily-painted mule-drawn hacks, farm-carts, wagons. Men in the embroidered jackets of wealthy gentlemen or the rough leather britches of vaqueros guided their horses among the press, making them caracole, regardless of traffic, when they glimpsed ladies of their acquaintance in the carriages. And in spite of Consuela's airy assertion that no one in the city walked, pedestrians were everywhere, talking, stopping mid-street to buy lottery-tickets or cigarettos, shouting at one another over the din.

Soldiers were everywhere. *Léperos* were everywhere. Priests and monks were everywhere.

Flies were everywhere.

As they passed the doorway of a church, a funeral emerged, the body of a dead child borne in the arms of a black-haired Indian mother while family and friends danced around her, clapping and singing with gladness and waving banners of cut paper: the child in innocence would go straight to Heaven, and miss the pain and poverty and grief of life. It was a time to rejoice.

The American chargé d'affaires in Mexico, Anthony Butler, had a large house on the Paseo de Bucareli, not far from the shade-trees of the Alameda, the city's central park. As January had feared, Butler was one of Andrew Jackson's less inspired choices, a tight-mouthed Southerner who'd followed the lure of cheap lands into the Mississippi Territory some years previously and had made enough of a fortune planting cotton to be of use to the President in his 1828 campaign. His secretary, a thickset young man with pale, suspicious eyes, asked twice if January's master had sent a message before he'd even take his card in to his employer, and Mr. Butler himself never quite appeared to grasp that a black man could be unpossessed by anyone, or might require the protection of the United States government as much as what he called a "regular" man would.

"No wonder they don't let black men vote," fumed January after he and Rose were seen out the door by one of Mr. Butler's slaves. "You couldn't get *us* to put anyone into office who'd appoint a knothead like that."

"Nonsense." Rose drew down the veils that decorated her wide-brimmed straw hat. "There are just as many black imbeciles as white—and that goes for women, too, if civilization ever advances to the point of permitting *us* to express our opinions about who makes the laws." She climbed into the carriage, even though the house of the British minister was within a few minutes' walk: Cristóbal and Sancho had fallen into step with them the moment they'd emerged from Butler's door, to keep the beggars at bay.

"Señor, my store in Jalapa was ruined by the fighting. . . ."

"Señor, my family and I once had a hacienda in Cohuila, we were driven off by the taxes. . . ."

"Señor, I am crippled and can no longer support my family. . . ."

"Señor, I have a beautiful sister. . . ."

Maybe the ragged man wrapped in the blanket *had* been a *hacendado* once upon a time. Feeling like the Rich Young Man who was the butt of so many Biblical parables, January tossed a handful of small coins in the direction of the outstretched hands, the stinking bodies, and watched men who should have been tilling fields or minding stores or raising families scrabble for the tinkling metal in the dust.

In New Orleans, nobody begged who wasn't forced to by physical infirmity or mental degeneration. Mostly if you wanted work you could find it, hauling boxes on the levee or sweeping out a saloon if nothing else.

Here, there was no work. There was no choice for these men to be anything but what they were—the flotsam of decades of war.

Sir Henry Ward and his staff occupied another of the magnificent palaces farther along the Paseo that had been built by some Count or Marquis with money from silver-mines and cattle-ranges the size of German principalities. The Cathedral clock was striking eleven, the bells of every church and convent in that city of churches chiming in like courtiers dutifully laughing at a sovereign's joke. Such was the press of carriages in the street that it took them nearly fifteen minutes to make the short journey, but January had seen enough of the city's beggars by then to know that they couldn't have covered the ground much more quickly by foot.

As Consuela had predicted, the carriage and servants accomplished what good clothing, spotless white kid gloves, and proper English probably wouldn't have, had January and Rose been unattended and afoot. A well-dressed mestizo servant showed them up to the wide *corredor* that overlooked the immaculate flagstones of the central court. An elderly English footman brought them coffee, and even bowed.

"My dear sir, think nothing of it," said the British minister when January apologized for interrupting him at his work. "One doesn't work, here, really—God knows there's little enough to do, and precious few books to read. I cannot imagine what the local people do to get through the evenings."

"Well, obviously as a stranger you're at a distinct disadvantage, sir," remarked Rose as Sir Henry bowed over her hand. He was a spry, sturdy man with a fair complexion much reddened by sun, dressed as he would have dressed had he been in attendance on his own King at the Court of St. James's, in strictly formal knee-smalls, striped stockings, a dark-blue long-tailed coat, and a white cravat of the type January hadn't seen for street-wear since his earliest days in Paris, nearly twenty years ago. "The local people all have each other's families to gossip about, which are extensive enough that I should imagine it takes up a great deal of their time."

Sir Henry laughed, invited them to sit—the chairs were tapestried and far finer than those of Mictlán—and sent the servant for *pandolce*.

"Most of my colleagues look down their noses at the local delicacies, but personally I find them delicious. What is the point of travel if one doesn't broaden one's experience? And I have a wonderful cook."

January had required no more of Anthony Butler than to introduce himself and make sure that in case of trouble, the American chargé d'affaires would at least remember that such a person as Benjamin January existed. To Sir Henry Ward he explained his case; that he was the friend of a British citizen who had been accused of murder, who was being held more or less under house arrest, and who had asked him—an American—to see to his interests.

"I cannot say that I am an American citizen," said January quietly, "because I am not, exactly. New Orleans is my home, but I have the right neither to vote nor to bear arms nor to hold any public office, nor even to publicly smoke a cigar. I have thought of myself all of my life as a Frenchman, but when I lived in France I was spoken of as an American. And to further complicate matters, I was born under the flag of the King of Spain. And all because my father was an African who through no doing of his own was kidnapped and enslaved. All I ask from you is your leave—your tacit support—in helping my friend, who is unjustly accused of a crime he did not commit."

"Your friend's—er—lady-friend explained the situation to me back in early September, when this happened." Sir Henry folded his hands, gloved in pearl-gray kid, upon his knee. "Had he been formally arrested and charged, of course, I would have been obliged to intervene, but he was not."

"If he is," January reminded him, "he may not be able to communicate with you before he is tried—maybe before he is executed. A letter to Capitán Ylario to the effect that you wish to be officially notified before any steps are taken would go far toward assuring that justice actually is done."

"I shall write one," agreed Ward with a brisk nod. "Though from what I have seen of the corruption at all levels of the courts these days, I'm not sure what good it will do if this Capitán Ylario is determined to make an example of Sefton. However, I am not a policeman, nor do I have armed constables on the embassy staff. And by all accounts there doesn't seem to be much doubt that Mr. Sefton committed this murder."

"I appreciate your willingness to write," said January. "It may be of great help. In fact, I think there is room for doubt that Mr. Sefton killed his host's son."

"Is there?" Sir Henry raised his brows. "Madame Montero did not seem to think so, and she should—er—know." He glanced apologetically at Rose, as if asking forgiveness for speaking of activities that human beings had been engaging in since the dawn of time. "The mere fact that Mr. Sefton did not trouble to present himself here—made no effort to establish credentials of any kind with the representatives of his homeland upon his arrival in Mexico—causes me to doubt his motives and his character. According to Madame Montero, he is a man of ... irregular habits, a drunkard, and an opium-taker. A vile weakness." Genuine anger suddenly envenomed his voice. "A trade that is a disgrace to my own nation, and makes me blush when England boasts of her righteousness and good will."

"But weakness does not necessarily make of him a killer," replied January gently. "Or exempt him from the right to justice."

"No," agreed Ward, and rang a bell on the corner of the coffee-tray. The elderly English butler—like Sir Henry, stifling in knee-breeches and a high white stock—brought a small portable desk from the study, complete with pen, ink, paper, sand, and sealing-wax, and the minister thought for a moment, then wrote a short paragraph in a strong and beautiful hand. "No, you're quite right.... And it would not be at all proper for the King to abandon even the guilty to the sovereignty of another nation. Is there anything else that I can do?"

"Only write me a letter of introduction and recommendation," said January. "I'll certainly need it to get in to speak with the Prussian minister in my efforts to locate the dead man's valet, who not only brought his master tea minutes before Sefton brought him brandy, but who, I have reason to believe, subsequently lied about the time of his death."

"Indeed?" The minister again raised his sun-bleached brows, his interest clearly piqued. "Could one put poison in tea without impairing the flavor? Coffee I could understand, particularly as they make it here, but tea..."

"I don't know," said January. "It's one of the things I propose to find out."

As they descended the tiled staircase to the velvety shade of the courtyard below, it crossed January's mind to wonder whether Hannibal had simply neglected to introduce himself to the minister upon his arrival—which would be very like Hannibal—or whether, in fact, his friend had deliberately stayed away from a man who might recognize him from his former life.

In the three years he'd known him, Hannibal had spoken of being up at Oxford, of aunts and cousins who were members of England's social elite; of the family gamekeepers and coachmen and of the countryside in the north-west of Ireland, where so many English landowners had holdings. His manners were as polished as his Latin, and even in the extremities of his illness, half-delirious in one of the back-sheds or whorehouse attics where he mooched a living, he was unfailingly polite and unwilling to give trouble. Yet he had never spoken of what had separated him from his family, or how he had found his way—a penniless consumptive with a hundred-guinea Italian violin—to New Orleans to eke a threadbare living among the black musicians of the town.

The second of November, thought January as the carriage inched its way through the wide Paseo, around the traffic circles with their stone benches and fountains and back to the narrower confines, the higher buildings, of the Calle San Francisco, and thus toward Consuela's flat again. In the market-places he could already see among the ant-larva tamales and mango fritters the sweet breads baked with the shape of bones upon their sugared surfaces, the little skulls of sugar decorated with flowers among the camote and spiced peanuts. Marigolds—the flowers of the dead—had begun to appear among the poppies and roses of the flower-sellers, huge gaudy basketfuls of them, to decorate the altars that would be raised in every home.

The Days of the Dead were coming, as certain as the slow waning of the sun. Ten days' grace at the outside, and less than that if Santa Anna left town, or Don Prospero grew bored with Hannibal. . . .

Or went mad again.

The recollection of the smell of blood in the darkness returned to him, and of Casimiro's frightened eyes. January reached into his coat and touched the letter of introduction, with its official crimson seal of lion and unicorn, and wondered how much information that seal would buy him.

And he still hadn't the faintest idea of where to begin.

ELEVEN

"My box at the Teatro Principal is not in the fashionable tiers," explained Consuela, emerging from her room gorgeously decked in indigo satin thick with gold. "Not down with the wives of the grandees—or the lady-friends of those who now make up Santa Anna's government."

Color was fading from the square of sky visible above the town house's high walls. Down in the courtyard, candles had been lit on the rough tables, and the voices of Señora Garcia's first customers of the evening rose, along with the smells of tamales, stewed pork, pulque, and cigarettos. From the street came the wailing voice of the charcoal-man, and the higher-pitched song of an Indian offering to trade fruits for outworn household goods.

"But you'll find no shortage of company," Consuela went on. "And many of the men who will come up there to play cards tonight—if the croaking of that crow they have singing the lead doesn't put everyone off their game—will be Fernando's fellow officers." As she spoke, she tonged chunks of dark muscavado sugar into two of the three small coffee-cups that Lita had brought out onto the *corredor* while January waited for the women to get ready: Rose was still in Consuela's room. After taking *comida,* Rose and January had slept, with every intention of going to the house of the Prussian minister to present January's newly-acquired credentials in the pre-twilight cool.

But waking with Rose lying curved against him in the straw-smelling gloom of their room was not conducive to any inclination on January's part to spring out of bed and institute expeditions anywhere, no matter how desperate Hannibal's situation. By the time he and Rose finally did get up, bathed, and had consumed a leisurely cup of cocoa on the gallery, the courtyard was deep in shadow and it was time to get ready for the opera, which, Consuela assured them, was where everyone who was anyone in Mexico City was to be found. Even on nights like tonight when she did not sing, she attended. "For what else does one do?"

"You won't run into trouble for inviting us to share your box?" he asked. In New Orleans he and Rose would not have been permitted into the section of the theater where whites sat.

Consuela paused, a cup of coffee in either hand. "Of course there will be raised eyebrows," she replied. "And if you did not have money it would be a much different matter. But you do have money . . . and you will lose it at cards to them, lose a great deal, and men always talk over cards. And then again, much of how you are treated in this country depends on how others see you being treated. There are so many mestizos here who have paid to have the records altered to say they are white, and so many bastards who have paid to have themselves declared legitimate, that no one points fingers so much as they used to. No one really knows anymore who has what blood in their veins."

"I think in my case," said January with a wry expression, "there won't be much trouble hazarding a guess."

"No—but then, you are not trying to establish yourself in society. No one has to worry about you appearing at their house or proposing marriage to their daughter. All you want is for them to talk for an evening. And I assure you, they will talk."

She rustled away to her room again; January heard Rose's voice as the door was opened for her, and their mingling laughter and that of their maids as it was closed. He settled back with his own coffee, a little regretful that he could not be part of the group in the bedroom. He knew many men who were impatient with—and contemptuous of—the froufrou of women as they got themselves ready for the opera or the theater or a ball. Having been married for ten years to a dressmaker, he had been initiated into the intricate codes that women use, the color and cut of their clothing, the fashion of arranging hair and flowers and jewelry, the secret language that says all manner of things: *I'm beautiful* or *I'm spoken for* or *I'm more important than any woman in this room* or *I'll lie with you if you give me money.* He found the bustle and flutter of women both fascinating and erotic.

Down in the courtyard, Señora Garcia the coffee-seller's wife chatted and laughed with the men who came in for supper, single men mostly or groups of male friends, muleteers with their faded shirts and dark-tanned faces, water-sellers who carefully set down their huge clay jugs, *cargadors* and lard-vendors and men who sold lottery-tickets. By the way they greeted the big woman, January understood that Señora Garcia was more than the source of a medio's worth of tortillas and beans every night: she was wife and sister and chum to men who were essentially alone. Most of them had only a single room in some barrio hut, without even a bed, much less a place to cook; many had to share such a room, and the muleteers didn't even have that.

Their voices ascended from the torch-sprinkled gloom of the court, friendly and at peace, mulling over the chaff of the day with people they saw in this place every night or nearly every night. *Good luck on the journey to Puebla tomorrow. Did your cousin have her child yet? Those Army men, they nearly got me today. I had to run around an alley and hide in a load of hay. . . .* Laughter. Someone playing a guitar.

"*Tortillas de cuaaajaadaaaa . . .*" wailed a vendor from the street.

Lamplight splashed through an open door, and January heard Zama's loud, free laugh, and two women came along the *corredor. . . .*

January had to look twice at the taller, resplendent in a gown of black satin, masked with a small domino such as adventurous ladies sometimes donned for assignations, flashing with diamonds, voluptuously curved and nothing like . . .

"*Rose?*"

Behind the mask the familiar gray-green eyes sparkled, the carmine lips curled in a smile. "Alas, no, M'sieu. Rose will not be with us this evening. Since the company tonight will be so raffish—and men will talk more freely in front of a single woman whom they feel will not disapprove of anything they say—Consuela thought that perhaps Rose's place should be taken by me, her evil twin sister, Elena."

"Oh, did she indeed?" January got to his feet and stared in startled bemusement at the woman before him, seeing where Consuela's theatrical experience had altered figure and face and hair and bosom into something that would never have been associated with the gawky and reserved New Orleans schoolmistress. He supposed he should act like a normal husband and thunder words to the effect that no wife of his was going out in public like that—evil twin sister be damned—but he was far too entranced. Besides, it was an excellent idea.

The perfume she wore was unfamiliar, vanilla and musk, and it went to his head like liquor with visions of crushing her to him, biting the silky dust-colored flesh of her shoulders.... "And are you—like your virtuous sister—also so short-sighted that you cannot see your hand in front of your face?"

"Alas, I am, M'sieu. But my mother—*our* mother, my virtuous sister's and mine—did not believe any man would ever wed a girl who wore spectacles. So up until I was fourteen I became very good at identifying people by shape, and by voice, and by the way they moved, and never knew there was another way to be."

She tucked a dark, oiled curl back into a coiffure much augmented with false locks and braided into the exotic loops and twists considered fashionable and topped off with an enormously tall tortoiseshell comb. Sprays of white jasmine made the darkened chevelure seem darker still. "My mother was a plaçée, remember, M'sieu, and attempted to raise me—and my virtuous sister, who loves you very much—to follow in her path. I think I will not have too much trouble tonight."

"Not while you're at the theater you won't," said January somberly. "But the moment we are alone, *Mademoiselle,* I warn you: you may tell your virtuous and loving sister that her virtuous and loving husband proposes to take revenge upon her for her trickery by giving her evil twin sister the punishment for which she is so shamelessly begging."

"Oh, M'sieu." "Elena" lowered her mascarae'd eyelashes breathlessly and unfurled her fan. "I can hardly wait."

They were joined for the carriage ride to the Teatro Principal—which had had several other names depending on the political regime—by a sleek young gentleman whom Consuela introduced as Don Tulio de Avila y Merced, "Formerly the son of the Marquis de Merced," Consuela assured them, who was now making his money as a genteel gambler, his family silver-mines having been utterly ruined as a result of the years of war. "He knows everyone in town, and is related to everyone...."

"Isn't that so, Aunt Trudis?" smiled the young man at Doña Gertrudis, who shared the carriage with them in affronted silence; she turned her face coldly aside. When they reached the Teatro, he and January immediately got up a game of vingt-et-un at a small table at the back of Consuela's box; it was all they needed to draw every one of her visitors into acceptance of January's presence, and into conversation over cards.

As in nearly every theater January had attended—or played at—in Italy and France, virtually no one paid attention to anything that transpired on-stage. A pity, since *Fidelio* was one of January's favorite operas, but it couldn't be helped. The theater itself, formerly splendid, was filthily shabby, and the corridor outside the cloakrooms had to be smelled to be believed; from what he could see of the production, the costumes seemed to have been chosen at random from what was on hand, Leonore bedecked in trunk-hose and doublet vaguely reminiscent of the Renaissance, while the evil Pizarro pranced about in Roman armor. But every box was filled, and long before the first strains of the overture sounded, Consuela was playing hostess to a steady stream of brightly-uniformed officers, to men in short jackets of embroidered velvet who'd made fortunes selling useless horses or cardboard boots to the Army of Operations, and suspiciously wealthy government officials and their even-wealthier hangers-on.

The company reminded January forcibly of the riffraff nobility who'd clambered to prominence in Paris in Napoleon's bloody footprints thirty years previously, with their talk of contracts and favors and special privileges to do things like broker food-purchases to the soldiers (with a little cut for themselves, naturally) or lend out at interest the money allotted them for gunpowder, ammunition, and food.

An experienced hostess, Consuela had brought her own candles, candleholders, brandy, and her butler, Sebastian, and Sancho to serve it. As predicted, Don Tulio's presence at the table with January acted as an introduction to men who would ordinarily not have sat down with a black man. The gold and silver mingled with the red and black of the pips, all glittering in the candle-light on the polished marquetry table-top, drew the men's attention like honey. They saw January being treated as a man of wealth by a man they knew, with whom they had played cards before.

And as Consuela had predicted, they talked.

They talked of parties they had been to, and horse-racing, cock-fighting, dogs—none of those brilliantly-uniformed officers ever seemed to have actually drilled troops in his life. Young Major Cuchero, one of Santa Anna's aides who'd been at Mictlán three days before, got a big laugh by describing how he'd gotten his prize fighting-cock drunk before a match so it would be cut to pieces by one of Santa Anna's, thus endearing the Major to the President's heart and getting him a promotion to console him. Another officer named Lajazar mentioned seeing the President with a new little game-pullet....

"You mean poor Fernando's bride?"

"She's had a narrow escape. You remember the time he bought an evening with La Perfecta, and then beat her so she couldn't work for weeks?"

"Sounds like Fernando," remarked January, lighting a cigar that would have gotten him jailed in New Orleans. "I knew him in Berlin— or met him, anyway, I'm sure he wouldn't remember the likes of me. Was he going to be married, then? That doesn't sound like him."

"If you knew anything much about him," laughed Cuchero good-naturedly, "you'd know how *much* that doesn't sound like him."

"Personally," said Lajazar's mistress, a flashily-dressed girl with a jeweled comb a foot tall in her Indian-black hair, "it's not Fernando I'd have worried about if I were Natividad, but Werther." She drew a long breath of smoke, holding her cigarette with a tiny gold clip to avoid staining her fingers with the nicotine. "I wouldn't have put it past him to put Spanish fly in her rouge."

"What became of Werther, anyway?" asked January. "Does anyone know?"

"Walking the streets, I should imagine," said a portly man who'd recently bought the right to tax every *pulqueria* in the city. "There's the woman who'd know..." And he nodded at Consuela, who had been playing ombre with Don Rafael and, January noticed, had quietly made enough to run her household on for several months.

Consuela shrugged. "My brother paid him, and his chef, and his grooms out of his own money, not Don Prospero's," she said, something January had already ascertained from Don Fernando's ledger. "He did not like the servants of this country any more than he liked the food, he said."

"My uncle Don Salvatore hired the chef," provided Don Rafael with a worried glance at the house-lights, to make sure he got back to his mother's box before she started looking for him. The de Bujerios were seated nearly opposite Consuela, but down a tier on the more fashionable level. Since his arrival at the party, Don Rafael had been assiduous about keeping in the shadows of Consuela's box.

"Werther came to me asking for work," said Major Cuchero, shrugging so that the gold braid that plastered the collar and breast of his crimson uniform glittered in the candle-light. "But aside from all else, the man spoke only German, which is a language for horses, not men. Of what use is such a valet?"

"You tell us, eh, Cuchero?" taunted Lajazar, whose mistress Cuchero had been eyeing across the drifting blue smoke that filled the little chamber. Cuchero leaped at him with a roar of rage, so that January and the pulque-merchant had to separate them amid a great deal of shouting and demands that the remark be taken back, so loud that even those playing cards and gossiping in the boxes to either side called out to them to hush. The entire subject of Werther Bremer was swallowed up in challenges to a duel and the quest for seconds, and then a long argument about whether the half-dealt hand that had been interrupted should be continued or scrapped, and in that case who had the deal . . . ?

January had witnessed similar scenes at every ball and party where he'd ever practiced his profession as a musician; it didn't seem to make any difference whether he was in Paris or New Orleans, or whether he played for Americans, French, or free colored—or, evidently, Mexicans. Someone would make a stupid jest in his cups, someone would take offense, and if they were Spanish or French or the Creoles of those races, challenges would be issued and seconds sought. The Americans were just as likely to go after one another on the spot with bowie-knives, boot-heels, and pistols.

He'd played enough entertainments among the free colored to know that the sole reason there weren't formal challenges to duels on those occasions was that duels were forbidden to men of African blood. There were certainly swollen eyes and bloody noses from back-lot encounters, and if there weren't quite as many fights as the white men had, it was because the free women of color had fewer polite scruples than the white ladies of good society, and were likelier to tell their menfolks not to act like fools.

Throughout the whole, Doña Gertrudis sat with her veils pulled down over her face at the front of the box, watching the opera in stiff-backed silence. January envied her.

Before the hectic splendor of the concluding chorus died away, the whole scene in Consuela's box packed itself up and moved back to her flat, expanding there to include several more card-tables and many additional gallons of brandy. January—and Rose, who compared notes with him the following morning over coffee—picked up a good deal of miscellaneous information about Fernando de Castellón, but little that they had not known before. The picture of the cold, finicking, stingy, and brutal martinet emerged like a white marble statue from among a garden of persiflage concerning the provisioning of the Army, the number of Texians each officer proposed to personally kill, the number of rifles sold by this or that middleman and at what enormous profit—though no one seemed to have tested these guns to see if they would actually shoot—the size of each officer's tent and entourage, and the merits of his blood-horses, to the disparagement of every other beast in the officers' corps. Bets were laid on the bull-fights to be held in the President's honor on Sunday afternoon: "Truly you must come, Señor Enero," urged a half-dozen of January's new acquaintances, mellow with the money they'd won from him and with copious amounts of Consuela's brandy. "How could it not be a glorious spectacle, with de Bujerio bulls in the running...?"

And Don Rafael bowed stiffly to them and smiled happily, in the midst of explaining something about the cut of his coat-back to an apparently enthralled Consuela. As far as January could tell, Don Rafael completely failed to recognize Rose's evil twin sister, Elena—who, with her quadroon complexion, French-accented Spanish, and narrow, delicate features, though she certainly would never have been taken for a white woman, might have been from anywhere along the Caribbean shores.

But then, he doubted Don Rafael's ability to recognize anyone not in his immediate family or connected with his own immediate interests.

There was another fight—over a Colonel calling the pulque-seller "Señor Escalada" rather than "Don Julio," as the merchant considered his right—with a great deal of shouting and the screaming of the women everyone had brought with them, broken glasses, and accusations of boot-licking, profiteering, and stealing sheep and selling them back to their owners. After the last guests departed close to dawn, and Sancho and Sebastian were cleaning up spilled brandy, peanut-hulls, mashed *pandolce,* shattered glassware, and the stubs of innumerable cigarettos and cigars, January heard, as he walked along the gallery to his room, the soft notes of a pianoforte being played very quietly: the duet from the second act of the opera they'd seen that evening, "O na-menlos Freude."

He stopped beside the half-open doorway and saw in the single candle's light the still, calm face of Doña Gertrudis de Caldofranco as she sat at a small six-octave square instrument of the kind that had been built in Germany forty years earlier.

"You play very beautifully."

Her hands paused on the keys. Consuela passed in the gallery: "I've nothing further for you this evening, Aunt Trudis. There's rehearsal again tomorrow morning, so be ready after breakfast."

"Yes, Señora."

Consuela's heels clicked away down the tiled *corredor.* January heard her call out for Pepita.

In a cool, small voice, Doña Gertrudis said, "In my day it was considered an accomplishment for a woman of family to play—in the bosom of her family, which was where she remained."

Her hair, dark streaked with silver, shimmered in the dim light under the shabby black point-lace of her mantilla, and she turned to regard January against the blackness of the silent courtyard beyond him. "In my day we were taught to be what our families needed of us; my brother to manage the estates; myself to raise children of decency and responsibility, to work with the Church in caring for orphans and the poor. For the honor of my city and my country, I wish that you could have seen New Spain as it was then. Now my husband and children are all dead, and my brother is a penniless bankrupt; our lands are gone because we had not enough men to work the mines, and the rebels burned out the villages on our estates. There was a time when I thought I would have the courage to die before I would see myself the servant of an opera-singer who is the daughter of a mestizo whore."

In her voice January heard the echo of Francisco Ylario's, when the Capitán spoke of the Principles of Universal Law to men who casually bought and casually sold justice at their whim because they liked the way a man played cards or the violin. When he spoke of the Emperor, who had, for a few brief years, seemed to be about to establish in Mexico a nation of wealth and honor.

"I have cut sugar-cane in the fields," January told Doña Gertrudis, "beside men who were the sons of Kings. Men do what they must to live, Doña. And women also."

"All we have is what we remember," said the woman. "Of our families, and of how we once lived, and what we once were. And even that, if we wish to spare ourselves pain, it is better that we forget. Good night."

As January turned away, he closed the door. The soft voice of the pianoforte followed him into the night.

TWELVE

The following morning January made enquiries for Señor Benedicte dos Cerritos among the letter-writers who set up their portable desks, their ink-wells and their sheets of pink and blue paper among the candy-stalls and vendors of mangos and oranges in the dense shade of the arcade along the western side of the Plaza Santo Domingo. He was directed to a house a short distance up a narrow street, like Consuela's, formerly a noble town house, now let out to a variety of tenants whose barefoot brown children darted in and out of the old carriageway into a laundry-hung courtyard. Señor dos Cerritos himself—like the original owner of the house in which Consuela lived—retained a few rooms in the rear, above the kitchen court. The servant woman who answered January's knock looked him up and down warily, as if holding his black skin and African features up next to his subdued European dress and spotless linen.

She took his letter of introduction and went in, leaving him in the harsh spatchcocked light of the bare arcade. A moment later she returned with the grudging information: "Señor dos Cerritos will see you."

January tipped her and went in, to find a fragile, elderly gentleman who rose politely from his chair in the bare and tiny *sala* and offered him a seat on the other side of the clean-swept hearth.

"Thirty years ago, of course, there would have been no need to even ask about inheritance," he replied to January's question. "Don Prospero

de Castellón was the Comte de Mictlán before Mexico became independent of Spain, and all his lands were entailed to his eldest male heir:
his son Damiano and then to Damiano's son, Luis. Both of them died
about this time last year while traveling to Vera Cruz—a most insalu-
brious city." He sounded as if he thought the city fathers of that malarial coastal town had simply been too lazy to do anything about the heat
and the damp swamp miasmas that bred disease.

"While I am of course unable to discuss the specifics of Don
Prospero's provisions, I feel able to assure you that the principle of pri-
mogeniture has always been a guiding beacon to the Comte—to Don
Prospero."

January remembered the opinions expressed concerning such ladies
as Coatlique and Helen of Troy. Not a man to trust money or property
to a woman, however many women he might marry or take under his
wing. "So it would be likely that his grandson, Casimiro Fuentes, will
inherit at least the real estate?"

Dos Cerritos gazed stolidly past January's shoulder. "You may draw
such inferences from my words as you please, Señor." Would the old
man have been more forthcoming to a man of his own race? January
was inclined to think he would not. Dos Cerritos was a lawyer to his
fingers' ends. Questions, from white men or black, Spaniards or *indios*
or mestizos, had only one answer: *I am of course unable to discuss the
specifics....*

"Does Don Prospero have a will?"

Señor dos Cerritos's mouth pinched; the delicate nostrils flared.
"I'm sure I could not say, Señor."

Either he doesn't, thought January, or it's the sort of thing you'd expect from Don Prospero: absurd enough to infuriate everyone but not
quite insane enough to throw out. Given the upheaval and corruption
in the legal system, he wondered what absurdity it would take to get the
will of so influential a man set aside.

"Would you be able to tell me something of the status of Señorita
Valentina? Correspondence of hers was involved in her brother's death,
so when the matter comes to court, I'm sure there will be questions
about her position in the household, in the light of her mother's deser-
tion."

"Ah." The old man's lips pursed tighter, as if even his breath were
money that must not be allowed to leak out. "I warned Don Prospero...."

He shook his head. "It is fashionable nowadays to speak of the equality of all men, Señor, but when it comes to it, blood will always tell. Doña Marcellina Alba de Medellín—the mother of Damiano and Doña Josefa—though she was born in this country was of perfectly pure Spanish blood; Doña Maria-Exaltación de Borregos was, of course, of an old Spanish family. Melosia Valenzuela..." He helped himself to snuff from a golden box on whose lid the miniature of a girl was painted in ivory. The old man's clothing would not have been out of place in a portrait fifty years old, a full-skirted black coat and knee-smalls, with ruffles of very fine linen, worn nearly to cobwebs, at his scraggy throat and blue-veined wrists. He wore a wig, too—January could glimpse an old-fashioned wig chest through the doorway of the bedroom, which was crammed with law-books, dishes, all the salvage of what had once been contained in many rooms.

"I understand that efforts have been made to convince Don Prospero to repudiate Doña Melosia so that he may marry again. Does anyone know where she now lives?"

"No, Señor. That she left with a lover is certain. She took nothing but the clothing she wore, and the sapphire necklace that disappeared with her has never turned up for sale in this country. Don Prospero has never been fortunate with women."

January thought about Consuela's mother and the tortilla-press. "Don Prospero spoke of some scandal concerning his second wife, Doña Maria-Exaltación...."

"That was merely a tale put about by the servants." Some flicker of youthful annoyance snapped in Señor dos Cerritos's pale eyes. "Old Yannamaria, I daresay, if the Devil hasn't carried that old witch off by this time. Doña Maria-Exaltación was never in good health, always throwing out a rash or down with the vapors. Her death in 1817 was no more than her sickliness catching up with her. Had the cook not been handsome, and had she been taken sick in the middle of the night instead of just after luncheon, there would have been no peasant jabber of poisoning or illicit affairs. At the time, even Don Prospero did not believe it, although she—"

He checked himself, coughed unconvincingly, and settled back into his chair. More mildly, he continued. "Don Prospero did not even fire the cook."

January strongly suspected that Don Prospero wouldn't have fired a good French cook whom he *did* suspect of poisoning his wife, but he only asked, "Was this M'sieu Guillenormand?"

"No, the man before him, a Monsieur Pourpoint. A young man, as I have said, and I suppose one that women would call handsome." He took another pinch of snuff and dusted away the residue with a lawn handkerchief as worn and mended as his cuffs. "He left Don Prospero's employment shortly after Doña Maria-Exaltación's death as soon as it was deemed safe to travel by sea, and returned to France."

"Do you know of any reason why Señora Lorcha would call M'sieu Guillenormand a poisoner?"

Dos Cerritos's thin lips curled. "Because she grew up eating tortillas and beans and thinks anything else is foreign and suspicious, like many today in higher stations than she." Such a flash of animation suffused his narrow face that January wondered whether Natividad's mother had ever come up here in the hopes of influencing this dry and precise old man. When, in a rush of anger, the old lawyer went on, January was sure of it.

"She thought she had that—that *disgraceful* daughter of hers settled for life, if not with the buck, then with the kid, and well-served she is for her folly. Sacripant Guillenormand is a most conscientious man for a Revolutionist heretic, and dedicated to his art, as indeed was M'sieu Pourpoint—and, as far as I can tell, the same could be said for the Frenchman Giles Laurent, whom Don Fernando brought with him from Prussia. Doña Maria-Exaltación was always sick with one thing or another, as is her daughter, Doña Isabella. Poor Don Anastasio has become quite a crank about her health, the way he's becoming a crank about Don Prospero's madness, something he took in stride before Fernando and his doctors got to him. He's convinced now that Don Prospero is growing madder by the day, when all of us who know him know that he has been holding conversations with the Jaguar-God since he was quite a young man."

Coming down to the courtyard not much wiser than he had ascended, January found Cristóbal in conversation with a brown and wrinkled little man who kept one of the small shops in what had once been the store-rooms of the house. The servant saw January coming and at once returned to the horses, but January held up his hand. Through the door of the little man's shop he saw plank shelves ranged with pots of black Indian pottery, and above them, bunches of herbs hung to dry. "Apothecary?" he asked, hoping he had the correct word in Spanish. *"Farmacia?"*

"Botica," agreed Cristóbal.

The shop was gloomy, and scarcely larger than a kitchen table; its proprietor barely spoke Spanish, and Cristóbal had to translate much of what January asked. Some of the medicinal plants he recognized from his sister Olympe's stock of voodoo remedies—spikenard for chest colds and aloes for bruises, chinchona bark to induce abortions. Others—yerba mansa, matarique, escoba, and jojoba—were new to him, and he listened with interest as the *panamacac* explained how one used a tincture of the first to wash dirty wounds, or salves of the second for sprains.

But when they spoke of local poisons, what January learned was not only unhelpful but puzzling. He had assumed that there was some local preparation that killed by suffocation within an hour or two of consumption, and that Werther Bremer—or someone else—had obtained it through an Indian *botica* like this one. But not only was there nothing that could be concealed in light China tea—*"Chichinaca,"* objected the shopkeeper when January held up the dark dried leaves of the manioc: *bitter*—but there was nothing in the shop, and nothing that the man knew of, that would kill that way at all. *Tlapatl,* which drove horses and cattle mad and killed men, did so through convulsions, headache, and thirst; the deadly arrow poison of the southern jungles was resinous and aromatic and completely harmless if swallowed. The only poison that came close to time and symptoms would have been the ground-up seeds of the death cama—the hog potato—and those would not only have left a noticeable residue in the glass, but would have preceded their major effects by massive salivation, which Hannibal could not have missed observing.

There's something here that I'm not seeing, thought January as he and Cristóbal rode through the narrow streets and out into the gaudy sunlight of the Cathedral square. *Something that I'm missing, or not looking at the right way.*

The answer is here somewhere.

Only it's disguised as something else.

He left Cristóbal beneath the trees of the great square, climbed through the brilliant pitches of the flower-sellers on the Cathedral steps, and entered the extraordinary shadowy vastness of that huge fane as the great bells in the towers were speaking noon. In one of the chapels, a dusky cavern of candles and gold, he waited with half a dozen market-women, and when his time came, confessed to killing a man in the high sun-baked pass a week ago today.

"He was a bandit?" the priest asked, and January said, "Yes."

"And he would have killed you had you not killed him?"

"I wounded him defending my life, yes, Father. He was terribly injured; he could not live. I gave him my rosary, as it is lawful for Christians to do if there is no priest near, and told him his sins were forgiven him. After he kissed the crucifix, I shot him, to put him out of his pain." January remembered the face of the bandit, streaked with filth, and with blood coming out of his nose and mouth, tears of agony tracking through the dirt.

There was long silence on the other side of the grille. Then the priest said, "Are you troubled about what you did, my son?" The voice of a young man, young enough to be January's son.

January thought about it for a moment, and said, "No. I am a surgeon. I knew that the man could not live."

"Nor had he lived, I think, in any real sense, for a long time before your paths crossed. Not as a man lives, in the sight of God and in his own eyes. Your act of mercy—of giving him the chance to whisper his prayer of repentance into God's ear on the threshold of death—opened for him the door between Hell and Purgatory: these are acts that saints do, Señor. He will be in Purgatory a long time, but when he finally comes out and meets you in the streets of Heaven, I believe his first words to you will be words of thanks. Say three rosaries for his soul and light a candle to the Virgin. Your sins are forgiven you."

So January told the beads on his battered old rosary, and breathed the musky potpourri of incense and candle-wax and the sweaty humanity of the people around him, and watched the candle-shadows waver over the dizzying exuberance of carved shapes around the altar: saints and flowers, birds and beasts, the Tree of Life with its twining branches and a jungly undergrowth of curlicues that reminded him of the carven reliefs still visible through the dirt and roots of that dark stone room within the Pyramid of the Dead. Before the altar in a coffin of glass lay a statue of Christ dead in his tomb, gory with the blood of his martyrdom: *God loved you this much.*

In a misgoverned land without hope of either law or justice, there was some comfort, he supposed, in that.

"For all old dos Cerritos had no use for Melosia Valenzuela," remarked Consuela later that afternoon when her stylish carriage maneuvered through the axle-to-axle jam of traffic on the Calle San Francisco toward her father's town house, "he has been quite good about coming up with reasons for my father not to repudiate her—one has only to look at Natividad Lorcha and her mother to see why. And then again, he has done what he can to protect Valentina, and the alliances my father can make if she is his legitimate daughter."

"Did you know Melosia?" asked Rose as the carriage halted for the dozenth time, blocked by a dilapidated hack filled with *poblana* ladies and their children. *Pelados* crowded from the flagway, hands outstretched. Juan lashed at them with his whip. Mostly, January suspected, to keep them from holding up a quick bolt for the next break in the traffic.

"Oh, yes." Consuela plied her sandalwood fan—the day was a warm one and the tall, tile-fronted houses shut in the heat around them. "Father married her in 'twenty-three, just before I went to the conservatory in Milan—in fact, it was she who urged him to pay my passage. She was very young, only a year or so older than I, and utterly mortified by my father's madness. Like my sister Isabella, she loved town life, and would not willingly forgo the opera and shopping in order to go out to Mictlán to be bored. And one can scarcely blame her."

The team leaped forward into a gap between a donkey-cart and a curtained carretela and Consuela cursed; Doña Gertrudis, seated beside her facing backwards, merely gritted her teeth. "In the end, when my father bore her out to Mictlán and refused to allow her to leave, Melosia simply ran away."

Juan blew three sharp notes on his brass horn and turned the team toward the carriageway of a four-story town house whose rich green stucco façade was laced with tilework, statues, and twisted pilasters like a cathedral's. A manservant in Don Prospero's purple livery opened the gates; Sancho sprang from the back as the vehicle halted, and bowed like a dancer as he put down the step.

"You will pardon me if I put you into Grijalva's hands here—Grijalva is the butler—and leave you." Consuela waved to the graying and dignified little man who came out from beneath the ground-floor arcade to greet them. "I have to be at the Teatro early to dress, and I want to stop at the de Bujerio town house, where they are having a party for their daughter Pilar. . . ."

"Pilar who's going into the convent?" asked Rose, startled.

"*En verdad!* When a girl of good family takes vows, you understand, for three days beforehand she goes from party to party, dressed all in lace and silk and wearing all the jewels she will never wear again. . . . It is only a few doors up the street. Sancho will show you when you are ready. I have sent a note to the Prussian minister inviting him to a little *tertulia* at my flat after the opera tonight. Tulio will be there, and nearly everyone who was there last night, so if you can manage to go on losing . . ."

"I can manage," sighed January, stepping down and holding out his hand to Rose.

"I must inquire," remarked Rose in French as the butler Grijalva led them up the marble steps, "to see if my wicked twin sister, Elena, has plans for this evening." Her eye caught January's, and she smiled.

The de Castellón town house was one of the few January had seen in Mexico City that had not been broken up or rented out. Like that of Sir Henry Ward, it was exquisitely and expensively furnished in the style of the 'eighties: spare lines, pale bright brocades, china from Dresden and Limoges. Most of the furnishings were under Holland covers, and the windows shuttered and barred. The place seemed to have only two servants, Grijalva and a footman, and the plate of candies and mango that the latter brought them with coffee had, January guessed, been bought in some haste from a street vendor for the occasion.

Grijalva showed them everything they asked to see, and, after January tipped him, even volunteered information: "Don Fernando tried to find green notebooks like that here in town, sir," he explained of the twenty-nine identical green-bound ledgers that January discovered on the shelf in Fernando's bedroom, dating back to 1820, when the boy had first gone to Prussia. "When I could not, he ordered them from a stationer in Berlin. They had to be the same, he insisted, green with gold stamping. He became most angry when I offered him the morocco-leather that Perez sells over on the Plaza Santo Domingo. He ordered the ink from Berlin, too, finding none to suit him here."

"Would you object to having the ledgers sent to Señora Montero's for me to look over?" *There's something I'm missing.* The thought glided again through January's mind like the shadow of a shark half-seen in deep water. *Something I'm not seeing . . .*

"With her permission, of course, Señor."

January looked around him at Fernando's room. Like the Creole French of New Orleans, the *hacendados* spent on their town houses what they would not think to waste on a mere country place. Fernando's room was plastered, wallpapered with Chinese silk, and rolls of Brussels carpets lay against the walls all around. An inlaid armoire held uniforms—the gold-braided crimson of the officers of the Tenth Berlin Guards, and the blue-and-crimson of Mexico—and a few civilian coats of finely-tailored brown velvet, of the old-fashioned cut that Germans still favored. A shelf held a few military books and Frederick the Great's *Histoire de la Guerre de Sept Ans,* as well as several volumes of racing studs.

A connecting door led to a penitential closet—Werther's room—that contained a low bed barely larger than a pallet, a couple of rough shelves holding volumes of Schopenhauer, von Ranke, Schiller, and Grimm, and a small leather trunk. Among the white linen shirts and silk stockings therein, January found an ivory miniature, the first picture he'd seen of the deceased Fernando—startlingly like what Don Prospero must have been in his youth, with sharply-defined features, a savage beak of a nose, and chill blue eyes. With the portrait was a sheet of notepaper, folded and sealed: it contained brushings and clippings of fine light-brown hair.

His glance went quickly to the butler.

"Very fond of his master, Werther was," said Grijalva expressionlessly. "None of us here understood it, for Don Fernando treated him—and indeed treated us all—worse than any dog. He beat one of the stable-boys nearly to death for stealing a few cups of oats. Werther seemed to think that as the master's favorite, he had the right to do the same when anyone displeased him."

"Do you know where Werther is now?"

"No, sir. When word reached us that Don Fernando had died, Laurent—our chef—at once sought employment elsewhere. Señors

Katz and Schnitten, his two grooms, made arrangements to leave the country. . . ." A world of backstairs power-struggles, of cold glares and petty revenges, glinted briefly in the mere pronunciation of the two names. "Meaning that they stole and sold a silver tureen and a number of silver cups from the dining-room. They were gone by the time Werther returned from Mictlán, which was on the Fiesta de San Miguel, about three weeks after his master was killed. Filled with rage, he was, that the world did not rush to avenge his master's death."

The butler's voice remained low and without inflection, but something in the softening of the corners of his lips hinted at just how much satisfaction he'd taken in telling Werther Bremer that there was no more room for him in the establishment on Calle San Francisco. He closed the door behind January and Rose: "Along here is the room prepared for Don Fernando's bride."

January regarded the enormous chamber with its carved American bed of black walnut, its refulgently-flowered brocades, and its bouquets of pink-dyed ostrich-plumes for a moment in bemused silence before he asked, "What was Bremer's reaction to the news that his master was to be wed?"

"He dropped the tray of things he was carrying—the good Limoges coffee-service and a decanter of brandy—and fled from the room, Señor. He was gone for several hours. Later that night he had a most disgraceful argument with his master, shouting and wailing that you could hear all through the house." Grijalva's lips pinched, reminding January of Señor dos Cerritos: if he wasn't completely Spanish himself, the butler had been raised in the old traditions of Spanish etiquette, and the German concept of natural emotions freely expressed clearly met with no approval here.

January raised his eyebrows, and the butler shook his head, with more than a trace of regret in his voice. "As they spoke completely in German, I could understand no words, Señor. . . ." He pocketed the silver reale that January handed him nevertheless. "But I know of no other reason that Werther would be in tears."

"How long was this before his master's death?"

"Ten days, Señor. Don Prospero arranged to have furniture delivered and the room made ready for Señorita Lorcha the following day. Only a week later Don Anastasio de Saragosse sent word of Don Prospero's madness."

Hooves clattered in the courtyard—the carriage returning, empty, there being no room, presumably, in the de Bujerio courtyard for it. In the stillness of the immense house the noise echoed eerily. No thump of looms downstairs, no laughter of the vaqueros; no chatter of servants passing back and forth. January wondered if Grijalva considered the single footman—far more Indian in complexion and feature—beneath his dignity to speak to, or if the two of them had some companionable lair back in the empty kitchen quarters where they spent their evening hours. But he did not know how to ask.

Carefully, he said, "If in his grief—perhaps in distraction of the mind—Werther Bremer sought to purchase . . . oh, perhaps something to make Señorita Lorcha ill . . ."

But his eyes met the butler's, and they both knew that it was not Señorita Lorcha who had died.

"I do not see how he could, Señor," Grijalva said in the tone of one who regrets having to do justice to the subject at hand. "He spoke no Spanish, you see. He is a very young man, Señor. He might perhaps have cut up Señorita Lorcha's shawls, or even put salt in her coffee, but I do not think he had the knowledge of even the household sub-stances—like turpentine or oil of vitriol—that can cause illness or death. Moreover, I think that if he did somehow purchase such a sub-stance for such an end, Señor, he would have used it on himself."

But he didn't, thought January. Or . . . "You don't think Werther Bremer might have killed himself, do you?" he asked Rose as the car-riage passed beneath the shade of the carriageway and endeavored to find a crevice in the mass of carriages, riders, beggars, and foot-traffic in the Calle San Francisco that would let it proceed the some hundred feet to the de Bujerio town house. "After accusing Hannibal and not getting any satisfaction from Ylario either?"

"Since I've never to my knowledge laid eyes on the young man," replied Rose, watching with interest the argument, on the opposite side of the street, between an old woman with a basket of poppies on her head and a priest with a little dog, "I have no way of knowing that—but I wouldn't think it likely. Not with his vengeance unachieved. My worry is that he's left the city and is hiding in one of the arroyos near Mictlán with a rifle, waiting for a clear shot at Hannibal . . . assuming he can shoot. That is the *beau idéal* of the hearty young Teuton these days, isn't it? The free-spirited *Freischütz* trekking through the forest green?"

"I'm assuming he can't shoot," replied January grimly, "from the fact that he hasn't done so already. What on earth is going on up there?" He rose from his seat in the carriage—which was stopped while Juan waited for two grooms to quiet a kicking horse in the harness of an elaborate old coach—and looked ahead down the street.

In the slanted golden light of evening he could see the problem, a small marching band in green livery emerging from the carriageway of a town house whose yellow stucco front was adorned with what appeared to be statues of the entire Heavenly Host. Streamers of cut paper and standards of brilliant flowers bobbed and dipped above the heads of the crowd; clarionettes, kettledrums, flutes skirled in a lively quick-step march. As January watched, a carriage emerged behind the band, and Don Rafael de Bujerio stood up beside the driver, throwing out handfuls of coin.

No wonder the street was impassably jammed. An army of club-bearing footmen surrounding the carriage to keep the *léperos* at bay didn't help the traffic problem any, but looking over the heads of the crowd, January understood the need for the escort. Doña Imelda, sitting in the carriage, flashed with diamonds enough to cause a second French Revolution, though they were paltry compared to the jewels bedecking the white-clothed young girl at her side.

"That can't be Pilar!" gasped Rose, horrified. "She's only a little girl!"

But the very young lady in the gown of white satin, a crown of diamonds on her head, and a little ornamental shield of goldwork and enamel in her hand, could be no one else. Juan backed the horses to let the procession edge past, and January saw the girl's face, basking in the hysterical attention with the full intentness of a fourteen-year-old's self-perceived martyrdom, solemnly reveling in being the cynosure of every eye. Pilar de Bujerio's lap was filled with pink roses, her smile flashing now and then with delight that held little comprehension—knowing only that for one time in her life, she was the most important person in her world.

January saw Doña Imelda's face, too, filled with the same purring satisfaction he'd heard in her voice at Mictlán: *Now, Josefa, envy is only to be expected.* Saw the bitterness in Josefa's eyes as she looked at her father from the opposite end of the dining-table, anger that smoldered with the slow patience of the robbed.

Gems winked on the little crown in the evening sunlight as the carriage proceeded slowly up the street, to the next party, the next celebration, music and brightness and flowers following in its wake. Like the musicians that had followed the woman January had seen the previous morning, who bore in her arms the corpse of her child.

"Ai, *what* a bore! And *what* a crowd!" Consuela scrambled up into the carriage and settled herself beside Rose with a flounce. Sancho, who had both pushed the crowd aside for her and defended her passage, swung nimbly up behind. "And if I had to endure one more second of Isabella going on about how *her* daughters would have gone into the Incarnation, if either of them had lived, and what a martyr she is that they did not—as if Anastasio would have permitted *any* daughter of his to become a nun!—and all her sorrows about losing her sons and her grief at her brother's death . . . *and* coming to the party in full mourning, though she never so much as bothered to visit Fernando in the whole eight months he was here in Mexico . . . I have had enough of respectable people for one day, and enough of family for a lifetime! Let us go to the opera, where people at least are greedy and reasonable!"

THIRTEEN

Well aware that no matter how much money he'd lost to them the previous night—and no matter how shady their own antecedents—none of Consuela's raffish hangers-on would even consider visiting a black man's opera box, much less appreciate a black man visiting theirs, January settled down in peace and quiet and enjoyed *L'Italiana in Algeri* as much as it was possible for him to do so.

But his racing mind could not let go of the butler Grijalva's voice saying *". . . He would have used it on himself."* Of Ylario: *"The jealous lover would have poisoned the girl."* Of the sight of a torn-out heart, swimming in a vessel of blood.

Beside those thoughts, Rossini's frippery version of life in a North African harem paled to absurdity, and January remembered only how the dark eyes of his first wife, Ayasha, had snapped with exasperation as she'd compared the absurdities of the tale with her own upbringing in her father's small harîm. Remembered her extravagant gestures in the café afterwards at the Palais Royale, and the scents of rain and coffee.

Ayasha was dead, too, he thought, and his mind tangled once more in uncertainty and fear.

Someone had bought poison *(From whom? What kind?)*, and had introduced it into something Fernando ate or drank after dinner *(before or after Hannibal spoke to him?)*. And Hannibal, who had never hurt a soul in his life, would hang for the crime.

If he lived through the Days of the Dead.

Rose, though she usually derived more enjoyment from the stage machinery than from the music in any opera, kept up a wry commentary on the logical failings of the plot ("Has that man ever actually read anything about how the sultans treat their women?"), though now and then he caught the worry in her sidelong glance. During the entr'acte she and January played their usual game of inventing tales about the spectators in the other boxes, a pastime enhanced rather than diminished by the fact that they knew virtually no one. They provided them with names—The Purple Prince, Madame Guêpe, Captain Falstaff, Abbé Frollo—and life histories, and speculated as to why gentleman A bowed so deeply to gentleman B, and why mothers and duennas smiled so sweetly upon gentleman C while subtly elbowing young Major D almost over the railing and into the pit.

January spied Don Anastasio in attendance upon a fragile-looking, fair-haired woman in mourning black—presumably his wife, Fernando's full-blood sister Doña Isabella—in the box with Doña Imelda and an excited and radiant Pilar. In another box, close by the stage in the most fashionable tier of the theater, Natividad Lorcha chatted with a revolving battalion of uniformed officers: "I see she's out of mourning already." "Nonsense, Benjamin, you wrong the poor girl! I'm sure that under all that pink silk she's wearing a black corset." January laughed, but the distraction was momentary: *The answer has to be here somewhere.*

What am I not seeing?

At Consuela's afterwards—amid the same talk, the same drinking, the same rounds of vingt-et-un and ombre in the overheated candle-lit *sala*—January was approached by his hostess with a tall, florid-faced dandy in tow, a fair-haired gentleman in lavender kid gloves and a buttonhole the size of a cabbage. "Benjamin Janvier, of New Orleans," introduced Consuela in her lilting French, "His Excellency Egon Rupert von Wolfbüttel, Graf von Winterfeldt and minister to the King of Prussia."

"I am deeply honored." January rose from the gaming-table and bowed profoundly, thanking the Fates that New Orleans had a large enough population of Germans to have given him a command of the language.

"My dear sir, a pleasure, a pleasure." The minister replied in French, which most of the old German aristocracy preferred to the tongue their peasants and soldiers spoke. "You're not here in connection with the Texian question, are you? I didn't think so—dreadful men, and they never cease spitting." He held up his gold-rimmed quizzing-glass to study January more closely. "I felt sure a man who would wear a waist-coat like yours could not be associated with them. Surely that waistcoat is Parisian? From Monsieur Joliffe's in the Avenue de la Pepinière, if I'm not mistaken..."

"You have a wonderful eye, sir." Warned by Consuela that the minister was something of a dandy, January had been careful to wear his best pale-green silk vest, which was indeed from Joliffe's. "I lived in Paris for many years before returning to New Orleans. And I suspect the Texians would have little use for a man of my hue, except possibly to pick their cotton."

"Well, the more fools they. Although it goes without saying that anyone who'd believe *any* promises of peaceful retreat given them by *any* relation of the President... Well, enough of that." He waved an airy hand and let the glass fall to the end of its violet ribbon. "They'll see their mistake when Santa Anna's Army of Operations marches into view. And how may I serve you, sir, since Henry seems to have given you *carte blanche* in that letter of introduction dear Consuela told me about? She always has that determined glitter in her eye when she wants me to do her a favor."

January laughed. "It's only a simple enquiry, your Excellency. I'm searching for a man named Werther Bremer, a servant. He was valet to—"

"Dear heavens, yes, Werther." The minister nodded. "Fernando de Castellón's valet. Terrible about Fernando." He sighed. "A good soldier. Santa Anna will miss his talents, particularly now that he's trying to whip those poor savages into an army capable of taking on the Texians."

"Do you think he'll succeed?" asked January, thinking of their Tennessean fellow-passenger John Dillard.

Von Winterfeldt raised his pale brows. Despite his paunchiness—carefully concealed with good tailoring and a merciless corset—he had an air of physical strength: a fencer, guessed January, or a devotee of sin-glestick. Not a man to cross, and be damned to your lavender gloves.

"Santa Anna cannot afford to fail. It isn't so much that he wants Texas—the land's good for very little except the running of cattle, you know. But if the Texians declare themselves to be an independent republic, and are simply let to go, the Americans will almost certainly move on to colonize Santa Fe and the fur-trapping lands to the north, and declare *them* to be independent republics also. California on the Pacific, too, for all I know. It has decent ports, I understand.

"Santa Anna's already put down one rebellion in Zacatecas, and not in a fashion likely to win him much loyalty from other states. The Yucatán and Oaxaca have barely anything in common with Mexico City already. I don't completely agree with the *centralistas,* but once a Federal union starts to divide along sectional lines, there's no stopping it—it's astonishing that Jackson was able to keep South Carolina from seceding from the United States over that tariff business a few years back. And once that starts happening, it's only a matter of time before the individual states start being used as bases for European powers."

"I understand the Army here leaves a great deal to be desired."

"It leaves everything to be desired, my dear sir. Including funding, by the way. They say the bull-fight tomorrow afternoon is in honor of the President, but it's really to raise money to buy the poor wretches boots and guns. Not that they'll get a thing worth wearing. I know the man Santa Anna gave the contract to, an absolute bandit! Have you been to a bull-fight in this country, Sir Henry?" He turned to address the English minister, who had appeared at his side, shepherded by the indefatigable Consuela.

"Barbarity," snapped Sir Henry, shaking his head.

"Now, Henry, any Spaniard will tell you it is the observation of bull-fights that makes Spaniards manly. I understand they'll be fighting bulls of the de Bujerio line, and the Potosí—quite fierce animals, and of impeccable bloodlines. Certainly they could trace their lineage back a number of generations further than most members of the government these days. If you're looking for Werther Bremer," von Winterfeldt added, raising his quizzing-glass again to regard January, "that might be a good place to find him. I offered to pay the poor lad's fare back to Lübeck, the most I could do, although since he's a Holsteiner I have no actual responsibility for him. But the Duke of Schleswig-Holstein has no minister in Mexico. I felt sorry for him, poor boy. But he refused, saying he must remain and avenge his friend. I understand he was seeking employment at the bullring when he could find nothing among de Castellón's fellow officers." He shook his pomaded head again and peered at the nearest knot of plumed and beribboned colonels and aides. "Fools. I understood from Fernando that Werther was a most excellent servant. And why would one wish to address a servant anyway?"

On his way to Mass the following morning—with the sky still opal-gray above streets deep in strange blue shadow—January saw posters for the fights: six bulls from the ranches of de Bujerio, Potosí, and El Grande Zacatecas, to be killed in the bullring of San Pablo, in order to raise money for the Grand Army's debts. No mention of the men who would fight them, though the names of this *torero* or that had laced the talk at the card-tables the previous night. Even over the cards, the talk had been more about the bloodlines and ferocity of the bulls. The Graf von Winterfeldt had given him the use of his box for the fight, sparing him the expense of paying treble price for tickets that brokers had fought for in the mobs at the ticket office earlier in the week.

In the quiet of the Chapel of the Angels, January knelt among the market-women and the servants—the only other people who attended Mass this early—and sponged his mind of worry and thought, opening his heart to the words of the ritual and his soul to the silence of God. A week ago he had killed a man—maybe more than one—in the dusty pass on the road down from Perote. A week ago they had buried the white-haired Swiss valet Da Ponte in the churchyard at Chalco, torches burning golden in the gathering dark of evening.

Hail Mary, full of grace, the Lord is with thee. . . . Pray for us sinners, now and in the hour of our death.

For the bandit in the pass. For the old Da Ponte in his lonely grave in foreign soil.

For his dear young friend Artois St. Chinian, who had died in last summer's agonizing heat in New Orleans and who would have been in Paris by this time, ecstatic with delight at the education his white uncle would have paid to provide him, away from the city and the land where men would look at him and think: *nigger.*

For Ayasha, always in the darkness in the center of his heart, like a flower perfuming an empty room at night.

Hail Mary, full of grace, the Lord is with thee.

Pray for us. . . .

For Hannibal, facing death at the gallows. *I'm sorry now that I ever wrote to you . . . stand not upon the order of your going. . . .*

It might be best to get Hannibal out of here. . . .

The smell of blood in the darkness.

Guide me to Werther Bremer, Mother of God—and put the right words in my mouth when I meet him.

Hannibal charmed every woman he met, thought January. With any luck the Mother of God would look kindly upon him, too.

When first he had gone to France in 1817, the baiting of bulls with dogs was still common. January had always hated those inn-yard spectacles, the tethered animals bellowing in terror and rage, uncomprehending of why they were being set upon in circumstances that they could not escape; dying in a welter of blood and agony so that men could bet on how long it would take them to do so, and how many of their tormentors they could take with them into the darkness.

Perhaps, he thought, it was because he himself had once been a slave.

The *corrida* was different from these gory outrages: ritualistic, a passion-play in which the tragic hero was the bull, the man cast as implacable Death, with always the titillation of the unpredictable, the possibility of the roles reversed. And of course—it went without saying—the brutal fascination of pain.

Nobody apparently gave a thought to the horses disemboweled and dying in agony—they were a sideline, a footnote to point up the peril the man was in, like the nameless Greek infantrymen Hector slaughtered on the way to his duel with Achilles. Rose said, after the first matador rammed home his sword between the disabled and exhausted bull's shoulder-blades, "I'm sure if the point of the exercise is beef, there are easier ways to obtain it," and left, accompanied by the disappointed Zama, to eat ices and read Jane Austen in the carriage.

January remained through two more *corridas,* watching the faces of the people around him in the shaded boxes, and out beyond on the benches in the westering sunlight. Listening to the sound of the crowd.

He found himself remembering the wake for his young friend Artois St. Chinian only a few months before. The boy's wealthy white uncle had come to the gathering, which had been held in the house of January's sister Dominique. In the stuffy heat of the bullring box, with the sun glaring across the red-splotched sand—with the gaudy colors of the crowd, with the harsh blue stink of cigarettos and the gold scents of ginger-beer and candy in his nostrils—January recalled the look of shock and bafflement in that old white man's face. It had been a typical wake of the free-colored community, men and women who knew the dead boy only slightly howling in grief in the bedroom, then passing into the parlor to get roaring drunk while they laughed and chatted with friends and listened to January play the piano.

All was done in love, in understanding that the dead Artois would want his friends to laugh as well as weep. The tunes January had played had been the boy's favorites, lively and quick-stepping. People had smiled as they sang.

The old man had not understood.

And January was aware, looking at the faces of the men and women on the plank seats in the sun below the boxes—listening to the cries of respect, of approval, of awe that swept like wind across the packed crowd—that he did not understand what was going on here. He saw there was skill and artistry involved, as well as brute courage. One of the matadors had it, though another was so nervous, he made all kinds of mistakes, jeered and laughed at by the *aficionados,* until he finally had his thigh ripped open from groin to knee. Even the clowns, who leaped and capered about the ring, or ate mock banquets before the charging bull only to spring aside at the last second in showers of breaking plates, had a panache and timing that some of the graver *toreros* lacked.

And he saw how it was a spectacle of bravery, even though the bull was carefully and systematically disabled by having its blood let and its heavy neck muscles—the muscles that controlled its ability to gore— sliced with lances and jabbed with darts, while it was confused, panicked, maddened by the firecrackers attached to the banderillas and bursting all around it.

Yet seeing all that, the cruelty of it revolted him. The cruelty, and the assumption that because men were men, they had the right to torment and kill; the right to encourage the spectacle of death, for their own amusement or for what they perceived as their own spiritual fulfillment.

He left the box and descended the rickety wooden steps in semidarkness, for evening was coming on. Once outside, he sought for a way around the rough-plastered adobe wall of the ring to the back, where he knew the corrals must be. This was not easy, for the San Pablo bullring stood in the tangle of small streets between the city's heart and the grubby barrios that fringed the lake on the east, and there were houses of adobe, and other, more ramshackle buildings of mud and thatch built up against its wall. By keeping the bullring wall in view on his right, January threaded his way through the narrow alleys till he found one wide and thick with trampled mud and cow-dung, and this he followed to the square beside the Church of San Pablo, where the makeshift corrals and chutes had all been set up to separate out the bulls from the small herd of steers with which they'd traveled from the ranges where they'd run wild for years.

He'd watched the men working the ring, the assistants running up and down the narrow shadowy slot between the *barreras* and the first row of seats, carrying jugs of water for the *toreros*, or spare swords or extra capes. Had observed the carpenters who swiftly repaired the barriers when one of the bulls rammed into it; the physician who waited for the gored matador to be carried out. With the exception of the physician, most of these workers had looked to be either *indio* or mestizo, and January assumed that a Prussian valet could not, in the weeks since his master's death, have acquired enough of the *torero*'s obvious skills to have sought that kind of employment.

That left either the hawkers of oranges and ginger-beer who made their way up and down the aisles—and he knew Werther had insufficient Spanish to understand that many people shouting orders to him all at once—or the handlers of the cattle before they got into the ring.

With luck Werther—who might be a dark-haired Bavarian for all January knew—would at least be distinguishable from the lower-caste Mexicans among whom he worked.

And so it proved. The shadows were lengthening and the dust in the air was like shimmering golden soup among the cramped pens built in the square, but as he picked his way through the labyrinth of rough pine-pole fences, January could see at a distance the only man who might remotely be of German extraction: tall, blond, and what was generally described as "strapping." The young man wore no hat, and though his face and throat were burned a painful shade of magenta, January could see he was extremely handsome, almost beautiful. One of the picadors, riding out of the black arch of shadow that led to the space beneath the tiers of benches and so to the ring, called out something to the blond man, and January heard him shout back, *"Ja, ja— schrekliche Kuh..."*

Then he turned and saw January striding toward him across a small open corral.

And bolted as if January had been aiming a gun at him.

Startled, January plunged in pursuit. His mended white shirt like a flag in the sun, Werther vaulted over a fence into a pen full of steers, snaked through the dusty, shifting mass of horns and hooves. January slipped under a fence, dashed through a narrow chute to head him off. He yelled, "Halt!" as Werther sprang over the fence at the far side of the steers, who were now milling angrily—rangy Mexican animals with enormous horns, wild and nervous as deer. January scrambled between two flimsy railings, dashed into another corral, and skidded to a stop as Werther shot open a gate at the far side of the open space, to release from its chute a bull the size of the Mexico City Cathedral.

The bull came out of the chute like a steam locomotive and charged January without so much as an instant's hesitation. January bolted for the nearest fence, though he hadn't seen a fence in Mexico that looked like it could stand up to a determined ramming, and this one was no exception, four or five skinny trunks of stripped lodgepole pine lashed to an upright with hanks of rawhide. He slid through it and into the next pen and the animal hit it full-on, snapping one of the poles out-right and wrenching the ends of two more in their bindings. The bull let out a bellow and piled up and over the fence, head tossing, small black eyes furious. January had heard how fighting bulls were bred to charge anything that moved, and he understood, terrifyingly, the courage of the matadors now, to stand still and control that rank, raw-smelling onrush of flesh and rage.

He vaulted over another fence and the bull crashed that one as well, horns glinting wickedly, so close January felt the hot drops of its spittle strike the back of his head. He pelted across the pen beyond, sprang up the next fence. There was nothing beyond that—a chute and the back wall of a mud-brick *pulqueria* that bordered the square. The bull smashed the fence full-force while January was still atop it, the impact of half a ton of blind animal rage nearly hurling him down on top of the bull. He caught his balance as the beast backed for another charge. Its neck muscles rippled as it flung its head sideways, then charged the post to which January clung. January leaped down into the chute, heard the bull bellow behind him, its horns snagged.

"Andele!" cried a high voice above the thunder of hooves, the stink

of cattle and dust. January backed along the chute, ready to leap onto the fence again if the bull followed him in; he saw the picador to whom Werther had been speaking—and Rose, of all people, on foot with her long pink skirts gathered in one hand and an eight-foot pike in the other—driving half a dozen dusty-flanked steers through the nearest gate into the pen with the bull.

"I'm gonna kill that fool cabbage-eater!" cursed the picador—who, January saw with a certain degree of surprise, was a woman. As Rose shut the gate behind the steers, the picador worked her horse through the maze of chutes around the pen: "You, Sambo, this way, eh? And slow—wait till he pulls his head free.... He don't see so good, that Señor Cojones, eh?"

January waited until the bull had pulled his head back out from the entangling pieces of the chute, then cautiously followed the chute around until he was away from the pen. Enraged and filled with terror alone, once among members of his own kind, the bull seemed to forget January's existence completely.

January was shaking all over as he made his way around to where Rose and the picador waited in one of the small holding-pens.

"*Mierda!* My little boy, he got more sense than that cabbage-eating German, eh?" The picador pushed the gate shut behind him with her pike. "Now we gotta run in one of the substitute bulls, an' they're both crazy bulls, you know? Potosí bulls, you never know which way they charge. That bastard there, he's a good Gran' Zac', at least he charge straight. But they learn fast, bulls. Now he know it's the man he gotta go after, not that stupid little red rag they wave. So he's spoiled for the ring."

She spat on the ground. She was a lush-breasted mestizo girl, her black hair braided into a *torero*'s pigtail and dented steel shin-guards glinting dully over tight buckskin breeches.

"You work fast, honey," she added to Rose. "How you know so fast we gotta get the steers in around Señor Cojones, eh?"

"I grew up in the country." Rose shaded her eyes, looking up at the woman. "On Grand Isle, someone was always doing something silly and getting chased by a bull." She'd lost her hat in her rush to rescue, and her soft brown curls lay over her shoulders; she might have been discussing the cultivation of hollyhocks.

"She was headin' for the steers' pen the second that bull come outa that gate. What'd you do to that unfertilized egg, eh"—the picador used the word *huero,* a common term in Mexico for a blond—"that he didn't want to talk to you that bad?"

"I've never met him in my life," January said, and slapped the dust from the sleeves of his jacket. "I need to speak to him, yes, but I can't imagine why he thinks I'd mean him harm."

"Well, maybe that's just how they say hi to their friends in Germany, eh?" She laughed at her own joke, high and rough, like a child.

"You don't happen to know where I could find him in town, do you?"

"What, you think I follow him home at night for his blue eyes?" She shook her head. "He just a peon, you know? They need so many to push the steers around and keep track of the bulls. With the Army out lookin' for anybody that got two good legs these days, they hire whoever they can get here. Old *Huero* knew the difference between a steer and a bull, so they hire him even though he can't talk Spanish. I ain't never seen him around my barrio, but that don't mean nuthin'."

From the dark maw of the arch someone shouted something. The woman yelled back, "All right, keep your pants on!" She reined her scrawny horse around and tucked the pike up under her arm. "I gotta go. One thing I tell you, after givin' the best bull of the day lessons in what he gotta chase, you can bet *Huero* ain't gonna be back here." And she tapped her mount's sides with the spiked rowels of her spurs and trotted back into the dark beneath the gate.

Beside him, Rose said in a thoughtful voice, "You really shouldn't have shouted, 'I know you murdered Fernando,' you know."

Taken by surprise, January laughed so hard, he had to lean against the fence. From the pen the bull watched him, suspicion in its piggy eye.

"If it's any comfort," Rose went on, linking hands with January as they edged through the chutes and pens, "I should say that Werther's immediate reaction of attack and flight at the sight of you should put paid to Ylario's contentions of his innocence. Whether Ylario will believe that or not is another matter."

January shook his head. "It has to have been Ylario who told him I was seeking him," he said. "He reacted *on sight*... and as I'm probably the only black man in Mexico City other than Anthony Butler's slaves,

I doubt he was mistaking me for someone else. Or... *would* he have had a reason to flee one of Butler's slaves?"

They stopped in the first *pulqueria* they passed, for January to get a shot of the curiously mellow-tasting liquor to stop his hands from shaking. The place was empty, its proprietors and its entire clientele being at the *corrida*. It was the first time January had been afoot in Mexico City that he hadn't been mobbed by *léperos*. They were all at the ring as well—he could hear the shouting, like gusts of wind sweeping the clear evening sky.

A round-eyed *indio* girl dippered the liquid from a barrel, staring in wonder at the well-dressed, dust-covered couple—one of them a black man at that—who came in to buy. The pulque was virtually raw and had a punch like Señor Cojones's charge. When permitted to age, pulque was barely stronger than a good German beer.

"I can't imagine why Anthony Butler would even know of Werther Bremer's existence," Rose mused. "Much less send his slaves after him, particularly when he has in his employ gentlemen like our friend Mr. Dillard and that pig-headed rhinoceros of a secretary who kept asking who your master was. If I were Butler, I wouldn't let my slaves out of the house at all, given that if they ran away here, there'd be no legal way of getting them back."

"They may not be slaves at all, you know." January cracked a peanut, turned the papery shell over between his huge fingers, as if he expected to find the answer to the riddle written inside. "I mean, legally, of course, they're not, here, but they may be freedmen back in South Carolina as well. I wonder how I'd go about finding that out."

"Mr. Dillard would be able to tell us."

"He would," January agreed. "If you can think of a way of asking him without the question being immediately relayed back to Butler."

Rose said, "Hmmn."

Consuela's coachman was gone, doubtless comfortably ensconced in the sun-side seats of the bullring, watching some other innocent brute being tormented and killed. Zama, too, had disappeared. The crackle of firecrackers splintered in the fading air from over the bullring wall, and the hungry sea-surge howl of the crowd. The street was lined with carriages, but not a coachman or footman was to be seen. Only old Cristobál, apparently asleep with his back against the wall of a dilapidated convent on the opposite side of the street, a rifle across his knees.

January had to look twice to realize that every carriage was where Cristóbal could see it.

"Anthony Butler may be innocent as the day is long," said January, helping Rose into the carriage. "Ylario was certainly keeping things from me when we talked, and just because he sincerely hates Santa Anna's favorites taking the Principles of Universal Law into their own hands doesn't mean he wouldn't feel justified in doing so himself to protect Bremer. But if there's some reason it's Butler's slaves that Werther is afraid of, we have to go carefully. Any approach I make to anyone in Butler's household is going to be reported back to Butler one way or another—and me being just about the only black man in Mexico City, he's not going to have too much of a problem figuring out who's asking questions."

"I wouldn't be so sure of *that*," said Rose around a mouthful of hairpins as she fixed her coiffure. "But it's probably best to be safe."

"Werther is alone," said January. "And in hiding. Therefore, I'm going to do exactly what our friend Lieutenant Shaw back in New Orleans does when he needs information about the free colored or the slaves—worlds in which he cannot move inconspicuously any more than I can move inconspicuously through the barrios here."

"You're going to ask your mother?"

January laughed, and took a silver reale from his pocket. "I'm going to ask someone who, I suspect, knows as much about the barrios as my mother does about the private affairs of every free-colored family in New Orleans."

He tossed the coin once in the air, catching it in his palm, then flipped it far out into the street. And though anyone would have sworn that Cristóbal was asleep, the old Yaqui's arm seemed to lengthen out like a gecko's tongue, snagging the little silver disk as it flashed in the dusty light.

FOURTEEN

It took Cristobál four days to locate Werther Bremer in the mazes of the capital's back-streets and barrios. During those intervening, nerve-racking days January tried patiently to track down every other fact he could about Don Prospero's household on the eve of Fernando de Castellón's murder, in the hope that—if they could not find the valet—they might at least find some clue that would lead to some answer other than the staringly obvious fact of Hannibal's guilt.

"The poison may not have been swallowed, you know," remarked Rose the day after the bull-fight—Monday—as Consuela's carriage inched along the tree-lined causeway that stretched from the city across the brackish western marshes. "It would be an easy matter to smear curare poison on the thorn of a maguey-leaf, palm the thorn, and give Fernando a smart slap on the shoulder with it. The puncture would never be noticed by candle-light as they were cleaning the body, and of course after this much time in the grave I doubt it could be detected at all."

Around them, every carriage and cart in Mexico City and about half its pedestrians as well streamed sluggishly along the causeway, bound for the Bosque de Chapultepec and Santa Anna's grand review of his Army. The pedestrians at least had the option of walking between the gray stone arches of the aqueduct that stretched from the city, across the acres of reeds and sedges and the gleaming sheets of what had been

Lake Texcoco, to the freshwater springs on the granite height of Chapultepec Hill. The roadway lay along the aqueduct's feet, less than a yard above the level of the squishy lake-bed; more than one driver glared enviously at the market-women and Indians who picked their way past the clogged traffic by leaping from grass-tuft to grass-tuft. Farther out on the lake-bed, where the water was deeper, small reed boats could be seen where Indians fished as they had fished when the pyramids of Tlaloc and Huitzilopochtli towered against the sky instead of the Cathedral's gilded towers.

January sighed. "Leaving out the thickness of the average military uniform coat," he said, "who would have done this, and when? Curare kills almost instantly. The door from the *sala* into the study was bolted, and there wasn't a time when someone wasn't in the *sala,* either clearing up after dinner or playing cards. The door from the *corredor* into the study was within sight of Consuela and others from the moment Hannibal emerged until Werther went in and found his master dead . . . and cold."

"This was much easier when we were on the *Belle Marquise.*" Rose's light tone covered the real unhappiness in her eyes. "I think I preferred speculating about whether or not Fernando wore armor to bed. Even if Natividad does attend this review, how good are our chances of getting to speak with her?"

"Oh, we should have little trouble if we can get to her when she is not with Santa Anna," replied Consuela. She turned—gratefully, January suspected—from listening to Don Rafael, who had urged his horse up beside the carriage to recite to her the family histories of the various bulls who had been killed in the ring the day before, and the individual details of every other *corrida* he had ever seen in his life. His mother's carretela lumbered in the press of vehicles behind Consuela's barouche, the dark-green curtains of its windows parting now and then for shadowy faces to peek through. January wondered if little Pilar was one of them. "Though what you expect Natividad to tell us I do not know."

"Nor do I," replied January grimly. "But she was there on the night of the murder, and I haven't talked to her yet. And unless you can think of a way to elude your father's vaqueros *and* Capitán Ylario some night to get Hannibal away from Mictlán and to the coast—and possibly evade the American chargé d'affaires as well—I think we need to at least hear what she has to say."

The fortress of Chapultepec, ruinous and weather-damaged, towered on a height of rock on what had once been the lake's original shore. Woodlands of cypress surrounded it, draped in Spanish moss and watered by the springs and by rain-tanks. "They say the ghost of Montezuma, the last Emperor of the Aztecs, can be seen in the night, walking in these woods," remarked Consuela as the carriage finally rolled into the dense shade. "He had gardens here, and a fortress of his own upon the height—you can see the whole valley from the walls up there. They say also that La Malinche—the Indian woman who was the brains behind Cortés—haunts these woods, too, but myself, I do not believe any such thing. One of them, of a certainty, but not both... And if the priests will have it that La Malinche did such a good thing to bring all this land under the heel of the Spanish to make good Christians of everyone, why should she walk, indeed?"

Don Rafael nodded wisely, and proceeded to recount how Doña Marina—an Indian woman enslaved by the Aztecs—had contributed to the Aztecs' downfall by acting as Cortés's translator, a tale with which every member of the party was familiar and to which Consuela appeared to listen with interest. Considering the amount of money she'd taken off Don Rafael at ombre Saturday night, reflected January, it was the least she could do.

Beyond the woods the Army lay encamped, straggling knots of thatched shelters, old blankets slung over stretched ropes, corrals of brush holding sheep, cattle, and some of the most miserable horses January had ever seen. By the smell of it, few of the men had any idea of the sanitation required under such crowded circumstances. Among the makeshift bivouacs, the white tents of the officers rose like New Orleans steamboats among the scrum of keelboats and pirogues on the levee: French, German, or English pavilions and markees, cook-shelters where servants prepared meals, lines of blood-horses and sleek mules to carry the officers' baggage. On the parade-ground before the camp, January watched them pass in review through a fog of yellow dust: superbly mounted colonels, majors, generals in brilliant uniforms, the glitter of bullion almost blinding in the sun. Horses pranced and caracoled; plumed hats were swept off in unison to the man who was both

President and Generalissimo *Benemerito en Grado Heroico,* who sat his white horse before them, his face solemn and thoughtful, as if he'd spent the night reading the *Meditations of Marcus Aurelius* instead of working his own fighting-cocks in the Plaza de Voladores.

"If he could have been induced to remain a general instead of indulging in the illusion that he knows the first thing about politics, this whole country would have been better off," murmured Don Anastasio, who guided his leggy black thoroughbred mare up beside the carriage to pay his respects. "He's an excellent general, and like your President Jackson, he knows the value of a hard strike in making sure that a second strike is not needed. If he knew the meaning of the word 'loyalty,' he would be a true hero."

Rose raised her eyebrows. "If George Washington had known the meaning of the word 'loyalty,' there would not be any United States for Mr. Jackson to be president of."

She spoke playfully, but though Don Anastasio returned a rueful acknowledgment of the truth of her irony, his smile swiftly faded. The infantry was passing before them now, thousands of feet beating dull time on the hard-packed earth. Uniformed ranks, some of them; others in the white billowing clothing of farmers, or the embroidered shirts of the Mayas from the Yucatán who spoke no Spanish. Marching in sandals and crude rawhide *zapotes* because they did not have boots, carrying pikes and spears because they did not have guns, or carrying guns that even January could see were ancient, broad-muzzled smoothbores from another era, many of them virulent with rust.

"Santa Anna's decision to embrace the cause of liberty was what brought about Iturbide's victory, and our freedom from Spain," said Don Anastasio softly. "And it was his defection that left Iturbide defenseless to his foes, and opened the floodgates to all the madness that came after: this strongman and that seizing my poor country by the throat. And all because Santa Anna took offense when he was told he could not sit in the Emperor's presence." He shook his head. "For him that was typical—that all things are personal, having nothing to do with the good of the country. And such an outlook can lead only to disaster."

They are marching to their deaths, January realized, watching the grim brown faces of the marching men, the heads held defiantly high. They had the stoic courage of men who work patiently to wring a living from unpromising land, but all of Friday night and Saturday night, while listening for word of Werther Bremer at Consuela's, January had heard the brags of the men who'd sold powder and balls to the Army and made a fortune doing it, adulterating the powder with coal dust, and buying up the balls in job-lots wherever they could without the slightest effort to check that they would even fit down the muzzles of the guns.

Courage would do those men little good if they had weapons that wouldn't fire, or if they were trying to march the eight hundred miles to Texas—in the dead of winter—on rations of cornmeal that were three parts sawdust.

"They deserve better," he said.

"Better?" Don Anastasio's laugh was a puff of bitterness. "They deserve *something* instead of the nothing they're getting. Look at them! Not those poor Yucatecs from the jungles, who haven't even seen snow in their lives—not that Santa Anna has given a thought as to what the Sonoran Desert is going to be like in February. Look at the others among them. Santa Anna's recruiters have emptied the jails: pimps, pickpockets, beggars, and thieves—at least those thieves who haven't the family or influence to buy themselves out of the Army."

Genuine distress twisted Anastasio's face. Following the direction of his gaze, January saw the slouching forms and wary eyes that watched, not the officers, but the other men, calculating their chance to make a break for it and take with them whatever they could in the way of other men's pay, and whatever weapons could be sold for the price of a few glasses of pulque.

"In a way I suppose it's efficient," sighed Anastasio. "If men must die, it's far better that they be scum like that—thieves and idlers and drunkards who are of no use to the state or to themselves—than men with families, men who can raise healthy children or healthy crops. But to give comrades like that to true soldiers is as criminal as giving them defective guns."

At his own carriage his wife was gesturing him back. He shook his head and bent down again over Rose's hand. "One day maybe both of our countries will come to their senses." He rode away through the crowd, his mare picking her way with the delicacy of a lady crossing muddy ground in satin slippers. January saw him bend from the saddle to kiss Doña Isabella's hand, and those of Doña Gertrudis and

Consuela, who sat in the carriage beside her. Turning his gaze, January scanned the other carriages for some sight of Natividad or her mother but could see no glimpse of either. Anastasio would certainly know where he could write to Señora Lorcha to arrange a meeting, he supposed, but to do so would be almost an announcement of intentions, always supposing the lady would deign to write back to—or receive—a visitor of color.

Much better to encounter her by chance at a place such as this.

"Good Lord," said Rose, shocked. "Is that their artillery?"

January turned. "Are those pieces you'd show off if you had others available?"

Rose made a face. "I can almost find it in my heart to be sorry for Santa Anna."

"Save your pity for his men," January said. "And for the Texians should Santa Anna defeat them—or should any fall alive into his hands. He has a reputation for massacre, and he doesn't particularly care how many of his own men perish in achieving his victories." He sprang down from the carriage, and as the last dust settled behind the few cannon and limbers, followed them to the park beyond the trees, where they were being drawn up.

No one stopped him. A few guards loitered in the trees, mostly occupied with smoking cigarettos and flirting with the *poblana* girls. Gentlemen of Don Rafael's type strolled among the guns with ladyfriends, but January's eye was drawn to a solitary figure in gray corduroy, half-hidden in the shadows of the cypresses.

January dropped back into the trees himself, and circled so as to come behind the man, who was in any case so deeply involved in making notes in a pocket memorandum-book that he didn't turn until January was nearly in touching-distance. Then he spun, his hand going to the pistol he wore at his waist. . . .

"January," said John Dillard, and relaxed. "Come to see the parade?"

"Such as it is," said January. "I've seen better artillery turn-outs at Fourth of July militia parades down Canal Street."

Dillard pocketed book and pencil and held out his hand to shake. "They're bringing in cannon from Vera Cruz next week, I hear."

"I hear that, too," agreed January, clasping the American's hand in his own and wondering how he could unobtrusively bring up the subject of fugitive German valets and Anthony Butler's slaves. "Those'll be the cannon they took from the Spanish fifteen years ago: they haven't been fired or cleaned since then."

The Tennessean's blue eyes narrowed sharply. "Where'd you hear that?"

"At the opera," said January. "Playing cards at the back of one of the boxes with about half the Mexican officer corps." Dillard had looked as nonplussed as if January had said he'd been slipped battle-plans at a church-service. "Those cannon are so fouled with rust, I'd be surprised if you can stuff a ball down them, even if the men who're selling powder to the Army weren't adulterating it with coal dust and sand."

"Bastards." Dillard spat, indignant in spite of himself. By the amount of tobacco-juice in the grass, he'd been standing by the artillery park, making notes, for some time.

"You're still outnumbered, though," said January quietly. "Badly."

"We'll manage."

"I pray you do. You remember what happened six months ago, when the state of Zacatecas tried to rebel against Santa Anna in favor of the old Constitution of 1824, as Texas is doing now. Not only were all the militia slaughtered, but Santa Anna turned his troops loose on the civilians as well."

"I guess Mr. Houston'll just have to keep that from happening," said Dillard, and spat again. "I appreciate you telling me about the cannon and the powder and all," he added. "I'll pass that word along to Mr. Butler. They said when I came here it wouldn't matter that I didn't speak the language, but Lord—" He broke off, eyes going past January, and he let out a low, bemused whistle. "Well, now, will you look at that?"

January followed his glance to the extremely stylish barouche drawn by four matched cream-colored horses to a shady spot on the fringes of the reviewing-ground. In it, Natividad Lorcha fanned herself with spangled yellow silk and followed Santa Anna's wide-shouldered scarlet form with parted lips and admiring gaze. When the Generalissimo turned her way, she lifted her hand in greeting. Santa Anna made his horse caracole for her, and swept off his plumed chapeau bras.

January was about to pass along Rose's remark about a black

mourning corset when realization dropped into place; he asked Dillard, "You know the young lady?" and was astonished at how off-hand his voice sounded to his own ears.

Dillard chuckled. "Well, we were never introduced. But I do know the last time I seen her, she was walkin' out with one of Santa Anna's best friends."

January nodded wisely, with as much a man-of-the-world grin as he guessed a white man would tolerate about a woman who, if not precisely white, wasn't black either. "A pretty good friend, I'd say." Both men laughed.

But Rose, when he recounted the conversation to her minutes later, said, "*Dillard* is Valentina's lover at the garden wall?"

"He has to be," said January. "Where else would he have seen Natividad and Don Prospero together?"

"Then Butler's slaves—or freedmen, as the case may be..."

"...suddenly have a connection with Werther Bremer after all," finished January softly. "Though why Butler would have sent slaves or former slaves after Werther when he had Dillard and his other secretaries for the job still escapes me."

"Possibly it wasn't Butler who sent them, but Dillard himself."

"Possibly. Either Dillard saw something or learned something— God knows what—on the night of the murder, or more likely Valentina enclosed a note of some kind with the parcel she passed over the wall. Hannibal isn't the only man in the Valley of Mexico capable of translating Spanish to English, though there doesn't seem to be anyone on Butler's staff endowed with that particular talent...."

"That's very harsh of you, Benjamin," reproved Rose, angling her head to peer over her spectacles. "You can't expect Mr. Dillard to entrust his love-letters to the pig-headed rhinoceros. In a way I'm relieved that it isn't Ylario taking the law into his own hands...."

"And he may still be."

"True. But it does leave us with the problem of how we're going to get around Butler...." She switched effortlessly to Latin as Consuela and Doña Gertrudis, trailed by the faithful Sancho, appeared beside the carriage and climbed in. "How we shall deal with the butler if we cannot find the valet."

By the time January reached the cypress grove near the artillery,

Natividad's carriage was empty. One of the soldiers guarding it—there were six of them, more than were in charge of keeping Texians with memorandum-books from counting the field-pieces in the artillery park—informed him for the sum of a reale that La Señorita had indeed gone to take her *comida* with the Generalissimo and his officers. With as much of an appearance of leisure as he could muster, January strolled among the picnickers who had now spread themselves out among the cypress-trees around the fringes of the parade-ground, scanning the crowd for sight of Natividad's mother. He saw no sign of the squat, black-clad figure, though he did see a number of cock-fights, a dog-fight, dozens of assignations, and Don Tulio de Avila y Merced running a faro-bank for an enormous crowd of young officers and gentlemen, with every sign of carrying on into the evening.

As January, Rose, Consuela, and Doña Gertrudis returned across the marsh to the town, the smell of smoke and cooking from the Army camp and the drifting music of a dozen bands followed them for miles.

Before departing for the review that morning, January had sent a note to Dr. Hernan Pichon at the Hospital of San Hipólito, and Rose had dispatched another to Consuela's aunt in the Convent of the Bleeding Heart of Mary. Upon their return, they found replies to both these missives, Dr. Pichon bidding them to visit on the following day—Tuesday—and Sor Maria-Perdita arranging for Rose to call on Friday afternoon.

In France it was still considered an amusing way to pass an afternoon, in some circles, to visit mad-wards and watch the antics of the lunatics, though this was no longer as fashionable as it had once been. Some of January's friends in Paris—writers and artists of the Gothic genre, mostly—claimed they did so out of a desire to "more deeply understand the human emotions through the dreams of madmen," though January suspected this argument as less than honest. As a medical student, he had visited the wards of Charenton and the Salpêtrière, and had found nothing either enlightening or amusing in the stink of excrement smeared on walls or voided into clothing, in the droning chatter of those chained figures in the shadowy cells, in the howls that echoed from the wards where the maniacs were confined.

Canst thou not minister to a mind diseased? Macbeth had asked, and two hundred and thirty-five years later, it seemed, no one was any closer to an answer.

The hospital administrator, a gravely elegant man who looked like a French marquis, greeted them in the entry-hall of what had formerly been the monastery of San Hipólito, and led them across the wide central garden. Men lay stretched on the grass beneath the pepper-trees, or walked about under their lacy shade. At one side of the cloister a man stood with his face to a pillar, his arms wrapped about it as high as he could reach. Another was spreading out children's clothes over the rim of the fountain, talking rapidly to himself, and stopping every few seconds to bend and drink deeply from the water. There were two other well-dressed couples in the garden who January guessed—by the European dresses of the women and the way they put their heads together, talking and pointing—were simply curious visitors, perhaps in quest of deeper understanding of human emotions.

"These in the garden are the privileged ones, you understand, the quiet ones," explained the administrator. "The furious are kept in the monks' old cells. . . ."

"BASTARDS!" a man's voice screamed. "Bastards, robbers, murderers . . . !" A man burst from the big door at the far side of the court, stark naked and swinging a three-legged stool like a weapon. He dashed straight for the outer gate, January and Rose springing to one side out of his path and the administrator to the other. "You can't make me! You can't make me . . . !"

Dr. Pichon and a burly attendant who reminded January strongly of Werther Bremer's bull pounded after the escapee, running him to earth near the man at the pillar, who buried his face against the stone and clung to it as if it were his sole hope of life.

"Hold him!" yelled Pichon as the attendant wrestled the naked patient on the ground—the patient struck at his attacker with the stool, shouting words seemingly at random: January caught "principles" and "justice, yes, we need—we can't make a world—yes, darkness—we can't—yes. . . ."

January caught the stool and wrenched it away—the man's strength was terrifying. The administrator seized the patient's thrashing legs and sat on them, and one of the visiting gentlemen ran up also to assist, while the two ladies clung to the remaining tourist and shrieked.

Around the garden the other "quiet" patients began to mill and shuffle, crowding away or running to look or simply dashing excitedly back and forth in the arcade.

"Get them out of here!" yelled Pichon as he dipped a bucket of water from the fountain, leaped up on the stool, and dumped the water over the heaving patient's chest and face. Water splashed everywhere. The gentleman visitor sprang back with a cry, and the leg he'd been holding down flew up and smacked January—now holding an arm—across the temple. "Another," Pichon gasped, thrusting the bucket at Rose, who obediently dipped it full from the fountain again. An attendant raced up with a second bucket, and for some minutes the mad-doctor stood on the stool, dumping bucket after bucket of water over his patient, while January, the administrator, and the first attendant all got as soaked as if they'd stood in a shower-bath.

"The rats," screamed the madman desperately, "the cats and the rats—rats chase the cats...!" Water poured into his mouth and January wondered that he didn't drown. He was probably halfway to it when the attendants dragged him, gasping, to his feet and into the nearest open cell. During the whole of the chase and the water-treatment the men confined around the cloister had howled, pounding on the doors of their cells. "Get the others inside," commanded the administrator to the dripping attendant at his side. "Señor, if you will excuse us...there is no danger, none whatsoever, but it is better if these quiet ones are taken away until the shouting is over."

"Of course." January was mentally charting the fastest route to the gate that led from the cloister back to the vestibule, or, at a pinch, looking for which open cell was the closest, into which he and Rose could dive in case of real trouble. The two visiting couples clung together in a corner of the garden, the women still shrieking, the young men gawking as if at a stage-fight in a melodrama. The man who'd been laying out the children's clothes had sunk down beside the fountain, weeping, and wept still more when the attendant wouldn't let him gather up all the little garments again and take them with him; he clutched what he could to his chest as he was herded toward the door of what had been the monastery refectory. The man at the pillar stubbornly refused to release his grip on it.

"I am trying to do my job and you all refuse to let me! Let me alone, let me do what I need to do...."

In the end they let him.

"Will you help me?" Pichon asked January. "You are Señor Enero the surgeon, as you said in your note? This man should be bled at once, before he regains his breath or his strength."

January followed Pichon to the cell. He was no great believer in bleeding but knew so little about illnesses of the mind that he was unwilling to argue what might be legitimate treatment. In any case, it would certainly quiet the madman down. The madman still lay on the stone floor of the cell where he'd been dumped, dripping and sobbing; January unbolted the door and held the man's arm while Pichon took a scalpel from his pocket, uncapped it, and, using the bucket from the fountain as a bleeding-bowl, drained close to a pint of blood from the man's arm. Even in the dim illumination that came from the judas-hole in the door, January could see the madman's arms both laddered with the half-healed cuts of similar operations. Under the straggling beard his face was young, gaunt, and twisted with terror.

He put up no fight as January and Pichon lifted him onto the bed—after losing that much blood he probably couldn't—and the doctor chained him to the wall by neck and feet. "I shall have the shackles taken off in a few hours if he remains calm," said Pichon as he carried the bloodied bucket from the cell and January bolted the door behind them. "In a little while I shall puke him—that seems to calm him. He is the son of a shoemaker in the barrio of San Pablo—he started cutting up animals as a boy, and last year viciously assaulted the child of a neighbor. He said voices coming out of the shoes in the shop told him to do so."

He shook his head, deeply troubled. "The administrators of this hospital would have it that he—and others like him—became this way because of their sins. When I came to work here they were still 'whipping the Devil out of them.' Barbarians."

In the cloister, a damp and rumpled Rose was still talking to the man at the pillar. "Since I have been here, the output of sugar has grown from one kingdom to three," the man was explaining. "And all because of my efforts—which these fools here don't understand."

"One day they will," Rose assured him quietly. "You may be sure of that. Here is my husband—I must go, sir. But thank you for explaining to me about the sugar, and the lightning in the air; I didn't know that before." She rejoined January and Pichon, touching January's soaked sleeve. "Do you feel saner and calmer after the water-treatment?"

"Much," January replied gravely, and Pichon looked at him with startled enquiry before realizing it was a joke. "Dr. Pichon, thank you for making the time to see us; we know you're busy here."

"Busy? God, what a jape! A hundred and two madmen and not a thing to do for any of them but keep them from hurting themselves and hope they get well. One feels a fraud."

Pichon shook his head, his hard, naturally disapproving mouth bracketed with lines of frustration and disgust. "Intemperance or love is mostly what brings them in here, but other men drink too much, love too much, and survive it. Why not these?" He sighed. "Well, my thanks to you for your help, Señor Enero, in any event. You said in your note you wished to know about Don Prospero de Castellón, I believe?"

January nodded. "I've been empowered by Sir Henry Ward of the British ministry to look into the events surrounding the death of Don Fernando." He made a move to take out the letter of introduction, but Pichon waved it away.

"Appalling." The mad-doctor grimaced. "Simply disgraceful. Is that fiddler of Don Prospero's still walking around free?"

"If you can call being held prisoner at Mictlán *free*," said January. "When did Don Fernando first speak to you about his father?"

Pichon considered for a moment, mustache and eyebrows both bristling with the pursing-up of his face. "March," he said at last. "After arriving in this country two months earlier."

In the cloister around them, the imprisoned maniacs were gradually quieting. They were hampered in this by the two young gentlemen and their lady-friends, who went from door to door, peering in—one of the young men put the end of his cane through the judas-hole and then jerked it back again as if something had grabbed at it inside. All four laughed, the ladies holding perfumed handkerchiefs to their noses.

"Don Fernando said he wished to establish a permanent conservatorship over his father's property, which he feared his father would dissipate in what he termed 'freakish fits.' He and Don Anastasio de Saragosse were able to provide me with considerable evidence about the worsening of Don Prospero's condition, even before this latest attack on September fourth. Don Prospero's pattern was one of extreme

172 — Barbara Hambly

excitation of the nervous tissue, followed by prostration and a return to lucidity. In this case, the excitation continued rather than collapsed. When my colleague Dr. Laveuve and I were there, the patient had not slept in three nights, and was completely incoherent. Neither cold baths, nor bleeding, nor blistering seemed to have much effect, and there was . . . a division of opinion concerning restraint."

"Between yourself and Dr. Laveuve?"

"Between myself and that ruffian who commands Don Prospero's vaqueros," responded the doctor with asperity. "This man—Vasco is his name—seemed to regard de Castellón's ravings as perfectly natural and said that if his master were restrained he, Vasco, would be forced to put us from the property. The matter very nearly came to blows with young de Castellón, and only the intervention of Don Anastasio prevented violence."

"But Don Prospero was eventually locked up?"

"For his own protection," said Pichon. "And for that of certain members of the household. I hope that I am a good son of the Church, Señor, but when that uneducated imbecile Padre Ramiro attempted to exorcise Don Prospero . . ." His breath blew out in an exasperated hiss. "Don Prospero was locked up but not restrained. Bolts were put on the outsides of all three doors leading into his room. The young Señorita Natividad especially was troubled about being in the room next to his, and requested that her room be moved. Don Fernando seemed to think this cowardly. Perhaps he was right. . . ." Pichon shook his head again. "But in the end, nothing came of it, for her mother—horrid woman—insisted that she remain where she was."

January's glance crossed Rose's, remembering the attempt to sneak a priest in to perform a hasty marriage. "And Don Fernando had the keys of all three padlocks?"

Pichon nodded. "He had the key to one of them—I believe the one on the door from the study into his father's room. I had the other two. When Don Fernando's body was taken down to the kitchen court to be washed, that scoundrel Vasco must have gotten the key, for while the body was being washed by the women, Don Prospero himself came down to the kitchen, with Vasco and some of his vaqueros, and demanded a drink of wine."

Pichon's mouth hardened again, and a bitter resignation flickered in his eyes. "After that, of course, we were simply told to leave. Vasco gave us the padlocks back when we rode out the following afternoon with Capitán Ylario. He said, 'These are your property, Señor,' and he grinned as he said it, as if his master had scored a triumph over us—which I suppose he had."

The quieter madmen gradually resumed their places under the trees where, it appeared, they spent most of the day. The man with the children's clothing returned to the fountain, still clutching his armload of little frocks and trousers, muttering and shaking his head. He refused to speak to the two visiting couples, who immediately went over to him and pressed him with questions, jests, and witty remarks. At last one of the young men said, "This is no fun. Let's go over to the women's ward at Holy Cross. I hear there's a girl there who's been in a hysterical trance for two years, ever since she was raped by a gang of muleteers. She relives her experiences over and over again. It's supposed to be extraordinary. . . ."

"It was you who pronounced Don Fernando dead?" January asked Pichon.

"I did, yes. He quite obviously died of some poison that induces suffocation. . . ."

"Would you have any idea what poison?"

Pichon frowned, then shook his head. "Some Indian poison, I assume. All the soft tissues of the throat were swollen closed, the tongue protruding and the face swollen and blue, most terrible to see. He was dead when we came into the room, and had been dead for, I would say, at least two hours."

"Would you be able to swear to that in court?" asked January. "Or testify to that effect to Capitán Ylario?"

Pichon's lips tightened again. "I could, for all the good that it would do for a man of Spanish birth—a hated *gatchupin*, a *greigo*—to testify to anything before that worshipper at the feet of his precious country. But of course I will testify."

"Dr. Pichon . . ." The attendant, still noticeably damp, came hurrying back up the path from seeing the tourists out.

Pichon nodded. "If you will excuse me . . ."

"One more question," said January. "And my thanks to you for taking the time to help us. How dangerous is Don Prospero?"

"How dangerous is any man in this country, Señor?" The mad-doctor shook his head. "Sometimes you will have a patient who goes for years peacefully minding his own business, like that one...." He nodded back toward the man at the pillar. "And then suddenly they change, no one knows why. Any man is dangerous to those around him, Señor. And particularly men who have power. We would all of us be safer if we each clung to our own pillar, and never exchanged a word with husbands, or presidents, or those who sit beside us silently drinking in the taverns, with knives stuck in their belts. I think Don Prospero is dangerous, myself. But it is not Don Prospero who killed his son."

FIFTEEN

"You might try driving through the gardens of the Alameda," suggested Consuela over a *comida* of kid stew and sweet tamales later that afternoon. "You would be sure to encounter either Natividad or her mother there, or if you drove along the Paseo de Bucareli or out along the canals. Those are the places where the fashionable ladies go, to see and to be seen."

She folded up a tortilla as neatly as if it were a love-letter, and scooped up beans with it; food as excellent, thought January, as any of M'sieu Guillenormand's French creations. "Though even if Señora Lorcha had somehow stolen the key to the padlock between Natividad's room and Don Prospero's, she would still need that of the lock between Don Prospero's room and the study, *and* would have to get into the study to unlock that door from that side. I do not see how it could have been done."

"I don't either." January made an impatient gesture, wanting to sweep the dishes from the table, to stride up and down the long room, to do something to relieve the anger and impotence and fear. "I'm grasping at straws, and I know they're only straws. But until Cristobál locates Werther Bremer, there isn't much I can do."

"Even straws can form up a trail that leads somewhere," added Rose, propping her spectacles with one forefinger. "I will drive out to the Alameda this afternoon and see if I can encounter Señora Lorcha: I suspect she would be more approachable by a woman unaccompanied than by us both, Ben. . . ."

"You mean she wouldn't want to be seen speaking in public with a black man—she barely glanced at me the whole evening at Mictlán, as if I'd go away if she didn't acknowledge me. But a quadroon woman could get away with it."

"You can always come along disguised as a footman," said Rose judiciously, and Consuela shook her head.

"It cannot be this afternoon. I have a performance tonight—*Cosi Fan Tutti,* if they can find a violinist who comes anywhere near Hannibal's skill . . . or any skill at all. Tomorrow evening . . ."

"I can take a hack to the Alameda, and walk when I get there," said Rose. "Because of the fence, there are no beggars to trouble me, and it looks quite unexceptionable."

"It is, but that is not the point! Only people who are nothing walk!"

"I will walk," said Rose firmly. "I haven't walked more than five feet since I came to this city, and I feel that if I don't get some exercise soon, you shall need to pour buckets of water over *me.* Benjamin, you can ride out to Tepeyac and pay your respects to the Virgin of Guadalupe, which I know you've wanted to do. Perhaps burning a candle there will be of some assistance, and in any case I think you'll feel better."

So it was that he did ride out, three miles across the tree-lined old causeway over Lake Texcoco, and knelt among the scattering of village women in the cavernous shadows of the great basilica, contemplating the curious image on the cloak. And he did feel better, though if the Virgin had any answers to the puzzle, she did not vouchsafe them there. Returning in the near-darkness, he had a long and annoying wait at the customs barrier and was nearly bitten to death by mosquitoes; he dreamed about the Virgin that night as she was pictured on the cloak, a brown-skinned Indian girl.

But he did not see her, in his dream, among the ruins of the Temple of Tonanzin, where the Indian Juan Diego had seen her. Rather, he kept glimpsing her from the corner of his eye as he worked back at the night clinic of the Hôtel Dieu in Paris, where he had trained as a surgeon. The clinic was as he remembered it, with its stone floors slick and filthy with the black acid mud of Paris that everyone tracked in; with its smells of unwashed bodies and wounds too long untreated; with the yelling of drunkards and opium-fiends in delirium and the hysterical sobbing of a young blond woman cradling a dead toddler in her arms. And as he bandaged knife-wounds and cleaned the gashes left by broken bottles, as he washed the bruises of whores or housewives beaten by their men and tried to tell the police that just because a poor woman's child had died didn't mean she'd murdered it, he kept seeing her out of the corner of his eye: that smiling brown Indian face, the shadowy blue of her cloak, the fugitive sparkle of stars in the air around her night-black hair.

Dr. Jean-Clair Laveuve, when they visited him the next morning—Wednesday—in his small and very comfortably furnished private asylum in the palace of a bankrupt and dispossessed Count, gave them substantially the same story they'd already heard from Pichon. "Franz de Castellón sought my advice about his father within months of returning to Mexico," he told them, one pale-blue eye blinking huge behind his monocle. "At first Don Anastasio was opposed to the restraint of his good friend—naturally enough—but upon looking at the situation with fresh eyes, he came to agree, something one does not always find in those who have made up their minds."

As he spoke, he threaded a large needle with heavy white silk. January and Rose had been escorted to the mad-doctor's workroom in what had been the drying-room of the house, a high-ceilinged, whitewashed chamber now fitted with shelves for medicines. In contrast to the combination of confinement and neglect meted out to the city's insane poor, Laveuve was a man who practiced all the newest methods being experimented on in France for the treatment of disordered nerves.

January read the labels: opium, calomel, cayenne, camphor, fish oil, beer, Indian hemp. A white porcelain head marked with the localities of traits—Causality, Ideality, Constructiveness, Foresight—gazed serenely at a rack where a row of brass clysters grinned like obscene teeth. On the wall a larger chart explained by means of a diagram that a woman's "region of virtue" lay in her breasts and her "region of insanity" around her pubis. "Self-esteem" appeared to be located in her right shoulder.

Through the door, in what had been the coal-room, January could see that a swing had been fitted up, the newest method of treatment—he had read about it in *Lancet*—for calming lunatics by constant, steady motion. The strait-jacketed man tied in it moaned and cried under his eyeless, buckled hood as an attendant pushed him, again and again, in a long, dizzying arc.

The coal-room was also fitted with two "tranquilizing chairs." Better than the chains above each cot at San Hipólito, January supposed.

"And on the eighth of September, you locked Don Prospero into his room with padlocks on the bolts of all three doors?"

The Frenchman nodded, a square-headed, fair-haired man wearing, like Dr. Pichon, a long-tailed coat and trousers rather than the older styles affected by the Mexican grandees. "He had attempted to kill his daughter's confessor—who rather ill-advisedly sought to exorcise him. . . ."

"How?" asked Rose. "With a knife?"

"By stuffing his rosary beads down his throat. But between that, and his hallucinatory delusions . . ."

"Was that the first time," asked January, "that Don Prospero had attempted to kill a man? Or an animal?" he added, remembering the shoemaker's son in San Hipólito, and the rabbit's heart swimming in its dish of gore.

"Aside from shooting at visitors who annoy him?" Dr. Laveuve raised an eyebrow and poked the needle through his sleeve to keep track of it as he began to mix bromide and opium into a sedative draft. "Personally, I suspect the—er—pot-shots are sometimes entirely for effect: Don Prospero is a most astonishingly accurate marksman when he has a mind to be. And mind you, there are any number of other gentlemen in this country—warranted by their relations as quite sane—in whose presence I would not care to be were they armed."

An attendant—a burly man with an Indian's impassive face—led a patient in, a horribly gaunt young woman whose shaved head showed bandages under the linen cap she wore. Laveuve switched to Spanish and asked her gently, "How are you today, Doña Francisca?" and she began to weep, tears flowing soundlessly down a face marked with old scabs as if it had been repeatedly raked with her own nails. The attendant helped her sit, as carefully and lovingly as if she'd been his own daughter, and held the opium draft for her to drink. Then he held her head between his hands while Laveuve took the needle out of his sleeve and pinched up the skin at the back of the girl's neck, piercing the needle clean through the flesh. Her nape was dotted with little sets of twin punctures from previous procedures. Laveuve arranged a towel across the girl's shoulders with the needle and trailing thread hanging down on it.

"It drains the excess liquids from the nervous system, reducing the excitation of the fibers," explained the doctor. "Is that all right, Doña Francisca?" He patted her shoulder. She continued to weep without a sound. The attendant laid one huge hand on her strait-jacketed wrist, and murmured encouragement to her in a voice too low for others to hear.

"Did Don Damiano ever speak to you about his father when he was alive?"

"Once," LaVeuve answered. "Just after I opened my sanatorium here. That was back in 'twenty-five, when things looked—well, different than they do now, politically. Nothing ever came of it, though. Don Damiano was too cowed by his father and too habituated to the situation at the hacienda to pursue the matter seriously. He traveled a great deal, Don Damiano, and spent much of his time at Don Prospero's other haciendas, in Jalapa and the low country near Vera Cruz, and in Catorce, where Don Prospero has mines. Of course Don Prospero demanded that the boy Luis be left at Mictlán. It was only chance that Luis was with his father in Vera Cruz the summer before last when yellow fever broke out in the town."

The doctor shrugged, and walked with them to the workroom door, which opened onto what had been the main courtyard. An elderly man sat there reading in the shade of a cypress-tree beside the small stone fountain; another was planting seedlings in one of the several big terracotta jars of earth along the sunny southern arcade.

"It was Don Anastasio de Saragosse who brought Don Damiano here, as a matter of fact," Laveuve said. "But in those days he was mostly concerned about how to deal with his friend rather than whether or not he should be restrained. There was no talk whatsoever of restraint. And though Don Anastasio tells me now that Don Prospero has become worse in recent years—and indeed in recent months—personally, I can't say that I see much of a difference.

"Of course," he added, "by the time it was apparent that there *was* a problem with Don Prospero, Santa Anna had come to power and would not hear of his being restrained as a lunatic. Possibly he suspected that Don Fernando would not be as forthcoming as his father in the matter of gambling-debts and loans. And the vaqueros, of course, find his behavior not in the least discomposing. Don Prospero pays them well—and keeps the Army recruiters away."

Glancing through the doors that led into what had been store-rooms, a wood room, and a room for making chocolate, January saw that they were furnished with cribs, coffin-like slatted boxes on legs. Again, he supposed, more humane than chains, but the thought of having a lid down that close over his face made his flesh creep.

"Is there any possibility," he asked bluntly, "that Don Prospero might have gotten free of his room before his son's death? Dr. Pichon said that the vaqueros let him out...."

Laveuve sighed and shook his head wearily as he removed his monocle to polish on a handkerchief. "God knows. Myself, I don't think he could have restrained himself from showing off his escape if Vasco had let him out beforehand. But I do not, as the lawyers say, know of my own knowledge that Vasco—or that dreadful Lorcha woman, with her marriage contracts and her drunken priest—didn't somehow obtain a key and unlock one of the doors in the hour or so after supper. I know only that after Don Fernando's death, and after Don Prospero was out, Vasco took the keys from poor Pichon at pistol-point; and I observed when I was there the other day that the bolts had been removed from the doors."

"What will happen," asked Rose, "should Don Prospero have another fit of madness?"

The mad-doctor shrugged, and bowed a little to her as the attendant on duty opened the courtyard's outer gate. "Nothing, I should imagine. If by some chance he should behave so outrageously as to force the issue, I believe that the old man's only surviving grandson, Casimiro Fuentes, would have legal conservatorship under the guardianship of his mother. But personally," he sighed as Consuela's carriage pulled forward from where it had been causing a traffic impedance for the past half-hour in the Paseo de Bucareli, "I cannot imagine what it would take to overcome the President's fondness for a man who finds mistresses for him and obliges with money on demand."

That afternoon, when siesta was done, Consuela outfitted January in the largest obtainable footman's livery—in which he could barely move—a powdered white wig, and spectacles. "Now, whatever you do, don't get down from the box," she instructed. No worry there, January reflected, his breeches would no doubt come apart at the seams if he tried to so much as bend forward. "The seat is high, so that Señora Lorcha will see only that there is a black footman, and not that you are tall, which I think is what most people see of you even if they do not look at your face. Juan," she added to the little coachman, "when the carriage stops, you give the reins to Señor Enero and help the Señora in or out."

The coachman looked deeply offended but made no argument, and in any case there was no call for such a diminution of his status that day. The low-slung red-lacquered barouche, drawn by its peacocky chestnuts, promenaded along the Paseo de Bucareli until lamplight softened the gathering cobalt gloom of the evening, jostling for wheel-space with what appeared to be every other volante and carretela in Mexico, without obtaining sight of either Señora Lorcha or her daughter. January felt close to despair. It was already Wednesday evening: Santa Anna was due to depart for his hacienda in Vera Cruz on Saturday, after Sir Henry Ward's reception Friday night, and there was still no word from Cristóbal about Werther Bremer. January's only scrap of comfort lay in the fact that Rose, on her promenade of the Alameda the day before, had encountered Lady Ward, the only other woman there on foot.

The two women had immediately recognized each other as kindred spirits—sharing views concerning the education of women—and as a result, Rose and January had been invited to Friday's reception.

"So we'll have a chance to speak to Natividad then, if nothing else," said Rose once the carriage had returned to the Calle Jaral and January was gingerly dismounting the box. "And possibly to suborn one of Anthony Butler's slaves for information, if he should happen to bring one along. I asked Lady Ward and she says there are three of them, the tall footman we saw, Butler's valet, and a female cook, she thinks. She spoke of them as slaves but doesn't actually know what their legal status would be back in South Carolina."

"I wonder if my time wouldn't be better spent trying to speak to the cook while everyone in Butler's household is at the reception," said January, easing himself out of the too-tight crimson coat. "If Cristóbal hasn't located Werther by that time I may have to. But how I'll get into a walled town house after dark..."

"...is something to be thought of Friday, not today," said Rose. "As Don Quixote said: *Patience, and shuffle the cards.*"

The following morning—Thursday—they searched—without success—through the enormous dim-lit chambers of the Monte de Piedad—the government pawnshop across the plaza from the Cathedral—for Fernando de Castellón's green-and-white Meissen tea-set, and in the late afternoon set out on a promenade again. This time they rode along the Paseo de la Viga, which stretched for miles south of the city, through the marshy verges of what had been the southern end of Lake Texcoco. A tree-lined canal connected the city's markets with the freshwater lakes of Xochimilco and Chalco beyond, and the road that ran along it to the little towns of Iztapalapa and Coyoacan was nearly as crowded as the Alameda or the Paseo de Bucareli.

And it was there that they saw, sipping pulque and nibbling peanuts at one of the makeshift tables set up along the canal's verge, the squat, black-clad figure of Señora Lorcha.

"Girls have no gratitude anymore," sighed Señora Lorcha as Juan—with a perfectly stony expression—helped her into the barouche. "After all I did for my Natividad, all my efforts...Since our return to town a week ago I have seen nothing of her, nothing! Not a word, not a note..."

Not a medio, added January silently, perched on the box beside Juan in his ill-fitting crimson uniform. He was certain that Rose was choking not to say the same words.

"I have walked here along the Paseo, her favorite place in all the world, in the hope of catching a glimpse of her! Of my own daughter! And I so depend upon my child...!"

Her voice cracked with grief. On the canal, flower-boats were returning from the city markets, the long, low canoes brilliant with left-over marigolds, poppies, blue and purple irises, and lilies of every color from blood to snow. Families of Indians poled them, men playing the guitar and singing; along the grassy verges, other canoes had tied up, and impromptu dances begun. Farther out on the lake, birds flew among the *chinampas,* the long islets of withes piled with dredged mud from the lake-bottom and planted with vegetable gardens, so that the open water was a sort of Venice of vegetation and canals.

"Isn't that just like men," exclaimed Rose, "to take a daughter from her mother and then to treat them both as if they were of no account!"

Had she wound up Señora Lorcha with a key, she could have received no better recital of that lady's grievances, anger, and version of the events of the eighth of September, interspersed with liberal personalities about Don Prospero, his son, his daughters, and his cook: "Nasty, finicking *fregón,* always fussing about his kitchen—as if a real man would know anything about cooking! And guarding every scrap of food after a meal as if it were the Sacred Host! And what Prospero pays him—fifteen hundred pesos a year, when he cannot spare a few coppers to keep his own son's *novia* from starving in a garret. . . ."

"Fifteen *hundred?*" repeated Rose, considerably startled. As well she should be shocked, thought January—provincial governors didn't make much more.

"Fifteen hundred," affirmed Señora Lorcha with bitter relish. "And whatever else he skimmed out of the bills he'd submit, for cheese imported from France and white flour, and imported French *mierda* belike to spread on his imported French raspberry bushes! If you ask me"—petticoats rustled and corsets creaked mightily as the Señora leaned closer to Rose—"if you ask me, that drunken fiddler wasn't the one who poisoned Fernando at all. It was that cook. He knew Fernando wouldn't pay him anything like that much once old Prospero was clapped up."

"Really?" Rose was laying it on with a trowel—she sounded enthralled. "But . . . but how could that *be?* Didn't everyone at dinner eat of the same food?"

Spite and satisfaction dripped from Señora Lorcha's voice—and delight, apparently, at Rose's expression of round-eyed awe. "Faugh! As if the cook of a house wouldn't know exactly which dishes each person favored, and which Valentina would turn up her pretty nose at, or Natividad, who's so dainty in her ways that she wouldn't eat more than a kitten. . . ."

An untruth—January had watched Natividad at dinner and she'd run a close second behind her mother in the shark-like heartiness of her feeding.

"There were thirty dishes on that table, and some took from one and some from another! Fernando was finicky as a lapdog, always complaining about this dish or that. After eight months, of course, the cook would know what he'd eat and what others wouldn't! But that imbecile Ylario wouldn't figure out that Cain killed Abel when they were the only two men in the entire world! *Policemen!*"

"I've often thought," said Rose in a conspiratorial voice, "that it would have served the lot of those puffed-up *ampulosos* right if you *had* brought about the marriage of Don Prospero and Natividad—which goodness knows both of you had every right to expect...."

"Expect? The dirty old goat *promised* marriage—and not with that son of his, either, who had as much use for a woman as an ape for a top-hat! And I would have brought it about, key or no key, doctors or no doctors who thought themselves so smart! I would have had the bolt off the wood of the door! But no, that ungrateful girl had to get cold feet, and sigh, and weep, and say she was afraid . . . afraid! Like she was afraid of Fernando as well, when I told her, 'What's a few licks?' I said. 'Every woman gets them from every man!'

"But that spying sneak of a valet caught me at it—listening at doors, he was!—and Fernando put me from the room . . . put me from the room as if I were a child! And had me watched. I told him, I'm not one of your soldiers, I said, and he only laughed at me: *You may thank God that you're not,* he said. *For you'd soon see what befalls those who disobey the master of this house.*"

Her voice thickened with anger and self-pity. "Called himself the master of the house, he did, as if his father were dead. Whoever poisoned him like the dog he was did no more than justice, and good riddance from the world."

Hacienda Mictlán
Wednesday, 27 October 1835

(Written in German—not read by Benjamin January until midnight Friday)

Amicus Meus,

For God's sake, get me out of this place before Friday evening. I'm sending this missive via Don Prospero's footman Bonifacio, enclosed in a love-letter to Consuela, and praying that Bonifacio will be sufficiently wing-footed as to deliver it before Sir Henry Ward's reception commences.

Valentina-like, I'm making preparations to escape on Friday, but the only way I can do so unnoticed is on foot, and I cannot get far without your help.

Don Prospero informs me that he's leaving Mictlán to attend the reception on that night. I very much fear that the moment our friend Capitán Ylario realizes Don P. is out of the way he'll hot-foot it out here to show Santa Anna that no Dictator can bite his thumb at the Principles of Universal Law while Francisco Ylario is around to defend them, so there. And it will horrify you to hear— it certainly horrifies me—that this is not the paramount reason behind my decision to fly.

Some very odd things are happening here.

Even odder than my host conversing with Quetzalcoatl in the sala *and drawing up a menu with the chef as to what Fernando would like when his spirit comes calling next Monday night, and rather more disquieting.*

As Cleopatra says to Anthony, all strange and terrible events are welcome, but comforts we despise—but one can have too much of that sort of thing.

Owing to a miscalculation of the kind one usually makes with one's finances—a too-greedy consumption of pages 143 through 304 of Les Liaisons Dangereuses *on Monday night—like the foolish virgin burning her lamp-oil I arrived at the accounts of Valmont's death, the Marquise de Merteuil's come-uppance, and the remaining two hours of my usual wakefulness at roughly two o'clock this morning. (I should know better than to commence reading with less than half an inch of pages in my right hand. Ah, mad love!* Da me basia mille, deinde centum. . . .)

It was in any case pitch-dark and deathly silent when I stepped out into the corredor—*the moon was down and even Don Prospero's jolly henchmen had sought their honest couches—and I crept along to the study, where I knew there to be a copy of Procopius's* Secret History, *always a reliable source of late-night entertainment. I admit that I crept, being in mortal terror of waking Don P. and becoming entangled in yet another orgy of specula-*

tion concerning Helen of Troy. (We had engaged in this activity for some hours earlier in the evening. It had, I admit, enabled me to well and truly fleece my host at picquet while his mind dwelt with indignation on the marital relations of the King and Queen of Sparta, but while I yield to none in my belief that one-third of all human wisdom can be found in Homer, still there are limits to what flesh and blood will bear.)

Upon reaching the study, I found to my surprise that the door stood open, though I could perceive no light within. Stepping inside, I immediately smelled both candle-wax and hot metal, as if someone had only that moment extinguished—or covered and concealed—a lantern. Like a simpleton, I did not immediately return to my chamber, but instead reached in my pocket for a lucifer-match, at the same time calling out, "Who's there?"

The result of this—as you will have foreseen—was that before I could get the match to strike, I was assaulted from the side by someone who smote me over the head with the 1672 London edition of L'École des Filles, *seized me by the throat, knocked me into the wall with considerable violence, and then—I assume, I was too stunned to follow the exact sequence of events—absquatulated, as the Americans would say. I don't think I was actually unconscious, but the next moment there were candles, torches, servants, Don Prospero, and Valentina of all people—fully dressed including her corsets—crowding into the study and helping me to my feet.*

It was quite plain that the place had been ransacked. There were spaces on the shelves where books had been pulled off and stacked on the floor, and you could see bare wood on the desk where papers had been likewise treated. Don Prospero took from behind the desk one of the bull's-eye lanterns from the stables, still lit but with its slide closed. I told my story, and in spite of the fact that I can come up with no reason why I would have hurled myself against the wall and smashed myself over the head with the 1672 London edition of L'École des Filles, *I could see that he didn't believe me.*

He hadn't spoken to me one way or the other about my remaining here during his absence, but since last night he has conferred with Vasco and I don't like the way Vasco has been looking at me. I wouldn't put it past the two of them to lock me up, which will cer-

tainly make it easier for Ylario to find me when he arrives, as he inevitably will.

I really think it is time for me to depart. There is a ruined
curing-house some little distance from the village of Saragosse, Don
Anastasio's hacienda, which lies some miles to the west of Mictlán:
a remnant of agricultural experiments gone awry. I will leave
Mictlán as soon as Don Prospero departs, and make for that
curing-house on foot—there is, at least, water at the stream near-
by, and shelter. I beg of you, meet me there with horses on Friday
night. Whatever is going on here, I suspect that Don Prospero's departure will render the situation worse.

Mictlán is empty and hollow these days, and indescribably sinister. Playing picquet in the sala with no one present but Don
Prospero and, to judge by his occasional remarks, Tezcatlipoca, is
an eerily unpleasant experience, notwithstanding the money I took
off them both. Eerier still is retiring to bed, with all rooms empty
and silent now save for little Casimiro down at the other end of the
corredor and, presumably, Fernando's ghost.

Whatever else may be happening, I am not looking forward to
remaining here alone with Doña Josefa, the lovely Valentina, and
whoever that was in the study, searching for . . . what?

Another rabbit, perhaps?

Nor, however, do I relish the thought of being escorted back to
town by Ylario and his constables and facing the noose.

I can only trust that you've located Werther Bremer—or some
viable alternative candidate for the role of First Murderer. Failing
that, it's O for a horse with wings and a rapid retreat to either Vera
Cruz or Texas with all possible speed. I fear that Mictlán is becoming as unhealthy for me as it proved to be for the execrable
Fernando.

Hoping this finds you well—and soon.

Your friend,
Hannibal Sefton

January attended the opera Thursday night—*Il Pirata,* appallingly done—in a mood of deep disquiet. Señora Lorcha's speculations aside, Rose's conversation in the carriage that afternoon had served only to cut away more possibilities that there was an alternate explanation for Fernando de Castellón's death. Don Prospero had almost certainly been locked in his room. Despite the spiteful woman's allegations, January couldn't imagine a way in which the cook—no matter how much he stood to lose should Fernando indeed take over management of his father's estates—could have poisoned one diner out of twenty-four at table.

So he listened to the gossip around Cousin Tulio's faro-bank while the evil Elena flirted with colonels and tax-farmers and minor diplomats, and neither of them learned anything that they didn't already know—at least not anything that concerned Don Prospero de Castellón and his immediate family. Don Rafael expounded on the proper theoretical means of playing écarté and lost nearly a thousand dollars to Consuela in the process: January was beginning to understand how the diva could support the flat, a carriage, a half-dozen servants, and Doña Gertrudis, not to speak of the indigent Hannibal. On-stage, the villainous Duke of Caldora flounced about, resplendent in the ever-faithful suit of Roman armor, for the benefit of Santa Anna, in the most expensive box, with Natividad Lorcha at his side. After the performance everyone repaired to Consuela's flat, and it was nearly three in the morning before the last guests departed, amid torchlight and servants and a clattering of carriages, handshaking, and laughter and jests.

Only when January was mounting the stairs from the courtyard did Cristóbal slip in quietly through the gate past the final departing carriage and emerge from the shadows to touch January's sleeve.

"I've found your boy," he said.

La Accordada prison stood, incongruously, on the fashionable Paseo de Bucareli, a tall building of red bricks with a long grilled niche in the front where corpses were laid out for identification by—and possibly the edification of—anyone who happened along. January had no problem getting in: a small contribution dropped onto the guardroom table, where half a dozen lancers in dirty uniforms were playing ombre, earned admittance and any number of respectful bows.

"The man I seek has offered me violence before this," said January in his loftiest Spanish, and handed another peso to the sergeant in charge. "I would appreciate it if one of your men would be on the lookout for trouble."

"Of course, Señor." The sergeant bowed. "Rios!"

Corporal Rios was winning and didn't look happy about leaving his place at the table. January slipped him another peso as a *douceur* once they were out of the sergeant's sight, knowing that officers frequently took a cut of bribes tendered to their men. Even in the guardroom the smell of filth was horrific, and flies buzzed everywhere above the blue drifts of tobacco smoke. As January followed Corporal Rios down a long stone-flagged gallery—trailed by the club-bearing Cristóbal—the stench grew, until by the time they stepped into the harsh sunlight of the main courtyard of the men's side of the prison, the stink was like a solid wall: dirt, rotting food-scraps, unwashed clothing and bodies, and mostly too few privies and far too many men who saw no reason not to relieve themselves in the corners of the yard.

"Most of the bad ones, the recruiters got last week," provided Rios helpfully, shouldering his rifle. "We got a couple in last night, from a big fight at the Wandering Jew. Some old *indio* started it, then slipped out the back, they say, when we showed up, so we just caught those who weren't clever enough to get away."

January glanced sidelong at Cristobál, who definitely had a black eye and a cut on one cheekbone, but the Yaqui merely gazed ahead of him in his customary silence.

The noise of shouting and curses burst on them as they stepped forth into the yard. Breakfast had just been put out—meaning baskets of tortillas prepared by the women prisoners on the other side of the high brick wall—and the men were clumped around them, shoving and thrusting one another and yelling. Most of the noise seemed to come because one man had been turned upon by the others: as January watched, the man was pushed from the food and stumbled a few steps on the filthy flagstones, turning back to curse the greater group.

"Schweine!" he screamed, lunging back at them again. *"Heiden! Schwartzen papistischen Wilden!"* He was tall enough and strong enough—like a young Teutonic god—to have easily taken on any of the aged and crippled *léperos* in single combat, but the men banded together, swarming over their opponent like rats and dragging him to the ground.

"That one, he been nothing but trouble." Rios shook his head and started forward. "He spit on this man or that, he don't show no respect—you don't got to know what kind of crazy language he speak to know he callin' you papist. . . ."

The prisoners saw Rios's uniform and scattered, leaving the blond man lying in the filth among the broken baskets. Bremer—January easily recognized the linen shirt, the buckskin breeches, though the valet had lost the boots he'd had on at the bullring—rolled over, shaking his head, blood trickling from a cut lip.

"Ich verlange . . ." began the young man furiously, catching sight of Rios, his finger jabbing at the retreating *léperos,* but he got no further. The next second he saw January, his eyes widened with shock, and he lunged at Rios—who by this time was within a foot or so of him—and tried to wrest his rifle from his shoulder.

Rios reacted far more quickly than his hangdog appearance would have led anyone to believe he could. He elbowed Bremer sharply, at the same time hooking his knee; Bremer tripped, fell, scrambling backwards, shouting *"Schwartzer Teufel! Räuber!",* his wide, scared eyes on

January's face. *"Meuchelmörder!"* He rolled to his feet and bolted, the other prisoners in the yard drifting aside to make way for him, watching with a kind of mocking indifference, calling out jocular advice.

Cristóbal and Corporal Rios spread out to either side of the fleeing youth as Bremer dove into the shadows of the arcade. January kept to the center of the yard, knowing there was nowhere else for the young man to go. He shouted "You won't be hurt!" in German, but Bremer was past listening; he crashed into one old man who was weaving hatbands out of horsehair and beads, tripped, and grappled with him for a moment, then came up with a small knife in his hand.

January yelled "Bremer!" again as the young man lunged straight at him, had just time to duck aside and catch the knife-hand in his own massive grip. Bremer was nearly January's height and very strong; he tried to wrench his arm away instead of switching the knife to his other hand, the way an experienced fighter would. January grabbed the other hand and Bremer kicked him, pulled his grip free, and stabbed, the small weapon tearing through January's sleeve as Rios and Cristóbal seized him from behind. Cristóbal smote Bremer down with astonishing strength; Rios struck him hard over the kidneys with the rifle-butt, and the young man screamed in pain. January held out his hand to stop another blow.

"I won't harm you, you donkey," January panted. "Who the hell do you think I am?"

The young man looked up at him, blue eyes filled with tears and with naïve shock at hearing himself addressed in his own tongue, as if he had assumed that no one in all the land would speak his language but himself.

"The bandit..."

"El Moro?" January remembered the dark face through the churning dust of the fight in the pass.

Werther swallowed hard, but some of the tension went out of his body. "I don't know what he was called." He wiped the blood from his chin. "He and his men tried to murder me in an alley—pursued me...."

El Moro or one of the men of color—slave or free—in Butler's employ. Like Señora Lorcha, Bremer hadn't looked further than a black man's skin.

January signed to Cristóbal to help Werther to his feet.

"Well, I'm not El Moro," he told the valet. "My name is Benjamin

January and I have been appointed by the British minister to look into the matter of your master's death."

"Thank God!" Bremer burst into tears and made to grasp his hands in thanks; Rios and Cristóbal pulled him suspiciously back. Though the entire conversation was taking place in German, a dozen of the loiterers in the yard moved closer to listen, the way cows will gather around an artist sketching in a pasture. January signed his myrmidons back, took Werther by the arm, and led him to the shade of the arcade again. This proved not to be a terribly good idea—the sheltered wall closer to the corner of the yard seemed to have been universally used as a privy—but it was the closest thing to privacy on hand.

"I had begun to think there were none in this godforsaken country to believe me!" Werther gulped, clutching again at January's arms. Close up, January saw that the man was barely twenty, the light down on his cheeks glittering like a white baby's hair. "No justice, no law, only dirty papist savages and weak excuses, and that vile old pander playing up to the President. . . ."

January's heart sank as the image of the murderous lover dissolved before the reality of an angry, terrified boy. No wonder Ylario's instinct was to take Werther's side, he thought. *I'd take it myself if the only other possibility wasn't Hannibal.*

He held up a stern finger. "But you must tell me the truth if I am to help you. I am a surgeon, so I know you lied about Don Fernando speaking to you before he died. As a soldier's servant, Bremer, you should know that no man grows cold within minutes of the breath leaving his body."

Werther sniffled, wiped his nose on his sleeve, and glared at him sulkily. "It doesn't change the fact that that degenerate fiddler poisoned him."

"Doesn't it? Could not the poison have been slipped into the tisane you brought him in an unguarded moment, after you left it there?"

"There was no unguarded moment!" protested the valet. "In that filthy household, with flies and insects everywhere? I locked the study door when I came into the room from the *corredor,* and you can be sure I watched from the pantry to make sure no servant would enter and break the dishes out of spite, or steal the spoons! I brought that set all the way from Potsdam! I lived in terror that it would be broken, for then what would I do? He could not endure to have things mis-matched, Fernando—my master."

"And you saw no one unknown, no stranger, near the house? No sign of an intruder?"

"No," insisted the young man.

"Did you go beyond the walls at all?"

"On that night of all nights, when my master needed me? Never!" Tears spilled from Bremer's eyes again. "There was no mysterious stranger, no outside evil-doer. It was Sefton who murdered my master! Does everyone in this country prostrate themselves before that dreadful old man's wishes?"

"What became of the tea-things afterwards?"

"I took them away and washed them, of course!" Werther appeared horrified at the implication that he would allow even his grief at his master's death to interfere with his duties.

"And when you left Mictlán?"

The valet sobbed in anguish, "I—I left them in my room! I didn't think—I should have thought! I know I should have remained there to look after all of Fernando's things. But Don Prospero was in such a rage that I'd touch a hair of that opium-sodden *Norte*'s head. . . . And I felt that I had to speak to the Capitán or die! He was the only one who . . . who understood what lay between my master and me! He spoke to me so kindly—that first morning, when he came upon me weeping in my room. He laid his hand upon my head—spoke to me of Goethe and Schiller, in the language that I understand. I know he understood! And then when I came to him here in town, and he did not believe me . . ."

"About your master's final words?"

"About the will, imbecile!" Werther flung up his hands. "He said there was no will, he found no will. . . ."

"Will?" January, his mind still trying to fit John Dillard into the picture, felt as if he'd stepped off a curb in the darkness, and into a bot-tomless ditch.

"Don Prospero's will!" Werther shouted at him so that Cristóbal and Corporal Rios moved forward again, and January signed them back. "Does not *anyone* believe me? Are you all ignoramuses? It was ly-ing on the desk in plain view! Poor Fernando was driven to distraction by it!"

"Did he tell you what was in it?"

"Of course he told me what was in it! How else would I know why that weakling beast wanted to murder Fernando? Over screwing that minx Valentina? Who would care about that?"

"What was in it?" January had the impression of having been suddenly blindfolded and whirled around. Ylario hadn't even mentioned a will, but he must have known. . . .

"It was the document of a madman!" cried Werther, pressing his palm to his forehead so that his fair hair spilled down over his fingers. "A hundred thousand pesos and a sugar hacienda in the *tierra caliente,* not to Sefton, you understand, but to those stupid idols, those images that were all over the room! But Sefton was to be their conservator, to look after them and take care of them. . . ."

"*What?*"

"What can you expect of that vile old man?" Werther's voice scaled up to almost a cry. "Who but a madman would stipulate that all his money was to be given not to his only son, but to that son's unborn child? Who but a lunatic would make his *chef* the heir to twenty thousand acres of prime cattle land and a hundred thousand pesos? Or grant thirty thousand pesos, and a thousand acres of land, to a papist convent, a *tomb,* that a half-mad harridan and her daughter might seal themselves into that corrupt sepulchre forever?"

Tears were running down his face again, and he was trembling, so that January offered him his silver flask of brandy, the mere smell of it bringing the little ring of inquisitive *léperos* closer. Werther drank gratefully and sniffled again, and January offered him his clean extra handkerchief as well—which Werther examined before he used, as if he suspected January of fobbing him off with soiled linen.

"Fifty thousand pesos and the town house to that Montero slut! *Herrgott!* My poor Fernando was tearing his hair out, trying to sort out this on top of all the other inanities: the hundreds of thousands of pesos spent on dirty old books, on Greek pots and statues of heathen gods; the mortgages and debts he bought up only to let his debtors go on living as pensioners, with their greedy, degenerate superstitious families! Had my master lived, he would have put all that right. He would have made Mictlán a paying proposition, have cleansed the house of musty books and heathen idols—yes, and leveled those foul pyramids for good building-stone as well!"

Personally January doubted this: it would take Pharaoh and all the children of Israel working under the lash to dismantle those five silent hills. The Conquistadores had certainly never managed it.

Passionately, Werther went on. "No decent country—no true law-court—would have supported such a pile of imbecilities! And then that wastrel musician, that laudanum-swilling tormentor of cat-gut..."

"And this will was on the desk the night Fernando died?"

"I tell you, yes!" Werther shrieked—January had never encountered someone who shrieked words like the lesser characters of Gothic novels were always doing. "It lay on the desk with the ledgers and the bills and the promissory notes and the deeds and all the other trash, under the eyes of those insane gods! No wonder my poor Fernando was driven distracted! What a cursed day that Fernando and I ever came to this awful land!"

As January handed him the silver flask again, he reflected that it was no wonder poor Señor dos Cerritos didn't want to discuss the will. Contemplation of such provisions probably made him want to shriek, too.

And with a hundred thousand pesos and a sugar hacienda at stake, he thought, his belly sinking with dread, it was no wonder Ylario had no doubt that it was Hannibal who'd poisoned his benefactor's son.

Damn it, he thought bitterly, *DAMN it...!*

"He never meant to come back to this country, you know." Werther wiped his nose and ran a weary hand over his face. His eyes were sunken and he looked like he hadn't slept or eaten in days. "He wanted to put it behind him, to make a new life for himself in a new world. I don't know if you understand."

"Yes," said January softly, thinking of the gray streets of Paris, and of men who addressed him as "vous" instead of "tu," like a child or a dog. "Yes, I understand."

"We were—he was so happy in Prussia. He despised his father, and used to tell the most dreadful tales of him to the other officers. I would hear as I waited on them, for naturally in those days he would not confide in a servant. Which is as it should be—he deserved better company than a servant. In those days he had his friends about him. Only when we were here, and he was alone... so alone."

His voice trembled, and he took one last drink and handed back the flask. "Herr Damiano managed the estates—it was only due to his care that my master's allowance came to him, and was not all spent on dirty statues and heathen books. When Damiano died, my master knew he must take over the management of things here himself, before all flew to the Devil."

"And you came with him?"

Werther drew himself up. "I have served Fernando de Castellón since I was fifteen. He was like a brother to me. More than a brother. No one understood him as I did, his moods, his needs, his greatness. Not his father, not Don Anastasio—that sterile scholar of weeds! Not that pinchbeck Napoleon Santa Anna, who would not so much as chide that monstrous old man for keeping his murderer alive about his household, only that he might have someone to play cards with! Not that cowardly whore von Winterfeldt, who thought only to get me out of the country, and not how to avenge my master. . . ."

January reflected wearily upon how everyone seemed to imagine that ministers to a foreign government had *carte blanche* to meddle at will—an impression apparently shared by some of those ministers themselves. What, he wondered, had Bremer imagined von Winterfeldt could have done to a British citizen without Santa Anna's approval and backing? Marched troops on Mictlán and besieged it?

"Yes, I lied. Fernando was dead when I came into the study at half past ten. Dead and cold. He must have died minutes after that *Scheisskerl* Sefton gave him the poisoned brandy. But I had to lie! No one was doing anything, not even Capitán Ylario, who of all men I thought must understand. 'I found no will,' he said, as if Sefton would not have stolen it when he murdered my master!"

His eyes filled with tears again, and he leaned against the crumbling stucco of the arcade, striking it with his forehead like the frantic patients of San Hipólito. "A pettifogger and a coward, like all the rest! A betrayer . . . My poor Fernando! Betrayed by everyone save I alone! By those lazy, thieving pagan servants at the town house, who turned me out! I don't doubt they were in league with that *Schwartzer* pig El Moro and the scum he commanded, and told them where to lie in wait for me in the alleys beside the town house, so that I dared not even claim my rights! Betrayed by those overdressed cowardly *Affenschwanzen* who were Fernando's fellow officers, who would not do a thing to avenge him—who would not even take me on!

"And all because I tried to stand by my friend. My poor Fernando trusted me and needed me. He had so much to bear. He was a brave man, Herr Januar, a noble man, and for that nobility alone they poisoned him, as everyone poisons and cheats and mocks the brave!"

His voice broke. Most of the other prisoners in the yard had returned to their own concerns, rolling cigarettos or smoking them, some of them weaving hatbands of horsehair and beads—for sale via the guards, presumably—or making baskets. But a few remained, watching Werther with open incomprehension and scorn; January was aware of the glint in their eyes as they attempted to figure out how this encounter might be turned to their own good.

From his own brief brushes with the law in New Orleans—his own stay or two in the New Orleans Cabildo—January knew there are always men who watch for their chance to prey on those who falter, who are confused or have no friends to watch their back.

And Werther, he guessed, didn't understand this.

Yet.

He had spent only the tail-end of one night in the prison yard.

"He was of the true nobility, Herr Januar. A Knight of the Holy Roman Empire, descended in pure blood from the days before it was split and decayed, when the true Spaniards and the true Germans stood as one and ruled over the whole of Europe under God. But he was born too late, into degenerate times. Only *I* understood this, understood him. He was good to me," the young man finished baldly. "Would you not do anything that you could, Herr Januar, to stand beside a friend?"

It has to be one of Butler's men, thought January as he walked with sinking heart along the stone passageway to the guardroom. What would a countryside bandit like El Moro be doing, lurking in wait in the alleys of the town to beat up wandering strangers? Not, he reminded himself, that he knew the local customs of Mexican banditry—perhaps it was usual to switch venues like that. But in three nights of listening to gossip at the card-tables, he'd heard complaints about *léperos* and burglars and house-breakers, but never about organized countryside gangs coming in to terrorize the streets.

And he'd heard El Moro's name mentioned several times, always as a highwayman who preyed on coaches and travelers outside the town.

But somehow he couldn't picture a black man, slave or free, giving orders to white Texians either, and Bremer had spoken of the black leader commanding men.

He turned back and glanced over his shoulder, where the shadows of the arcade framed the great glaring arch of the sunlit yard. Bleak and desperate in his heart, wondering what the hell he was going to do now. Try to insinuate himself into Butler's town house tonight? Werther Bremer hadn't seen anything of John Dillard, anything outside the walls at all. Try to force the truth out of Valentina by threatening to expose her lover?

God knew what counter-charge the girl would come up with.

The evidence is fairly damning, Hannibal had written. . . . Damning? It was irrefutable. And tomorrow Santa Anna would leave for Vera Cruz, and there would be no rescue the next time Ylario rode out to Mictlán. Hannibal would be lucky if he survived a night in the prison yard before being hustled onto the scaffold.

He could see Werther sitting with his back to one of the arcade pillars, his arms folded around his knees, looking fearfully around him.

Hungry, almost certainly. And perhaps beginning to suspect what would happen once the sun went down.

The temptation was strong simply to walk away. It would be days before Ylario heard his protégé was here. . . .

And Werther, January knew, wouldn't last days.

A voice in his mind whispered, *It would solve a lot of problems. . . .*

But there were things he knew that he could not do.

In the guardroom he dug in his pocket and handed the sergeant five pesos. "Would you see the German boy gets put in a cell by himself?" he said, knowing that such accommodation was available on the upper level of the arcade. "And see that he gets his share of the food. Capitán Ylario will be asking for him, and will want to find him safe and sound."

Forgive me, my friend, he thought as he walked down the stone carriageway to the street, his boots echoing in the shadowy vault. *But those of us who work for friendship's sake must help one another as best we can.*

"Well, it explains at any rate why Ylario was so certain of Hannibal's guilt." Rose dipped a rag swab into an infusion of the *tecomblate* that Zama had bought for them at the local *botica* and squeezed the astringent wash gently into the wound on January's arm. "But I'll take oath Hannibal knows nothing of the will."

"If it existed at all." January put a finger on the knot of bandage for Rose to tie. The cut was superficial and had all but closed by the time he'd returned to the Calle Jaral, but the lack of cleanliness prevailing in La Accordada made January willing to go through the pain of reopening and cleansing the flesh. "What Fernando found may have been only a draft drawn up by his father to force him into a marriage any sane man would draw back from. Don Prospero himself may have put it on the fire the minute the room was clear. God knows he'd never have heard the end of it if Doña Josefa learned about the thirty thousand pesos to the convent... presumably the Bleeding Heart of Mary."

"About which you can be sure I'll ask Sor Maria-Perdita this afternoon." Rose washed her hands in the second bowl of water on the windowsill of their chamber and tidied up the swabs. "Don Anastasio would know about the will, if anyone would, and he's certainly not mentioned it—will we see him at Sir Henry's tonight, do you think?"

"I doubt it. Anastasio has no great opinion of Santa Anna. But he'll be at the Chapel of the Bleeding Heart this afternoon when Pilar de Bujerio takes her vows."

"Will you write to Ylario about Werther?"

January nodded with a sigh. "I have to," he said. "He'll find out soon anyway. Werther's testimony about the will won't make much difference to a judge who's already made up his mind to put Hannibal on the gallows; at least now we know what we're up against. I'll send a note to von Winterfeldt also. Even if, as a Holsteiner, Bremer is no business of the King of Prussia's, von Winterfeldt may be able to do something for him. Certainly the guards at the prison won't know the difference between one German principality and another."

"And I somehow suspect," murmured Rose, "that one need not fear von Winterfeldt being overly scrupulous about the Principles of Universal Law."

Coming into the *sala* in search of notepaper, January found his hostess with a basket of marigolds on her arm, arranging the brilliant flowers in a series of terracotta pots on a little table set up in a niche at the far end of the room. Among them, carefully folded, lay an old reboso of faded black and gray; a necklace of red beads with a silver cross; a cheap rosary; a pair of brass earrings.

It reminded January a little of the altars his sister Olympe, and the other voodoo queens of New Orleans, would make to the gods of

Africa: images that spoke of their nature, and the things they were said to love, liquor and tobacco and flowers of certain colors.

But this was smaller, and not a place of the worship of spirits of power but of single memories reverently held: four clay toy bulls with the paint nearly all worn off them, a doll whose face had been nearly rubbed away but whose black-dyed sisal hair was neatly braided. A plate of coconut candies lay between two gourds of aguardiente, a double line of tidily-arranged cigarettos, a bowl of spiced peanuts, a plate of tiny skulls wrought of sugar and painted silver and gold.

"They like to be remembered," Consuela said, glancing back at January over her plump shoulder. "Mama and Teresa and Joselito. It's not like a big family *offrenda,* not like the one my father will have out at Mictlán, or Don Anastasio's at Saragosse, as big as a cathedral, for all the various branches of the Avila family going back three hundred years. But Mama would always have one for her mama—my Abuelita Tita—and her mama in turn, and all my aunts and uncles. When you have very little, it's important that you hold to what you have. And sometimes all you have is the memory of being loved, when there was nothing else."

In his dreams that afternoon, as he lay with Rose in the drowsy siesta dimness, January decorated his own family altar with flowers in his heart. On it he put his first wife's single gold earring that had belonged to her mother in the deserts of northern Africa, probably only a few hundred miles north of where his own father had been born. He arranged her thimbles and her needles, and the feather aigrettes she'd put in her hats, and on a plate put honey for the sweetness of her kisses, and fire—in his dream he saw it dancing in a little dish—for the love that had been between them, fire that had never gone out. Of his father he had nothing, yet in his dream the altar was crowded with the magic light of the songs he'd sung, and the gift of music that he'd passed on to January as a tiny child. The pressure of a big, reassuring hand on January's shoulder, telling the child he had been in those days of slavery and fear that everything would eventually be all right.

The memory of being loved.

From that beautiful altar he turned to the three-hundred-year-old altar of the de Castellóns, and he saw it strewn with trash and sprinkled with blood.

Half a piece of dry bread on a French china plate.

Natividad's bridal veil, and a green-and-white Meissen tea-cup with a rabbit's heart in it, floating in blood.

A tortilla-press with blood and hair on its edge.

And above all, the staring skeletal image of the God of the Dead.

SEVENTEEN

A bell clanged softly, the only sound within the dim-lit church. January crossed himself, and around him whispers swelled to a murmur like the rustle of wind through leaves. "It's absolutely barbaric," murmured a voice in his ear, and Don Anastasio slipped into the row beside him, far over to the side of the aisle but close to the immense grating of turned wood that divided the Church of the Bleeding Heart of Mary from floor to ceiling, like the bars of an American prison cell. "I'm surprised to see you here, Enero. You impressed me as a man of greater education than most of my relatives."

"I have learned never to have opinions about anyone's relatives," replied January in an undertone. "But I try to continue my own education wherever I find myself."

"An education indeed." The Don's thin mouth bent sourly under his neat black beard. "Where else can one look directly through a window into the fifteenth century?" He folded his hands as he spoke, though January observed that unlike most of the crowd who packed the church from the wooden grating to the outer doors, he carried neither rosary nor prayer-book. His black trousers and his close-fitting jacket of black linen were unrelieved by any touch of color—mourning for his brother-in-law Don Fernando?

Or for the young girl about to leave the world?

From the painted vaults of the ceiling hung a black curtain, a good thirty feet down to the floor. The floor itself was wrought of blocks of onyx, worn by the bare feet of penitents through the centuries. Despite a bound and bleeding St. Sebastian, a primitive-looking Virgin in a pink gown entirely covered with some of the largest pearls January had ever seen, and Stations of the Cross whose graphic gruesomeness would have made Goya queasy, the grating and the curtain gave the small church the air of a theater, as indeed, January supposed, it was. Those who knelt shoulder-to-shoulder with him, packing the cramped sanctuary to the doors, jostled and conversed much more like the audience at the opera than the witnesses of a solemn ceremony.

Don Anastasio went on. "As if this country has not better things to do with its young women—girls of intelligence and breeding like Pilar, girls whose family could afford to give them decent educations—than to convince them from the time they're able to walk that God wants them immured in prison to waste the rest of their lives in self-torture and grief. At least in India they give women the chance to bear and educate children before they burn them to death."

January said nothing. Having come early, he had secured a place not far from the grating that separated the public portion of the convent church from that reserved for the nuns. He wondered how Rose was faring, and whether Sor Perdita would cut short their conversation to participate in this ceremony. A few rows ahead of him he could see the de Bujerio family, lacking only Doña Imelda: among that swarm of unmarried and presumably dowerless female cousins, second-cousins, sisters, aunts, and great-aunts he recognized Doña Isabella, decked out in what Rose irreverently referred to as "Mexican mourning," a black gown of extremely opulent fabric and cut worn with a parure of diamonds. Beside her knelt Doña Josefa, veiled and unadorned, her emaciated hands folded. There was no sign of the girl Paloma, or of Casimiro. Did Don Prospero ever permit them to leave Mictlán?

A muted stirring just this side of the grille drew January's attention. A dozen musicians filed in—guitars, cornets, violins, a bass-fiddle, and two clarionettes, like the orchestra for a dance. The organ in the rear of the church groaned out a sonorous note, and from the small square outside, January heard the crackle of rockets being set off into the afternoon sky. At the same moment the band burst into lively music—the Overture from *The Barber of Seville*, which made January wonder if the person who'd chosen it had ever seen the thoroughly irreverent opera.

From the narrow door that had admitted the musicians, Doña Imelda emerged, gorgeously gowned in sea-green and gold and literally flashing with jewels. She took her place among her relatives and the music ceased, and with a faint squeaking of pulleys, the black curtain behind the grating lifted, for all the world, thought January, like the opening act of an opera....

In spite of himself, he thought, *Yes, and the opera is Act Two of* Robert le Diable, *with the chorus of mad dancing nuns....*

Don Anastasio was right. Whatever one felt about the Church, there was something in the scene beyond the grating that struck him as slightly hysterical and infinitely tragic.

Candles blazed around the altar, the gold that plated every pillar, swag, and curlicue throwing back the soft waxlight in a thick, dusky glory that is unlike anything else in the world. Banners, drapings, tassels of crimson, burned like blood; painted statues of saints gestured, bled, and blessed. At a table to one side, the Bishop of Mexico City sat, gold and scarlet himself, stout and benevolent, flanked by attendant priests. And on the floor before the altar, stretched prostrate in robes of funereal black, lay the nuns of the Convent of the Bleeding Heart of Mary, faces pressed to the floor, hands stretched above their heads grasping thick candles of white beeswax whose faintly honeyed smell rose above the musky pungence of incense.

The nuns softly chanted, *"Veni, sponsa Christi, accipe coronam, quam tibi Dominus praeparavit in aeternum..."* to the girl who knelt among them, delicate and beautiful in her party-dress of pale-blue silk and lace, veiled beneath her crown of diamonds, her shield of gold and paint held like a bridal bouquet in her hands.

January glanced sidelong in time to see Doña Josefa throw back her own veil, and the expression on her face was almost shocking to see. Hungry, furious, eyes blazing with envy and rage as she silently mouthed the words of what might have been prayer.

"Adducentur regi virgines post eam...." The nuns rose, singing, then knelt again and touched their faces to the floor, their voices sweet and eerie in the painted vaults of the church. *"Proximae ejus afferentur tibi in laetitia...."*

A priest came forward and raised Pilar, and led her to the bishop. The curtain came down and the band played again, Mozart this time, gay German dances, and again the chatter rose, exactly like that during the opera's entr'acte. Don Anastasio looked as if he'd bitten into sour fruit, but he remained. It was true what Consuela had often said, that family was everything: one did one's duty no matter what one felt. When the curtain went up again, January thought, *Act Two—the wicked Elena is turning me into a heretic like herself*. . . . But his smile faded at the sight of the girl Pilar lying prostrate on the floor before the altar, dressed in black and covered with black sack-cloth: jewels gone, lace gone, crown gone, as if she were truly dead. The nuns knelt around her, singing: *"Me expectaverunt peccatores, ut perderent me: testimonia tua, Domine, intellexi . . ."*

The girl was raised, still fighting to keep a good face on the matter, but in her eyes January saw that she was beginning to realize just what her life would be, forever, until she died. She knelt to the bishop and kissed his ring, then moved from one dark-clad phantom to the next, embraced by each like a sister, as if with each embrace she was being drawn further into the world of the shades. The fatter of the two attendant priests elbowed his way through the nuns to the grating and delivered a sermon about how Pilar had "chosen the good part, which could not be taken away from them."

"Ass," whispered Don Anastasio savagely. Doña Imelda clasped her hands before her breast and cast her gaze ceilingward in an expression of joyous martyrdom, not even looking at her daughter. Doña Josefa's face was like iron, cheated bitterness in her eyes.

The girl came forward to the curtain, looking out into the church. The last people she would ever see who were not nuns, thought January.

Tears were running down her face.

The black curtain came down.

"Honestly!" Doña Josefa nearly spat the word as her sister and Don Rafael helped her to her feet. "That girl's ingratitude sickens me, Imelda! What I would do—what I *have* done already—to stand where she now stands. . . ."

The men were lighting their cigars the moment they got into the sacristy, where trestle tables were spread with *pandolce* and punch. "What's this I hear," January said as he and Anastasio edged through the press, "about Don Prospero leaving money to the Convent of the Bleeding Heart in his will?"

"*What?*" Anastasio stared, cigar forgotten in his hand. "What will? Where did you hear that?"

"From Ylario. He asked the other day if I knew anything about it."

"Where did he hear it? It's absurd." But the *hacendado* looked deeply shocked, and glanced around them at the crowd that pressed toward the refreshments. Liveried servants dippered flavored pulque into cups.

"*Ylario* told you? Surely it wasn't in the papers on the study desk? I looked, to make certain there was nothing there that harridan La Lorcha could use...."

"He wouldn't say where he'd heard it. It didn't sound as if he'd seen it for himself."

"Good Lord, I should hope not!" Don Anastasio stepped to the nearest candle to light his cigar. "If it exists, it'll play hell with the will he wrote a year ago, after Damiano died. Though, of course, now that Fernando is dead... But leave money to the convent? That's insane...." Then he seemed to hear his own words, and laughed ruefully. "So in fact it may be true after all. But if that's the case, why...?"

"'Stasio, *mi corazón.*" Doña Isabella appeared, fanning herself with what looked like a half-acre of stiffened black lace and extending a fragile mitted hand. "You simply *must* find me a chair in all this! I'm quite faint, and feel absolutely unable to breathe. Your sister has been *prosing* on about how *dreadful* her lot in life is until I promise you I see spots before my eyes!"

"*Mi corazón,* if you're seeing spots before your eyes, it's from the candy you've doubtless been eating...."

January slipped away from the sacristy with a sense of relief. He circled the convent church, observing as he did so the stones low down in the walls where the broken stucco showed carvings of Tlaloc with his huge ringed eyes and protruding tusks. The old Indian woman who minded the convent gate went inside at January's knock—through the iron-barred judas in the gate January could see a patio beyond, riotous with late roses, and the heavy doors of the convent itself.

A few moments later Rose appeared, dusting powdered sugar off her fingers. She handed a coin to the Indian woman—a servant, not a nun to judge by her dress, and the woman slipped it into her bosom—and stepped through the outer gate, which closed behind her with a clang. The church's bells were ringing as January walked her back along the narrow lane to the square. Fireworks cracked, showering glittering blossoms through the twilight sky.

"Did you ask Don Anastasio about the will?" she inquired as Juan brought the carriage up.

January nodded. "He'd never heard of it. There's evidently a will already in existence, written after Damiano died. Goodness knows what its terms are, but Anastasio made no comment about its sanity or insanity, so it must be fairly normal. I could think of no polite way to ask him further questions, but I will." He gazed worriedly up at the darkening sky, stitched with the brilliant red and white of fireworks.

"I talked to Sancho—he knows of no robbers here in town who are black. So Werther must have seen either Butler's men or El Moro, though God knows what El Moro would be doing playing sneak-thief in an alley. As I recall, Santa Anna asked Don Prospero to be at the reception tonight, and if he is there, we have to somehow convince Santa Anna to issue an order *in writing* officially remanding Hannibal to Don Prospero's custody. It's the only way I can think of to buy us more time."

"It may be," said Rose worriedly, "if it works. But aside from the issue of whether Ylario will respect such an order, it will infinitely complicate any effort of ours to get him away. Was Josefa at the church?"

"In the front row. With an expression on her face of the most devouring fury that Pilar was where she, Josefa, longed to be."

"Mmmn." Rose did not look surprised. "Sor Perdita spoke of the hatred in Josefa's letters, envy so deep that she expressed not even gladness for the girl's sake. She wrote to Sor Perdita nearly every day, you know—including a most condescending description of my morning in the chapel with her: *I feel that worldly and frivolous as she is, my example helped show this woman some glimmering of God's light. . . .*"

"*Worldly and frivolous?* Are you sure she spoke of you and not your evil twin sister, Elena?"

"One wonders indeed." Rose's eyebrows drew together as the carriage jolted over the rutted pavement of the Calle Tacuba. "I don't understand religious people very well," she said after a time. "And I've never comprehended the concept that God wants some people to tell other people how they ought to live. Having read history, I know very well that some people are quite willing to kill others over what they think God has told them is their right: to appoint priests and bishops, for instance, or whether to hang a cross or a crescent in certain old buildings in Palestine, or whether they should pray in Latin or German. But what Josefa herself would actually *do* . . . I don't know."

"Did Sor Perdita have an opinion about Josefa's sanity?"

"You mean about whether Josefa would actually kill her brother in order to gain a place in a convent? Not directly. But Sor Perdita—whom I never actually saw, by the way, our entire conversation was conducted through a barred window that was curtained on the other side—spoke with some concern about what she called Josefa's *immoderate enthusiasm* for the religious life. Coming from a woman who voluntarily sleeps without a blanket on a narrow plank with a one-inch stringer of wood nailed up the middle to keep her from getting too comfortable, this does not sound like sanity to me."

January said, "Hmmn."

"She did," added Rose, "offer to copy out and send to me Josefa's entire account of the wedding-feast and Fernando's murder, which Josefa said was willed by God: she read it to me and there isn't a thing in it that Josefa didn't say to me last Wednesday. She had reams of Josefa's complaints about her brother—only to be expected, Sor Perdita said, considering the way Fernando's mother disgraced herself when she was a novice in the selfsame convent."

"I'd forgotten that." Momentarily distracted from his speculation as to how to break into the American minister's house, January wondered if the conduct of Don Prospero's second wife while in Holy Orders had anything to do with his unwillingness to let his daughter enter them.

As the carriage turned into the courtyard of the old palace, Señora Garcia was already dishing up tortillas and beans for the local men. Rose and January glanced at each other. God knew when Consuela would be back from the festivities at the de Bujerio town house, or whether she'd given the servants the night off. In Rose's eyes January saw his own thought: Sir Henry Ward might invite them to his reception, but even if food was being served, there were almost certainly men there who would take exception to a black man eating it from the same table as they. Even January's friend Lieutenant Shaw of the New Orleans City Guards would sit at an adjoining table when they had coffee in the market-stands by the levee.

"Have the carriage ready in an hour," said January to Cristóbal, who had ridden on the footman's perch. "And have bath-water in our room when we come up. Señora"—he turned to Señora Garcia—"what can you do for myself and my wife in the way of supper?"

•　　•　　•

"All right," he said to Rose over tortillas, beans, and some truly excellent stewed kid, "tell me how Maria-Exaltación de Borregos de Castellón managed to disgrace herself while in Holy Orders."

"She became pregnant," said Rose. "By one of the confessors, evidently. Sor Perdita concurs with the general consensus that she was an unconscionable flirt and extremely charming. She managed to attract Don Prospero's eye while in her delicate condition, no mean feat when coupled with a novice's veil."

"Sor Perdita told you all this?"

"Oh, after a long talk and a great many confidences exchanged. As headmistress of a girls' school—and I am one again, or will be as soon as we get back—I learned the right questions to ask and when to ask them. It's astonishing how much like a girls' school the atmosphere there feels, always supposing there are girls' schools in which it is considered appropriate for the pupils to starve themselves, wear spiked iron belts under their clothing, flog themselves so that the walls of their rooms are spattered in blood, and occasionally—as a special treat for their friends—strip to the waist in the dining-room at meals so that others may admire their suppurating sores."

"I don't wonder no one eats much." January poked his stew, suddenly less hungry.

"They take turns wearing an iron crown of thorns," said Rose, taking another spoonful of corn pudding. "I only hope they rinse it off between-times. It sounds like a most insanitary practice. Maria-Exaltación de Borregos was sent to Mexico by her family from Sevilla in 1803, at the age of fifteen. Given the conditions in Spain at the time, Mexico was considered safer for a young girl. She was fair and extremely pretty, with light-brown hair like Fernando's. I saw her portrait, done with her 'shield of God,' those painted circular things they carry. By the amount of lace, gold, and pearls on both the shield and the diadem she's wearing in the picture, there was no want of money in the de Borregos family."

"At five thousand pesos to enter the convent," remarked January, "there mustn't have been."

"As you say. She was fragile and rather sickly, but that was considered 'interestingly delicate' in those days—I don't imagine a steady diet of dry bread and water rendered her any more robust. She had no trouble turning every head she encountered. The priest by whom she was suspected to have conceived was sent away, and she bore the baby—a boy called Orlando—in the convent. Evidently there was discussion about whether to send her and her child back to Sevilla, but with fighting going on all over the high seas then, it wasn't considered safe."

"It wasn't considered safe eight years later," said January, "when I was trying to get trained as a surgeon and the best I could do was study with a M'sieu Gomez in New Orleans. Not that he wasn't an excellent teacher," he added, remembering the dapper, sardonic quadroon who'd guided his initial studies in the miracles of human bones, nerves, and flesh. "But there is only so much you can learn by observing and reading."

Rose, who had had her own struggles being educated, nodded, a small crease of bitterness tugging at the corner of her mouth. "By that time the brother who'd brought Maria-Exaltación over here had died, apparently only weeks after contracting marriage to the lady who is now Valentina's duenna. It would seem one keeps such ladies in the family, to provide for their support. And it was a moot point anyway, because several months before little Orlando's birth, the widowed Don Prospero saw Maria-Exaltación while on a visit to Sor Perdita, who is his cousin. He was captivated."

"I don't expect Sor Perdita was pleased."

"Well, she had nothing to say on that subject and said it at great length. But Don Prospero was no easier to deal with then than he is now. He made arrangements for little Orlando to be adopted by cousins on the other side of the family—Sor Perdita told me the boy died when he was thirteen or fourteen—and wed Maria-Exaltación in 1805."

"After which she continued to flirt," murmured January, "until her death in 1817, when Fernando was ten. At least I have Señor dos Cerritos's word that she continued to flirt, though in fact if she was of sickly constitution, I think it likelier that she died of food poisoning of some sort than that she had an affair with the cook and was murdered with a praline."

"Which are quite delicious as they make them here." Rose picked a fragment of one from the plate of *postres* Señora Garcia offered them, darker and more strongly flavored with muscavado, and embedded with peanuts instead of New Orleans pecans. "Sor Perdita and I had a long chat about food, of which there is plenty available in some convents: the servants brought me some truly excellent camote, though Sor Perdita said—as if it were a color that was not agreeable with her complexion—that she did not indulge."

January left a reale on the table to pay for the supper, and crossed the court hand in hand with Rose, uneasy tension winding tighter behind his breastbone. He wasn't certain that his wife could convince Santa Anna to sign anything—certainly Don Prospero would be less willing to deal with a woman. With Santa Anna gone, would Butler and his household remain in town? He remembered the way Santa Anna had regarded Hannibal, that casual interest, as if looking at the weaker of two dogs going into a dog-fight, knowing it would be torn to pieces and not caring. Remembered, too, the smell of rabbit's blood in the darkness, and the sinister glint of dead skulls' crystal eyes in the shadows of Don Prospero's study.

Santa Anna would leave for Vera Cruz in the morning. Before dawn, then—written order or no written order—he and Rose would have to depart for Mictlán. The thought of putting himself once more in the realm where that crazy white-haired despot was all-powerful made his hair prickle. He'd have to talk to Cristóbal about getting the horses packed....

Beneath the fast-running ice-stream of these thoughts, Rose's voice went on, light and inconsequential. "Sor Perdita said she didn't miss the delicacies of her former life; she complained that she is subject to devastating migraines when she drinks chocolate, which I can sympathize with—not that I can remotely imagine giving up chocolate. But my Aunt Francine on Grande Isle had migraines if she ate bread, although fortunately she could limit herself to rice and beans with no more inconvenience than the occasional stigma of eating like a peasant. Goodness knows how people manage if they have that sensitivity in France, or England, where corn and oats are fed only to horses. I suppose it's true, that one man's meat..."

January stopped in his tracks at the foot of the stairs, without warning back in his dream—back in the stinks and clamor of the night clinic of the Hôtel Dieu, binding the wounds, washing the bruises of the poorest of the Paris poor.

Feeling as if someone had tapped him on the shoulder.

A blond-haired woman weeping and sobbing with a dead child in her arms. The harsh-faced gendarme standing before him: *Of course she killed it, like she killed the one before...*

And the woman sobbing, *I did not! I did not! Oh, my poor little child.... O Blessed Virgin, help me...!*

Rose had stopped beside him, looking up at him questioningly, the cresset-flame from the courtyard reflected in her spectacles. And he said softly, "... is another man's poison."

She started to speak, then was quiet again. Running over in her mind fragments of conversation, of information about other things....

Slowly, they ascended the stairs and walked along the unlit *corredor* in silence to their room.

"I know some people are... are *sensitive*," Rose said as January opened the door. "To strawberries, or chocolate, or aubergines, for instance...." She shut the door behind her as January lit a match from the small store he carried in his pockets—they were unobtainable in Mexico City—and illuminated half a dozen candles. "And come to think of it, everyone always says that Doña Isabella is forever throwing out a rash, or having a migraine, or the vapors."

"And the vapors," said January, "is a sensation of choking, isn't it? Of not being able to get one's breath. It's often brought about by panic, or anxiety—usually exacerbated by tight-lacing. But in some cases it's brought on by something one ate."

"But could it... could it *kill* you?" Rose sounded incredulous. As the mistress of a girls' school, she had encountered too many cases of the vapors that had simply been an excuse for having one's own way.

"Oh, yes," said January. He shook out the match. An extra can of hot water, muffled in towels to keep it warm, waited on the windowsill; Rose's good green silk was laid out ready on the bed.

As he unlaced her, January went on. "During the six years I worked at the Hôtel Dieu in Paris, we had a woman come in twice... no, three times. Two of her children died—and the third almost did—from choking for no known cause, and at roughly the same age. The second time, I had to talk the police out of arresting her, and I think they would have had she not been so distraught, so clearly devastated. I feared for her sanity. Both the same, they turned blue and their faces and tongues swelled; what the poor woman went through from her neighbors whispering I don't even like to think.

"But after the third one, barely a toddler—who hadn't even been born when that eldest brother died, also a toddler—Madame Valory said that all three had eaten whelks just before their fits began. And in all three cases, since the children were so young, it was the first time that each child had eaten a whelk, or indeed any sort of shellfish. They lived out in Pigalle, far from the river. It was only when they grew old enough to walk down to the quais with their mother that they came into danger, and a sister who was born between the first two suffered no ill effects. The youngest child didn't have the same degree of sensitivity as the others did, and by slipping a tube down her windpipe I was able to keep her breathing until the attack passed and the swollen tissues relaxed."

He stood still by the end of the bed, cheek resting against the bedpost, looking at Rose, her stays loosened, her hair unpinned and lying over her shoulders. Seeing not her, but the shrieking, sobbing girl clinging to the other orderly at the clinic, and the swollen face of the terrified, convulsing child.

"I asked one of the senior doctors, Dr. Pelletier, about it later, at the clinic," he went on. "He said that some people do have these—these *morbid sensitivities,* he called them. Galen wrote about them in the second century A.D. Dr. Pelletier said he'd personally encountered cases in which a child was stung by a bee, and died of it, with much the same symptoms as my poor little whelk-eaters. Pelletier thought that most people in whom such sensitivities manifest must die as children, with no one knowing the cause."

"And Fernando didn't..."

"Obviously, because his father refuses to eat any of the foods native to Mexico," said January. "Then before he was old enough to go about on his own, he was sent to Germany—where he wouldn't encounter such things as chilis, or cactus, or peanuts, or deep-fried ant-paste tamales—whatever that is. He didn't know he had a sensitivity to such a morbid degree."

"Then his death was... was an *accident?*"

"That's what it sounds like." January stripped off his shirt and trousers, poured hot water into the basin. "There was something in one of M'sieu Guillenormand's dishes that everyone else at the table could—and did—eat with impunity, but that killed Fernando, as surely as arsenic or monkshood."

"Good heavens." Rose gazed for a time into the darkness beyond the candle-glow, appalled, bemused, and fascinated by the scientific puzzle. "And if poor Hannibal hadn't chosen that moment to try to speak to him I suppose he'd have been only one suspect of many. Though how we'd go about finding out what it was. . . ."

"It should be easy enough to find out," said January. "M'sieu Guillenormand knows every ingredient of every sauce like a father knows his children—always supposing the father isn't Don Prospero. What *I'm* worried about," he added, "is how the hell we're going to convince Capitán Ylario that this isn't just something I'm making up to get Hannibal's head out of the noose."

"My dear Herr Januar, I trust that your object in accepting Sir Henry's invitation tonight wasn't to try to actually *speak* to President Santa Anna." The Graf von Winterfeldt bowed profoundly to Rose, shook January's hand, and raised his quizzing-glass as he turned to survey the crowd in Sir Henry's *sala*—something the Prussian could do with almost as much ease as January could, being nearly January's six-foot-three-inch height. "Most of these poor fools will be lucky if they get near the Napoleon of the West before he departs to rest himself before descending upon the northlands in the character of the Hammer of the Texians."

"I'm afraid I must take my chances among them," said January quietly. "The matter is one of life or death."

"My dear sir, every one of these gentlemen here considers his problem one of life or death. I myself have been trying to speak to the man for months about the tariffs, as have my counterparts from Russia, Britain, and France. Everybody else just smuggles, and I can't imagine why the King doesn't simply give me bribe-money for the customs inspectors. It would make everything easier."

"Yes, but think how dreadful that would look in the account-books." Rose unfurled her fan: with her spectacles on and her hair in neat loops and braids, there were few who would identify her with the wicked Elena of Consuela's *tertulias*—except, possibly, the Prussian chargé d'affaires himself.

Von Winterfeldt laughed and said, "You probably have the right of the matter, Frau Januar; I cannot imagine Frederick Wilhelm permitting an entry to go to the Privy Council as 'bribes.'"

"He could simply list it as 'laundry,' I suppose. Or you could."

"I could at that," mused the minister. "The King would even probably approve the tripling of the laundry bills in the interests of cleanliness—I shall have to try."

Across the room voices rose, General Cós—Santa Anna's brother-in-law—bellowing at one of his subordinates over the punch-bowl. The assembly being largely diplomatic, there was less of an air of jumped-up vulgarity than there had been at Consuela's or even at the opera, but January recognized quite a number of the President's wealthier supporters—and most of his general staff—gathered around Cós in an atmosphere of expensive brandy. Capitán Ylario, rigid in his neat black coat, stood with a group of von Winterfeldt's younger aides: "I should go tell him about Werther Bremer," said January softly.

"That's kind of you," said Rose, and January shook his head.

"With luck he'll stay in town tomorrow to visit Bremer in prison, and we'll have a head start getting out to Mictlán."

On his way across the room he was stopped by Sir Henry Ward, asking news of his mission: "After trying to run interference between the Army and that meddling ass Butler—because God knows what will happen to British investments in this country if America comes in on the side of Texas—it's quite a relief to deal with a simple puzzle of how one man can be poisoned at a dinner from which everyone else walks safe away."

January smiled a little at the minister's jest. "I think I've arrived at an answer for that, sir, but I'd rather not say until I'm certain."

"Wise man. When you find out, though"—Ward leaned close and stage-whispered behind his hand—"let me know, because there are any number of people one meets in my business for whom one would not weep, if they did not survive the dessert course."

"I'm sure I have not the slightest idea to whom you refer, sir," replied January with mock gravity, and Ward sighed with equally exaggerated martyrdom.

"Just as well, my good sir, just as well."

"If you can arrange for me to have a few words with the President..."

"Well, I shall do what I can, of course," said Sir Henry doubtfully. "But the Generalissimo has a nasty habit of staying for half an hour and then disappearing—I understand there's a cock-fight of particular ferocity taking place somewhere in the barrio of San Pablo later tonight, so I don't hold out much hope of his remaining long. Still, I'll see what I can do...."

The minister passed on, to join his wife in talking to Rose, two of the very few women in the room whose dresses were not a decade out of date and plastered with jewels. The babble of voices reminded January of the white folks' parties he'd played at in New Orleans, French and Spanish striving over the gay strains of a small orchestra in the room beyond the *sala*.

Then a voice cut into his hearing in English: "I don't care if he's a Brit, it's a goddamn insult to ask white men to drink under the same roof as a nigger."

January turned his head sharply, to see, as he'd expected, a little cluster of men standing around Anthony Butler, like an island of black in the flamboyant colors of the rest of the assemblage. Butler didn't even look embarrassed, though he saw January over the heads of the crowd. The speaker—the same pig-headed, pale-eyed secretary who had taken January's card in to Butler a week ago—met January's glance with a kind of defiance: *You gonna make somethin' of it, boy?*

"Hale, you don't know what the hell you're talkin' about." John Dillard set down his punch-cup on the sideboard. "You step with me this way an' I'll introduce you to a man who fought under General Jackson at New Orleans—*against* the damn Brits. An' if you need a better reason to shake a true man's hand, you better tell me what it is."

Every line of Mr. Hale's body and face shouted *He's still a nigger*, but he followed Dillard through the crowd. "I'm pleased to make your acquaintance, sir," lied January in his most perfect English when they were introduced, and Hale bowed stiffly, shook his gloved hand, and lied back, "And I yours."

No "sir," of course, but one couldn't have everything. January even got a condescending handshake from Butler, and congratulations for having followed Old Hickory into battle, though, of course, Butler wasn't going to waste much time on a man who'd never be able to vote. January wondered if he'd brought his footman with him, and how he could find that out.

"Santa Anna's been dodgin' Butler like he owed him money," muttered Dillard, remaining at January's side when Hale and Butler's aides and secretaries had gone on their way. "Probably thought he was safe here tonight, Butler bein' the last person to drink champagne with the Brits, him havin' fought in 'twelve when they burned Washington City. You'd think Santa Anna would actually stick around and rule the damn country once he'd won the election, instead of disappearin' all the time.... What kind of a president is that? No wonder the country's bein' run like a back-alley crap-game. You see Old Hickory gettin' homesick and lightin' out for Nashville every couple weeks when the weather in Washington City don't suit him? Faugh!" The Tennessean shook his head. "But we'll get him this time. He's been dodgin' our petition about Texas since our boys whipped Cós's arse at Béxar—we'll make him at least *admit* we got a side in this, too."

"You think it'll do any good?"

Dillard glanced sidelong at him. "I think it'll at least show Old Hickory that we're not just a shipload of owl-hoots and filibusters come out from New Orleans to stir up what trouble we can so we can get some profit out of it."

"Andrew Jackson is a sick old man," January said bluntly. "And at the end of next year—or the end of next month if he takes a chill—he'll be succeeded by a slick little New York ward-boss who isn't going to risk his position among northeastern businessmen by starting a war with Mexico. He's not going to help you."

Dillard's chin came forward, and he drew breath to say something along the lines of *What the hell you know about it, nigger?* But by his eyes he knew January was speaking truth.

Quietly, he said, "Then we'll fight without his help."

"I know you will," said January just as softly. "Santa Anna has nearly thirty thousand men. Ill-fed, untrained, badly armed—but they're brave, and they're tough, and they've got a general who doesn't care how many of them die to win him his victory. Twenty-five hundred women and noncombatants were slaughtered in Zacatecas. It's not a situation I'd want to take my wife into. Are you married, Mr. Dillard?"

"Not yet," said Dillard. "Soon, I hope. And I hope—I know— Señorita... that is, the young lady... understands that there are things a man must fight for."

The music of the orchestra halted; there was a small commotion around the door. A footman's voice called out in French, "His Excellency President Antonio López de Santa Anna; Madame de Santa Anna; Don Prospero de Castellón!"

"De Castellón!" Dillard's eyebrows went up; his face altered and brightened and looked suddenly young, as he had in the *diligencia* when Rose had asked him about the land that was the home of his heart. "What the hell's he doin' here?" And looking sidelong at him, January saw that the light in his eyes had nothing to do with Anthony Butler at last getting the opportunity to present a petition of Texas grievances to the President of Mexico.

As von Winterfeldt had prophesied, every diplomat in the room promptly surged toward the splendid crimson-clothed figure in the doorway. It was like being caught in a rip-tide. January was separated from Dillard in a discreetly elbowing flood of ministers, secretaries, and chargés d'affaires all clamoring in politely modulated shouts for attention. January backed to the wall, knowing that the last thing Santa Anna would appreciate would be the sight of a large black man tossing diplomats aside by the scruffs of their velvet-collared necks to address him. He wondered how much Ward would remember of their conversation—like von Winterfeldt, the British minister had his own life-and-death questions of tariff and trade to fight for.

Santa Anna's plumed and gold-laced aides formed a flying wedge around the dictator, while the Napoleon of the West himself nodded gravely and extended a palm gloved in spotless white kid to shake this waving hand or that. As always, the dictator appeared unruffled, grave, philosophical, and a little sad, as if he were a martyr to reason and progress in a world of chaotic folly. Señora Santa Anna, a tall and skinny woman in an extremely fashionable blue satin gown (*The Josephine of the West?* January wondered), had already been enfolded in the coterie of diplomatic wives.

"Señor Enero!"

Startled, January turned to see the lovely Natividad emerge from the fringes of the press like a foam-borne Venus rising in a pungent aura of attar of roses.

He bowed low, even as his mind discarded the idea of asking for Natividad's help. With Santa Anna's wife present, there wasn't a chance she'd even be able to speak to the dictator—he wondered if she was going down to Vera Cruz with some appointed stand-in to take a furnished house near the President's hacienda, or whether she'd be passed along to someone else before departure. "Señorita."

"My mother tells me that your wife asked after me. That was so kind of her." Natividad spread her fan and raised velvety eyes to his. Frank, sweet eyes, without much intelligence but without malice, either. "I was sorry to depart from Mictlán without taking leave of you and your wife. She was so good to me. Not like . . . well, not like some of the other ladies there."

Given that Natividad's marriage to Don Prospero, had it materialized, would have resulted in Valentina's being repudiated as a bastard and Doña Imelda's losing her sole chance of marrying her son to the daughter of the man who was supporting her and her entire family, January could scarcely blame the other ladies for being cold. But looking down into that child-like face, he guessed that the scheme had been the mother's, and not Natividad's.

At a guess, Señora Lorcha would have been horrified to see her daughter speak to a black man where others could see her do so.

"I understand," January assured her. "And Señora Enero does, too. Of course, the President, with all the press of Army business, had to depart promptly, and it was only reasonable that you should not make him wait."

She beamed with relief at his understanding. She was clothed in opulent yellow silk—in what was clearly supposed to be the latest Paris mode—and her nearly-uncovered bosom was draped in enough diamonds to blind Argus. January remembered the Yucatán peasants, marching in sandals in their ragged cotton trousers, and wondered who had paid for the jewels.

Natividad glanced back at the group near the door—which seemed to be getting thicker, if anything—and said, "I feared that . . . that Don Prospero was very angry at me for leaving so . . . so abruptly. Did he speak of it?"

Still close beside the door, Prospero was smiling, shaking hands with profiteers, colonels, mine-owners, and men from the Army quartermaster's office, a startlingly dapper form in old-fashioned court-dress, gold-laced velvet coat, and white knee breeches of the kind that hadn't been seen since the days when the Bourbons had ruled Mexico. Yet the garments themselves were brand-new. There must be tailors somewhere in Mexico City still eager to turn out whatever sort of apparel Don Prospero considered appropriate. January guessed if he'd turned up in an Elizabethan doublet and trunk-hose, he'd have been welcomed as lavishly by those who sought to sell things to the Army of Operations.

Prospero seemed sane enough, and jovial. With luck he'd go along with January's request for a written order, and wouldn't object on the grounds that he wanted to wait and see what Fernando himself had to say about his own murder. Santa Anna was looking restlessly at the door—anything in the nature of a fuss or argument, January guessed, would be met with "Speak to me of this later...."

Natividad's soft voice continued behind him. "Mama tells me it's foolish, but...I hope Don Prospero's feelings were not hurt. Of course I know he was ready to...to have me marry his son...and Mama says that means he cannot truly have cared for me. Still, he was so kind to me, and I would not want to wound him."

Inwardly January shook his head at the thought of such concern for the feelings of a man who would blithely have condemned her to live under the same roof with the jealous Werther and the vindictive Fernando. There had to be some pagan goddess somewhere looking out for this child's affairs, for naturally no saint would have rescued her....

Or did the saints, too, petition for unspecified miracles from God under false headings like "laundry"?

Tactfully, he said, "It's difficult for me to tell what Don Prospero is actually thinking, Señorita. He is volatile, as you know, and he has...a bitterness about women that may misinterpret perfectly innocent actions."

Natividad heaved a long-suffering sigh that threatened every one of the few square inches of her bodice. "Don't I know it! Whoever that Helen was that he's always talking about..."

"Helen was a woman in a story," said Rose, joining them. "She, too, ran away from her husband, the way Don Prospero's third wife did from him." She followed Natividad's gaze to Santa Anna's wife, in her circle of ladies.

"Well, if Helen's husband was always going on about people in stories, or having conversations with gods or with the flowers in the vases, I'm not surprised she left him. Did you find who really killed Fernando? Or at least did you get poor Hannibal out of there and safely on a boat? Because I know he can't have killed Fernando. He wouldn't do such a terrible thing." Her brown eyes filled with tenderness, and January wondered exactly what her relations with Hannibal had been. He decided not to ask.

"In fact," said January, "there may be the possibility that Fernando's death was an accident. That's why it is imperative that I speak to President Santa Anna before he leaves tonight."

Her eyes and her mouth made a succession of perfectly round O's. "You mean someone gave him poison by mistake?"

"Something like that," January said. "I'm not sure yet. Was there anything—any sort of common food—that Fernando couldn't eat? That made him very sick?"

"Oh, *everything*!" The young woman rolled her expressive eyes. "He wouldn't eat aubergines because they gave him indigestion—the one time poor Señor Guillenormand served them, Fernando was up half the night moaning, with Werther running back and forth with cups of tisane and threatening to beat Señor Guillenormand, and Don Prospero saying he would shoot them if they as much as touched his cook. And strawberries gave him a rash. And if the sugar wasn't white enough—it had to be scraped off the very outside of the loaf—he would have the migraine. Myself, I couldn't imagine him leading soldiers anywhere where he couldn't have his own cook and Werther running after him with steam kettles and lavender water. Not like... well, not like the President, for instance."

She cast down her painted eyes shyly and January knew that whosever arm she'd come in on, it was with Santa Anna that she would leave.

"But had Fernando ever been really sick? Deathly sick?"

She frowned, puzzled, then nodded uncertainly. "Yannamaria told me when he was a little boy, before he went to Germany, he used to have choking fits when he got very angry, or sometimes for no reason at all. Is that what you mean? Once it was so severe, they were terrified that he'd die, and Isabella stayed up all night, praying for him. Poor little boy." She frowned, and toyed with her fan, her exquisite face looking suddenly very Indian in repose. "It isn't kind to say so, but I'm glad I don't have to marry him, no matter what Mama says about needing the money. And the President"—her eyes glowed softly as she spoke his title—"is very kind. Kinder than Don Prospero."

"I'm sure he is," agreed January, still watching the scrum around Santa Anna the way Juan the coachman watched the traffic on the Calle San Francisco, waiting for a momentary hole. "The night of Fernando's death, did he have any quarrel that you know about with Señorita Valentina? Or to your knowledge, did anyone see a stranger near the *casco,* an intruder?"

"No." Natividad shook her head, all the diamonds flashing in her hair. "Other than Valentina's lover, you mean? I don't think Fernando knew about him," she added, seeing January's startled expression. "Oh, please don't tell Prospero—Don Prospero," she corrected herself hastily, "or poor Don Rafael, or . . . or anyone. I think it was too bad of her to encourage Hannibal to write love-letters to her at the same time. She might have broken his heart!"

January privately reflected that a broken heart was not what Hannibal was likely to have gotten out of any relationship with Valentina, but held his peace. "Do you happen to know if anyone encountered this lover of hers that night? Werther, for instance?"

"Werther." The girl made a face. "He wouldn't have, because he sat the whole evening in Fernando's room, waiting for him. I know, because I could see him through the doorway from where I was sitting. I was cold and wanted to get my shawl out of my room, but I . . . I didn't want to walk past the door when Werther was looking out. He . . . he was so mean sometimes."

January wondered whether it would comfort her to know that Werther had been paid—at least a little bit—for some of his meanness.

"Señor Enero?"

January turned, to see Sancho signaling to him from in back of the crowd around the door.

He bowed over Natividad's hand, then made his way, with some difficulty, to where the footman stood. "This came for you this afternoon."

Sancho held out a single sheet of paper, folded neatly into a letter and sealed. January recognized Hannibal's writing.

"This afternoon? I was there two hours ago."

"It was enclosed in a letter for the Señora Montero," said the man apologetically. He contrived, even in his best crimson livery with ruffles at his chin, to look a little feral, like a bandit in a not-very-convincing disguise. "The Señora did not return from the de Bujerios' until an hour ago. She said it was important...."

The seals were cracked. Of course Consuela had read it. But standing beside the sconces on the landing to peruse the enclosed tale of escape attempts, assault, and strange intruders in the night, January hoped that even as he read, she was organizing horses and saddles for a fast ride to Mictlán. "Thank you," he said, and handed Sancho a coin. "Please ask Juan to bring the carriage around."

No hope in getting to Santa Anna, not without violating every canon of the etiquette by which these people lived, and the hour or so of maneuvering that it would take might cost Hannibal his success in getting clear of Mictlán. With luck they'd arrive at the Saragosse ruins before the vaqueros ran him to earth, and be able to get him clear of the place before Don Prospero's return.

He swam through the crowd again toward Rose and Natividad. He glimpsed Don Prospero as he passed: the *hacendado* was still standing beside Santa Anna, but with everyone crowding around the Generalissimo trying to get his attention, no one was paying particular heed to the old man. There was a discontented glint in his eye, a restless anger in the way he looked about him, and January remembered Consuela saying, *God forbid the bride should have more attention paid to her on her wedding-eve than he....*

Natividad's slim waist was now encircled by the green satin arm of the young Major Cuchero. Momentarily abandoned, Rose was looking around the room as if searching for someone. When January came up beside her, she looked up at him and said softly, "Ylario's left."

"Damn. When?"

"I don't know. I was just thinking, that as long as Don Prospero is here in town for the night, tonight and tomorrow might be an ideal time—"

"—to get Hannibal out of there." January handed her Hannibal's letter. "If Ylario gets him now, he's a dead man—I'm not sure Don Prospero would bother to come into town after him if it would involve sitting in the customshouse line to get through the gate. I've sent for the horses; we can—"

"You are a scoundrel, sir!" bellowed the harsh voice of Mr. Hale over an explosion of uproar around Santa Anna and his entourage. "A liar and a rogue! We are not Mexicans, but Texians!"

"By your oaths you are citizens of Mexico!" returned Santa Anna above an almost indescribable din of shouting in Spanish, French, English, and Italian. "And as such you are traitors and spies! Arrest them!"

"You have no right...!" shouted Butler, striding toward the President at the same moment that Hale yelled, "You dare call me *traitor*!" And he lunged at Santa Anna's throat. Dillard and Butler grabbed Hale's arms as Santa Anna's aides closed in around them—the President's hand went to the ceremonial sword at his side, and for a moment January thought he was going to go after the men himself. January grabbed Rose by the wrist and tried to thrust his way past the whole boiling mess to the door, but at that moment Don Prospero—who had bowed to Natividad when first he'd come into the room—now caught sight of her and the handsome Cuchero and reacted as if he had just seen her for the first time.

"Whore!" he screeched, wrenching the sword from the President's hand. "Trojan hussy! Traitoress!" He threw himself at the young woman, who—precipitately abandoned by her escort—dodged behind January, clinging to his coat and screaming while the bodyguards shoved and struggled to follow the retreating Texians. "I have witnessed your harlotries, Tlazolteotl—I, the Jaguar-God, the avenger!"

January caught Don Prospero's wrist, and though his own strength was tremendous, the madman's made nothing of it; it was, for an instant, terrifyingly reminiscent of the shrieking young lunatic at San Hipólito. The old man was howling "The Jaguar-God will be avenged!" while Rose hustled Natividad toward the nearest door. Natividad dropped her fan en route and darted back for it—January thought Rose was going to slap her, for Don Prospero nearly twisted out of his grip and hurled himself at the saffron-clothed beauty. January succeeded in wrenching the sword from Don Prospero's hand only moments before the Graf, Sir Henry, the papal nuncio, and several assorted Colonels swarmed over the enraged *hacendado.* Staggering free, January made for the door, sword still in hand, and was seized from both sides by Santa Anna's bodyguards.

"Not so fast, *Norte....*"

There wasn't a Texian in the room.

NINETEEN

"This is an outrage!" thundered January in the most upper-class Spanish he could muster. "I am an agent of the British minister...!"

One of the guards who was shoving him along the Paseo de Bucareli hooted with laughter. "Tell me another, Zambo!"

"Yes, and those other *greigo* swine are all agents of the *American* minister," snarled the guard at his other side, but the sergeant in charge of the party took a closer look at January's well-cut clothing and clean linen by the jolting torchlight.

To him January said, "If you will look in the right-hand pocket of my coat, you will find the minister's letter of authorization."

The lancer on that side released January's manacled arm and groped under the tail of his coat for the pocket—not easy, since the squad pushing him along the street didn't halt. It was early in the evening by Mexican standards, not yet one in the morning, and the Paseo de Bucareli was alive with carriages, riders, stray soldiers from the camp, and the inevitable *léperos,* whining for alms or warily looking out of the candle-lit darkness of the *pulquerias* to watch the guards and their prisoner pass by.

The lancer pulled out Sir Henry's letter and January's purse of money, both of which the sergeant snatched. He held the letter over by the nearest lancer's torchflame and studied it far too quickly to read what it said, but at least, January hoped, he would recognize the seal of the lion and the unicorn. Then he shoved it—and the purse—into his own pocket. "We'll see about *that*," he said.

"Señor...!" Corporal Rios was in charge of the watch-room, and came out into the stone-flagged gate-passage as the lancers shoved January toward the iron gates at its end.

"You know this one?" the sergeant demanded.

"I do, sir. He came this morning, on business from the British minister."

The sergeant studied January again, clearly gauging the amount of tip implied by Rios's reverent air. "Take him upstairs, then. After tonight the British minister's lucky *he* isn't spending the night here, too."

The moon had set. As they crossed the dim, star-lit pavement of the yard, some of the men huddled in the shadows raised their heads; most slept two and three together, under their combined serapes for warmth. The torchlight touched others, crumpled in the corners, without those striped Indian-weave blankets that so many men wore like cloaks—the fate of those who have no one to guard their backs.

Then they climbed the stone steps to the upper gallery, and January wondered if he'd end up sharing a cell with Werther Bremer.

"Can I fetch you anything, Señor?" asked Rios as he unbarred an iron-strapped wooden door halfway along the gallery. He held the torch inside and a rat went whipping away into a crack. Neither of the two men dozing there—strangers to January, but each with his own blanket and both better dressed than the men in the yard—so much as stirred.

"A blanket," said January, though he knew he wouldn't sleep. Nights on the high Mexican plateau were cold.

Rose would come in the morning, if she hadn't been arrested herself. He hadn't seen her as the sword had been wrenched from his hand. Everything had happened so fast—being slammed against the wall by Santa Anna's lancers, his wrists bound behind him, being thrust down the stairs. Corporal Rios unlocked the manacles and even dipped a little bow as he departed; January wondered whether Rose would be able to see Santa Anna—dear God, he was leaving for Vera Cruz later in the morning!

Sir Henry would be able to do something, he told himself, his heart beginning to pound hard. Von Winterfeldt would be able to do something. At the very least, Sancho would carry word to Consuela and she would take the necessary steps to get him—and possibly Rose—out of prison. He wouldn't be left here, as so many of the native Mexicans were, for weeks and months, waiting for the *alcalde* to hear his case....

But even a day would be too late for Hannibal.

Damn it, he thought desperately, pacing the two strides that took him from one side of the cell to the other, then the two strides back. *DAMN it...!*

Pounding on the door would only get him off to a bad start with his cell-mates, whom he might have to deal with in a few hours—in the worst case, perhaps for a day, or two days....

Virgin Mary, please don't let it be two days....

Rios came with a blanket, thick and warm and not even particularly buggy. January thanked him—"I will not forget"—and settled down to wait, wrapping himself as he sat in the corner farthest from the one the rat had disappeared into, as the torchlight faded again from the judas-hole, leaving the cell in pitch-darkness. At least, he reflected, he wouldn't have to worry about being quietly sold to slave-dealers, something that occasionally happened to those free men of color in the smaller town jails in Louisiana if they were unfortunate enough not to have families on hand to bail them out.

Hail Mary, full of grace, the Lord is with thee.... January dug in his pocket, felt the chipped blue beads of his rosary, like the promise of daylight in darkness. *Pray for us sinners, now and in the hour of our death.*

Somewhere bells struck two.

Get me the hell out of here.

The wary skitter of rat-feet whispered in the dark.

Bells struck three.

Torchlight. Boots, and the fat, unshaven sergeant's voice, then the grate of the bolt in its sockets. "All has been regularized, Señor." The sergeant even bowed. "Your servants are waiting for you at the gate. We hope you have not been inconvenienced...."

January's purse was considerably lighter when the sergeant handed it—and the letter of introduction—back, but he gave the man a peso nevertheless, and Rios another—and slipped him a third when the sergeant turned to lead him down the gallery stairs.

January almost didn't recognize Rose, standing in the torchlit dark of the gate passage. She wore a vaquero's leather knee-breeches and a striped serape like a muleteer's, her spectacles flashing under the wide brim of a leather hat. "I got a few of your things from Consuela's but we must ride fast. The gates at the causeways are still shut, but Cristóbal says he can lead us through the marshes and around to pick up the Chapultepec causeway."

In the torchlight January recognized Sancho, more bandit-like than ever with a cigar at a jaunty angle and a couple of rifles slung on his back.

"Santa Anna was still trying to smooth Don Prospero's feathers—I didn't dare bring up Hannibal's status for fear of setting him off," went on Rose as their horses wound their way from the Paseo—still lively with homebound revelers—into the night-black barrios that ringed the town. "But I did get a pardon for you. Even if we can't meet Hannibal at Saragosse, we can probably intercept Ylario on his way back to town with him. It's too much to hope that Hannibal was able to get away."

Stars powdered the sky above the low black shoulders of those crowding hovels, but no trace of its fragile light penetrated the alleys below. January was conscious of scufflings and whisperings in that darkness, like the rats in the cell he'd just left: *"Rifles... four of them... they have horses... no, too many for us..."*

Then the stinks of privies and sties lessened, and the oozing ground underfoot gave way to the wider gleams of water. In the starscape of ink and silver, it was impossible to tell where firm tussocks became beds of reeds; Cristóbal lit one of the lanterns he carried on his saddle, but even with his guidance January and the others frequently ended up hip-deep in brackish mud that reeked of sewage going back to Montezuma's day. At least, January reflected, there weren't crocodiles to contend with, though the mosquitoes were bad enough. Far to the south, an edge of snow marked the breast of Popocatepetl, and above it, a thin plume of smoke veiled the stars.

Even when they reached the tree-lined causeway at the aqueduct's feet, and passed the stench of the army camps beneath the shadow of Chapultepec Hill, their progress was slow. Though he knew that the absolute darkness that kept them all to a walk would likewise keep any bandit company in its lair, January strained his ears for the beat of hooves, the clatter of tack that would tell him that El Moro and his cohorts were on hand and they'd have to fight. The four of them might have been too much for the unarmed *léperos* of the barrios, but against outlaws he knew they wouldn't stand a chance.

Once light began to stain the sky, they picked up speed. Ylario, too, would have been slowed by the darkness, but he had a long start on them, and January now strained his eyes over the harsh roll of the deforested landscape, seeking the sight of a plume of dust that would speak of riders coming back toward the city. They found the ruined storage building across the stream from the village of Saragosse but saw no sign that Hannibal had ever arrived there. Riding on, they passed Indians with their burros, coming into the wakening town with baskets of marigolds whose butterscotch hue flamed like the music of trumpets in the early light.

"Look, they're already setting up the frames for the fireworks in the churchyard tomorrow night." Sancho pointed with his cigar toward the rust-and-golden tilework of the stumpy church tower, visible beyond the willows. "No one, not the tiniest child, will be forgotten."

No, thought January as they rode on. He thought of his mother, and his sisters, Olympe and Dominique, in the cemeteries of New Orleans, cleaning the marble and polishing the iron, remembering even the babies who had died. Two of Olympe's six children, dead before they learned to walk, and the infant that Dominique had birthed during the fever summer. Thought of the graves he wanted to visit: his young friend Artois St. Chinian's, and that of his old teacher Gomez. Should he die here in Mexico, his name would be remembered, if not by his mother then by his sisters. His mother was so snobbish about being half white that she could only barely be gotten to admit that someone as dark as January was her son in the first place.

It crossed his mind to wonder what Hannibal felt on the advent of this feast of families—on all those Days of the Dead in New Orleans, when the city was decked with flowers for those who, though gone, were not forgotten.

Had his own family, of whom he never spoke, forgotten him?

Dust above the cottonwoods, catching the morning sun like gold.

"If you're going to take on the *policia*," said Sancho, "it's better if Cristobál and I hide in those cottonwoods there, so we can cover them with the rifles."

"This isn't a military ambush," protested January. "I'm going to see

if I can make Capitán Ylario see reason about there being another explanation for Don Fernando's death. I don't propose to get into a gun-
battle over it."

"No, of course not," agreed the footman. "But if we do get into a
gun-battle, I should rather do it in those trees, where there is cover."

"Besides," added Rose, tossing a spare bullet-pouch to Sancho, "it's
always easier to make another man see reason if you have him in a
cross-fire. Are those cottonwoods in range, Sancho? Wouldn't you have
a better line of fire from those rocks?"

"Most assuredly, Señora, but the rocks are low, and I cannot fold up
my horse like this handkerchief and put him in my pocket."

"I'll hold him."

January sighed.

Moments later, the approaching riders crested the little rise: Ylario,
three uniformed constables, and a disheveled Hannibal, his wrists
lashed to the saddle-horn and the Capitán himself holding the reins of
his horse. January set his own mount sideways across the road at the little hill's crest, with Rose stringing out the spare mounts to block the
way around him. Ylario and his men drew rein; January held up his
hands to show them empty.

"I wish only to talk, Capitán."

"Then ride with us back to the city and talk on the way." Ylario's
face was dusty and grim, and like January, he still wore the neat black
coat, pale pantaloons, and immaculately tied linen cravat he'd had on
the previous night.

Like January, he was covered with grime, rumpled, considerably
worse for wear, and probably extremely cross.

"Those scoundrels de Castellón pays to run his cattle for him will
be after us—and myself, I have had enough 'talk' from Don Anastasio."

He urged his horse forward, but January didn't budge. When they
were almost knee to knee, Ylario stopped.

"I ask only that my friend should have justice," said January. "You
have no proof—none—that Fernando de Castellón did not die of some
other cause."

"That will be for the judge to decide." Ylario stared up at January,
his eyes bitter with years of frustration and disillusionment. "He's waiting for us in his rooms even as we speak."

"*Non vultus instantis tyranni,*" said Hannibal quietly, "*mente quatit solida.*" Under the layer of filth his eyebrows stood out blackly against chalky exhaustion; he did not look as if he'd slept in nights. One of the constables struck him across the shoulder with his quirt; Ylario snapped, "None of that. The man is a murderer but not a dog." He turned back to January. "If you're so certain of your friend's innocence, ride back with me and speak to the judge. Tell him your evidence, as I shall tell him mine. Myself, I am not interested in your opinion. I ask only that the laws men died for in this country be upheld, and that punishment be meted out to all criminals equally, and not merely to those who have not curried the favor of a dictator's friends."

"You have no proof. . . ."

"What more proof do you think I need?" The Capitán's mouth twisted, and he tried to rein around January, who moved again into his path. "You *Nortes* seem to regard my country's laws as if they were the rules of a children's game and not binding upon you, the adults. But I tell you, protector or no protector, *Norte* or not . . ."

"And I'm not," sighed Hannibal, as if he'd given up on convincing anyone otherwise.

". . . he will hang for his crime, and I will see it done." Ylario reached to the holster on the front of his saddle. "Now, get—"

Before his hand could touch the pistol, a shot cracked, as loud as a cannon in the thin, clear air. One of the constables threw up his arms with a cry and at the same time from the rocks beside the road Sancho yelled, "Señores, look out!" January saw gunflash from the rocks as riders thundered up from the gully a dozen yards away, ragged men on starved-looking horses, led by the red-clothed black figure he recognized instantly from the mountains above the Vera Cruz road.

"El Moro!" shouted Ylario's sergeant quite unnecessarily, and January's horse squealed and leaped as a stray bullet stung its flank. As the constables scrambled for their rifles to return the bandits' fire, Rose spurred her horse into their midst, caught the lead-rein of Hannibal's mount out of Ylario's hand, and galloped away along the rim of the gully toward the more settled lands of the now-distant village of Saragosse. January plunged after them, glancing back in time to see one pursuing bandit shot off his horse by Cristobál. He'd left the spare mounts, and they mingled with the remounts led by Ylario's men, kicking, screaming, and plunging in all directions as the bandits fired again.

At the first possible break in the gully's lip, Rose urged her mount

down into the thick of the cottonwoods and paloverde that grew along
the stream, the two men following her into the concealment of that
windless shimmering green-and-gold world. "The spare horses should
keep them busy." Rose drew rein and sprang down; January was already
pulling his knife from his belt to cut the rawhide strips that bound
Hannibal's wrists. "Are you all right?"

"*Vitae summa brevis spem nos vetat incohare longam.* I will be as soon
as I get some feeling back into my hands." The fiddler dropped from
the saddle and stumbled to the edge of the stream, where he knelt, flex-
ing his hands cautiously in the trickling water. "Though I am rather
tired of being cursed as a *Norteamericano* when in fact I'm a subject of
King William's—not one of his favorites, to be sure, but then, I daresay
Mr. Jackson wouldn't have much use for me either."

He bent, and shoving back his hat dashed handfuls of the bitter-
cold water on his face. "You have no concept how exquisite it is simply
not to be under the domination of a madman. No wonder Valla's
duenna drinks. If I didn't drink already, it would certainly drive me to
it. And speaking of drink..." He hunted through his pockets for his
square black bottle of laudanum and sherry. His hands, wet from the
stream, were shaking badly. "Did you get my letter?"

"Last night. Consuela didn't return home until late...."

"I might have expected it. *Mulier cupido quod dicit amanti, in vento
et rapida scribere oportet aqua....*"

"I think she was at a party celebrating the entrance of Don Rafael's
sister into a nunnery."

"Doesn't matter. *Her end is bitter as wormwood, sharp as a two-edged
sword....*"

"I think you've been listening to Don Prospero on the subject of
Helen of Troy entirely too long," said Rose severely.

"A single evening," sighed Hannibal, "of Don Prospero on the subject of Helen of Troy... Well, nevertheless. I did try to escape when the
vaqueros were at supper, only they weren't, not all of them. I was laugh-
ingly escorted back to one of the store-rooms and locked in. Vasco
seemed to think it a huge joke, and it probably is, for him. Nobody's
going to hang *him* for Don Fernando's murder. Barely had rosy-
fingered dawn stolen o'er mead and meadow when Ylario and his
bravos galloped in and held up the lot of them at gunpoint. If I get out

of this country alive, I shall spend the remainder of my declining years in a condition of bemused astonishment. Did you speak to Sir Henry?"

For answer, January held up the letter of introduction. "And to Don Prospero's long-suffering man of business, and to the equally long-suffering Señora Lorcha, and, more to the point, to Werther Bremer—after he turned a wild bull loose on me in the mistaken belief that I was El Moro, who apparently assaulted him on his way back from Mictlán."

"And I spent a vastly entertaining afternoon at the Convent of the Bleeding Heart of Mary—I truly did—" Rose said, "and Benjamin has a theory about how Fernando might have been poisoned even though he ate the same supper as everyone else."

While January slipped the heavy Spanish bits from the horses' mouths and poured oats from one of the saddlebags onto a stream-side rock for the tired beasts to eat, he explained about poor little Madame Valory in Paris and her children who could not eat whelks. "It's conceivable that Fernando could have lived till the age of twenty-five without his sensitivity becoming active because he lived fifteen of those years in Europe," he said. "I'm guessing whatever he was sensitive to is a New World food, and one that isn't eaten even now in Europe, at least not by the upper classes. Potatoes don't count, everyone in France and Ireland eats them now."

"It has to be one that isn't eaten by the upper classes here either." Hannibal leaned his back against a deadfall cottonwood. "Certainly not in Don Prospero's household. Could it be what killed his mother?"

"Having been raised in Spain," said Rose thoughtfully, "Doña Maria-Exaltación might not have known she had a sensitivity to whatever it is, either—if it was even the same thing. At the convent they said she was always sickly in the same way Fernando and apparently Isabella are. But at the Convent of the Bleeding Heart she wouldn't have eaten anything other than dry bread and water, which would be enough to make *me* marry even a lunatic if it would get me out of there. Hannibal, did you see anything resembling a will on Don Prospero's desk when you went back to search for Valentina's letters? Capitán Ylario has them now, by the way."

"I wondered what had happened to them. No, no will, but I wasn't looking for one. The Declaration of Independence could have been lying on the desk and I wouldn't have noticed it, Argand lamps notwithstanding. I guessed I wouldn't have much time to search. Now that I think of it, the papers were much disordered, much more so than when Fernando had been at them for two days."

He frowned. "There seem to be rather a lot of people searching that study. If Prospero mentioned the will to anyone—which he certainly didn't to me..."

"Well, you inherit a hundred thousand pesos and a sugar plantation in Vera Cruz," said Rose. "Which isn't going to do you any good if Ylario sees it."

"Thank you for modulating my transports of joy before they endangered my health. I wonder if he actually meant to sign the will. It sounds like exactly the sort of thing he'd do to get a rise out of Fernando. Thank you," he added as January handed him a couple of tortillas from the other saddlebag, along with slices of white cheese from the small block that Rose had packed. "*We will eat our mullets / soused in high-country wines, sup pheasants' eggs / and have our cockles boiled in silver shells.* One of the things I most love about you, *amicus meus,* is that you never forget the essentials of life."

After eating, January changed his much-scuffed evening clothes for the rough trousers, shirt, and boots Rose had lashed on behind his saddle, and the three friends moved on, seeking a break in the gully wall that they could follow up to return to the city. Throughout their rest he had been straining his ears, not only for the sounds of pursuit but for any sign of Sancho and Cristóbal. January hoped the Yaqui had been able to track them. If not, better perhaps that both returned to the city.

It was past noon now. Their spare horses gone, it would be well after nightfall before they returned—and then there remained the problem of how to get Hannibal safely to the coast.

"We've ruled out Don Prospero as a culprit," said Rose as they moved on foot through the dense rustling heat within the gully. "Though that business with the rabbit's heart still makes me very uneasy."

"Makes *you* uneasy?" Hannibal's eyebrows laddered a series of parallel wrinkles all up his forehead. "You try playing picquet with him until four in the morning, with every other blessed soul in the *casco* asleep, and those obsidian sacrificial knives grinning at you from the shelves. I asked Vasco about the rabbit, by the way—about whether Don Prospero had ever done something of the kind before—and he only shrugged."

His boots slipped in a puddle, and he caught himself on his horse's bridle and added, "*Do bravely, horse, for wot'st though whom thou mov'st?* The servants seem to think he's always been this crazy. It isn't as though he hasn't plenty of company in the British aristocracy. I had an uncle who used to dance and sing in unknown languages—he claimed they were Hittite and Japanese, of which he was not a student—all around the upstairs gallery of the hall, and all the family ever did with him was keep a padlock and chain handy for when there was company for dinner. He was quite reasonable otherwise, and would help the servants polish the silver."

"Rabbit or no rabbit," Rose said, "Don Prospero seems to have had little trouble keeping the family fortune intact during eighteen years of continuous civil warfare, which is more than can be said of most of his neighbors. Do you think Don Anastasio has returned to Saragosse, by the way, now that poor little Pilar is safely entombed in her convent? He might be prevailed upon to give us fresh horses—possibly even to keep Hannibal hidden until we can make arrangements to leave for Vera Cruz. As a botanist, he might even have some idea of what could have found its way into the food to kill Fernando."

"It might be worth scouting to see," agreed January, pausing to scan the bank above them again. "Once we get out of this gully, that is.

> " '*Non vi dispiaccia, se vi lece, dirci,*
> *s'a la man destra giace alcuna foce*
> *onde non amendue posseamo uscirci,*
> *sanza costrigner de li angeli neri*
> *che vegnan d'esto fondo a dipartirci,'*

as Dante overheard Virgil say under similar circumstances."

"You'd think after months as Don Prospero's house-guest I'd know how to get back to the city," sighed Hannibal. "But this is the farthest I've gotten from the hacienda. I'm not even sure we're off his land yet."

The thick yellow heat seemed to congeal in the gully with tormenting clouds of gnats before they found a watercourse that cut the bank, barely wide enough for a horse to ascend and almost too steep to climb. Now and then January would hear the dry clatter of rattlesnakes—long experience in the bayous of Louisiana had caused him to cut a snake-stick, and he'd been poking the brush and rocks with it as they'd walked.

He scrambled up the water-cut to the plain above, looked around cautiously, and saw nothing but tumbled rocks, a few clumps of cottonwoods marking the course of the smaller stream, and three or four grazing steers. Clear and hard, the mountains stood to the east and north. He would be glad, he realized as the wind dried the sweat from his face, to get out of this land and back to the world he knew.

It took him and Rose nearly a half-hour of shoving, coaxing, and care to bring his horse to the top of the bank; Rose remained on guard at the top while January went down for the others. None of the beasts wanted particularly to climb the bank; January was hot, cross, exhausted, and covered with filth by the time he and Hannibal got the third horse to the top.

There they found that Rose had been joined by Vasco and four of Don Prospero's vaqueros, standing around, grinning, with guns in their hands.

"You're very lucky, Señor Enero." The handsome vaquero chief shook a reproving finger at January. "It might have been that heathen bandit El Moro and his men who happened along, and not us, when you came out of that gully. What would you have done then, eh?"

January sighed. "I can't imagine." He could guess where they'd been hiding, among the cottonwoods near-by. Of course, all they'd have to do once they tracked the three horses into the gully was to follow it to the next break on the Mexico City side and wait out of sight.

"Or that Ylario." The scar-faced Quacho clicked his tongue. "He had already talked with El Moro when we met him, I think; he was on foot, and without his constables or horses. Two of the boys took him back to town."

"He must have been so grateful to you," enthused Rose without a trace of irony in her voice.

The men all bowed to her, and Vasco kissed her hand. "He was, beautiful Señora. He was pale with it and nearly in tears. Will you and your husband come back with your friend"—he indicated Hannibal, who was already being put on a horse by two of the men—"to Mictlán for supper? We know you are honored friends of the Padrón. Or if you wish, one of us will ride with you back to the city, to keep you safe from El Moro and his men."

"We accept Don Prospero's hospitality with grateful thanks." January bowed deeply. "And our thanks to you for taking such care."

The least he could do, he reflected wryly as he mounted once again, was get an interview with the cook. And perhaps, if he was lucky, join the queue to search Don Prospero's study before the *hacendado* himself returned.

As things turned out, he was wrong about that, but it wasn't until he was fleeing from these same vaqueros with bullets snarling around his head that he had time to reflect on what a bad idea returning to Mictlán actually was.

TWENTY

By the time they reached the Hacienda Mictlán, supper was being laid on the table. Don Prospero had not yet returned from the city, so Doña Josefa occupied the foot of the long table in solitary raven splendor while little Casimiro presided at its head. "Grandpapa must have stopped for *comida* with Uncle 'Stasio," said the boy, wielding his silver fish-fork with adult adeptness over M'sieu Guillenormand's milk-poached trout. "I wonder if Aunt Bella came out with him this time. She doesn't often—she likes Mexico City, and seeing her friends, and riding in the Alameda."

"It is not polite to speculate about other people in their absence, Casimiro," stated Doña Josefa repressively. "Gossip is abominable in God's sight."

January did not consider it especially polite to correct a child in front of company, but said nothing. Casimiro's thin cheeks colored and he looked at his plate. Apparently it was also considered improper for the young girls of the family to sup with company in the absence of the head of the household, for neither Valentina, Paloma, nor Doña Filomena was present. Out of consideration for Josefa's sensibilities— and sheer exhaustion from the day's adventures—Hannibal was also among the missing, leaving January and Rose to the undiluted company of Doña Josefa and Father Ramiro in the long, echoing, candle-lit *sala*.

January said to Casimiro, "Then perhaps you can tell me about Doña Pequeña instead. Is she well and happy?"

The child brightened at once. "Yes, Señor, she enjoys excellent health. She caught a mouse yesterday and killed it, and laid it on Aunt Valla's bed. Aunt Valla wasn't pleased one bit. But it shows that Pequeña is a real dog. . . ."

"Did someone say she was not?" asked Rose, raising her brows. Like January, she was outfitted in borrowed garments, having expected to return to Mexico City after her excursion through the countryside. Being much the same height and thinness of Doña Josefa, she was now clothed in a borrowed gown of black silk bombazine, a color flattering to few women of African descent.

January wasn't sure who had been the original owner of the short jacket, finely-tucked shirt, and gray Mexican trousers he wore, but they fit him no better than his footman's livery had earlier in the week.

Casimiro's brow clouded. "Uncle 'Stasio said that little dogs like Pequeña were bred that way by the heathen Indians long ago, to be killed for the gods so that useful dogs could live. He says he will give me real dogs—hunting dogs—as if Pequeña were no good, and should be killed just because she's little."

"Well, I don't know, but I don't think that's what your uncle can have meant," said January gently, though it flashed across his mind how Anastasio had looked on the ragged jailbirds in Santa Anna's Army and had said, *If men must die, it's better that they be scum like that.* "Because Pequeña isn't useless, you know. She killed a mouse, didn't she? And she keeps your Aunt Valentina from being lonely, and makes you and your sister happy. I don't believe God frowns upon happiness when it is innocent, do you, Doña Josefa?"

The widow stiffened, black-mitted fingers touching the stem of a blue-and-yellow Venetian goblet full of water. With apparent effort she admitted, "No. But we must distrust anything, even seemingly innocent pleasures, that divides our minds from contemplation of Christ's suffering, which He undertook for our sake."

"Of course." January inclined his head.

"Uncle 'Stasio's dogs are from England. They pick up the birds after Uncle 'Stasio shoots them. Uncle 'Stasio took in Uncle Fernando's dogs, too, when Uncle Fernando died. . . ." The child glanced uncertainly at his mother, as if unsure whether the topic was forbidden, but

Doña Josefa seemed to be praying, her eyes closed and her hands folded before the untouched fragment of white bread that lay on her plate. On the other side of the table, beside Rose, Father Ramiro's piggy black eyes shifted hungrily back and forth between January's *poulet bonne femme* and *soufflés des volailles* and Doña Josefa's bread. The priest was careful, January noticed, not to consume his own bread a mouthful more quickly than she.

"I drew a picture of Uncle Fernando's hunting-dogs to lay on the *offrenda* for when he comes back. Would you like to see it?"

When the servants came to clear away the supper dishes, Casimiro took the smallest of the branches of candles from the table and led January and Rose to the far end of the *sala,* where the *offrenda* stood in a niche surrounded by more candles still. Vases of coxcombs and marigolds stood on the little table among the burning lights, and the petals of the marigolds thickly strewed the table-top in a carpet of gold and red. Instead of the rather disrespectful little images January had seen on Consuela's altar—crudely-fashioned skeletons in the robes of priests and nuns, and one skeletal pope—the de Castellón altar was chastely decked with saints, around whose feet were arranged apples, oranges, persimmons, grapes—the brilliant colors of life.

"No bananas or chirimoya, I notice," remarked Rose under her breath in French, and January grinned. Evidently the ban on foods eaten by the Indians held true here as well. The candies were European, too: dainty marzipan, sugared orange-peel, candied walnuts, and marrons glacées. No candied yucca or camote or cut lengths of cane dripping sweet green sap, no peanuts, and certainly no tobacco. As in Consuela's humbler shrine, objects loved and used by the dead were mingled in these offerings: miniatures of men and women, a worn shawl smelling of aromatics and camphor, a child's shoes. January looked for Uncle Fernando in his uniform of crimson and gold but saw no picture of him—only half a dozen lead soldiers uniformed in Prussian white. Surely Werther had not taken the only one? He did see a nun's beautifully-painted shield—Maria-Exaltación's? The hawk-nosed young man whose mouth and chin so resembled Doña Josefa's must be Don Damiano in his youth; the boy beside him, in a startlingly macabre panel framed in gold, so much resembled Casimiro that it had to be Damiano's son, Luis, laid out in his coffin in a suit of white satin, his head decorated—in bizarre reminiscence of Pilar's—with a little jeweled crown.

What did Casimiro think when he saw that?

Casimiro's dark eyes, so like his mother's, were repeated over and over in the other portraits and miniatures, hanging on the sides of the flower-wreathed niche: stiff gentlemen in starched ruffs that framed their heads like dinner-plates, chilly-eyed dames in the lush somber velvets of Hapsburg Spain. Other aunts in veils and crowns pointed significantly to their shields. A smoke-and-age-blackened uncle gestured with a crucifix and raised a warning finger to three shadowy Indians, bowed in chains at his feet, and folded next to it, Casimiro's childish drawing of two fiercely slavering hounds.

For three hundred years they had ruled here like kings, January reflected. Off-hand he could not think of one European dynasty that had held power for so long.

"Casimiro," reproved Doña Josefa, "you must not bore your guest with *indio* superstitions. Señor Enero is an educated man. He knows that ghosts do not really come back from Purgatory to visit their families. With the joys of Heaven before them, they would not put off that blessed Union with God by so much as a moment, by taking that moment away from the rightful expiation of their sins. You must forgive my son, Señor. And my father, whose whim it is to have the altar decked in this way. Try as I will to keep my brainless sister Isabella from prattling to my children of superstitions such as these, she is as much a child as they. It is she who sends over the candies, which are no good for children and only teach them superstition in their turn."

As Doña Josefa swept from the room with her tame priest in tow, Casimiro lingered daringly to whisper to January, "Hannibal told me..." He looked uncertain, and distressed at the mention of Hannibal's name. "Before—before my uncle died, Hannibal told me a story about how the damned in Hell all get Sundays off, like peasants in the village; he said he read it in a holy book. Also in another book it said that Judas Iscariot gets to leave Hell on Easter Day, and sit weeping on a rock in the Atlantic Ocean with sea-gulls making messes on him, and that a ship full of Irish monks saw him there when they first sailed to America.... Is that true?"

"I've certainly read the same book," smiled January. "Whether it's true or not—who knows? It was a saint who wrote the book, St. Brendan of Ireland."

The boy sighed, his dark eyes troubled in the light of the flickering candle-branch he held. "Hannibal...he didn't really poison Uncle Fernando, did he? Everyone says he did, but...he *wouldn't*. Not Hannibal."

"As far as I can learn, he did not," said January gently, squatting on his haunches to speak to the child, whose dark head barely came up to his elbow. "I think that your uncle ate poison by accident. But I need to find proof of that in order for Hannibal to go free. And that's going to be very difficult. And in the meantime, everyone will go on thinking that he did it, and he'll be in danger until he can get away."

"That's hard," said the boy gravely. "Sometimes I get blamed for taking things that I didn't take, like Aunt Valentina's sapphire earrings. And killing someone is worse. That policeman came from the city and took Hannibal away this morning—I watched from over the wall, though Mother said I shouldn't. My mother will not let me speak to him now, or listen to him play music. He was teaching me the violin a little, and to say funny things in Latin. I didn't know you could be funny in Latin. Can I help you find the proof you need?"

"I don't think so," said January. "But I'll tell him that you believe in his innocence, and that will help him. And with luck, I'll find the proof I need tonight."

When January reached the kitchen, lamplight glowing amber through the thatch and wattled walls, Sacripant Guillenormand was gently sponging and rinsing the delicate glass goblets in a bowl of warm water and shouting to Lupe and Yannamaria to be careful scouring out the pots. That the two women had scoured these same pots nightly for twenty years did not seem to cross his mind, for as January entered the firelit shelter from the dove-colored twilight of the yard, the chef was reminding them just how much it had cost to bring the vessels over from France, and how much French scouring-chalk cost per barrel.

"We are not made of money here, no matter what the Don may say! Those pots are irreplaceable, for who brings in such wares nowadays, eh? Tell me that! Get out of here, you lazy limb of Satan....Not you, M'sieu Janvier..."

And indeed, January was crowded out of the doorway by Padre Ramiro. "The Doña has sent for coffee and cakes for her guests...."

"You mean *you* want coffee and cakes, eh? To sit in your little cell after delivering a sermon on abstinence, cramming your face! Glutton!"

"Atheist!" The priest loaded up a plate with the delicate cream-filled profiteroles at which Doña Josefa had turned up her nose after supper. "Were things as they should be still in this land, the Inquisition would look after you!"

"Were things as they should be in this land," retorted the Frenchman, "idlers like you would be turned out of their parishes and put to do honest work! Alas," he added sadly as the priest flounced from the big ramshackle shelter, "that even Napoleon himself could not remedy the evil of the Church. What may I do for you, my friend? I trust the dinner was to your satisfaction?"

His good will, however, turned to outraged horror at the mere suggestion that young Don Fernando might have met his fate as a result of eating any morsel that originated in Guillenormand's kitchen.

"Ridiculous! Preposterous! You women," he added sharply, switching back to Spanish—he and January had spoken French. "Get out of here! Leave the pots—but mind you, come back for them when we're done here! I'll send Joaquin.... That's the most absurd thing I've ever heard!"

He swung back around to January, florid face blotchy in the sweltering glare of the open hearth. "A what-do-you-call-it—a sensitivity? I've never heard of such a thing!"

"It is not unheard-of in medical circles...."

"It is unheard-of in any medical circles I've ever encountered!" The chef slammed his washrag down onto the table. "Medical circles, pah! Like those piss-scryers Fernando and Anastasio brought in, as if Don Prospero isn't perfectly capable of running this manor until he dies of old age as his father did! And his father, I'm told, used to paint himself blue with yellow stripes and run about naked with feathers in his hair, and what of it? Nothing in this kitchen was the slightest bit unwholesome...."

"Of course not! It's only that if young Fernando had such a sensitivity to something that grew only here in the New World—to chilis, for instance, or to chocolate—"

"There has *never* been a chili in this kitchen! Nor any other fragment of Indian fare!" Veins throbbed in the chef's thick neck. "How *dare* you imply that I would sully the true art of cookery with...with peasant make-dos? With old women's pottages of beans and corn-moulds? Next you will accuse me of putting salamanders in the *etouffé*, or of serving up tortillas! I said get out, you drunken bitch!" he added as Doña Filomena tiptoed through the door. "Get that little trollop's cocoa when I'm finished! Every morsel, every crumb"—he swung back and stabbed a finger at January, his voice rising in hysterical rage—"that comes into this kitchen is the true stuff of real cookery, and you *cannot* suggest otherwise! That meal by which you claim that I—*I*, Sacripant Guillenormand!—poisoned my master's son..."

"M'sieu Guillenormand, I never claimed anything of the kind!"

"That is exactly what it amounts to, with this *couillonnade* of 'morbid sensitivities'! 'Morbid sensitivities' forsooth! Poisoning is what you speak of! That supper contained not one bay-leaf, not *one* drop, not one marrow-bone of substance that could not have passed at the finest tables in France! Certainly nothing that the boy had not been eating all his life in Prussia! A *ratatouille jardinière* with garlic, eh? *Quel horreur!* Beef *à la Maréchale* and veal *à la broche,* removed with a rice casserole and *poulard à la crème*...Deadly, no doubt! I wonder the whole company did not turn purple and expire in their chairs! *Côtelettes de mouton* and an *etouffé* of quail raised on this very hacienda, with leeks, onions, and truffles from Don Anastasio's beds...Ah, I strangle just thinking of such a thing!"

He flung out his arms, causing Father Ramiro, who had stolen silently in and was refilling a plate with slabs of cold pigeon pie, to nearly drop his spoils as he bolted out the door.

"When a man dies of poisoning, or a child for that matter, it is because someone who wished to profit from their death gave them poison, not because of any 'morbid sensitivity'! You are deceived, M'sieu! Deceived by your worthless opium-eating friend as you were deceived all those years ago by some murdering heartless mother's false tears! Yes, what is it?"

"Señor Guillenormand," panted Bonifacio the footman, framed in the cobalt darkness of the doorway, "it is Don Prospero! He has come, he and Don Anastasio, and Don Rafael is with them, and Don Rafael's mother! He is demanding supper...."

"A thousand curses! Take that tray—and the dishes—where is that lout Joaquin? Build up the fire again.... I pity you, M'sieu," he said, turning back to January and leveling a ladle at him as if it were a sword. "But I tell you, you shall not accuse Sacripant Guillenormand of bringing harm to any man, and you shall not accuse Sacripant Guillenormand of allowing the smallest fragment of Indian food to find its filthy way into *his* kitchen! Now, get out, all of you!" he bellowed at the scurrying servants. "Bring wood! Fetch the Brie from the cooling-well! Bring the cream, and you—!" He stabbed the ladle again at January. "You get away from me with your insane ravings and never come into my kitchen again!"

"Did you expect anything different?" Hannibal turned his head on his pillow and regarded January with philosophical weariness in the single candle's light. He still wore the dust-covered riding-clothes he'd had on during the rescue that morning—and presumably for his escape attempt twenty-four hours earlier—being too exhausted even to take them off; his untouched supper-tray still sat on the windowsill, where a servant had left it some hours ago. In the *corredor* outside, the voices of servants brushed past the open door like fluffs of evening breeze, candles flickering as they hurried to make up a room for Don Anastasio. Horses stamped, saddles creaked in the courtyard below, and Don Prospero's harsh voice could be heard querulously demanding why supper was not ready to be laid upon the table—what did servants *do* here all day?

A passing glance through the door of January's own room had showed him Rose still absent, presumably in the women's court, trading convent reminiscences with Doña Josefa. The dust-smeared and muddy garments he'd worn, both to Sir Henry's party the previous night and later during the excursion through the gully, had been taken away to be cleaned. He thought he heard Sancho's voice, but glancing through the door at those dim, hurrying shapes, it was hard to determine: the footman and Cristobál might easily have made their way to the hacienda and be bedding down among the vaqueros by the corrals.

The morning would be soon enough to know.

Hannibal sighed and made a move to get up, then sank back again. The red welts left on his wrists by the rawhide ropes had turned to bruises. Deep lines had settled into the corners of his eyes: he'd once told January he remembered, at the age of twelve, everyone talking about the Peace of Amiens and the hope that Napoleon would be content with the Consulship of France. This would make him a few years older than January's forty-two; tonight he looked a decade beyond that.

"Whether or not chilis or chirimoya or deep-fried ant-larvae found their way into the *ratatouille,* Guillenormand will be the last to admit the possibility, especially if the will is ever discovered. Which is what he was seeking in the study, if that was him Tuesday night...I don't think Josefa has the strength to throw me against the wall like that, not to mention that a work so indelicate as *L'École des Filles* would undoubtedly have left tell-tale scorch-marks on her sanctified fingertips. And in any case, far better to put the blame on a worthless opium-eater whom no one will ever miss and whose life for the past twenty years has been to all intents and purposes a waste of air and water. Like poor little Mademoiselle Pequeña, I am not of the useful breed of dog."

January grunted and gently pulled off Hannibal's boots. "And here all my life I've fought for the right not to be useful to every American slave-owner who comes along."

The fiddler's dark eyes twinkled. "*Touché*—I admit that I have less to complain of than you, *amicus meus.* At least I *had* opportunities to fritter away. And even being the prisoner of a madman awaiting the opinion of a dead one is less daunting than the task of convincing Compair Ylario of the existence of morbid sensitivities. I wonder if something of the kind was what actually slew Achilles?"

Soft scratching sounded on the door; to Hannibal's "Enter," it opened, admitting the footman Bonifacio. "I'm very sorry, Señor," he said. "But Don Prospero is finished with his supper, and insists that you come out and play for him."

The muscles in Hannibal's jaws tightened hard at the thought of getting up, much less making music for several hours while the men smoked and played cards in the gallery. From the darkness outside, Don Prospero's voice could be heard, sharp, with a dangerous note, like broken mica in the sun: "Tired? Nonsense! If the man's tired, it's his own fault. Now get him out here. I've missed his company, and I want to ask him about that rascal Ajax, going mad and murdering sheep on the plains of Troy—all a hoax, I say, a lie put about by Odysseus!"

"Much as I would love to play duets with you again, *amicus meus,*" said the fiddler as he reached wearily for his boots, "I should advise you not to remind Don Prospero of how much he'd like you to remain for a few days. Get out of here at daybreak if you can—I'm sure Don Anastasio would put you up at Saragosse...."

He groped under his pillow for his bottle of laudanum-laced sherry and took a quick sip, wincing at the bitterness beneath the musky sweet. "You could ask Don Anastasio about Doña Isabella's sickliness, and he may even have some ideas about how to convince Capitán Ylario that just because he hasn't heard of complicated medical conditions, that doesn't mean they don't exist."

But January was not destined to benefit from Anastasio's knowledge. After a stealthy visit to the corrals—where, as he'd suspected he would, he found Sancho and Cristóbal bedding down with their saddles for pillows—to make sure their horses would be ready at daybreak, he returned to his room. There he found Rose sitting quietly in the darkness of the unlighted doorway, listening to Hannibal play.

They went to bed soon after. It had been a very long two days.

The first cracks of light through the shutter woke him, and the silence. He'd meant to rise early for Mass, but—oddly—heard no bell. On a Sunday one would think Father Ramiro would be more assiduous, not less, in impressing Doña Josefa with his piety.

Or had the previous sleepless night in the cell, coupled with the long ride, so worn him out that he'd slept through the peal? There was no sign of a breakfast-tray—Guillenormand was evidently still furious with him—and no hot water in the can outside the door. As he washed in leftover cold water, and dressed, January became aware that no sound of servants passing came in from the arcade. No laughter or joking of the vaqueros down in the court.

Something was wrong.

He pulled on his boots and riding jacket, and slipped from the room, quietly so as not to waken Rose. As he opened the door he heard the vaqueros in the courtyard, talking rapidly and quietly, clustered together by the empty workrooms.

A knot of servants crowded around the mouth of the passageway to the kitchen courtyard. Guillenormand would undoubtedly fling pots at him—imported or not—if he entered the kitchen court, but at least he could find out from the vaqueros what was happening. He descended the stair, started across the dusty open quadrangle. . . .

"MURDERER!"

January spun and dodged in the same heartbeat that a rifle barked, and a ball tore the ground where he had stood seconds before.

"ASSASSIN!" screamed Don Prospero's voice. *"BLACKGUARD! SAVAGE!* NORTE *VILLAIN!"*

The old man on the gallery above the gateway that led to the women's court wore only his nightshirt and had Vasco and two other vaqueros with him, all armed; Don Prospero seized Vasco's rifle, and January, alone in the midst of the courtyard and the only possible target, plunged sidelong and ran.

"TAKE HIM!" the *hacendado* screamed, and January, realizing that whoever was dead, now was not the time to stand still and ask for information, bolted for the little group of vaqueros leading their horses toward the main gate.

One of the men fumbled with his pistol; two others ran to intercept January, but January simply smashed one aside with the back side of his fist—it was like hitting a straw dummy—and as the other one seized his arm, elbowed him hard across the face, sending him flying. The third man got his gun up, but by that time January was within arm's reach of him. He tore the weapon from his grasp, threw himself on the largest of the three horses, and lashed the animal's flanks with the quirt that hung from the saddlebow.

"Shut the gate, you imbeciles!"

But January had a long start on them. He ducked as he passed under the archway, bolted out among the trees and water-carriers and flocks of turkeys around the hacienda gate. He heard shots behind him and knew it would be only moments before pursuit was organized, and lashed the tough cow-pony harder, reined around, and headed for the nearest tree-filled gully. Don Prospero's shrieks of grief and outrage followed him, hanging like dust in the yellow morning air.

TWENTY ONE

For all it had been the largest of the three available, the cow-pony was a small animal. Under January's massive weight, it stumbled, and January slowed to a jog. In the green-and-yellow shade of the cottonwoods in the arroyo, he listened but heard no sound of pursuit. He stepped from the saddle, led the mustang swiftly along the round smooth rocks of the dry stream-bed, picking the stoniest ground. North of the hacienda, the land was broken by a maze of gullies, where winter rains washed the eroded soil down toward the shallow lake. January turned down one water-cut, then up another, remembering again Dante and Virgil traversing the narrow canyons of Hell, always listening behind him.

Always making his way as well as he could around the hacienda north and east, working toward the yellow, brushy heights that rose behind the Spanish walls in a line straight as the haft of a war-club: the pyramids of Mictlán.

Virgin Mary, he prayed as he walked, *get Rose out of there before Don Prospero takes it into his head to hold her hostage for my return.*

And once you've dealt with that miracle, he added, *could you please somehow let me know what the hell this is all about?*

The Don had sounded awfully certain that whoever was dead, January was responsible.

Even in the clear morning light, silence immersed the pyramids of

Mictlán as if they'd been sealed in glass. January concealed the cow-pony in the deep, overgrown depression of the old ball-court, then war-ily crossed the broken tangle of bunch-grass and ocotillo to the Pyramid of the Dead. He climbed the eastward face, despite its steep-ness, to keep the bulk of the hill between himself and Mictlán, and the morning sun blazed dizzyingly strong on his head.

But when he attained the broken crown and stood among the rub-ble that the Conquistadores had left of the temple, he could see far off the yellow plumes of dust where pursuit galloped now here, now there across the range.

No one was coming anywhere near the pyramids.

Having watched the vaqueros on this spot a week ago, January had been fairly certain that left to themselves, they would not enter the woods that crowded so thickly around the old mounds' feet. The si-lence here seemed deeper than in the open cattle-ranges, or in the gul-lies farther west toward Saragosse. The music of birds seemed to whisper echoes of flutes and horns long consigned to the Inquisition's fire, of players who lingered here still. The sudden buzz of an insect had a quality here that it had nowhere else, alien and frightening, as if a long-silenced voice were trying to frame forgotten words.

The gods were here—those gods that, as a Christian, January no longer believed in. They had never left.

He sank down with his back to the square base of what had been a pillar. In a tangle of mesquite, a worn carving showed hook-nosed war-riors holding a victim stretched over the altar—*Usually an enemy war-rior,* he remembered Don Anastasio saying. *They were thrifty that way, rather than wasting warriors of their own.* Rather like Santa Anna's re-cruiters taking *pelados* from the jails, he supposed.

A lizard flickered over the stones.

A rattlesnake buzzed, far off but clear as the tolling of the church-bell in the village.

Savage, Don Prospero had screamed. *Assassin . . . !*

Why was he so sure that the killer was me?

Even as he framed the question, January threw up his hands in dis-gust. *His voices may have told him so. Tlaloc may have appeared to him and said, By the way, the black* Norteamericano *is the one who killed . . .*

Killed who?

Someone whose life meant more to Don Prospero than his son's, anyway.

From the pyramid's top he could see the *casco* itself in the preternatural clarity of the forenoon light, tiled roofs and the dark-green of dusty cypresses. Yellow and blue tilework gleamed on the façade of the chapel, whose bell clanged small and clear, calling the faithful to a belated Mass. Dust hung heavy around the yellow walls as riders came and went, swift and tiny as fish in clear water. The light flashed on the reed-mottled silver of the lake. In the village streets January could discern where marigold petals had been strewn, blazing pathways to lead the dead home to their families tonight. Another plume of dust marked more riders galloping from the gate.

Evidently, if Rose and Hannibal had protested that January had been continuously with one or the other of them all night, Don Prospero wasn't listening.

I must go back for her. His heart lurched and he wondered how he'd manage it. There was no reason to think the Don would turn his rage against her, of course. . . .

January remembered the rabbit's heart, and shivered.

Good God, he doesn't think I'M the one who murdered Fernando, does he? Had Guillenormand, in fury . . . or fear? . . . accused him of the crime?

No. Someone else. Someone who died last night.

He closed his eyes.

And for whatever reason, he thinks I'm the killer.

The air grew burning, and seemed to thin with the rising day. Forms moved about in the village churchyard, arranging baskets, pots, bottles of marigolds on the graves. A framework of bamboo for fireworks, as there would be also at Saragosse. Musicians set up chairs in the shade, and January remembered Compair Lapin, setting out to play the dead up out of the earth with his fiddle, and to make the Devil dance.

When he was sure no riders were anywhere near, he descended the precipitous slope to the crypt passageway on the eastern side, wondering what kind of concealment the little chamber would offer him in the event of a search. If Don Prospero sent for Ylario, it would take more than the shadows of ancient gods to keep that coldly rational lover of justice away.

Or would Don Prospero take vengeance on his own? If he—or Don Anastasio—led the pursuit, they'd search the crypt. God knew where January could conceal his horse, although if worse came to worst, he could release it, and steal another from the corrals. The *casco* was within an hour's walk of the pyramid's western slope, with sufficient brush and trees to cover a man afoot. He'd need a place to lie low if he was going to stay until darkness—and the confusion of the feast—gave him the chance to go back for Rose.

But even in the passageway he smelled the musky pungence of marigolds. Morning sunlight glinted on shapes and colors within that had not been there before.

January checked his steps, the hair prickling on his nape. Then he moved forward slowly into the dimness of gold and shadows.

Around the ghastly carving of Mictlantecuhtli, the Death-God, an *offrenda* had been raised. Garlands of marigolds circled the skeletal neck, and two late-blooming pink roses had been inserted into the hollow sockets of the God's empty eyes. They were already losing their petals, which lay like waxy tears among the marigolds heaped around his feet. Elaborate designs had been worked on the stone in red and gold flower-petals, mingled with cigars, with pottery cups of pulque, rum, and expensive cognac, with bits of candy creeping with ants. Mixed with these things were bones: rabbit, chicken, sheep. The skulls of cats grinned horribly amid the flowers.

A green-and-white Meissen tea-service was arranged there: pot, slop-bowl, saucer, cup, water-pot, even the two gold spoons. A pair of white gauntlets embroidered in gold with the crest of the Royal Military College in Potsdam. An officer's sabre in a red velvet sheath. Half a dozen lead soldiers whose regimental companions January had already seen on the household *offrenda* in the *sala* at Mictlán, and a small portrait of Fernando in the crimson uniform of the Tenth Berlin Guards.

I have found little altars among the pyramids . . . January heard Don Anastasio's voice whisper in his ear. *It is not only food that has fed those returning spirits.*

Did Anastasio guess even then who had raised them?

Gingerly, January picked his way around the broken altar-stone, the gaping black maw of the holy well, and stood where the doorway's brightness haloed the *offrenda* spread upon the steps. The flowers weren't fresh—they'd been set in cheap clay pots of water, perhaps as much as two days earlier.

Before Prospero left for Sir Henry's reception in town, thought January.

The passage of the sun would soon leave the ruined sanctuary in deeper shadow, and the slits and niches in the walls already gaped like windows into Hell. He dug in his pockets for his tinderbox and retreated to the sunlight outside, where he cut a short sapling for a torch and a longer one for a snake-stick. He'd already seen scorpions darting among the broken stones with their barbed tails curved high.

Would Don Prospero lead the searchers here? To this secret sanctuary, this hidden *offrenda* to his dead son?

Probably not—but he might very well come and look himself.

January's first thought had been to see if there was a way to conceal himself down the cenote, but a closer examination of its rim showed only sheer walls. Holding his torch down that black throat, January could see a narrow ledge about ten feet down, and beyond that only shadow. A dropped pebble clinked on stone very quickly, so it was at least dry and not abysmally deep. Still, there was no way to descend that wouldn't involve a tell-tale rope, and if he were stranded there, it was a near-certainty he'd be left to die of thirst. If the behavior of the vaqueros was any clue, no one but Prospero himself ever came here.

An examination of the crypt walls proved more promising. The gaps and niches in the stonework were mostly too small to conceal even a man of Hannibal's slight frame, much less one of January's height and bulk. But one, cleverly tucked into an angle of the wall, led back to a tiny space within the rear wall of the chamber itself. January could barely squeeze himself through the aperture, but found, when he did, a little hollow in the stonework, some four feet by four feet by seven, the ceiling blackened with ancient soot and the floor paved with cut stone. Straw cushions almost reduced to dust still lay on a low bench built out of the wall that separated this room from the sanctuary, and in the wall were three holes, the lowest of which was rimmed in a fading glim of the light that came through the sanctuary door from outside.

He was, he realized, behind the image of Mictlantecuhtli himself.

January felt immediately better. Not a superstitious man, he had nevertheless seemed to feel, all through his examination of the sanctuary chamber, the dead eyes of the Lord of the Place of the Dead fixed on his back. Now he felt as if some monstrous shape of nightmare had pushed up its mask and revealed itself as an actor, hired to play the part. The God of Death was merely an image on the wall—an image, to judge by the remains of the cushions, behind which a priest could kneel to whisper judicious messages to whatever royal officials came to consult the deity. Not so different, he decided, wriggling out through the hidden doorway into the sanctuary again, from the steam-driven mechanisms that mysteriously opened ancient temple doors in Egypt, to awe the worshippers.

It was good to step out into the sunlight again, to feel the hot, dusty wind on his face. He leaped and slapped at imaginary scorpions on his back only three or four times, when those breezes riffled his shirt. Regaining the top of the pyramid, he could see dust where horsemen searched the rangeland from arroyo to arroyo. But only a single rider approached the pyramids, coming up out of a gully and making a long circuit over the rolling scrublands and clumped agave to the east. January watched for a long time, until the big, thick-bodied black horse was almost among the woods that surrounded the pyramids, although he was fairly certain who that lone vaquero was.

Kneeling in the temple ruins, he whispered a prayer of thanks.

He descended the pyramid's northern slope, cutting back and forth because of its steepness, and then followed the line of heaviest cover around the bases of the pyramids of the Moon and the Rain. By the time he reached the last in the line of artificial hills, the rider had come into open ground at the foot of the Pyramid of the Sun and dismounted.

Spectacles flashed in the shadow of her hat.

She, too, had ridden cautiously, certain that she would find him here but not willing to take off the hat that covered her long hair and shaded her face until she was sure she was unobserved. In her right hand she held a red bandanna, an old signal between them that said *All is well.*

From the brush he whistled the first two bars of "Eine Kleine Nachtmüsik" and she turned, smiling, as he stepped from cover just enough to be seen.

"Thank God you're safe." Rose wore the vaquero gear she'd had on for the ride out to Mictlán. "I thought you'd make for . . ."

She broke off as January strode across the clearing and caught her in his arms with almost brutal ferocity, his lips taking hers as if the act of kissing could negate peril, fate, and death. Her mouth tasted of dust and sweat. "How did you get out?"

"I faked a faint," said Rose, "when everyone came barging into our room and the shooting started." She didn't sound in the least afraid.

"What the hell was going on?"

"My darling, if I had the slightest idea of that, I'd have been able to do something other than flee like a scared mouse the moment everyone's eyes were off me. I know perfectly well you didn't murder the cook."

"Murder the *cook*?" January stared at her, aghast. And then, despite shock and horror and bafflement, his sense of the ridiculous pinked him like an impish fencer and he clapped his hand over his mouth to keep from laughing. "No wonder Don Prospero was outraged!"

Rose chuckled, too, shaking her head, and tightened her arm around his ribs. "Of course. He keeps his own son's killer on hand to play picquet with him, but touch one hair of his cook's head . . . Poor Guillenormand!"

"What happened?"

She made a gesture of despair. "The shooting waked me—the shooting and Don Prospero screaming *Assassin!* I reached the door, wrapped in the bedsheet, just in time to see the whole boiling of them—Prospero, Anastasio, Don Rafael, Father Ramiro, and six vaqueros—come barging along the *corredor* toward our room. They burst in, all shouting at once. Father Ramiro yelled, 'See, there is blood!' and pointed to the chest in the corner. Don Anastasio found the key for it on the windowsill and they opened it. Your shirt and jacket were there—the ones you had put out to be cleaned . . ."

"Which anyone could have picked up . . ."

". . . along with a sack of money. . . ."

"*What?*"

"Don't ask me." She shrugged. "I know only what they pulled out. It was quite a substantial sack, and heavy, there must have been close to a thousand dollars in gold in it. Don Prospero let out a bellow like a

bull stuck with fireworks, and started cursing you for a thief and an assassin. At least I assume that you were the thief and assassin he referred
to, because he had your shirt in his other hand. Then someone—it
sounded like Sancho but I can't swear to it—shouted 'There he goes!'
from the main gate, which was absurd, because you were already long
gone. . . . To my unending relief, by the way, that you had the wits to get
out of there promptly. . . ."

"I would have gone back for you come nightfall."

"Then I can only be glad I got out of there when I did, because
you'd never have eluded all the searchers around the house. I fainted at
the first shout of 'there he goes,' and the minute everyone charged out
of the room I snatched up my riding-gear and my boots and dashed
into the nearest unoccupied store-room while everyone was running
down to the gate. I gather Sancho and Cristobál kept everyone dashing
hither and thither for some fifteen minutes just by shouting 'There he
goes!' periodically. When I slipped out, no one was in the main court—
even the women who grind the corn were all grouped around, listening
to Yannamaria go on about how she knew it was coming because the
French *tarugo* had been a heretic and an atheist. That was the reason I
was able to get water but no food."

She gestured toward the bottles slung from the saddle-horn; she
must have taken the time to collect them from every saddled horse in
the courtyard. "There were blood-smudges on the railing of the *corredor* and the stairs, and one quite large one on the doorjamb of our
room. It was about the level of where I'd have put my hand—shoulder
height—and of course about six inches lower than where you would
have left a mark."

"Hmmn." Rose was tall for a woman, nearly equal in height—give
or take an inch or two—to Hannibal, Don Anastasio, Don Rafael,
Sancho, Cristobál, Doña Josefa, Santa Anna, and about two-thirds of
the vaqueros.

"As I was dressing," Rose went on briskly, "I heard someone shout
to Hinojo the butler asking what was going on and he said that the
black *Norte* had cut Monsieur Guillenormand's throat and taken his
money. I went down, got the biggest horse I could of the several saddled
ready there, and rode out through the gate. *Did* you leave the key to the
trunk on the windowsill?"

"No, but whoever picked up my shirt and jacket could easily have found it, it was on the table next to the bed." He led her into the shadows of the trees, where his own little piebald mustang cropped weeds in the shade. All the while the thoughts returned, *She's alive. She's safe.* He felt more relief than he had about getting away safely himself. "Thank God you got out of there...."

"Oh, absolutely." Rose settled her hat back onto her hair, which she'd tied back under a silk scarf like the vaqueros did. "Anastasio mentioned to me when we were here last week that Don Prospero has grown unpredictable and vindictive lately."

"It's more than that," said January. "I'll show you, in the pyramid."

"I wouldn't put it past Prospero to hold me hostage to bring you in. I'm a little afraid he may decide to use Hannibal for that same purpose, though I'm not sure he'd jeopardize his card partner. Admittedly, my flight suggests complicity in your crime, darling, though what reason you and I would have to conspire to murder that poor chef..."

"Exactly," said January. "Why would I murder poor Guillenormand?"

"Other than for his money? Now I know how Joseph's brethren must have felt in the Bible when he got even with them by caching Pharaoh's tableware in their baggage and accusing them of theft."

"Rose, you and I don't *need* money. We *have* money. Not as much as we did before I started gambling at Consuela's parties..."

"That's only *our* story," Rose pointed out. "Don Prospero doesn't know anything about us, after all. Only that we're friends of Hannibal—and Consuela probably described us to him as impoverished, which we were the last time she saw us. Did Guillenormand tell you anything last night?"

"Only that neither chilis nor chirimoyas had ever sullied the *hauteur* of his cuisine. He became quite angry that I'd even suggest such a thing. Angry enough, obviously," he added grimly, "to fulminate to the wrong person about how I'd been asking questions that might lead to an enquiry about who else had been in the kitchen on the afternoon of Fernando's wedding-dinner. I had thought, you know," he added, unhitching his own mount's tether and leading both horses farther into the trees that grew so thick along the north side of the Pyramid of the Sun, "that Fernando had been poisoned by accident. Poisoned by some ingredient introduced without Guillenormand being aware of it. Despite his oaths to the contrary, people come in and out of that kitchen all the time, though I'd be a little surprised if Father Ramiro or

Señora Lorcha could get near enough to the food without being tossed out again. But this puts paid to that theory."

"Leading us to two questions," said Rose. "Who knew the family well enough to know there was a sensitivity to whatever it was? And which of those people was present both on the night of the wedding-banquet and last night?"

"Three questions, my nightingale," corrected January. "Which of them had a reason for wanting Fernando dead?"

In the tangled thickets that grew in the old ball-court, it was diffi-cult to hear the sound of approaching riders, and visibility was cut to no more than a few yards. Mosquitoes hummed above the stagnant pools. Checking the ground for tracks, January found the place where John Dillard habitually tethered his horse when he went to check Valentina's message-drop under the jaguar statue: he found the drop-pings of a grain-fed horse there less than a day old.

And a short distance away, tracks of a woman's feet, fresher still. Where the ground was damp, water was still oozing into them, coming and going—she must have worked her way to the place under cover of the trees while he was in the pyramid, only hours ago. While everyone was either at Mass or out hunting him, he thought wryly. Her father— or one of the servants—must have recounted to her what had happened at Sir Henry's. Of course she'd know—or hope—that Dillard would leave a message for her. . . .

And so he had. After prodding the hole with his stick to discourage whatever might have taken refuge there—nothing either emerged or rattled at him—January knelt to investigate, and brought out a folded rectangle of yellowing paper, the torn-out page from the back of some book. On it was printed, in laborious letters,

SARAGOSSE GRAVYARD———TONITE

The note lay on top of a rough wooden packing-box that proved to contain tortillas, white cheese, and several sweet bosc pears that had to have come from Don Anastasio's orchards by way of the unfortunate M'sieu Guillenormand's kitchen. January handed Rose half the tor-tillas, cut off a chunk of the cheese, and took two pears. Then he closed the box and pried farther into the hole, unearthing a light-blue piece of

paper, unweathered and fresh. In a hand that looked like that of a pro-
fessional scribe was written in Spanish, *Beloved, I must fly this city, and
the country as well. Will you come?*

"He must be hiding somewhere in the hills," January told Rose.
"Which means you and I should make ourselves scarce as soon as we
can. She may have left a signal of some kind for him. You don't think
Guillenormand caught Valentina stealing food . . ."

"And that slender little girl cut his throat for him?" Rose retreated
across the clearing, watching from the shelter of the trees while January
reached with his snake-stick to scuff and scratch out his own tracks. It
was tricky to do this without obliterating Valentina's as well—Dillard
would almost certainly read the ground when he approached the place
himself. January wished he knew more about tracking and signs.
Lieutenant Shaw of the New Orleans City Guards could tell by glancing at hoofmarks the age, sex, condition, and probable burden of a
horse—maybe the color of the rider's shirt as well, January wouldn't put
it past him. "Cutting a man's throat is something that's easiest done
from behind—not someplace a smallish girl is going to be in the midst
of a murderous argument with a man who's going to expose her to her
family. It's *possible*—"

"But partakes, as Aristotle—and Hannibal, I'm sure—would point
out, of the improbable possible rather than the probable impossible. I
think you're right." Beside the horses and once more in the heart of the
thickets, January unhooked the water-bottles from the saddles,
wrapped some of the cheese in a tortilla, and sat on a deadfall juniper.
"On the other hand, Valentina would certainly have heard from her sisters about Fernando's sensitivity to certain foods. She may well know all
kinds of things that no one has thought to tell either of us. Which, for
that matter, she may have passed along to Don Rafael . . ."

"I think any information of any sort being passed from her to him
is definitely in the realm of improbable possible." Rose tore into her
makeshift *comida* with an alacrity that reminded January that like himself, she had had no chance to eat since yesterday's supper. "Just waiting
for a break in his discourse could take you all night. But for what she
knew, or guessed . . . You know, if there was the slightest reason for Don
Anastasio to want Fernando dead, I'd say it had to be he. The mere fact
that he's as solicitous as he is about what his wife eats indicates he has a

suspicion about morbid sensitivities. You don't think Fernando insulted Anastasio in some unforgivable way, do you? Or that he nursed a secret passion for the lovely Natividad?"

"I think any man who nursed a passion for the lovely Natividad would have no trouble consummating it for a very modest sum," remarked January. "Besides, Fernando was working with Anastasio in getting Don Prospero confined. He has to have known that with Fernando dead, he'd have to deal with Josefa, which I can't imagine him wanting to do. As for Josefa herself..."

"It's true she'd know whatever Valla knew," Rose said slowly. "And she's intelligent, which is something people don't expect of religious fanatics. She certainly had reason to fear Fernando's ascent to power, and she would certainly be trusted by Guillenormand enough to be able to get behind him if he were sitting at a table doing accounts, for instance. But whether—"

January threw up his hand, and Rose fell silent at once. Into the silence January heard the rumble of hooves.

Rose clapped on her hat as January shoved the rest of the food into the big black gelding's saddlebag, jerked the cinches tight. *They expected me to be on top of the pyramid, watching,* he thought, *rather than down here....*

The nearest gully was northwest, so he and Rose headed out at as swift a trot as the horses could manage through the thick trees as far east as the old ball-court went. When they reached the end of the trees, he could see no riders in that direction, no dust. Only a wasteland of scrubby grass and gray-green agave, where longhorned Mexican steers ambled from waterhole to waterhole. "Come on," he said, "let's get clear of this place before the searchers get to the top of the pyramid themselves. Feel up to herding more cows?"

"I pictured myself engaged in many exotic activities when we came to Mexico," Rose reflected, following him toward the nearest bunch of steers. "But somehow driving cattle never occurred to me. My brother and I—my father's white son—used to take herds over to Chenier Caminada to sell, and swim them across the gaps."

"You think you can get that herd to Saragosse?" January pulled the knots free and unshipped the lariat tied on the black gelding's saddle, using the thick coil of rope to slap his mount's flank, as he'd seen the vaqueros do.

Rose urged the little piebald into a hard-gallop beside him. The horses, rested, moved friskily toward the cattle, clearly ready to do their day's work. "Of course. Though why we need to steal Don Prospero's cattle on top of our other sins..."

"They'll search around the pyramids first," said January, reining his mount sidelong to nudge the first of the steers back into the larger band. The heavy reins, and the massive Spanish bit, made the trained horse instantly responsive to the smallest gestures. "If someone goes up to the top of the pyramid to look for us..."

"... all they'll see is a couple of perfectly innocent charros taking a herd of cattle back to Don Anastasio's land." Rose nipped in front of another steer, the horse clearly knowing the work. "From there we can... what? Circle back to town and present our side of the problem to Sir Henry? I feel certain he's heard more eccentric things from Don Prospero than the mere murder of a cook. Get in touch with Don Anastasio himself? He'll be in the cemetery tonight—and we have to be there in any case to intercept Valentina."

"If—for whatever reason—Don Anastasio did kill Fernando," said January slowly, "I think it would be singularly dangerous to let him know we're not halfway to Vera Cruz and still running." He tried to imitate what he thought Rose was doing, veering back and forth across the heels of the herd, urging them in the direction of the distant village. He hoped that none of those few vaqueros who might have the courage to climb the Pyramid of Mictlantecuhtli on the Day of the Dead would be bright enough to wonder about the obvious ineptitude of one of those "innocent charros" he saw from the top. "Whoever murdered the cook did so because he—or she—saw that I was getting close to the answer. If I can't be driven off, I will need to be killed.... And now that you've joined me, you'll be presumed to know whatever it is I might have learned."

"I wonder if that's what the priest had in mind when he asked if I would take you for better or for worse. Hey up, Bossie, no you *don't*!" She swung her hat at a cow, who shook enormous horns at her but trotted back to the herd. "On the other hand, it's very likely Don Anastasio will remain at Mictlán for part of the day—to supervise the search for you, if he is the murderer, or to deal with Don Prospero at the very least. We might well learn something from a simple investigation of the hacienda de Saragosse if we're not too long about it. After that I suppose we can make it to Mexico City before mid-day tomorrow, and take refuge with Sir Henry."

"We could," agreed January, squinting at the angle of the sun. "But unless I'm much mistaken, tomorrow night is when Don Prospero is going to visit his private *offrenda* within the Pyramid of the Dead to ask his son about what he should do with his murderer. And whatever he thinks Fernando will tell him to do with Hannibal, I'd rather be on hand."

TWENTY-TWO

They concealed the horses in the ruined curing-shed at Saragosse, which stood across the village stream and about a half-mile from the small *casco's* red-washed walls. The shed itself had apparently been torched several years previously, by bandits or by soldiers in the endless struggles for military supremacy that had blotched Mexico's history since its independence from Spain; when January made a cautious foray into the weed-grown fields that surrounded it, he saw the remains of a fire beneath the ragged growth of soapweed and creosote as well.

"So much for Don Anastasio's efforts to bring peanuts into fashion among the upper classes," he murmured, returning to the striped shade where Rose was looking around for a vessel to carry water to the horses. From the debris along the walls he picked out a snarl of hair-stemmed vine, studded still with the dried remains of hulls. Broken tables down the center of the shed must have been for stripping and sorting the pods from the dried vines; the remains of two ovens and a woodshed outside showed where they'd been roasted. "Can you picture Doña Imelda settling down with a bowl of peanuts and a glass of pulque? Neither can I."

The village was quiet save for the voices of some of the women washing clothes on the flat rocks of the stream beyond the trees. After resting the horses and letting them forage among the tall grasses, Rose and January re-saddled and rode in a long circuit around the outside of the village to the churchyard that lay just outside the *casco* walls. A few men were still tinkering with the bamboo framework for the fireworks up near the church door, and others were just setting up tables for refreshments. Most of the graves had been decorated with flowers, and some with the little statues that mocked death: skeleton priests and nuns, ladies and gentlemen, and here and there with the loved toys of children whose parents had not forgotten them. As they passed the village, January saw thick trails of marigold petals running through the dust of the street, and into the doorways and courtyards.

But it was early yet in the afternoon. Only a few children darted among the graves, and they ran away crying, "El Moro!" at the sight of January's black face.

The tallest tomb in the center of the churchyard had been decorated lavishly with banners of fancifully-cut paper and rich profusions of flowers. Many of its marble slabs had been effaced by time: the earliest date January could read was 1577. Rinaldo de Avila de Saragosse y Merced, born in Barcelona in 1532. The remains of his wife were there as well.

The newest slab bore four names: Maria-Ursulina 1821–1830; Cicero 1823–1826; Maria-Proserpina 1826–1834; Porferio 1830–1833. Above them a smaller slab bore the name Orlando Iglesio, 1805–1818.

"Maria-Exaltación's child?" asked Rose, and January said, "It has to be. It makes sense if Don Anastasio is a friend of the family. . . ."

"How DARE you come into this place?" gasped a voice behind them, and turning, startled, January found himself face-to-face with a young man in a priest's black robe: thin, bespectacled, his well-born European features rigid with outrage. "I don't care who your patron is, I told you never to return—"

He broke off, blinked, stepped closer, and removed his spectacles to squint. January saw they were very thick and very old, the gold rims having been mended many times.

"I'm so sorry." The priest rubbed his eyes and replaced the framework of metal and glass on his beaky nose. "I took you for . . . I thought you were someone else."

"You thought I was my cousin, in fact," said January quietly, and assumed an expression of profoundest sorrow and shame.

The priest nodded, and there was no question, to judge by the pinched righteous anger of his expression, that it was El Moro he had thought to see.

"And that said," continued January in his best and most educated Spanish, "I beg you, Father, speak to no one of my presence here. My cousin would not appreciate hearing I was near-by."

"No," said the priest, "of course not. But I warn you, the Padrón who owns this land will return this evening, and he has employed your cousin—paid him off—to do jobs for him in the past. The Padrón may tell him of your presence."

"Oho." January raised his brows. "He rides high with the gentry now, does he?"

Spite and anger narrowed the young man's pale eyes. "Don Anastasio is an atheist and a heretic," he said, his voice soft but nearly spitting the words. "An unbeliever who tries to corrupt all the souls under my care with his books and his 'science' and his 'logic.' And they follow him, because he has learned medicine and can cure their ills, as he cured your cousin's and your cousin's followers. A *brujo*—a sorcerer—who has sold his soul to Satan."

Rose touched the grave-slab of the dead children and said gently, "From the dates on these slabs it seems to me that he has paid at least some of his debt."

"Rather, his poor wife has paid." The young priest sighed. "A lady of great kindness to all. It is only through her generosity and gifts that this village has been able to maintain a church living at all. Matla, the *mayordomo* here, tells me that Don Anastasio believed that he could save his children by watching and writing down every morsel of food that they ate, by withholding food from them—now meat, now fish, now fruit—as if he, and not All-Merciful God, holds the lives of *los niños* in his hands."

Rose said in precisely the voice she had used to exclaim over Señora Lorcha's accusations of Don Prospero's cook, "What an *extraordinary* delusion!"

The priest assumed an expression of somewhat peevish self-righteousness, like Hamlet's friends reveling in their secret knowledge: *We could, and if we would . . .*

"They tell me in the village that Don Anastasio has been thus— like a form of madness—for many years, since the death of a young gentleman who was raised in his household," said the priest. "Blas—the old scoundrel who ran the *pulqueria* in the village—had his establishment closed down because the young gentleman died there: choked, and turned blue, and perished in convulsions, as if invisible hands were closed around his throat. I am told—I have served here in Saragosse only this year and last—that the Don blamed his poor wife when their own children died, cursing her and saying she had poisoned them. But what harm is there in giving sugared peanuts to a child?"

January's glance crossed Rose's, and he said, "What harm indeed?"

"Do you think it was Don Anastasio who paid El Moro to attack Werther in town?"

"Someone did." January stripped the saddle off the black gelding in the curing-shed's slanting shade, rubbed the animal's back with a bunched handful of weed-stems. It was the time of siesta—the washer-women had abandoned the stream, and the gentle noises of the village street, dimly audible even at a mile distant beyond the screens of cactus and trees, had lulled. "The only other person who might have utilized the bandit's services would be Don Prospero himself—and Don Prospero wouldn't care if Werther knew the contents of his will. I only hope Ylario is able to protect the boy in prison, and that von Winterfeldt can get him out of the country. He's had a narrow escape."

"And Hannibal's going to have a narrower one." Rose settled on the edge of one of the great stone oil-presses that filled all of one end of the shed. The incandescent afternoon sunlight picked brassy splinters in her loosened hair and fragments of fire in her spectacles. "If we can get him out of there at all. He'll be at the churchyard at Mictlán tonight, playing for the ghosts of *los niños*. . . ."

"And Don Prospero will be watching him like a hawk," January reminded her. "Tonight is our only chance to hear whatever Valentina has to tell—I think we need to take it. I have an idea of how to convince Don Prospero of Hannibal's innocence."

"If you can explain to Don Prospero not only that morbid sensitivities exist, but that his son was poisoned with a handful of peanuts," said Rose, "I take my hat off to you, sir. I can't imagine even how I'd try."

January smiled. "That's because you don't have a *voodooienne* for a sister," he said. "It's all in how one puts things; and I think I know how to make Don Prospero hear."

The sun sank, and coolness seemed to rise from the earth like the breath of a sleeper, to bless the parched world. When January went out to water the horses again, he could see lights in the village, gold and amber jewels on the dove-colored velvet evening, and heard music from the churchyard, sweet and gay. He saddled the horses and he and Rose rode around to the churchyard, tying them out of sight among the willows by its wall. The gate of the cemetery glowed from the bonfires within, like a cheerful Hell-mouth, and the warm bright torchflame dyed the cinnabar tilework of the church-tower until it stood out like a column of fiery flowers against the darkening sky.

Lilies, marigolds, poppies, and coxcomb garlanded the tall gateposts, made ropes and swags around the necks of the statues on the little church's façade. January was amused to note that the Archangels Michael and Gabriel wore feathers in their hair, the mark of an Indian warrior, and held, not swords, but the obsidian-edged clubs of Quetzalcoatl and Huitzilopochtli: *In righteousness he judges and makes war.*

Under the gaze of those Aztec angels, the churchyard was a fairyland of blossom. Every tomb was now lush with the offerings of the living: baskets of tamales, brilliantly glazed pottery bowls of chicken and mole, little plates of cigars, bottles of pulque and wine. Golden oranges glowed in heaps, *pan de muerto* sparkled. Skulls wrought of sugar grinned cheerfully on all sides.

And among them the laces, the gloves, the tortoiseshell combs, and simple tools of those who had gone on to other worlds. In a green pottery dish, a necklace of amber beads: *whose?* A wooden model of a boat, with ADRIAN on its prow. A little owl wrought of lead. Music wove the gold-laced darkness. Men greeted one another with embraces, women with kisses. Children dashed about in sticky-handed excitement, brandishing pralines and stripped stalks of sugar-cane.

Candles flowed into the churchyard like a river, villagers bearing baskets of food and flowers, calling out to their friends. Indians and mestizos, villagers and the rancheros from the surrounding settlements, vaqueros and the rough muleteers who returned to their home villages on this night, to be with their families, living and dead. The women laughed together, dressed in their best: two-colored skirts stiffened out in approximation of wide petticoats, short-sleeved chemises, satin vests and sashes jingling with ornaments. The warm night gave back the scent of copal, from where, just out of the disapproving young priest's sight, a leathery old man in a peasant's white clothing was smoke-blessing men and women; the priest stayed by the doors of his church, greeting all who came to him.

Someone—probably the *mayordomo* and other *acomodados*—had laid offerings on the big family tomb, but it was clear by their sparse-ness that Don Anastasio had not yet arrived. Among the candy skulls and baskets of mangos was a bowl of sugared peanuts; January knelt and turned the pale, smooth legumes with his huge fingers, smelling the irresistible sweet-saltiness of honey and pepper and wondering if Anastasio would order them taken away.

From childhood he'd loved them—ground-nuts, they were called on Bellefleur Plantation, or monkey-nuts. When his mother had gotten a white protector and moved to New Orleans as a free woman, she wouldn't have them in the house. He'd had to sneak out and buy them from the old man on the corner.

"It has to have been peanuts, doesn't it?" asked Rose.

"I think so. Doña Maria-Exaltación died of eating 'poisoned candy'—it could easily have been a praline. And in a *pulqueria,* it's what young Orlando would have eaten the first time he slipped away at the age of fourteen to drink with the men and prove himself a man. Anastasio's one of the few people who could come and go from Guillenormand's kitchen without comment—it would be easy for him to carry a handful of powdered nuts wrapped in paper and dump them into the strongest-tasting dish he could find. If they didn't kill Fernando outright, they would certainly incapacitate him to the point that, if necessary, Don Anastasio could go into the study and hold a pil-low over his face until the job was done."

Rose, usually so calmly logical, grimaced. "But...why?"

January shook his head and stood up again. "It doesn't matter why," he said. "Maybe he did want to elope with Natividad Lorcha. Or he'd conceived a chivalrous passion for Natividad and couldn't bear the thought of Fernando laying a hand on her. Myself, I think there was something in that will that touched Don Anastasio, something we don't know about—and probably never will know about, since Anastasio was one of the first people into the study after Fernando's death."

"You're probably right," she agreed. Somewhere a child shrieked joyfully, and the band struck up a wistful barcarole. "Still . . . How on earth are we going to prove it?"

"We aren't," said January grimly. "We can't. All we *can* do—all we *need* to do—is . . ."

"Doña Isabella!" called out a voice, and January drew Rose aside, into the shadows of the gorgeously-decorated tombs. Three women in black made their way among the crowds, stopping to embrace this woman or that, their dark silks somber against the gay skirts, the embroidered blouses and aprons of the *poblanas,* the flower-stitched Indian *huipils.*

It was the closest he'd seen Doña Isabella, who bore a strong resemblance to the several portraits of her deceased brother that January had seen. But her narrow face, with its close-set hazel eyes, was pleasant and good-natured within the frame of her black point-lace veils. She bent to hug this child or that, laughing and kissing their mothers, almost like a sister. . . .

Or like the lady from the Big House, thought January, going down to visit the quarters at Christmas.

Santa Anna had boasted on a number of occasions that there was no slavery in Mexico. But January had seen in the city—and saw here now more clearly—the subtler enslavement of a land in chaos, where the weak must become slaves of the strong in order to feed their children. And unless that was secured, he thought, the legal right not to be bought and sold meant very little.

Valentina walked behind her half-sister, clothed like her in a black silk dress of European cut, kissing and greeting and clasping hands as Isabella did. Her mother's sapphire earrings glinted under the smoke of her mantilla. But the girl was clearly distracted, scanning the darkness beyond the light of the cressets and candles, her whole body stiff, as if beneath her corsets she could barely breathe from excitement.

Waiting for her moment, thought January. *Watching for the instant when everyone's back is turned, to casually wander away into the shadows . . .*

"Doña Gertrudis!" called out one of the village women, surging forward in a tinkle of silver ornaments, and the third black-clothed woman embraced her, and another, and another.... "So good to see you home, eh? So good to see you back!"

January's eyes met Rose's, startled. The third woman, with Isabella and Valentina, was definitely Consuela's duenna, the disapproving Doña Gertrudis, her lined, sour face now wreathed in smiles: "Auntie 'Stanza!" she greeted an old Indian woman who came up to them from the crowd. And to another, "Yolie, I've missed you! How are the little ones now, eh?"

"Oh, my dearest child," effused a stout, white-haired woman who looked old enough to have been Doña Gertrudis's nurse, "how I think about you, there in the city, in such a place! Whenever 'Stasio comes here, I ask after you—what kind of man doesn't go to see his own sister? I pray you are well." And they embraced.

It all depends on family, Consuela had said. It all depends on whom you're related to.

Now my brother is a penniless bankrupt: our lands are gone....

And Doña Isabella: *Your sister has been prosing on about how dreadful her lot in life is....*

January blinked, shocked, wondering why he hadn't seen it before. In the way Don Prospero treated Anastasio, exactly as he treated Rafael and his family: *He'll do as he's bid.*

Cultivate pears for me, bring me spinach or cattle or horses as I order....

Of course Don Prospero would buy up the debts of his daughter's husband—or would seal their purchase with such a marriage. He would have let them keep their town house, keep the management of the hacienda that had once been theirs.

He drew a deep breath, and let it out.

"Don Anastasio," said the young priest, rigidly correct, advancing from the church door to greet the *hacendado,* dapper-looking in his suit of embroidered black velvet. The next moment the Don turned and embraced Doña Gertrudis in a way that left January without the slightest doubt that they were, in fact, brother and sister, both ruined alike by the misfortunes of the past twenty-five years. Both pensioners, in whatever positions Don Prospero had chosen to put them.

We keep better count of money in Germany—in Germany we hire business managers....

Managers who didn't spend their money and efforts on a hopeless campaign to get the *criollo* grandees of the town to eat *indio* foods, anyway.

A flicker of black among the firelight and marigolds.

Valentina, slipping away.

At the touch of January's hand, Rose followed him deeper into the shadows. Around the north side of the church the darkness was thicker, the few graves to be found there unkempt and nameless: strangers passing through the land like the poor old valet Da Ponte, vaqueros who had no family, dead from bandit skirmishes and the government armies that had suppressed them. Pepper-trees overhung the graves, forcing apart the bricks of some of the tombs, and from the shadows January watched Valentina making for the heavily-sheltered north door of the church.

From a thick clump of laurel, Rose and January watched as the girl went straight to the statue of St. Paul that stood among the hoary trees, and took something from behind its crumbling pedestal. Then she crossed to the deep embrasure of the church door, disappearing into its dense shadows as if she'd dived into the lightless cenote in Mictlantecuhtli's pyramid. Beneath the soaring brassy notes of a Mozart contradanse, January heard the silvery rustle of taffeta in the darkness, caught a glimpse of white emerging from the mourning black like a moth from a chrysalis, then heard the clink of steel buttons brushing the tile that framed the door.

When Valentina reemerged, she was dressed in the *china poblana,* the bright-hued costume of the women of the people, complete down to her white satin shoes. A striped silk reboso covered her fair hair. She stopped to tie her long silk sash with its tinkling ornaments, and while she was thus occupied, January led Rose to the north churchyard gate. He pressed his ear to it for a moment to make sure the street beyond was empty; everyone was in the churchyard, laughing with family and friends. Slipping the latch, he stepped out into a dark street splashed with squares of lamplight in windows left unshuttered, the marigold petals seeming to glow where they crossed the golden beams of open doors. The night was redolent with cooking, with incense, with the beneficent whispers of the returning dead.

Miles away at the churchyard in Mictlán, it seemed to him he could hear the echoes as Hannibal played the violin for the spirits, like Compair Lapin, summoning the dead to dance.

Leaving Rose to follow on the other side of the street, he slipped across to where an alley gave shadow as dense as that in the churchyard door that had concealed Valentina's change of costume. In a few moments the gate opened again and a small figure in a bright pink skirt, a yellow apron, a white blouse trimmed with lace emerged, a carpetbag in her hand. *Dress and petticoats,* thought January. *She can't let those be found too soon.*

She turned and walked along the churchyard wall, north toward the last houses of the village, humble *jacals* where candle-light shone luminous through the cracks in the crude thatch of the roofs. No doors were closed, and through them January saw the families who remained to celebrate at home: gaggles of sisters in bright skirts, men in the white clothes of the field workers, laughing together, feasting with one another and with those they had loved and had missed with such daily pain for who knew how many years.

It is so good to see you again, my friends, even though we cannot actually see you. My beloved, I have never forgotten you—We're all so glad you haven't forgotten us, you who are happy now forever....

Beyond, the dark trees loomed, and the chuckle of water could be heard over the playing of the now-distant band. The women of the village had done their laundry here, he thought, for five hundred years at least. In the clear silver light of the gibbous moon, the girl strode out to the rocks along the stream, and January heard a man's soft whistle:

> *What will your mother say, Pretty Peggy-o,*
> *What will your mother say, Pretty Peggy-o?*
> *What will your mother say when she finds you've gone*
>   *away...?*

Valentina stood still. "John..."

John Dillard stepped from the shadows of the trees and caught Valentina in his arms.

TWENTY-THREE

January unslung the rifle from his back and said, "Hands up! Don't touch your gun." He stepped into the moonlight, where they could see him, rifle pointed, and added, "I won't do you harm." He repeated that last in Spanish for Valentina's benefit, for she reached down for the carpetbag in a way that made January guess she had a weapon in it.

"There are horses in the trees." Rose emerged beneath the cottonwoods, leading a string of five animals: two horses under saddle, two haltered spares, and a laden mule.

With a strangled cry Valentina sprang at her, and Dillard caught the girl around the waist and dragged her back, for Rose was armed, her pistol in her hand. Valentina thrashed against the Tennessean's grip, kicking and biting. "I won't go back! You can't make me go back!"

"No one's asking you to go back," said January in Spanish, stepping forward and lowering his rifle but keeping a wary eye on Dillard.

"He is a beast!" Valentina turned on January, panting, her fair hair tumbled over her shoulders and her eyes grim and wild. "I will kill myself before I return to his house! He is the Devil, and living with him—with him and with my sister!—is like being in Hell!"

Dillard, who quite clearly didn't understand a word of what was being said, looked warily from Valentina to January and said, "It's all right, *corazón*. It's gonna be all right...." His hand was bleeding from where she'd bitten him. To January he said, "I got the idea you was no friend to Prospero de Castellón—nor to Santa Anna neither. I swear to you my first order of business, once we get over the border into Texas, will be for me to make Miss Valentina my wife—and a braver and more intelligent girl you've never crossed paths with, exceptin' maybe your own lady Rose. And I swear to you on the Testament that before she's my wife I'll not lay a hand on her. I may have little in the way of worldly goods, but I do have my honor, and she has hers. Just because I'm not some Mexican grandee..."

"I believe you." January held up his free hand to stem what he guessed would be everything Dillard would have said to Don Prospero, could Dillard ever have come into that gentleman's presence. He suspected the Tennessean would take serious offense if he had said simply, *It isn't any of my business whether you seduce Valentina de Castellón or not*—which it wasn't, and if he'd made it his business, Dillard would have been the first to tell him that as a black man his opinion didn't matter.

Whites were strange that way.

Men were strange that way.

And he had a good idea that Valentina de Castellón was more than able to take care of herself. Her virginity, he was willing to bet, would not survive the night, no matter how much Dillard struggled to spare it.

He went on. "And I would not have stopped you tonight, except that for a friend's sake I must speak to Señorita de Castellón, and ask something of her that she may be unwilling to give."

He turned to Valentina, who had locked her arm tight around Dillard's waist and was following the conversation between the two men with the watchfulness of an animal. "Señorita, I will not stay you from leaving your father's house—"

"You cannot, and I would like to see you try!"

"*Corazón...*"

The glare she gave Dillard at this mollifying interjection promised a lifetime of half-apologetic, timid *corazóns*.

"I will not stay you," January repeated, "but nor will I let you leave without a written explanation—to your family and to the authorities in Mexico City—that you were never Hannibal Sefton's lover, and that the letters to you in his hand were in fact translations of clandestine correspondence from a *Norteamericano*. And your letters to Dillard would help."

Her chin went up. "It isn't anyone's business what I do." In the shadowy floods of her hair the sapphire earrings she'd inherited from her erring mother sparkled darkly. "I won't go back to be offered like a piece of camote to any man my father wants to ally himself with! To live under the threat that if I'm not a good girl he'll repudiate my mother and have me declared an *adulterina*, whom no man will marry! To have my room searched, to have my things taken away—even my mother's jewelry!—and given to his whores. What is it to anyone where I go or what I do or where I choose to seek my happiness?"

"It is something to Hannibal," answered January, a little surprised that he felt no impulse to box this defiant child's ears. "Because of those letters he will be hanged for your brother's murder."

Valentina blinked at him in astonishment. "The letters have nothing to do with it," she retorted in the tone of one who has never connected her own actions with other people's unhappiness in her life. "He poisoned my brother, and I don't care that he did. Fernando was a beast—more of a beast than my father, for at least Father you can talk to sometimes, when he's not thinking he's the God of the Night. Fernando was like a marble building, cold and locked up. Like a bank that will never lend you a copper medio if you are starving because it is not in the interests of the bank."

She stooped to pick up her reboso and pulled it over her shoulders, shivering in the chill by the water. "Bad enough that Father would have married me off to that old nanny-goat Rafael to get me off his hands ... and whose fault is it that no one who was not forced to do so would take a girl who could be turned out of her inheritance at the next twist of her father's madness? But all Rafael is interested in is keeping Fructosa hacienda, and having his mother live in the town house, and making everything look as if they were still rich and not as poor as the beggars on the Cathedral steps. And even so, Fernando was going to turn them out and put those lands into the hands of a 'good administrator' to make them produce more money for him!"

Her voice shook with passion, and Dillard, who'd been pursuing this back-and-forth with furrowed brow, ventured, "Dearest heart, if this man ..." He stumbled over the subjunctive clause and retrieved himself with "Does this man trouble you?"

Valentina made a gesture at him to shut up, as if she were shooing flies. "Fernando said he would give Rafael enough money to start a 'respectable business'—as if that clown wouldn't go through whatever Fernando gave him at the gambling tables in a week!—and he was terrified that if Don Rafael learned I'd written love-letters to another man, he wouldn't marry me. Then I'd be on Fernando's hands, like a carriage-horse that kicks, and would end my days like silly old Doña Filomena, having to be someone's duenna because no one would have me. Hannibal poisoned my brother because he deserved to be poisoned—"

"Hannibal did not poison your brother," cut in January.

"Oh, and you did not cut the throat of poor Señor Guillenormand, either, eh?"

"No, I did not."

"After practically accusing the poor man of murdering Fernando himself..."

"And where," asked January, "did you hear that?"

She shrugged. "I heard him ranting on about it to Uncle 'Stasio in the kitchen last night."

"Considering that Don Anastasio did not arrive at Mictlán until nearly midnight," pointed out Rose, "that was awfully late for a proper young lady to be in the kitchen."

"I was getting food," returned Valentina sulkily. "Food for this journey. Josefa told me how you had said there was a great quarrel between the President and the *Nortes*. I knew my John"—she pronounced it "Joan"—"would leave word for me in our secret place, and that I would have to go to him quickly."

"Which I take it you did," said January, "while everyone was out looking for me?"

"I knew he could not come close to the *casco*," said the girl. "I had meant to go while Josefa was at Mass."

"You're lucky," remarked Rose, "that none of your father's vaqueros—or El Moro's men—encountered you on your way to the pyramids. I take it you chose the pyramids as your post-box because few will venture there?"

"They're all cowards," sniffed Valentina. "Cowards and poltroons. I do not fear Father's moldy old gods."

"I swear to you, January," Dillard launched in again in English, "that I've loved this girl since first I laid eyes on her. If we've gone about this thing clandestinely, it's because that crazy father of hers wouldn't hear of a match between her and a poor man, a true American. But my intentions toward her have been of the most honorable from the first. After that hoo-rah at the British minister's, Butler advised the lot of us to head straight for the town gates and not even stop at our digs; most of the boys took off straight for Vera Cruz. But once Valentina's family knows she's gone, that's where they'll look for us. We aim to go straight up overland, across the Rio Grande to San Antonio Béxar—"

"And warn Sam Houston," asked January softly, "that Santa Anna's on his way? And exactly how many men he has with him, and in what state his artillery is? And join the militia he's raising as well?"

"Something like that." The young man's arm tightened protectively around Valentina's waist. And Valla, her head high, closed her hand over his, where it lay on her hip, as if she guessed what January was truly asking.

"If Mexico was the land it should be—that it *was* before Santa Anna took it over—we wouldn't have to be doin' this," the Tennessean added. "We could have dealt with a fair government here fairly."

January kept himself from remarking that the Americans—who'd just finished running the Louisiana Chickasaws off their land—would probably have rebelled against whatever government Mexico had, fair or unfair.

He merely turned to Valentina and asked in Spanish, "And that was what you were doing the night Fernando was killed? Stealing food and passing it over the wall?"

"Food, and some of my jewels," she replied. "Such of them as my father hadn't already stolen from me for his whore."

She turned to Dillard and said in halting English, "Joan, give him what he ask. All my letter. We come not back here again."

"You're sure, *corazón*?"

She nodded, and Dillard stepped away from her, and picked his way over to the pack-mule. While he opened one of the saddlebags, January heard again the drift of music on the night air: how long would it be before Isabella and Anastasio realized Valentina wasn't somewhere in the churchyard throng?

Certainly not until after Mass. Given the comings and goings among the tombs, the amount of wine and food and conversation, it might be two or three in the morning before anyone realized she wasn't

around—but it could easily be noon before they realized she hadn't returned to the *casco* and gone to bed.

Rose, January noticed, kept her distance from Dillard, her pistol
trained and ready. He didn't think she needed this. The Tennessean—
soon-to-be Texian—was at the moment engaged in trying to light a
small bull's-eye lantern. But Rose was not one to take chances.

To Valentina, January said, "If you had the food ready to pass over
the wall as soon as it grew dark on the night of Fernando's death, you
must have taken it from the kitchen earlier in the day. Did you see who
else came and went from the kitchen while Guillenormand was preparing supper?"

"Did I!" The girl threw up her hands. "I must have waited and
watched for an hour behind the door of one of the corn-stores, waiting
until the kitchen-yard was clear! Poor Señor Guillenormand was like a
madman when he cooked! I thought he would drive that weaselly valet
of Fernando's out with a frying-pan; and then Padre Ramiro kept hanging about, hoping to steal enough camote to last him through the
night. Uncle 'Stasio was in and out a dozen times, with pears and apples
and bottles of wine and bunches of grapes, and Father ordering him
about like a slave. . . ."

"Don Anastasio is Doña Gertrudis's brother, isn't he?" asked
January, and Valentina nodded.

"They do not speak of it, since Father made her go live with
Consuela. Their father was the younger brother of the Marquis de
Merced. The whole family was on the verge of bankruptcy when 'Stasio
supported the Emperor Iturbide, seven years ago, and Santa Anna
turned against him. Father kept 'Stasio from being put into prison, but
'Stasio lost everything—lands, house, cattle, even his books. Father
bought up his lands the way he did old Don Alejandro de Bujerio's, and
he lets Isabella go on living in their old town house. But they're as much
his peons as any of the *indios* in the village."

Above the trees, fireworks exploded with a loud crack, crimson rain
and golden lightning showering down through the darkness. Mellow as
butterscotch, the notes of trumpets soared into the sky.

" 'Stasio's another one, like Rafael, who smiles and bows and pre-
tends not to be insulted, only so that he may continue to have a roof
over his head. For Rafael it is his mother and his aunts and his sisters,
and making sure everyone has jewels and coaches and good food and

can put my cousins in the most fashionable convents. For 'Stasio it is his precious orchards and his precious library. And it all comes down to the same thing: they let themselves be ruled by the whim of a madman because they're afraid."

Scorn flickered in her voice—the scorn of one who has never felt hunger or cold or the despair of responsibilities that she is unable to uphold. "I am not afraid."

January studied her, that slim, beautiful girl in her gaudy skirt and borrowed reboso, and tried to picture her alone in a foreign land with a child or children to feed. When Santa Anna's Army reached Texas, Dillard would be in the forefront of the battle. And even with the amount of sand and sawdust in the Mexican Army's gunpowder, some of those bullets would find flesh.

Would she be afraid then?

Or would she stay on anyway, to become a Texas woman, the founder of a new state?

Another explosion, and the sky was filled with blue and green sparkles. "Sulphate of potassa," remarked Rose.

"Uncle 'Stasio makes them," agreed Valentina, sitting on a rock as Dillard came back carrying the lantern and a slim sheaf of papers. "He can make nearly anything." She took from him a lead-pencil, and tore off the bottom of one of the sheets. " 'I, Maria-Valentina de Castellón, daughter of Don Prospero de Castellón and of Melosia Valenzuela, do here attest and swear that the letters written to me in the hand of'—by the hand of?—'Mr. Hannibal Sefton were in fact only translations of letters received by me from my affianced husband, Mr. John Dillard of Smith County, Tennessee, and Nashville-on-the-Brazos, Texas; and in keeping silent concerning this fact Mr. Sefton was obeying my earnest pleas, and defending my honor.' There!"

She signed with a flourish and thrust the papers at January. Gravely, she added, "It will do you no good, but I do owe it to Hannibal that at least he not be accused of trying to seduce me. He did us all the greatest of services, poisoning my brother. Tell him I thank him for that. We all should, Josefa and Natividad and even Father, because it was Fernando who really wanted Father locked up. I mean, if Father had been locked up, Fernando would have taken over Saragosse as well, and put in a 'good administrator'—" Her voice twisted over the words, as if she said *slave-driver* or *whoremaster*. "But 'Stasio was afraid if he didn't help

Fernando, Fernando would have his way anyway and then would throw him—and Isabella—out into the road."

She put her arm through Dillard's. "And if we are taken," she added to January, "I will tell them that you forced me to write that letter—and all of these as well—and that you dishonored me afterwards. Let us go, *amor mio.*" She smiled up at Dillard. "We can be in Jalapa by morning."

"And God help him," murmured Rose as the Texian and Don Prospero's younger daughter mounted their horses and splashed away up the course of the trickling stream, "the day he runs afoul of that little cactus-blossom. Curious how it didn't seem to occur to any of them—not Rafael or Don Anastasio or Valentina—that being thrown out to make one's own living is not the end of the world."

"God forbid that the nephew of the Marquis de Merced should have to enter trade." January slung his rifle back over his shoulder and crossed the moonlit rocks back to where the overgrown path led up to the curing-shed. "Or learn how to deal with life that doesn't include being treated with respect by everyone he meets."

"For a woman it's different, of course." Rose uncocked her pistol and slipped it into her sash. "There isn't much else Doña Gertrudis *can* do except be passed along as a duenna to whoever in the family wants one—including the bastard daughter of a family friend who's no better than she should be. Whatever papers Don Prospero may have had regarding the status of his friend's lands and property must have been kept fairly secret—it doesn't seem to be something Ylario knows, for instance. But Fernando would certainly have come across them in sorting out Don Prospero's effects."

"And may have been so foolish as to mention his plans to Anastasio."

TWENTY-FOUR

They slept a few hours in an arroyo, and rode through the pre-dawn starlight to reach the pyramids of Mictlán just before first light. January saw no sign of fire, smelled no smoke as they circled through the gullies and woods that surrounded the old temples, then moved cautiously in for a closer look. They found horse-droppings in the woods, and the tracks of men—mended *zapatos* without the scuffing of a vaquero's protective *bota* attached—but no evidence that the riders whose coming had driven them away yesterday had ascended the Pyramid of the Dead.

"What will you tell Don Prospero?" Rose asked as they climbed the broken remains of the old stair to the flattened area outside the crypt passage. The soft dirt of the passage, and of the crypt around the broken altar, was unmarked by any boots but January's own.

"The truth," he replied, studying again the vases of marigolds, the dying roses weeping from the Death-God's eyes. The things that had been dear to Fernando. "Depending on how receptive he seems to be and how many other voices he's already hearing in his head. Last night was the night of *los niños*. The night of All Saints," he went on, coming out to cut a branch of scrubby sagebrush to scratch out his own tracks. "Tonight is the night of All Souls. Everyone returns, saint and sinner alike, presumably even apostates like Fernando."

He walked back down the passageway, brush branch in hand, and his shadow against the light made Mictlantecuhtli's features flicker, like eyelids stirring in sleep. The pale daylight gleamed wanly on the Meissen china, the curves of candy and bones, tea-cup and sword. "If Don Prospero intends to have words with his dead son, it will be tonight. And it will be here."

They spent the day lying on top of the pyramid in the dismantled shrine, alternately watching the hacienda and the surrounding range-lands, and picking out the worn shapes of priests and warriors, singing-girls and sacrifices, from the stones around them. The church-bell tolled in Mictlán, calling the people to the Mass of All Souls: *Dies irae, dies illa, solvet saeculum in favilla....* The wind bore up to them the scents of smoke from the village, where a second feast was being pre-pared, and in the streets January could see the women scattering more flower-petals, to lead the spirits home.

"Santa Anna may not even know about Don Prospero's purchase of the Avila de Saragosse lands," said January as he passed Rose a water-bottle. After checking on the horses and making sure of the loads in all their guns, she was stretched out full-length, reading Valentina's love-letters.

"But records of the transaction would have been among Don Prospero's papers. It's what Anastasio was truly afraid Fernando had mentioned to Werther Bremer—what he was afraid Bremer would tell Ylario."

"And poor Hannibal simply walked into it," sighed Rose. "Valentina may have been poorly educated," she added, turning over the love-letter in her hand, "but she definitely has a working knowledge of the more sensational romantic fiction available in Mexico. This business about *I am your humble and willing slave, you torture me but to try me,* is straight out of *Glenarvon,* and *In thy veins while blood shall roll, I am thine! Thou art mine! Mine thy body! Mine thy soul!* comes from *The Monk.* I know, because one of the girls in the school I taught wrote the same thing to a young poet she was enamored of. Poor Hannibal, to have to translate this tripe. Her letters are all in his handwriting as well, poor man. She must have dictated them. The signatures seem to be hers."

"Good," said January. "At least Ylario can't argue that he wrote her half of the correspondence to exonerate himself."

"Nonsense," retorted Rose. "Of course he can—and will. He'll say Hannibal deceived the poor girl into signing them—told her they were affectionate missives to her father or something—which I'm sure is exactly what she'll swear to if she's caught."

She sat up and brushed the dust from her elbows. It was the hour of siesta, and on the top of the pyramid the sun was brutal, but January dared not relax his guard. "Do you think he'll believe you? Don Prospero, I mean?" she asked.

January hesitated a long time, then said, "I think so. When a man has a valley-wide reputation as a wizard, it shouldn't be too hard to convince his friend that he was capable of brewing a potion that could kill one man out of a table-full and leave the rest without even a tummy-ache. I don't have to make a case that will stand in court. Only one that will convince Don Prospero to release Hannibal from custody, and smuggle him out of the country ahead of the law."

"It's a pity in a way," said Rose. "I think Hannibal is genuinely fond of Consuela. Goodness knows he looks better than he has since I've known him. What if Don Prospero doesn't come?"

January glanced down the hill-slope to the broken stone images at the bottom that marked the ancient sacrificial stair. "He'll come," he said.

Requiem aeternam dona eis, Domine: et lux perpetua luceat eis. In New Orleans his mother and sisters would be tidying up the grave of his mother's recent husband, Christophe Levesque, and the family tomb of the Janviers. White members of that old French family would be chatting with them comfortably, quite at ease with St. Denis Janvier's mistress and his daughter, "from the shady side of the street."

Maybe that's why everyone puts skulls on the offrendas, he thought, gazing off across the lizard-brown softness of the dry range. *Because Death strips away the smiling lips, the painted cheeks, the skin whose hue is so desperately important to so many people. "Get thee to my lady's chamber and tell her that though she paint an inch thick, to this end will she come."*

Under the skin, Death grins at us all.

The moon stood high before the sun faded, nearly full and glowing with burning silver light. Firefly sparks flowed along the village streets and a little jewel-heap of amber lights congregated beneath the shadow of the church-tower, but for the most part the night's feasting seemed to be in the homes. "We may not see him coming once it grows dark," said January with regret as the ruby globe of the sun dyed the snows of Popocatepetl. "And he'll see whatever light we kindle."

Faced with the prospect of a long vigil in the tiny chamber behind the stone image, he was thinking less and less well of his plan.

While Rose stood watch, January descended to scout the area, then saddled both horses in case of need for a quick getaway. While the last blaze of daylight still gilded the sky, they entered the crypt again, the light of their candles making every carving and shadow move with a gruesome underwater animation. Darkness tangled in the roots that thrust apart the crude corbeling of the ceiling, and lent the Death-God's skeletal countenance a malign expression of watchfulness. Directly below it, Fernando's bland, prim face appeared even more withdrawn, aloof and calculating between tea-cup and sword.

"Where will you be?" whispered January, handing Rose his rifle.

"Lying in the brush behind Quetzalcoatl's head." She gestured out the passageway, and down to the foot of the pyramid. "There's no real cover closer than that. I'll have to wait till he goes inside before I start to climb, so stall as long as you can."

She would be far too distant to be of real help in an emergency, reflected January, but that couldn't be helped. There was nothing closer, and it was highly unlikely Don Prospero would be accompanied.

"Let's just hope the sound of my voice coming out of the idol doesn't panic him into falling into the well." January took a snake-stick in one hand and a candle in the other, and edged his way around the gaping black circle of the pit to the tangled roots that concealed the entrance to the priest's nook behind the statue. "It won't do me any good to tell him that the gods want him to release Hannibal if he proceeds to break his neck—or if he sees either of us and realizes the voice of the god is a hoax."

"On the other hand, pushing him in the cenote may solve many of our problems," remarked Rose judiciously. "Let us keep it as a last resort in case of emergency. Do you have any little companions in that niche to keep you from growing lonely?"

"The last thing I want while I'm in there," growled January, holding the candle to the cramped throat of the nook, "is the patter of little feet. Yuh!" he added as a rather large brown scorpion scuttled out and vanished at once into the shadows.

"Better that you saw it go out than in," said Rose in the comforting tone of one who doesn't have to sit in an underground hole with scorpions herself.

January made no reply. The wavering candle-flame made every-thing seem half-alive, and deepened rather than revealed every tene-brous crevice between the ancient stones. What had appeared, in the open air of Saragosse's moonlit stream-bank last night, to be a brilliant means of freeing Hannibal now presented a gruesome series of logistical realities.

January unearthed and killed three more scorpions and a tarantula, which made him feel worse rather than better. Like mice or roaches, he suspected there were ten unseen for every one eliminated; he felt like the hero of a blood-and-thunder melodrama hewing at a wolf-pack in knee-deep Russian snow. At last he retreated to where Rose stood watching the moonlit hill-slope, and said, "I'm going to keep a candle burning in there with me. Will you owl-hoot when you see Don Prospero coming up the hill?"

"Do you think you'll hear me inside?" she asked. "Or that Don Prospero won't wonder why there are hoot-owls in this part of the country?"

"I'm not sitting in there without a candle."

She put her hands on his shoulders and tiptoed to kiss him, smil-ing. "Hannibal owes us both dinner at the Buttonhole Café," she mur-mured, "when we're all safely back in New Orleans."

The candle helped a little, though its uncertain light did nothing to dispel the inky shadows that clotted the little priest-hole like horrible lace. There was barely room for January to stand, and he could not sit without his back touching one wall or another. He was reminded of the dungeon in the Châtelet prison in Paris that had been called "Little-Ease," so constructed that the unfortunate occupant would be unable to either sit or lie and was too low to stand in, either.

No wonder the French rose in revolt.

That dungeon had probably been infested with roaches and rats, too, he reflected with a panicky twitch as he brushed at his shoulder for the dozenth time, fancying he felt the pricking feet of a vinigaroon when it was in fact only a fold of his shirt. At least, he decided, he was not of a fanciful disposition, or superstitious about crouching in the dark heart of the Pyramid of the Dead on the night when all the souls of the departed floated through the darkness. His childhood had been spent in a world of spirits and *loa,* of the platt-eye devil and a thousand Petro demons that needed propitiation. But even as a child in the slave-quarters of Bellefleur

Plantation, his attitude had been pragmatic. There were mojo-signs and conjure-bags and gris-gris to deal with such spirits as Onzoncaire and Guédé-Five-Days-Unhappy. Whatever there was to be afraid of in the darkness, his father had been able to say *Look it in the face. The bad spirits can't abide being looked at in the face, and the good spirits will look you right back.*

It was not that he did not believe that spirits walked the darkness, he reflected, watching the candle-shadows waver over the stone pits that were the idol's eyes, the stone tube that was the idol's mouth. They were still there: the spirits of the Aztec priests who had crouched here where he crouched; the youths and maidens who had lost their lives on the altar or in the cold, lightless waters of the holy well. Just as he knew his own ancestors walked the swamps of the Mississippi bayous when the sun went down.

You just looked them in the face, seeing them for what they were, spirits like oneself.

An owl hooted. With a silent prayer that it was Rose—and that something would happen fairly soon and not leave him for another three hours in total darkness with the scorpions—January touched the speaking-tube with one hand, and puffed out his candle.

Blackness, in which the silence seemed more crushing than the weight of the hill above him. A thousand scorpions the size of dogs emerged from the caverns of his imagination to ring his boots.

He was just wondering if that had been an actual owl—and how he could get his candle lit again—when a tiny rim of reflected gold bobbed on the inner surface of the speaking tube. Startlingly clear, he heard a man's breathing in the temple, and the scrape of boots; the rustle of clothing and the creak of belt-leather. Of course, he thought, this was a spy-hole; the acoustics of this hidden chamber must be designed to magnify the slightest whisper in the sanctuary outside.

His mind filled with tarantulas, January pressed his face to the curved stone of the inner side of the idol's skull-like head, and looked out through the speaking-tube of the mouth in time to see Don Anastasio lay the unconscious Don Prospero down in the shadows beside the inky abyss of the holy well.

Don Anastasio was dressed as he had been the previous night, in the black velvet garb of the wealthy gentleman that all thought him still to be, bullion glittering on his sleeves and pockets and hat. Only his silver-

streaked black hair was hidden under a scarf, like a vaquero's. Don
Prospero was likewise formally dressed, as if he'd fallen asleep—or been
drugged—immediately after dinner. His breathing was thick, and he
lay without moving, his long, white mustaches hanging limp. Don
Anastasio straightened, and stood looking down at him for a moment,
his face unreadable in the whisper of his lantern's light. Then he opened
the satchel he wore slung at his side and took from it handfuls of
marigold-petals. These he carefully strewed along the passageway to the
outside, and then, returning, on the floor all around the broken altar-
stone that stood beside the holy well.

That done, he took from the satchel a triangular-bladed obsidian
knife, probably from Don Prospero's own collection, and laid it ready
on the ancient altar beside the lantern.

He crossed to Don Prospero, took off his velvet coat, laid it carefully aside, and knelt beside him in shirtsleeves, feeling his pulse.

January thought, *Opiates. Or possibly some kind of Indian drug that
has some of the same effects . . .*

"I assure you that according to all the best authorities, what you're
doing is terribly, terribly unlucky," came a familiar voice, hollow with
the echoes of the tunnel from the hill-slope outside. "*Facilis decensus
Averno: sed revocare gradum superasque evadere ad auras, hoc opus, hic labor est.* In any case, the British minister will make enquiries if I'm not
properly hanged according to law, and Don Prospero will be exceed-
ingly annoyed." Hannibal's breath dragged sharply over the words as he
stumbled.

In slow Indian Spanish a man's voice replied, "The Don, he's already annoyed with me and José here, my friend. Besides, who's going
to tell him you were with us, eh?"

Don Anastasio straightened up, snapped, "Lobo! I told you not to
speak to the man, and I meant it."

"What harm, eh, *jefe?*" They emerged from the tunnel, two men
whom January had a vague sense of having seen before—El Moro's
men? Not vaqueros, anyway. Definitely bandits, their lean Indian faces
scarred and weather-beaten, their straight black braids hanging dirty
from beneath battered hats. Worn faces and tired, like animals who will
kill and eat anything to stave off hunger, like the bandit in the pass.
They dragged Hannibal between them; his hands were bound behind
his back and his long hair hung down around a face bruised and cut, as

if he'd put up a struggle at some point. He was in shirtsleeves, panting, and barely on his feet. His dark eyes went to Don Anastasio's face, then widened at the sight of the gaudy red and gold of the flowers around the grinning God of Death, and Fernando's portrait among the bones at its feet. Then to Don Prospero, stretched out unconscious in the shadows.

And to the knife on the altar.

Seeing what January saw and guessing what January now guessed about who had actually set up Fernando's altar, and for what purpose.

"I assure you, whatever testimony you seek in order to prove Don Prospero's insanity, I can provide you—without even violating the truth or coming anywhere close to its fullest extravagances..."

"The heretic, he's funny," said the shorter man—José—with a slight drunken slur to his speech, as the heavier, bearded Lobo set down the lantern he carried. "He told us a story about this Protestant who died and went to Hell—"

"I don't pay you to listen to his stories." Anastasio reached into his satchel again and brought out two small bags, handling them as though they were heavy. January heard the unmistakable clink of coin. José reached to take one of them, and Hannibal tried to twist free and run the moment he'd released his grip. José jerked him into a casual back-hand swat that made him stagger. Then he pushed him to the ground, inches from the black rim of the cenote, and put a foot on his back to take the money.

Rose, thought January, frantic, wondering what the hell he could do to delay them. *She saw who it was coming in, she's got to have guessed. She's got to be close....*

How close? How many minutes—seconds—did he have? Squeezing out of the tunnel he'd be a sitting duck, dead before he could so much as cry out. *Damn it, Rose....*

Anastasio handed Lobo the second bag and produced a silver flask, which he uncorked and handed to the bandit. While Lobo drank noisily of it—and José kicked Hannibal aside to go get his share—the Don stood over Hannibal and turned him gently over with one foot. "Do you really think Santa Anna would listen to the testimony of a laudanum-sodden opium-fiend? A man whom I doubt he would even take into that pathetic Army he's raising? No, my worthless friend. He must be shown, in terms that even *he* will understand, how mad Don Prospero is."

Hannibal edged away from the well's rim and tried to raise himself onto one elbow. "According to the *Iliad,* one can go mad just as convincingly by slaughtering sheep."

Don Anastasio reached down, dragged Hannibal to his feet by the front of his shirt, then tore the garment back over his shoulders and shoved him into the grip of the two bandits, who had managed, in near-record time, to finish the liquor in the flask. "The British minister," said the Don, picking up the obsidian knife, "would make less of a fuss over sheep. Probably not much less, but some."

At a nod from him, Lobo kicked Hannibal behind the knees, thrust him down onto the stone altar. The fiddler kicked and twisted, but the two bandits pinned him by ankles and shoulders exactly as the priests did in the ancient carvings on the walls. Don Anastasio started forward. . . .

"ANASTASIO DE SARAGOSSE!" January bellowed at the top of his lungs, not knowing how the speaking-tube might magnify his voice, and was rewarded beyond all expectations by thunderous echoes that seemed to come from everywhere in the darkness at once. Don Anastasio might not believe in the ancient gods, but he was startled enough by the sound alone to jerk back and drop the knife, and his two henchmen leaped away from the altar as if they'd been shot at.

Swift as a lizard, Hannibal rolled off the altar and bolted for the door, and January saw nothing of the proceedings for the next second or so as he slithered through the narrow passage to the sanctuary, pistol in hand. He writhed clear of its entrance in time to see Lobo catch Hannibal by the arm and fling him back in the direction of the altar. Hannibal collided with José, tripped on one of the lanterns, sending it plunging down into the dark of the holy well and falling himself on its edge. For an instant he lay gasping on the brink of the chasm, struggling to twist his hands free of their bonds. José strode over to him and he tried to roll aside, and before January could reach them or even move in that direction, with spiteful deliberation José kicked Hannibal over the edge.

A gunshot cracked in the same instant and José sprawled back into a corner. Rose ducked out of the doorway as Lobo raised his own pistol—January seized his wrist, hearing the bone in the arm snap as he flung the bearded bandit aside. In the doorway Rose cried out, "Ben!"

And turning, January saw Anastasio backed against the carved jamb of the outer door. He held Rose by one arm twisted behind her, the sacrificial knife at her throat.

January froze.

"Throw down your gun," said the Don quietly. "I have no desire to harm either of you. If you leave at once, tonight, for Vera Cruz, I shall see to it that your wife rejoins you there safely within a week. Thanks to her, I have a dead man, and a dead man is all I really need tonight; it scarcely matters who. I don't think anyone will believe a pair of *negros* any more than they'd have believed your worthless friend."

January stood a few feet from the edge of the cenote, his breath dragging hard. José, his chest blown to bloody rags, was still twitching and gurgling near the unconscious Don Prospero. His blood had splattered the far wall, dripping down the brown skeletal face of Mictlantecuhtli and the gaudy marigolds. Lobo crouched, moaning with pain, in a corner. The crowded darkness was filled with the stink of blood and voided waste.

"Any more than I believe you," January said.

"It scarcely matters whether you believe me or not," replied Don Anastasio in his soft, reasonable voice. "I assure you that what I am doing is for the best."

"And I suppose you're going to kill him, too?" January nodded at Lobo.

Anastasio shook his head impatiently. "What does he matter? I have killed him already. You don't think I'd trust men like that to run about wagging their tongues in every *pulqueria* in the Valley of Mexico, do you? I repeat, there is no one here now who can hurt me. Leave now, and no harm will come to your wife." He pressed the blade to her throat. "Interfere with me..."

"Without her as a hostage you're a dead man."

"That won't bring her back, now, will it?" Drawing Rose after him, Anastasio backed along the passageway. January followed him slowly outside, wondering desperately what he was going to do, what he *could* do. He dared not rush him, dared not risk his own reflexes—or Rose's—against those of the wiry, quick-moving Don. Yet he knew as surely as he knew his name that the man who had calmly handed those two poor bandits a flask of poisoned liquor—who had calculated the most worthless available victim whose death would oblige Santa Anna to have Don Prospero locked up—would never let Rose go free.

And if Anastasio was paying El Moro and his bandits, he himself might never reach Vera Cruz either.

Moonlight blazed on the steep slope of the pyramid outside. January saw horses tied at the bottom. He felt hypnotized by the sight of that black glass blade, after five hundred years still sharper than steel, pressed into Rose's skin. "Go down the pyramid ahead of me," said Anastasio quietly. "Take one of the horses and go. I swear to you she will come to no harm as long as you keep silent about what you have seen here tonight. This is purely a family matter. . . ."

"Are you counting Guillenormand as family? Or Hannibal? Or Werther Bremer?" But even as he said the words, January guessed that Don Anastasio didn't even comprehend his objection.

A servant? An opium-eater? A catamite?

Nothing.

No more than a woman of color, a woman of no family . . .

"I repeat," said Anastasio, "you really have no choice. Unless you . . ."

The rifle that cracked almost in January's ear made him leap aside, his heart nearly springing out of his body with shock. So silently had Don Prospero emerged from the tunnel behind him that January didn't even see the old *hacendado* until he fired. It was an astonishing shot for moonlight: Don Anastasio's head snapped back and his arms flew out, Rose ducking, springing aside from the falling body. For a half-second all January could see was Rose, stumbling to her knees and catching herself, still moving, still alive. . . .

Then he looked back and saw Anastasio reel backwards and tumble down the pyramid in a spatter of blood to the bottom, as the sacrificed victims had long ago rolled.

Beside January, Don Prospero stepped forward to watch him roll with interested eyes, leaning on the rifle while smoke curled from the barrel, white as the old man's hair in the moonlight.

Only when the body came to rest did the old Don turn to January, his pale gaze quizzical under those jutting, animal brows.

"It's a most extraordinary thing," he remarked. "Fernando says *Anastasio* killed him."

Rose got slowly to her feet, brushing dirt from her hands and, almost as an afterthought, wiping the thin streak of blood from her neck. *"What?"*

January ran down the slope to her, caught her in his arms, trembling with shock. The black glass knife lay where Anastasio had dropped it, in the dust at her feet. She shook her head a little—*I'm all right*—and laid her hand against his cheek; he felt dizzy for a moment, as if he was going to faint.

Hannibal, he thought then, *Hannibal falling into the pit in the temple....*

He scrambled back to where the Don stood, gently took the rifle from him, though having been fired, it was no danger now and Prospero showed no signs of re-loading it.

"Fernando told you?"

"Just now." The Don blinked at him, puzzled but not upset. "Back in the...Are we at the pyramid? How did we get here?"

He shook his head. In the bluish moonlight his face was empty of ferocity, relaxed, like that of a sleepy child. "The last I recall I was having a drink with Anastasio. Then I woke up, and Fernando told me Anastasio had murdered him—something about peanuts, though how peanuts could harm anyone...And he said to kill him."

The old man sighed, stroked his long mustaches into tidy order, and slowly descended the pyramid to where Anastasio's crumpled body lay. "It really is too bad," January heard him say without a backward glance. "He did raise astonishingly good pears."

TWENTY-FIVE

"Hannibal?"

The surviving lantern had been kicked into a corner of the temple and was guttering out. Kneeling on the edge of the holy well, January could see the tiniest smudge of yellow gleam reflected on rocks just below the narrow ledge, as if the lantern had rolled into some nook or cave beneath it. Even as he watched, it flickered out; his own torchlight showed him that Hannibal had not, as he'd prayed, fallen onto the ledge. But a moment later a faint, husky voice whispered, *"Darkling I listen, amicus meus*— Is Rose all right? I thought I heard her voice. . . ."

"She's fine." *Barely,* January added to himself, shivering again. He was beginning to understand those men who went mad and locked their wives up to make sure nothing ever happened to them.

Like Don Prospero.

"Are *you* all right? Where are you?"

"Under the ledge—the ground slopes pretty sharply once you hit. *Fallen from his high estate, and welt'ring in his blood. . . .* Only I don't seem to be weltering much, thank goodness, though I won't answer for my right leg." A dry whisper as weight shifted tentatively on stones, and the sudden harsh draw of breath that told January his friend was far from unscathed by his fall.

"Was that you who spoke to Don Prospero?"

"Me? Not a word. I've been lying here, pretending to be a virgin. I heard him say Fernando's name once, but that was all. Is the shooting done?"

"I think so. I have to go back to the bottom for a rope."

"*Be thou here again ere the leviathan can swim a league,* if you can manage it, *amicus meus.* There's something down here—I don't know whether it's a scorpion or a spider, but it's walked across me twice."

"*I'll put a girdle round the earth in forty minutes,*" promised January, breathless with relief at being involved again in one of Hannibal's ridiculous conversations, and strode out through the dark of the tunnel to the moonlit hill-slope beyond.

Rose was sitting on the domed head of a half-buried stone serpent at the bottom of the pyramid, her rifle across her knees. Don Prospero lay asleep on the ground near-by. She had dragged Anastasio's body straight and covered it with a ragged blanket. "I've had to chase away coyotes twice," she said when January came down the slope to search the saddles for rope. "We have to get him out of here soon. Is Hannibal all right?"

"Alive and quoting Shakespeare," reported January as he untied the rope and slung it over his shoulder.

"And Anastasio's henchmen? How many of them were there? It seemed like about a dozen. . . ."

"Two," said January. "One's dead. The other's poisoned—I'll have to do for him what I can, but I don't know as there's anything I *can* do. We'll have to get him back to town somehow. . . ." He found another small lantern tied to one of the saddles, lit the stub of tallow candle within it.

"So the police can hang him?"

January only shook his head. When he reached the temple again he found the bandit Lobo still twitching spasmodically, surrounded by puddles of vomit. The whole temple reeked of death.

I have killed them, Anastasio had said.

Killed them with the cold-blooded efficiency that regarded bandits and opium-eaters in the light of sacrificial animals, to be disposed of as stepping-stones to some larger scheme. Along with cooks and catamites, presumably, and the scum of the jails drafted into the Army to fight in Texas. January knelt beside Lobo and peered into his eyes, then covered him with the coat Don Anastasio had taken off, though he knew it would do little good. He had no equipment here to force whatever residue there was out of the man's stomach, nothing he could do except build a small fire with brush and sticks, in the hope of keeping him warm. The flaring yellow light of brush hastily pulled outside twisted over Mictlantecuhtli's grinning face as January anchored a loop of rope around the broken block of the blood-spattered altar, making him seem about to speak.

"Dear gods, I don't think I've ever been so happy in my life to hear anything as when you shouted." The jerking whisper of the lantern-light was just barely enough to show January the white blur of Hannibal's shirt below, and the pale shape of his face. He lay, as he'd said, in a niche beneath the ledge where the rubble of the floor had subsided sharply, like a farther pit of Hell beneath the first drop. There was no sign of the lantern. "Then, and a few minutes ago when I realized that you'd survived the shooting and that I wasn't going to be left down here to die of thirst. . . . Where's Don Prospero?"

"Asleep at the bottom of the pyramid." January set his lantern on a rock and knelt; blood glittered on Hannibal's face through a mask of dust and filth. "Do you think you can walk?"

"That would entirely depend on who was chasing me. God . . . !" he added as he turned over to let January cut the rawhide thong that bound his wrists, but when January helped him up he could stand on his left leg, his right arm over January's huge shoulders. "Naturally," he panted, breathless with shock and pain, "the one time I don't have a bottle on me . . ."

January made a loop of the bottom of the rope and passed it under Hannibal's arms, climbed to the top, and hauled him up, not the ideal way to bring up a man with an injured leg but preferable to trying to make the climb with the fiddler clinging to his back. He said, when they reached the top and Hannibal sank down gasping to the floor, "I could get Rose. . . ."

"And leave Don Prospero free to wake up and wander about as he will? I'll be well in a moment, *amicus meus,* I promise you. Give me but a minute and I'll skip like a ram in the springtime—let us only get out of here now, at once." The tiny brush-fire beside Lobo had already burned itself nearly out. Hannibal glanced over his shoulder at the shape of Mictlantecuhtli, brooding amid blood and flowers in the dark.

January paused only long enough to check on Lobo, who—not much to his surprise—was dead. Loath as he was to leave two men

unburied and unprotected, he could think of no easy way—and no reason beyond respect—to transport them to the city. They would have
enough trouble with Anastasio and Hannibal. The moment they left,
he reflected, the coyotes would arrive. Like everyone else tonight, they,
too, would have their dinner with the dead.

"Anastasio and his myrmidons came to my room only minutes after
I retired," Hannibal said as January helped him down the pyramid's
endless steep slope. His voice was shaky, and he spoke, January guessed,
to keep his mind from the pain in his leg. "I'd played for the ghosts in
the cemetery all last night, and damned interesting it was, too, even if
the vaqueros wouldn't let me leg it over the wall. . . . Which is apparently what the lovely Valentina has done. The whole place was in an uproar all day about it, with everyone accusing everyone else and Don
Prospero ranting. . . ."

"Never mind about that," said January. "I talked to her. She's elop-
ing with a Texian."

"I hope he beats her. Well, by the time it was ascertained that no,
she wasn't at Fructosa and no, she wasn't at Saragosse and no, Doña
Filomena hadn't seen her since they entered the Saragosse churchyard . . . It wasn't much of a party here tonight. Doña Josefa elected to
spend the night on her bare knees in the chapel; Don Prospero locked
himself in his study to brood about where he was going to get another
chef in time for Christmas—that was absolutely all he said, or seemed
to think, about poor Guillenormand's death. Casimiro and I sat up for
a little in the *sala* playing monte with Hinojo, but if any of the deceased
put in an appearance, they wouldn't have found it any more exciting
than a dull afternoon in Heaven. Did they add to the height of this
pyramid while we were inside? Surely it wasn't this far to the bottom
when we came up."

Hannibal was sweating, clammy, and trembling with shock by the
time they reached the bottom. Still, when January asked "Do you think
you can ride?" Hannibal replied, "To get out of Don Prospero's immediate vicinity before he wakes up, I assure you, I'll *walk*. Just get my
boot off," he added when January helped him to sit on the serpent-
head. "I've had these boots since I was up at Oxford, and if my leg
is broken, I don't want to have to razor it off. They're the only ones
I've got."

"I thought you won thousands of pesos off Don Prospero at picquet." Rose handed him the brandy-flask from January's coat.

Hannibal drained it without pausing for breath. "Back at Mictlán. With my fiddle..."

"We'll send Consuela for them once we get into town. Hold on. This will hurt."

"So will hanging." Hannibal closed his eyes.

Once Hannibal's boot was off, January felt his leg and thigh as carefully as he could, and found what he thought was a break in the tibia just below the knee. It was hard to tell, and he could only splint the place with the ramrods from his own and Rose's pistols, and lift his friend onto the back of Rose's horse behind the saddle for the ride back to town. Then he went to help Rose lift Anastasio's body onto the calmest and most dispirited of the other horses, slinging it over the saddle like game.

"Why not simply kill Prospero?" asked Rose softly as she roped a serape over the man she'd made dinner conversation with not two weeks before. Blood stained her collar where Anastasio would have cut her throat as he'd cut the chef Guillenormand's without the slightest thought that here was someone he'd known and respected—in Guillenormand's case, for years.

Only because it was an expedient thing to do.

"With Fernando dead, there was no danger to Anastasio's property. Not as long as Casimiro is a child. Why set up a fake ritual here to have Prospero declared mad?"

"*Declared* mad?" Hannibal, clinging to the cantle of Rose's saddle, raised his eyebrows almost to his retreating hairline. "My dearest Athene, we are past fine distinctions about hawks and handsaws here and deep into the realm of Lucia di Lammermoor, in case it has escaped your notice."

"I suspect," January answered, "because Santa Anna doesn't like Don Anastasio—and Don Anastasio couldn't be sure that Prospero hadn't told the President about Don Anastasio being his pensioner. Everyone in Mexico City must know that Doña Gertrudis was forced to become a duenna, even if they don't know the precise circumstances."

As he tied the body in place, he saw where Don Prospero's bullet, entering just above Anastasio's left eye, had torn away a huge chunk of the back of his skull; it must have passed within inches of Rose's cheek.

Let me know what I owe You for this, he whispered in his heart, his hand groping for the rosary in his pocket. *Anything You ask. Anything You want.*

"No, Don Anastasio was right," he said. "He had to have Prospero locked up, preferably in France or Spain, where any communication or instruction would have to come through him. It was the only way he could buy himself time to readjust the situation. And the only way he could get Don Prospero confined was to present Santa Anna with evidence of insanity so gross that it could not be ignored: viz., being found in a pagan temple with a sacrificial victim's torn-out heart in his hand."

"Giving a new meaning," mused Rose as she swung onto her horse in front of Hannibal, "to Othello's threat to 'cut out his heart in a church.'"

And Hannibal, looking like a corpse himself now in the moonlight as exhaustion and shock began to settle in on him, gave a single whispered chuckle.

January looked up at him for a moment, then, though his legs ached at the thought of yet one more climb, turned and set off up the pyramid again. His approach sent half a dozen coyotes streaming out of the black sanctuary cave; he averted his eyes, in the swaying lantern-light, from the corpses of José and Lobo.

As he picked up Don Anastasio's short velvet coat, he turned one last time to the *offrenda:* flowers and tea-cup, gloves and sword, candy and tobacco and bones. Blood spattered them and the vermin had already disarranged Don Anastasio's careful ordering of the fake shrine, but still they had an eerie beauty, an eerie power. His sister Olympe, he thought, could have warned Don Anastasio not to make an altar to the young man he'd murdered, no matter whom he wanted to convince of Prospero's madness. Or at least—if she'd been feeling charitable—she'd have warned him to keep away from it on the night of All Souls.

It was agreed that Rose and Hannibal should start at once for Mexico City while January rode with the dazed and sleepy Don Prospero to within sight of the hacienda walls. As Hannibal had said, even on the night of the Feast of All Souls, the compound at Mictlán was somber and quiet save for the lights in the servants' quarters, and one light burning in the chapel.

During the ride from the pyramids, Don Prospero had seemed half-waking and half in dream. But beyond repeating, in answer to January's question, that Fernando had told him that Anastasio had been responsible for Fernando's death—and that Fernando had said that it had something to do with peanuts—the old man was silent. Whether he recognized January, or remembered his murdered chef and the blood-ied shirt and bag of money in January's luggage, January did not know. When they came within a hundred feet of the *casco* gates, January helped him down and sat him on a deadfall tree, tied up the horse that bore Anastasio's body, then fired his pistol twice to bring the vaqueros, and rode away as fast as he could.

January had frequently had cause to comment on how simple life was for the heroes of the romances to which his sister Dominique was so addicted. They could gallop all night on horses that never grew tired, without the nuisance of changing saddles to a spare cow-pony who kicked—by the light of a convenient moon that never set, apparently—in order to show up "at daybreak" upon the doorstep of helpful friends, Renaissance Italian cities evidently not having customs barriers. After an hour of vainly trying to figure out a way through the marshes on the northwest side of Mexico City, he gave up. He joined the enormous queue of charcoal-merchants, wood-sellers, farmers with loads of veg-etables and enormous herds of cattle, sheep, swine, and geese bound for the city's markets, finding—several hundred feet closer to the front of the line—Rose and a nearly-unconscious Hannibal still waiting also.

The gates were open by then but the line was slow, owing to the number of merchants cutting ahead of those who couldn't afford to bribe the customs inspectors. January pulled his hat over his eyes, won-dering if he was going to be arrested for Guillenormand's murder—or for being El Moro—and watching the Indians glide by on the canals of the marshes, heading for the markets with canoe-loads of fruits and flowers.

It was the third of November. The Dead had returned to their homes in Heaven—or presumably in Hell—for another year.

At the Calle Jaral, Consuela was having breakfast with Don Rafael de Bujerio, both of them in dressing-gowns. "Hannibal is a dear man and I love him with all the passion that inflamed the heart of Dido for

Aeneas," she assured January as she hurried with him and Rose down to the courtyard, where Hannibal slumped at one of Señora Garcia's tables, being served cocoa heavily laced with laudanum by that obliging lady. "But after all, Dido was Queen of Carthage and did not need to be provident about her grocery-bills. Don Rafael's heart is broken...."

Or anyway his pride seriously miffed, thought January, but didn't say so. Perhaps the jilted *hacendado* was merely being provident as well: Don Prospero had given ample evidence that one daughter of doubtful provenance was to him pretty much like another.

"Bonifacio wrote to me Sunday that you had come to Mictlán," Consuela added, leading January and Rose—with Hannibal supported between them—into the old house's inner courtyard. The Garcias and several other families occupied what had been kitchen and laundry quarters around it, but a back stair led up to one of the smaller rooms of her own apartment, which Hannibal had occupied prior to his appropriation by Don Prospero two months before. It was a small, sunny, whitewashed room, and very quiet: books stacked in a couple of up-ended crates, sheaves of music, pots of ink. Consuela had already started storing extra trunks of dresses there. "Then last night Rafael arrived with the news that you had murdered my father's cook, for no good reason that I could understand...."

"It isn't true." January laid Hannibal—half unconscious—on the bed and took the razor Consuela fetched from the wash-stand to cut away the makeshift bandages and the trouser-leg. The whole leg was swollen from hip to ankle and Hannibal's right side was a mass of bruises; the tibia seemed to be cracked rather than broken through. January was astonished that the damage hadn't been worse.

"So Sancho assures me," said Consuela. "He arrived yesterday also, along with Cristóbal, having talked to all the servants at Mictlán. Lupe and Yannamaria both saw Guillenormand alive through the kitchen window long after the pair of you had retired together for the night. Guillenormand was talking with Don Anastasio, and so Sancho is prepared to tell that blockhead Ylario."

"Anastasio will have gone straight to the kitchen," January told Rose after Consuela had left to tactfully hustle her new lover on his way. "Did Don Prospero say anything to you while I was up in the pyramid, before he fell asleep?"

Rose shook her head. "And he may not recall that it was he who killed Anastasio. Unlike Hannibal, Don Prospero isn't sufficiently accustomed to opium to sort out dreams from memories."

"Do not speak slightingly of the God of Poppies," whispered Hannibal, opening his eyes. "Don Prospero has no need of Smyrna cocktails to hold conversations with invisible Jaguar-Gods. So no one would ask—or try to tell one act of madness from another."

Rose poured a little more laudanum into a glass and held it to Hannibal's lips. The ride—and the straightening and re-splinting of his leg—seemed to have taken the last of his strength; he appeared to January almost like a spot of sunlight on the worn linen of the bed, that would fade with the first cloud across the light.

"I have to admit Anastasio made his plans very cleverly." January pushed the fear in his heart aside and kept his voice brisk and matter-of-fact. "He laid a subtle groundwork by hinting to me—and almost certainly to others as well—that he'd found evidence of sacrifices among the temples. Killing that poor rabbit was an act of genius. After that I don't think a single one of us would have doubted that Prospero would later have killed a man."

"*Be thou as chaste as ice, as pure as snow,*" whispered Hannibal, "*thou shalt not escape calumny.* At least not if you're a lunatic, a catamite, or a votary of the God of Poppies. Did you ever believe I'd actually done it, *amicus meus?*"

January said, "No. I didn't know how you could have *not* done it, but I never thought you did."

The fiddler's mouth pulled sidelong in the ghost of a smile. "*Towering heaven in bronze and terror fall / and bury me and all the folk of earth / upon that day when I forsake my friend. . . .*" His eyelids slipped closed and the long fingers slid limp.

Breakfast with Don Rafael notwithstanding, Consuela ordered her traveling-carriage prepared and departed for Mictlán shortly before noon, to fetch Hannibal's violin and books. Sancho was dispatched to make the journey to Vera Cruz with money to pay passage on the first steam packet to New Orleans available, it being too late in the year to count on a sailing vessel. Doña Gertrudis was still at Saragosse with Isabella: "A fortunate circumstance," remarked Rose as she packed up their trunks preparatory to the swiftest possible departure that could be arranged. "Whatever Cristóbal and the other servants tell Ylario about who was where when M'sieu Guillenormand was killed, I feel that the fewer people who know of our presence here, the better."

January looked into Hannibal's room several times during the morning, always to find him sleeping, but when he and Rose entered after siesta, the fiddler was propped up in bed with a closed atlas by his side—standing duty as a desk—laboriously working on what appeared to be a letter.

"Consuela should be back sometime tomorrow," Rose told him, going to the cupboard to fetch a second book to provide stability under the ink-well. Sheets of paper and spare quills were scattered everywhere on the counterpane. "I think Cristóbal and I will visit Ylario first thing in the morning to find out if it's safe for Ben to be seen on the streets. I understand—from Cristóbal—that young Werther has been released from La Accordada, and is staying with Ylario, so I think that a hasty retreat is more than ever in order. The main question now is, how much do we tell of what happened last night? We don't even have to have been there, you know."

"Some of us earnestly wish we had not," agreed Hannibal. He was sweating with the effort of writing, and his hand shook so that he had to stop constantly to wipe his palm on the ruffles of his too-large nightshirt, but his lovely Italianate handwriting remained perfectly steady.

The air had changed with the ending of siesta; from the courtyard below the voices of children drifted, shrieking with joy in some kind of game, just as if the world they would grow up in promised them something other than poverty, drunkenness, and ignorance throughout their lives. Señora Garcia called them to order with a loving laugh; the cobbler tapped with his little hammers and last, and one of his daughters sang as she gathered in the laundry.

Over the city, all the bells of the churches chimed the hour, distantly answered by bugles from the Bosque de Chapultepec.

"By all appearances," Rose went on, "Don Anastasio and Don Prospero went to the Pyramid of the Dead together. They were attacked by bandits there, who killed Anastasio. It might even be a little difficult to explain our presence on the scene, though not nearly so difficult as an explanation of how Anastasio murdered Fernando."

"Of which we have neither jot nor tittle of proof, by the way," said January. "Only a staggering order of probability."

"But would it serve anyone, now, to have Don Prospero locked up?" queried Rose. She took the pen-knife and quill from Hannibal's trembling fingers and mended the point as she spoke. "Josefa would simply go into a convent—dragging her poor daughter with her almost certainly—and leave Casimiro to be raised by Isabella and whoever Isabella next marries. I grant you, Mictlán is no place I'd want to see a child raised, but..."

"I suspect," said Hannibal, "that things would be better all around if you did admit to being there, and did admit to seeing Don Prospero kill Don Anastasio in a fit of madness. It will complicate things, of course, and perhaps delay our departure, but... Thank you."

He fell back against the pillows, the pen sliding from his fingers. "Did you happen to see anything of what was in the well with me, *amicus meus*? In that little hollow under the ledge, where all things roll that fall there? The lantern fell on its side and the things never give much light in the best of circumstances, but..."

January shook his head. "Only shadow and darkness."

"Just as well." Hannibal brushed the letter with the feather end of the quill. "When you see Ylario tomorrow, Athene, take him this. Tell him if he doesn't believe it, to go down the cenote with a lantern himself. He'll find the remains of at least four women—I made it four, anyway, counting skulls and corset-bones. One of them was wearing a sapphire necklace."

In the end, of course—as January suspected would be the case—nothing much was done. Ylario investigated the well within the Pyramid of the Dead, but there was nothing to prove that Melosia Valenzuela and the other three women found there had been killed by Don Prospero. Santa Anna could not be reached, and the entire Avila clan united behind Doña Isabella in vociferously denying that a noble *criollo* gentleman would ever do such a thing.

No one, as far as January ever heard—through subsequent letters from Consuela, Sir Henry, and the Graf von Winterfeldt—was ever prosecuted for the murder of Sacripant Guillenormand.

On the seventh of November, Consuela Montero left Mexico City for Vera Cruz. She was accompanied in the carriage by her dear friend Rose and another dear friend, Doña Viola d'Illyria, in deep mourning for her husband and obliged to walk with a cane and a crutch as the result of a severe fall. Doña Gertrudis remained at the Avila de Saragosse town house with her widowed sister-in-law Isabella, and if some of the members of the military bodyguard provided by Capitán Ylario thought that Doña Viola *was* Doña Gertrudis, January did not enlighten them.

Riding beside the traveling-coach up the dry, rutted slopes of the Sierra Madre Orientale, January was rather curious as to what Hannibal and Consuela would have to say to each other on the six-day journey to the coast, but Hannibal appeared to accept Consuela's dismissal of him philosophically. Love was all very well, but there were always grocery-bills.

"And so long as Santa Anna remains in power, I doubt anything much will be done about my father—maybe not even after he falls. As he will fall if he takes on the Americans. And those who replace him..." Consuela shook her head. "My father is quite good at befriending those in power."

She stirred at the chocolate the innkeeper had brought them—rather rancid and made with goat's milk—and gazed into the embers of the fireplace in the corner of the big, chilly, dirt-floored common-room of the travelers' inn at Perote. The *diligencia* from Vera Cruz was in, and around the other plank table were grouped its passengers: ship-captains, a French merchant, an indignant-looking official in a black coat, and the man's wife and daughter, all smoking cigarettes that filled the room with blue fumes. The Yankee coachman sat by the door, contentedly spitting tobacco on the floor. January remembered staying in this same inn three weeks previously.

It seemed like another lifetime.

"It is as you said, Rose, concerning the families of those who are insane," Consuela went on. "How the madness of one affects them all. Sometimes I think it is the same in my whole country. That until its leaders cease fighting among themselves, and decide that just because they are of pure Spanish blood—or mostly pure Spanish blood—they do not have the right to ignore those of us who are not, there is not much that can be done for anyone here. And that, I fear, will take some time."

The Captain of the steam packet *La Sirène,* a Caribbean Frenchman, greeted with a shrug the information that Doña Viola was actually a man: the Captain had been around the Gulf for a long time. In a great reek of coal-smoke and shuddering convulsions in every beam and timber, the ship parted from the wharf, Consuela's small black form growing smaller across the stretch of green water, Cristobál and Sancho and Zama waving on either side. January watched the low flat shore of sand-dunes and blackened buildings recede in the lurid glare of the tropical morning, conscious of a sense of deep sadness.

He had not, he told himself, gone to Mexico expecting to find it a land of freedom just because it had abolished the slavery of men. But he had expected to find something other than he had. Perhaps, like Capitán Ylario, he had read too many philosophers, and had believed too much in what he read. Perhaps, like Werther Bremer, he had not been prepared for a world shaped by the kinds of slavery that one could not point to, or fight.

Every *indio* was still every white man's slave. Men still died like animals over pennies, as the bandit had died in the pass. Or died for nothing, like the *pelados* in the streets.

And blacks were treated exactly the way blacks seemed to be treated everywhere in the New World, as creatures without rights or name.

At least he hadn't been murdered, he reflected. And that was something. Rose was still alive, still with him. . . . And he'd had a few weeks when he didn't have to worry about being kidnapped and sold to the Territories.

That evening, after supper in the cramped and smelly passengers' cabin, he carried Hannibal up to the fore-deck and outlined to him— for the first time, given the near-ubiquitous presence of servants, escort, and assorted other supernumeraries on the journey—his theory of how Don Anastasio had known that the de Borregos family was prone to morbid sensitivities and particularly to that of *arachis hypogaea,* and had turned that knowledge to personal effect. Hannibal listened with interest, but said, "I can only be grateful that things transpired as they did, because God knows how you'd have proved that, even in an impartial court of law with a stiff wind behind you. Not that I appreciated at the time being pitched over the edge of that well, but I would much rather have a broken leg than hang—which is what I'd have done if you'd gone before a judge with a tale like that."

He sipped at his bottle of laudanum-laced sherry—it was the first occasion since departing from Mexico City that he hadn't been drowsy with opium as well. The agony of six days in a jolting coach was marked in the thinness of his face, the near-transparency of his fingers as he picked up his violin. Even this far from the engine-room the constant, bone-jarring jolt of the engines, the shuddering thunder of the sloshing screws nearly drowned the sweet music. Above the rim of the sea the stars leaned down, darkness luminous to the horizon's edge.

> *Sweet William is dead, Pretty Peggy-o,*
> *Sweet William is dead, Pretty Peggy-o,*
> *Sweet William is dead, and he died for a maid,*
> *The prettiest little maiden in the area-o.*

The hurricane season was well over, and though the air was as balmy as a New Orleans April, the northern wind had a chill to it.

Still, the thought of going belowdecks to the reeking little cubicles assigned to travelers was more than any of them could bear at the moment. *Every time I take a steam packet,* reflected January resignedly, *I swear the next voyage will be under sail. And then while we beat back and forth within sight of port for two weeks, waiting for a favorable puff of wind to take us in, I remember why I don't.*

"I didn't intend to try," he said. "Since I thought it was Don Prospero who had made the *offrenda* in the temple, I simply intended to tell him—through the mouth of the idol—that you were innocent and that he should let you go. God knows what I'd have done if he didn't believe me."

"Don Anastasio must have planned something of the kind from the start, you know," said Rose thoughtfully. "If he secured the tea-set as soon as Werther was driven off the hacienda. Your being accused of the crime was a godsend, of course. . . ."

"All my life," said Hannibal with a little riffle of notes, "I have waited to hear someone cry, 'You're a godsend!' And now I have. Somehow I do not experience the soaring elation I once expected to feel."

"It makes me wonder," Rose went on, "how many men have been hanged for precisely that reason. Not because of this particular circumstance—for, as you said, Ben, a sensitivity like that is something that usually kills in childhood, like your poor Madame Valory's children—but because of some condition of medicine that we simply don't understand. The way the Indians didn't understand, when Cortés and his men came here, that what they were dying of by the hundreds of thousands were smallpox and measles, things they'd never heard of. They didn't know any more than Fernando and his mother knew."

"Don Anastasio knew," said January grimly. "Growing up in New Spain, he would have been aware of how things commonplace to those in the Old World might be inimical to the inhabitants of the New... and vice versa. All he needed was a victim to prove Don Prospero's madness. He may even have intended it to be Werther, before Werther fled. After that he may have set El Moro to make sure you weren't dragged away to Mexico City prematurely."

"I cannot tell you how lowering it is," sighed Hannibal, setting his fiddle aside, "to reflect that I was the one adjudged to be the most useless out of all available candidates—including the local sheep, which were good enough for Homer when he wanted to display to his readers how mad Ajax was...."

"Never trust a man who doesn't know the *Iliad*." Rose laid a comforting hand on Hannibal's wrist.

And January, hearing real bitterness beneath his friend's jesting tone, added, "At least you were picked because someone *would* make a fuss over your death. Unlike Rose and myself, who didn't even rank that high."

Hannibal shook his head, and fingered his naked upper lip, where his mustache had been sacrificed to his personation of Consuela's duenna. He'd resumed masculine dress—including Don Anastasio's coat, which was better than his own—and his long hair lay braided back over his shoulders in a neat, old-fashioned queue. "The reflection is almost as depressing as the realization that I have, literally, no thanks to offer the two of you but... my thanks. Worthless and ephemeral as wind."

"Or music." January smiled. "We rabbits, sheep, and sacrificial dogs have to stick together."

"You know, I never expected you to come," Hannibal went on. "When you walked into Don Prospero's *sala* that day and kept Ylario from haling me off to Mexico City to be hanged, even more intense and enormous than my gratitude was my surprise. Because I truly thought that I was going to die in Mexico. And it seemed a very obvious conclusion to the problems I have all my life been faced with, including such questions as what the hell I was going to do when Consuela found someone else and turned me out into the street. And now that I understand that I'm free, and going to live, I find myself filled with terror. I feel as if I have been delivered from drowning, only to be set ashore in some completely unfamiliar land, like the heroine of *Twelfth Night*, to make my way as an impostor: *What country, friends, is this?*"

"Illyria?" asked January softly. "Or only Louisiana?"

"The land of the living. God help me."

And with a flick of his wrist he threw his opium-bottle far out into the starry following sea.

SANTA ANNA

Antonio López de Santa Anna marched north in January 1836 to crush the American colonists who sought to make Texas a separate nation. Though his Army of Operations suffered staggering losses due to blizzards and attacks by Comanche and Apache in the eight hundred miles of open plain, they still vastly outnumbered the 186 defenders of the Alamo, and after thirteen days of siege, on 6 March 1836, the Mexicans overwhelmed the makeshift fortress and massacred even those few who were finally taken alive.

As careless of his own men's lives as he was savage with his prisoner's, Santa Anna also executed the four hundred American prisoners taken shortly thereafter at the Battle of Goliad. On 21 April—six weeks after the Alamo—Santa Anna's forces were defeated by Sam Houston in eighteen minutes at the Battle of San Jacinto, mostly because Santa Anna neither posted camp guards nor set any kind of watch. Santa Anna fled the battle and was captured, alone, the following day.

Santa Anna's post-Alamo career surpasses most fiction. Astonishingly, he fast-talked Sam Houston into letting him go north to Washington, D.C., as a "goodwill ambassador" for Mexico (the Texans wanted to shoot him, and no wonder); ten years later, having been re-elected President of Mexico following the so-called Pastry War against the French, he attempted to regain the territory he felt the Americans had stolen from him and managed to lose California, Arizona, and

New Mexico as well. He lost a leg in the Pastry War—a fact he never subsequently let anyone forget—and had it buried with full military honors in a cenotaph in the Santa Paula cemetery in Mexico City. The leg was dug up and destroyed by an enraged mob on one of the later occasions on which Santa Anna was out of favor, but Santa Anna had several interchangeable wooden legs which he carried with him in a leather case: one for dress, one for every day, one for battle, etc.

In and out of exile, in and out of jail, in and out of the presidency, womanizing, gambling, switching sides at the drop of a hat, and displaying a brutal flare for generalship, Santa Anna ranks as one of the most colorful figures of the nineteenth century; his career would be hugely entertaining if not for the cruelty and unnecessary savagery that cost so many their lives. Despite pocketing for himself most of the ten million dollars paid by the United States to Mexico for the Gadsden Purchase in 1853 (during his fifth go-round as President of Mexico), he died broke, blind, and forgotten in Mexico City in 1876.

The American chargé d'affaires, Anthony Butler, was recalled by President Jackson in December 1835 for untoward interference in Mexican affairs in favor of the Texas dissidents. One can only speculate what this consisted of.

MEXICO CITY

The economic and social chaos and corruption rampant in Mexico during the 1830s and '40s are amply documented. Those who wish to read further about that amazing country during Santa Anna's heyday should locate a copy of *Life in Mexico,* the collected letters of the Scottish-born, American-raised wife of the first minister sent by Spain to independent Mexico, Frances Calderón de la Barca.

Frances Calderón de la Barca consistently refers to the capital city of Mexico as simply "Mexico"—I have departed from this aspect of authenticity simply to avoid confusion. Prior to its independence from Spain, the country, of course, was generally referred to as "New Spain." In the 1830s, Mexico City covered only a tiny percentage of its modern mega-sprawl, occupying the area of the "historic district" downtown, the site of the original Aztec city of Tenochtitlan on its island in the midst of Lake Texcoco. An eighteenth-century drainage project had begun to lower the level of the shallow lake, but it wasn't until the mid-nineteenth century that the land beyond the city's ancient boundaries was dry enough to support those appalling slums that now cloak the dry lake-bed to the horizon.

Within Mexico City itself, street names changed every block or so, and nearly all streets were re-named—some of them several times—during subsequent revolutions. The area northwest of the Cathedral square and west of the Plaza Santo Domingo (where the Calle Jaral of my story is located) is now part of the jaw-dropping excavation of the Templo Mayor, the great Aztec temple complex leveled, buried, and built over by the Conquistadores. The Cathedral square—known also as the Plaza Mayor and, after the 1840s, as the Zocalo—was at the time of the story as it is described, surrounded by trees like a rather larger version of the average Mexican town square.

Now, of course, the Zocalo is paved wall to wall and is one of the most awesome public squares in the world, dominated by the baroque towers of the Cathedral, by the broken shapes of the excavated pyramids, and by the enormous red, white, and green flag of Mexico flying in its center. Though the streets of the old city—and the floors of its ancient churches and mansions—are a rippled roller-coaster due to subsoil subsidence from the draining of the aquifer beneath, Mexico City is an extremely beautiful city, both gracious and awe-inspiring.

ANAPHYLACTIC SHOCK

The system-wide autoimmune reaction to proteins that the body mistakes for invading microorganisms—known as anaphylactic shock—is poorly understood even today. Symptoms can range from mild to fatal, and sensitivities can develop in adulthood, though the usual pattern is for symptoms to become evident in childhood. There are between 150 and 200 deaths a year from food-induced anaphylaxis, and many thousands of emergency-room visits for episodes that would certainly have proven fatal before the development of epinephrine. Those at highest risk nowadays are teenagers eating out with their friends away from home.

In the nineteenth century, such deaths would mostly have passed unrecognized amid the staggering incidence of infant and childhood mortality. (Looking back at old records, it's still sometimes difficult to determine exactly what illness any given child died of.) Before the development of modern medications, there was almost nothing that could be done about an attack.

Food allergies frequently run in families but are just as likely to occur spontaneously. Fish, shellfish, peanuts, milk, and eggs are the most common culprits, sometimes in quite minuscule amounts.

ABOUT THE AUTHOR

BARBARA HAMBLY attended the University of California and spent a year at the University of Bordeaux, France, obtaining a master's degree in medieval history. She has worked as both a teacher and a technical editor, but her first love has always been history. Barbara Hambly is the author of *A Free Man of Color, Fever Season, Graveyard Dust, Wet Grave, Sold Down the River,* and *Die Upon a Kiss.* She lives in Los Angeles, where she is at work on a novel about Mary Todd Lincoln, *The Emancipator's Wife.*